donegal generations

A Novel

BY TOM GALLEN

Copyright © 2011 by Thomas Gallen

This is a work of fiction. Names, characters, places, and incidents either are the product of the author's imagination or are used fictitiously. The author's use of names of actual persons, places, and characters are incidental to the plot, and are not intended to change the entirely fictional character of the work.

All rights reserved.

ISBN-10: 1482723972
ISBN-13: 9781482723977

*This novel is dedicated to my wife, Grace,
for her help and encouragement.*

Introduction

Donaghmore is a parish in County Donegal, Ireland. It is located along the River Finn between Ballybofey and Lifford. My Gallen ancestors lived there until the 1850s when my great-great-grandparents emigrated to America with their family. This book is based on the lives of my Irish ancestors.

These are the annals of three generations of a fictional family who lived in Donaghmore in the 18th and 19th century. The names of many actual characters and events from those years are used, especially those named in historical references, but they are used fictitiously in this book. Although the names of the principal family members and their neighbours are invented, I have tried to use the surnames of people recorded living in the Donaghmore area with my ancestors. My Gallen ancestors lived near McMenamins, Boyles, Bradleys, McCormacks, Gallaghers and others. Many names of politicians, landlords, and clerics may be accurate for the period, but these again, are used fictitiously. The names of some actual townlands are used in the novel while others are invented.

This book is a work of fiction. Names, characters, places, and incidents are either the product of my imagination or are used fictitiously. Any resemblance to actual persons living or dead, business establishments, events, or locales is purely coincidental.

Tom Gallen

BOOK 1 - PATRICK

Chapter 1
[1779]

In Meenahinnis on the lane to Lismullyduff, there is a turf cabin where an old hag by the name of Nora lives alone raising pigs. The pigs in her yard were once children that she stole from her neighbours. She has the magic to turn children into pigs which she sells at the Castlefin fairs. I ask my oldest brother, Seamus, if he believes this. He tells me that he heard that a number of children were missing in Sallywood. They went to the well for water but never came back home. The people of the townland searched high and low but couldn't find them. Someone in Meenahinnis noticed that the hag had more pigs in her care shortly after the children were missing. Seamus dares myself and my other brother, John, to see her for ourselves. John and I decide to catch a glimpse of this woman.

On a dismal grey day, we walk up the lane until her cabin is in sight. We are close enough to hear the snorting of her pigs. We stop to spy on the cabin long enough until Nora appears. From the distance I see that she is an ugly old witch with no teeth. She looks in our direction and starts to walk toward us on the lane. John and I run as fast as we can toward home. We never stop until we reach our cottage.

We tell Seamus about our adventure. He laughs and tells us that he is brave enough to walk past Nora's cabin and even speak to her if she is outside. We warn him not to do such a foolish thing. He says that he will carry a wee crucifix in his hand, and that will protect him from the hag's magic. John and I join Seamus as he walks up the path to Meenahinnis. We stop and wait in the lane as Seamus continues walking toward Nora's filthy mud cabin. As he strolls past, he looks at us and smiles. He is feeling both brave and safe.

All at once, Nora runs out of her doorway with a switch. She rushes into the lane and grabs Seamus by his collar. As we watch in horror, the hag drags Seamus into her cabin. Several minutes go by, and there is no sign of any activity from the cabin. What shall we do?

Finally I say, "We must go to the cabin and rescue our brother."

John is not so sure. "Ach. We warned him. He knew the danger there. I don't fancy spending the rest of my life eating rubbish."

"We can't leave. If you don't go, I'll go by myself. I'll go just as far as the door."

John does join me, and we walk up the path and gaze at the cabin door. The bottom half is shut, and we stare into the darkness within. We see nothing, and we hear nothing. Then we get the shock of our lives. The hag appears at the doorway, which quickly opens, and instantly she is standing before us with her switch. John almost trips over me as we run as fast as we can down the path toward home. When we are far enough away, we look back, but Nora is nowhere to be seen.

"She could be in the hedges over there," John says. "She seems to have the power to move through the air in the blink of an eye."

We bless ourselves with the sign of the cross and run away again home, not passing near any bush where the hag could hide. We know that Seamus is gone forever now. He is the new pig in Nora's pen. What will we tell Uncle Jimmy?

Uncle Jimmy is at the cottage when we arrive.

I ask, "Do you know the oul' one, Nora of Meenahinnis?"

He says, "Aye, you better stay away from her. She has some magic in her."

I tell him about our visit to Nora. He looks shocked.

"I better get some lads together," he says as he heads out the door.

We wait nearly an hour before someone struts through the door. It is Seamus and he is grinning.

"Wha'?" both John and I say together.

Seamus walks over to the fire. He must be enchanted, still under Nora's power. I go up to him and stare him in the eyes. No, he is still Seamus, as sure of himself as always.

"Nora's not a bad sort," he finally says. "She invited me in for some scone and buttermilk. I stayed and chatted with her."

"She dragged you in," I tell him. "We thought that you were being turned into a pig."

"I don't think so."

Then, he snorts like a pig. I look at John.

"Sorry. It must have been the buttermilk," Seamus says.

I can see that Seamus is having fun with us. He will never tell us what went on inside the hag's cabin. I'm sure that it had nothing to do with scones and buttermilk.

Uncle Jimmy shows up at the door with four neighbours. All are holding hayforks. He sees Seamus standing there with his mischievous grin, and turns to dismiss the rescue party.

My name is Patrick. This is the story of my life in Donaghmore Parish of County Donegal.

chapter 2
[1771 - 1779]

My mother died on the day I was born. Da couldn't take care of us after she died, and that is why we are being raised by my Aunt Mary and Uncle Jimmy. We live with our cousins, Aunt Mary's and Uncle Jimmy's children, in a wee cottage on a farm in Monellan, a townland south of the River Finn in the parish of Donaghmore. The eight of us sleep on two big mattresses stuffed with chaff in the back room of the cottage. My brothers, Seamus and John, sleep with cousin Willie and myself. Because I am the smallest, I sometimes wake up on the dirt floor. The girls, my sister Mary and my cousins Big Mary, Teresa, and Lizzie, sleep on the other mattress. My aunt and uncle sleep in the big room by the fire.

Uncle Jimmy is a tall, dark-haired man with a calm manner. The only time he isn't calm is when my brother, Seamus, gets overactive and goes berserk. Seamus is an excitable child and a bit of a bully to us younger children. Uncle Jimmy will yell at Seamus in his loudest voice, but it takes Aunt Mary to settle Seamus down. Aunt Mary is a short stout woman with straight brown hair. She is kind to all the children, and we think of her as our mother.

Being the youngest of the children isn't fun. If I'm not being used as a plaything for the girls, I'm being pushed and battered by the boys. My childhood seems to be a bunch of bad memories. Whenever I can, I try to be near Aunt Mary for protection. I follow her around as she cleans the cottage and prepares the supper in pots over the fire. With me constantly underfoot, Aunt Mary tries to teach me my prayers. I learn them by repeating them over and over. Sometimes Aunt Mary has tears running from her eyes, laughing at some of the things that come from my mouth when I attempt saying a word I don't know. She looks forward to Uncle Jimmy coming home so that she can repeat them, but I don't believe that anything I say is that funny.

My brief childhood is over soon enough. Now that we are all old enough, we all work on Uncle Jimmy's farm. He has about 15 acres and can use the help. The boys use our uncle's spade to turn the soil over so that Uncle Jimmy can plant corn, potatoes, and cabbage. We have a pig, which we will sell someday, and our sheep graze in the meadows shared by our townland neighbours.

Uncle Jimmy shears our sheep in the spring before they go into the hills. The girls have the job of preparing the wool. First they pick out the dirt with their fingers as they tease the wool from the fleece. After that, they use stiff brushes to card the fluffy stuff into long wispy slivers.

Aunt Mary taught her girls the skill of spinning the wool slivers into yarn using the spinning wheel in the big room of the cottage. They sell most of the yarn at the Ballybofey market. What they do not sell is woven at home into material for garments. Uncle Jimmy does most of the weaving in the winter when there is little for him to do in the fields. He uses an old hand loom that was given to him by his parents when he married Aunt Mary. There is great patience and dexterity required to slip the shuttle through the warp threads in the loom. At times, the girls try some of the weaving.

The girls are skilled at cutting and stitching the woven material to make dresses, shawls, and mantles. Most of our clothes, nevertheless, are purchased from men who sell them at the

Ballybofey market. The clothes from the market are the old clothes of wealthy people in the towns of Derry and Strabane who no longer wish to wear them.

The only time we see Da is when he visits on Sundays. He works as a labourer on the large estate of Robert Blair near Killygordon. His Sundays are free, and he goes to Mass at the new chapel in the village that we call the Cross. After Mass, he comes to our cottage and spends the day with us. I was named after Da. Uncle Jimmy and Aunt Mary call him Paddy, but they call me Patrick. He doesn't touch a drop of whiskey even when Uncle Jimmy offers it. After supper, we walk him back to his turf cabin on the Blair estate.

Da is a quiet man. He is strong and well built as are most of the farmers I have seen around Monellan, but he is shorter than Uncle Jimmy. When we see him on Sundays, he is usually well dressed. Mr. Blair has given him dark trousers and a long grey vest. His white shirt is clean but frayed at the cuff. Except when he goes to Mass in the chapel, he wears a knitted peaked cap instead of the tall hats that most of the men wear. "I have one of t'ose hats at the cottage," he tells us, "but it is a bit too big. It covers me eyes and ears." Seamus asks if he can see it when we get there.

Da tells me that I look like him when he was a young boy. Da has a dark reddish face with black whiskers. The shadow of his whiskers remains even after Uncle Jimmy shaves him before going to the chapel. His hair is thick, black and straight. I guess that my unruly hair will look like that someday.

During these walks to Da's cabin, he tells us a bit about our mother. Seamus is the only one of us who remembers her. Seamus was six years old when she died.

Da works on the Blair farm. Mr. Blair has Da work at his whiskey distillery in Castlefin as well. Mr. Blair likes him for his sober ways and his dedicated work. Although Mr. Blair is not of the true faith, he admires Da's devotion to God, but he doesn't care for the "idolatrous" rituals of what he calls the Papist church. Da prays for Mr. Blair's soul. My father lived in the cow byre on the Blair estate until Mr. Blair allowed him to build a cabin a way off from the manor house. The cabin is a simple one room hut with no windows. Mr. Blair charges Da no rent for the land.

Da met my mother, Margaret Scanlon, when she started working as a housekeeper for the Blairs. They married in 1764, and my brother Seamus was born shortly after that. They lived in Da's cabin. Soon my sister Mary was born, and after that there was John. Mam died when I was born in 1771. We were too young for Da to raise by himself, so we went to the home of Mam's sister and became part of her family.

As far as I know, I have no grandparents or other relatives besides Uncle Jimmy, Aunt Mary, and their children. Most of my friends have loads of aunts, uncles, and cousins. I often wonder why I have so few. Da never mentions his parents nor tells us if he had any brothers or sisters. When I ask him about his relatives, he just tells me that they are dead and buried. I question Uncle Jimmy. He tells me that Da's parents died only years after they were married, and he was raised by families in the parish. Uncle Jimmy says that my mother and Aunt Mary had family in Sligo but travelled here when they were young to work as housekeepers. They never returned to Sligo. He believes that their parents are dead now, but there may be other relatives left in Sligo or Mayo.

"As for myself," he says, "I came from Inishowen where I have a mother and a brother there still. I seldom return there, but I try to see me mother every few years or so."

Our uncle's last name is Dougherty and our name is Gallen. Sure it became confusing when we were introduced. I became known as Patrick Dougherty and I never correct anyone when I am called such.

Today, Uncle Jimmy lets me in on a family secret. He tells me that his son, Will, is actually a changeling, a fairy. I can't believe my ears. I knew that there was something different about him, but I couldn't tell what it was. One day, when Will was a baby, he was left alone in his crib. Aunt Mary returned and discovered a different baby in the crib. Her baby had very little hair; the one in the crib had a full head of dark hair and full eyebrows.

Fairies love human babies. They are always looking for ways to steal them. Unminded babies are the perfect victims. The fairies simply switch the human babies with those of their own.

My uncle tells me that Aunt Mary was beside herself with grief. She asked Uncle Jimmy what they should do. He said they should ask the parish priest. At the chapel, the priest told them he didn't believe in fairies and told them they must be mistaken. Babies change their appearance overnight sometimes. They weren't satisfied. They knew that the baby was not their own. Then they asked the neighbours what they should do. Some told them to pray to St. Anthony; others told them that they should catch a fairy and hold him hostage until their child is returned. For years, my aunt and uncle looked for fairies, walking at night and early morning about the fairy hills and holy wells. They never saw a fairy and therefore never captured any.

In the meantime, their changeling son grew older with his sisters Mary and Teresa. Later another girl, Lizzie, was born to the Doughertys. As you might expect, Lizzie wasn't left alone for a minute. Later still, my brothers, my sister, and I became part of their family.

What does Willie look like now? He looks somewhat normal but with large ears that stick out from his straight sandy-coloured hair. I would have expected his ears to be pointy but they are not.

Uncle Jimmy tells me that he is raising Willie as his own child. Willie doesn't know he is a changeling, and he acts like any other child. My uncle asks me not to tell Willie anything about his parentage and not to tell my brothers. Why did my uncle tell me this in the first place? From now on, I'll be looking at Willie in a queer manner. I don't know if I can handle the responsibility of keeping my gob shut.

There are some fairy mounds up near Cronalaghy. I talk Seamus and John into taking me there. I want to hear the music the fairies play inside their dens in the ground. I ask them to bring Willie with us. If anyone can hear the music, Willie should. It is a long walk but finally we get there. I listen and my brothers listen. No music. I ask Will if he can hear anything.

He says, "Aye. It is beautiful. There is a wee fiddle and a harp. I don't recognise the air that they are playing, but it is lovely nevertheless."

We all look at him. We get closer to the mound. Still no music. The wind makes a sound through the trees, but no one can call that music.

Seamus says, "You're mad, Will. There is nothing to be heard. It must be the sound rattlin' around in yer empty head."

We walk back down to Monellan. I want to tell my brothers about Will, but I vowed that I wouldn't.

Uncle Jimmy sits the boys all down on some winter evenings by the fire and tells us the stories about the ancient Irish heroes. The girls listen but don't seem interested. I look forward to the story nights. From the way Uncle tells the stories, I get the feeling that I am living in the exciting years of past centuries. Tonight, he tells us of Cuchulan, the famous warrior of ancient Ulster.

He tells us of Cuchulan's childhood and how he became the champion of the boy's troop of the Red Branch knights, the army of Conor macNessa who was king of Ulster at the time. He tells us of Cuchulan's training in Scotland and how he was given the magic spear called the Gae Bulga. When Cuchulan threw the Gae Bulga, it never missed his target. It was as if it had a life of its own.

Cuchulan also had another weapon in his arsenal. It was the "rage." When he became angry, his face turned into a terrifying mask. His head seemed to grow and his hair stood out. His eyes grew to twice their size, his face turned bright red, and his mouth opened wide showing long pointed teeth. To illustrate this, Uncle Jimmy makes a grotesque face with wild eyes and a mouth wide open to show his crooked teeth. We all are horrified at first but then we laugh.

He continues his story with Cuchulan as an adult, manning a fort and patrolling the mountain passes and fords leading into southern Ulster. With his magic spear and his skill at the sling and sword, he drove off all enemies of Ulster single-handedly.

On another story night, Uncle Jimmy tells us the story of Queen Maeve and how she captured the champion brown bull of Ulster under the nose of Cuchulan. The story is exciting and bloody. The day after each night of story-telling has me making crude swords and spears and challenging my brothers to battle. Unlike Cuchulan, I often lose to them and end up with many cuts and bruises.

Uncle Jimmy also explains to us how the English came here and enslaved the Irish people. He tells us about the great battle where the English defeated the army of the Irish lords. They punished us by taking away our land, forbidding us from going to Mass, and from speaking the Irish language. He says that this is why he must pay rent to Englishmen or men of English descent to stay on the land. I am puzzled by some of this. We are not forbidden to go to Mass. We go to Mass at the Cross every Sunday. Uncle explains that times are beginning to change. Up to just a few years ago, there was no chapel in which to attend Mass. Mass was held only in people's homes and at the old Mass rocks up in the hills. The English now allow us to have our chapels and attend Mass, but there are still restrictions. Father O'Flaherty and his brother built our present chapel at the Cross with their own hands. It is a simple building with a thatched roof. Our chapels must not be larger than the Protestant churches and must not have steeples or church bells. As far as the Irish language goes, I never hear anyone speaking it except some of the old people who visit us. They seem to speak the language only when they are cursing or expressing surprise. Uncle Jimmy has many visitors who discuss the local conditions. I can't follow many of their conversations. I only know that sometimes the discussions get loud and angry.

On some Sundays, Da and Uncle Jimmy take us down to the river to fish. We have to be quiet and sneak onto the land of the Protestant farmers to get to the river. We stand on the river's rocky bank and cast lines made of coarse twine tied to the end of a long stick into the water and wait for a fish to bite our bait on a hook. For bait, we usually use the grubs that we find early in the morning in the earth. On most days, none of us catch anything, but occasionally a trout or salmon will get caught on the hook. When this happens, we all leave and bring the fish home so that Da can clean and cut up the fish for Aunt Mary to boil in a stew over the fire. The taste of fish is hard to get used to, but I soon fancy the new flavour and greatly prefer it to our usual diet of boiled potatoes.

chapteR 3
(1779 - 1883)

Samhain, All Hallows Eve, is my favourite holiday. It is the night before All Saints' Day, the first day of November. We eat a large supper with potatoes, bread and bacon. After dinner we go to the crossroads at Monellan and watch the bonfire. Before we go, we blacken our faces with soot from the fireplace and wear our clothes backwards to confuse the spirits that are wandering the earth tonight. To the amusement of my Uncle and Aunt, Seamus even dresses in my sister's clothes. The fire at the crossroads is immense and the flames leap to the sky. The bigger children run around the fire in the dark and try to scare the younger ones. When we return home, we carve frightening faces on a few of our turnips and put them in the window to keep out the evil spirits, but we leave our door unlocked so that the spirits of our dead ancestors can come and visit. We put food out for them to eat if they come while we are sleeping. When I was younger, I was terrified of Samhain. I stayed awake all night listening to the howls and shrieks of the evil spirits outside, and I listened for the door opening when our dead ancestors would come. I wondered if my mother would come with them. Now, I just enjoy the excitement of the holiday.

It seems as if Seamus's purpose in life is to annoy John as much as possible. He does it by giving John a slap to the back of his head every chance he gets. If John retaliates, Seamus hits him again and stands just out of John's reach. Seamus always gets the last blow, and eventually John just shrugs it off. Seamus also makes fun of John by repeating the last thing John says. John then warns him to stop, and Seamus repeats John's warning. I am thinking that John will get even someday by clobbering Seamus when he least expects it.

Once a year we buy a piglet at the fair in Ballybofey. We keep the pig in the house as a pet during the first few months until he gets too big. He eats our potato skins and other cooking scraps. After a year, when he reaches a good size, we sell him at a decent profit and buy a new piglet to raise. This year Seamus asks Uncle Jimmy if he can name the pig. We mostly just call him "Pig." It doesn't pay to get too attached to an animal we plan to sell or slaughter. Seamus is insistent this year, and Uncle Jimmy tells him he can name the pig if he wants. Seamus asks his brother, "Would it be fine with you if I name him after yourself, John?"

John looks pleased that Seamus would consider such a thing and says, "I have no objection if that is what you want."

Seamus smiles and calls to the pig, "Here fat-arse! Here fat-arse!"

Uncle Jimmy frowns and John sulks. Seamus has gotten the best of John one more time.

Da and Uncle Jimmy sometime discuss changes of the law in Ireland. I don't follow many of their discussions, but it sounds as if some more of the laws against Catholics are being repealed. Now Catholics can bid on longer land leases. Before, the Presbyterian farmers had that advantage over us. Now, they must compete for land leases with Catholics and they aren't happy about it. In some of the villages in Ulster, Presbyterians are forming defence groups. Although Da works with several

Presbyterians on the Blair estate, he doesn't seem to notice any change in their attitude toward him.

In the meantime, Da is saving money for his own farm. In 1780, with Mr. Blair's blessing, he leases five acres of almost worthless land in the upper hills of the parish. We sadly leave our Aunt and Uncle to join him in the two room cottage he built for us on the land. I feel that Uncle Jimmy and Aunt Mary aren't all that sad about us leaving because their children are getting bigger, and they can use the space we are vacating. Big Mary is now 19, Teresa 17, Will 16, and Lizzie is 13. Our sister Mary is only 12 and will stay on at the Dougherty's for a while. As for ourselves, Seamus is 15, John is 11, and I am 9. We can help our Da clear the land of rocks, and get the land ready for the spring planting.

This is a new world for us here in the hills. There aren't many other farmers here. There are also the fairy mounds which shelter the wee people. When I pass them, I try to hear their music, but I still hear nothing except the wind. Maybe they don't live here anymore.

Our cottage is a simple stone building with a thatched roof. Da whitewashes it with water and lime from the kiln down in Monellan. The whitewash waterproofs the cottage and turns it gleaming white. The inside of our cottage is mostly dark because the window is quite small. It is a bit brighter in the summer when we leave the top part of our half door open. The bottom is kept closed to keep out animals. There is just enough room inside for our three beds with mattresses made from sewn flour bags stuffed with corn chaff. Da and John sleep in one bed and Seamus and I in the second. We are saving the third bed for Mary when she moves in with us from Monellan.

The harvest in 1780 isn't much, but it pays the rent when it is due in November. We even have a bit left over, and Da buys some distilling equipment from lads he knows at the Ballybofey market. In the winter, he boldly builds a still house on wooded, unclaimed land in the mountains of the next townland. In 1781, we plant barley as well as oats. Of course, we have a lazy bed of potatoes and a plot of cabbage. I am in charge of our pet pig as well as keeping the house clean. By 1782, we have a number of chickens and pigs who spend the night in the new byre attached to the cottage and a few sheep that graze in the pastureland above our farm. Da is able to sell jars of his poteen to our neighbours. Little by little, we are able to meet our rent on gale days and put something away to lease better land. When Mary turns 15 in 1783, she joins us and helps with the housework which used to be my responsibility.

We still attend Mass on Sundays, but instead of walking all the way to the Cross, we wait until the curate visits the Mass rock in Meenluskeybane. There, Mass is celebrated in the open air, and often in the rain.

On most days, we obtain our water for washing from a quickly flowing burn a way off from the cottage. For our water for drinking and cooking, we use a well nearby in Cronalaghy.

While exploring one day up the hill past Da's still, Seamus finds a hidden spring. It is a wee cascade of water spilling out of rocks in the side of the hill. The water falls into a pool and disappears into the earth. It is a pretty sight. The spring is deep in the forest and hard to find.

There is bogland high in the hills near County Tyrone. Many of our days are spent clamping turf from the swampy land and piling it up to dry. We have an endless supply to keep our fire going throughout the year as long as we continue putting in the long hours. There is considerable bogland in these hills, and generally no one cares who cuts turf on their land. On some of the bogs, nevertheless, the landowners pay labourers to cut the turf and bring the dried bricks to town where they are sold.

Da plants the corn crop in the spring; this year it is oats. He builds up ridges of earth with his spade and spreads the seed corn from a bag hanging around his neck. In the summer, the fields turn a glorious colour of gold. We harvest the grain in September. Da and John cut the stalks down with a sickle, and Seamus and I tie them into sheaves. After we get four sheaves, we "stook" them by tying them together and standing them in the field. The ropes we use are hand woven by us from straw. After about two weeks of good weather, the stooks are dry, and we stack them close to our cottage in a haggard with a thatched roof to keep the rain off.

The threshing is hard work. Seamus is typically given the job of vigorously beating the sheaves with our flails, which are two hefty sticks bound together by a leather strap. Seamus likes this work. He viciously swings his flail with all his might against the helpless sheaves while screaming, "Take that John! Take that!"

I believe that Seamus has a bit of madness in him. John just stands there looking at Da and myself as if to say, "Should we stop him?"

Da shrugs. He knows that Seamus is doing a better job of threshing than anyone in the townland. The effort Seamus is putting into separating grain from chaff will satisfy his call for violence. He just needs to release some of his excess energy. We don't believe that he really wants to harm his brother. It is just another way for him to torment John...I think.

After Seamus finishes pummelling the sheaves, the loose material is shaken into a large sheet of linen. Then we riddle it to separate the grain from the chaff by throwing both into the air on a windy day. The wind blows away the chaff. We then take the oats to the mill in Kilcadden to be ground into oatmeal. We save a bit of the oatmeal for ourselves for stir-about porridge. The rest is sold at the market.

In 1782, a stone bridge is built across the River Finn which greatly improves commerce between the Cross and Killygordon. It is located near the ruins of an old O'Donnell castle at Dromore. In the old days, there was a shallow ford at that location. Later wooden bridges were built that frequently washed away during floods.

Chapter 4
(1783 - 1789)

One day at the end of summer, I see Mary returning from the spring with her bucket of water. She looks paler than usual and rushes over to talk to me. "Paddy, I saw someone at the spring and I am frightened."

"Who was it, Mary, a redcoat?"

"No, when I came past the hedges, I saw a beautiful lady dressed in a long clean tunic. She had a silver cup and was drinking from the spring. When she saw me, she said nothing but looked at me and smiled. Then she ran off swiftly into the forest. Who do you think she was?"

"I have no idea, Mary. No one lives up there. You say that she ran into the forest and not down the path to the town."

"She did, and she looks not like any of us. Her face was smooth and clean and her clothes were not like any that I have ever seen. She could be a lady from the city, but what would she be doing here? There is no road for a carriage. Paddy, could she be a fairy like those Uncle Jimmy told us about?"

"Mary, the fairies don't show themselves to people like us. I have no idea who she is. Maybe we will see her again, and we can ask her."

Mary looks unhappy and says, "I hope that you boys will fetch the water for the next few days. I am afraid."

John and I fetch the water from the spring for the next couple of weeks but we see no one. We start to believe that Mary made up the story to avoid one of her chores. We convince Mary that she can visit the spring safely, and she never mentions the earlier incident again.

Da has built a shed that he calls a shebeen up the hill from our cottage. He stores his poteen there. One day, Seamus and John coax me into the shebeen to try some of Da's whiskey. They had opened a few jars in past weeks and tasted it and then replaced what they had drunk with water. Today I will be initiated into the world of the drinking man. The first swallow of the evil stuff is disgusting. I had known that it would be this way, but I didn't think that it would be such an effort to get the liquid down my throat. I only take three swallows as John and Seamus drink from different jars. They sit back and tell each other jokes and laugh. Most of their jokes are about Daddy, making fun of his serious discussions with us. They also make jokes about tending the sheep during the summer grazing in the hills but I don't get the point of their humour.

"Paddy, are ya not enjoyin' yourself?" asks Seamus.

"I am indeed," I reply.

Seamus is now a slight wiry lad with light brown hair. He must look like Mam because he doesn't look like the rest of the family. We all have black hair, except for Da whose hair is grey, and he is now going bald. Seamus always manages to get his chores done in the shortest possible time. Then he races about looking for other things to occupy his time.

John is heavier than Seamus. Mostly he is quiet and keeps to himself. Today he is more talkative. He says, "How are ya gettin' on with the lasses, Paddy?"

I am not getting his drift. "What do you mean, John?"

John says, "I mean are ya findin' anyone to your fancy, like Kate Bryson or Mary Quinn? They both were lookin' ya over at Mass."

I say, "Aye, they are nice looking indeed, but I'm having nothing to do with them. They act like eejits when I try to speak to them."

John says, fairly soberly, "Both of them have daddies who can spare a bit of land when their girls marry."

Seamus roars when he hears this. "John, you arse! What is it you're after? Do you want Paddy to move away so that you can get more of Da's land, or do you want to court the lasses yourself?"

John turns away and sulks. "I was only lookin' after the boy's interest."

The room begins to spin, and I leave them and go outside. I can't stand and I fall on my side when I try to sit down. I cannot stop laughing. It is a lovely feeling. We all fall asleep and wake a while later when it starts to rain heavily. We refill the jars to the top with water and walk down to the farm with our heads hurting and our stomachs uneasy. The sick feeling stays with me as I finish the day in the fields. Later after I feel better, I'm looking forward to visiting the still again, but Seamus tells me that we must not drink too much poteen. We rely on the sale of it to live here, and we will be pushing our luck if we visit the still too often. If Da catches us, Seamus is certain that he will destroy the equipment, and that will be the end of our good fortune.

The Samhain celebration up in the hills is more grand than in Monellan. We again wear outlandish clothing and head up to Carn Hill, the hill that separates the counties of Donegal and Tyrone. Large crowds walk up both sides of the hill to an immense bonfire at the graves of the giants who walked these hills in ancient times. There is singing, dancing, and boozing. From Carn Hill we can see all the way to the fires at Killeter and Aghyaran in County Tyrone. Da doesn't come with us, and so we get a bit wild. As the fire starts dying a bit, Seamus suggests that we play tricks on some of the farmers in Cronalaghy. He brought a large flour sack with him in anticipation of midnight mischief. We join him in creeping up to a cottage nearby. We help him climb the roof. He quickly pulls the sack over the chimney and jumps down from the roof. We watch from a safe distance as the farmer rushes out through a smoke filled doorway to see what the matter is. We can hear his curses as he struggles to bring his ladder over to undo Seamus's mischief. Seamus tells us that next year he has a better plan which he heard from some of the lads at the bonfire. We can take apart a farmer's carriage and put it back together in a shed or byre so the farmer can't get it out. We must scout out the best location for this mischief long before next Samhain. We will also need more lads to participate in order to keep the prank to the shortest time possible. In my mind, this is a long way off and it is unlikely that Seamus will remember to think of it in time by next year.

Before going home, we return to the bonfire which is dying out. Like the others there, we gather some of the burned embers to take home and to throw on our fields for good luck.

There is a dance and bonfire at the Cross in May of 1788 where I meet a beautiful, dark-haired, lass by the name of Anne Kelly. Anne has pale blue eyes and a lovely smile, and after speaking with her, I learn that her voice is as lovely as her smile. She sounds like an angel. She is wearing a white blouse, a grey skirt, and a grey linen scarf on her head. She looks somewhat saintly in the scarf that falls to her shoulders. I prefer the scarf to the silly looking bonnets that some of the other lasses wear.

Anne lives in Monellan, near my Uncle Jimmy, which gives us a topic for conversation. As our chat progresses, I am aware of an angry looking lad staring at me from across the fire. He walks back and forth as if enraged by my speaking to Anne. I ask Anne who he is, and she tells me that he is Hugh McLaughlin, a close friend.

"Why does he seem so irritated?"

"Ach, he is always irritated about something. He seems to think that he and I are betrothed, and he gets jealous every time I talk with another lad."

"Are you betrothed to him?"

"Not yet. My family likes him. He is a good farmer and his father holds a lease on a fair sized lot in Mounthall. Both his family and mine believe that we would be a perfect match."

"Do you believe so, as well?"

"I believe that we could have a good marriage someday. I haven't thought of marrying any other; we have been together our entire lives."

"Would he let you meet another lad just to be sure he is right for yourself? He looks as if he would like to kill me."

"Ah, that he does. He has quite a mean temper. We should probably say goodbye for now. He will be storming over here in another minute."

I say goodbye to Anne but I'll not forget her.

Seamus meets Mary McMenamin at this same ceilidh. Mary becomes pregnant by some miraculous phenomenon on that occasion. A wedding at the McMenamin house will soon take place. Ceilidhs, wakes and weddings are the principle way young lads meet young lasses in our parish, and I use Seamus's wedding as an excuse to get to know Anne Kelly. She is not known to either family to be invited, so I invite her myself. I walk down the hill to her cottage and meet her mother at the half-door. Her mother seems surprised to see me. She doesn't greet me with much enthusiasm, but she calls Anne away from her indoor chores. Anne comes to the door in her old everyday work clothes, her head unadorned. She still looks grand. I ask her if she would like to join me at the wedding. Her expression is a look of puzzlement as if no fellow ever asked her such a thing before. She thinks a long time before answering.

"I don't believe that Hugh would approve."

"You told me that you are not betrothed. Does he have to approve?"

"Ach, he will be quite angry if I go, won't he?"

"Anne, I would like to know you better. If you don't want to see me, just tell me so."

Anne bites her lower lip and looks at the ground.

"I guess that he doesn't have to approve of my going to a wedding without him. Can I not meet you at the wedding? Where will it be held?"

"It is at the McMenamins in Avaltygort. I'd be proud to escort you."

"Ah no, it's best if I go alone. My brother will take me there. You may escort me home."

It is a fine wedding at the McMenamin's cottage and farm, considering the haste of organising it. I am thrilled when Anne arrives. We talk and she seems genuinely happy to be with me. We manage a few dances to the music of a fiddler. Too soon, the party is over and I walk Anne back to her home.

Hugh McLaughlin is waiting at the Kelly's door when we arrive. He looks angry.

chapter 5
[1789]

Hugh is a big strapping lad, at least six inches taller than me, and outweighs me by at least two stone. I would not care to fight this fellow.

He asks, "Where were you two?"

Anne replies, "We were at the wedding of Patrick's brother."

Hugh says, "Why did you not tell me?"

I step forward and say, "I asked Anne to attend. Does she have to report her whereabouts to you always?"

Hugh walks up to me. His face is now red with fury.

"She does, and she will no longer have anything to do with the likes of you."

I look up into his face and see a bit of spittle is on his lips. He is fuming.

"I believe that Anne has a right to do what she wishes. If she wishes to see me, you have no right to stop her. You do not own her."

Anne joins in, "Hugh, Patrick is a friend. Don't try to intimidate him. I'll see him when I want. Get that into your thick skull."

Hugh now loses control. He grabs a barrow leaning against the cottage and throws it into the lane. He picks up dirt and sod and throws them into the air. Mrs. Kelly comes to the door.

"What is going on here? Hugh, what is the matter with you?"

Hugh cools down and apologises to Mrs. Kelly. He returns the barrow to the wall as I whisper to Anne, "I think that I better go now. Will you be alright?"

Anne tells me, "Aye, we are used to Hugh's temper. We will be fine. I hope that I'll see you again."

"You will. You definitely will. I'm sorry that you have to put up with a fellow like Hugh. You should end your relationship with him. It is not good for you."

I feel a bit like a coward leaving like this, but I don't see any good coming from my staying. It would lead to a fight with Hugh and me being the loser, a bleeding pile of flesh on the ground. What would that prove?

Seamus and his wife, Mary McMenamin, move into our household with Da, Mary, John, and myself. It is quite crowded. All of the floor space is taken up at night with our bedding. Then, Da's grandson is born to Mary McMenamin. Our hilltop cottage is so overcrowded that some of us are sleeping in the shebeen, and in the byre on nights that are not too cold.

One evening, Seamus asks me if I have an interest in any of the lasses of the parish. I tell him that I do, but I have to deal with an unstable and potentially violent rival for the lass's affection.

"Do ya want me to kill him for ya?"

"Wha'? Ah no, for God's sake. Are you mad? I'll take care of it myself."

It is hard for me to tell if Seamus is serious at times. What would he have done if I said yes to his question?

My sister Mary will be the next to get married. She had known Owen McCullough of Ballinacor since she was a child. He visited her often in our hills, and it seems that, in order to get away from her hard life in our bleak world, she talked him into marrying her. For convenience, they will be married at Aunt Mary and Uncle Jimmy's home in Monellan. Da will provide the food and drink, much of which is legal and taxed, although he will have a few of his own jars available when the legal whiskey runs out. After they marry, Owen and Mary will live on the McCullough farm in Ballinacor, giving us a bit more room in Da's crowded cottage.

This is another occasion when I can call on Anne to accompany me to the wedding. I know that Anne's parents don't approve of me. They would prefer Hugh even with his hot temper. Hugh is actually a good looking fellow. He is strong, handsome, and is an intelligent farmer. His parents will give him a farm in the fertile low lands of the parish when he marries. What is not to like about such a lad? Then there is me, a scrawny ugly runt working with his father on a scraggly piece of land in the mountains. What future do I have? What can I offer a lass from such a well connected family as the Kellys? Ah well. Although I haven't so much as kissed her yet, I love Anne, and I must try to win her over. I'll work on her family after that.

I escort Anne to my sister's wedding. There was no sign of Hugh at her cottage, and we don't mention him for the rest of the day. The wedding goes off without any problems, and all of us present have a good time. Anne enjoys my family. This is a good start for our relationship. On our way back to her cottage, we leave the path to sit by a wee burn gurgling down the hill. I decide to bring up the ugly subject of Hugh McLaughlin.

"How has Hugh been treating you lately?"

"He has been alright. He comes for supper with us every now and then."

I don't like to hear that. "Has he been holding his temper, now?"

"Ah, sure. He is an alright fellow when you aren't around, you know."

"Do you ever wonder how he'll be if yis marry, and you innocently look at another man?"

"I do wonder about that, but I think that he will do me no harm."

"Then you are still going to marry him."

"My parents are looking forward to it."

"Has he proposed to you yet?"

"He has. I told him that I'm not ready. I'm still a young lass, and I want to have a few more years of freedom."

"Do you like me?"

"I do, you know. You are a fine lad and you can dance, as well."

"Well, I like you very much, and I wish we could know each other better. It will be strange courting you when you are sure that you will marry Hugh someday."

"Aye, it is strange, but Hugh and my parents will have it no other way."

"We haven't kissed. Will you kiss me now?"

"I will. I would like that."

We carefully position our heads and bring our lips together. It is a brief kiss, but then Anne presses her lips on mine again. I embrace her and fall backwards on the grass. Anne is on top of me and our lips are still together. Finally our lips separate.

She says, "That was nice, wasn't it?"

It was nice, but I can't get over that she will not break off with a madman like Hugh. I'm certain that her life as Hugh's wife will be miserable. Why can't she see this?

She starts laughing. I ask her what is funny.

"I can just imagine Hugh seeing us kissing like that. He would kill you right on this spot, you know."

Pleasant thought. I guess that I'll continue with this unusual courtship in the hope that Anne will come to her senses. I take her home and kiss her again before she enters her cottage. Her mother sees us, and I can tell that she disapproves.

When I get home, Seamus wants to talk with me.

"Paddy, I saw a friend of yours at the weddin'."

"Many friends were there, which one?"

"Hugh McLaughlin."

Seamus has my attention.

"He was loiterin' about and seemed to be lookin' for someone. I didn't know who he was, so I asked him why he was there. He told me his name and said that he was Anne's friend. I figured that he was the lad who has been giving ya a bad time for seein' Anne. I told him to meet me behind the byre. He didn't want to go, but I convinced him with my knife."

"You didn't kill him, did you?"

"I did not. I just persuaded him that he should leave yis alone. I told him that, if he harmed ya, I would find him and cut his bollocks off.

Seamus is not a strong lad, but he has a wiry, feral look about him that intimidates strangers. His eyes can stare holes through you. I am always glad that he is on my side.

"Thank you, Seamus. Anne and I need all the help we can get."

Hugh McLaughlin and I alternate seeing Anne on Sundays. Hugh gets invited to supper at the Kellys. So far, they haven't invited me. Thanks to Seamus, Hugh doesn't seem to pay me any mind when I see him.

It is a queer courtship I'm having with Anne. It appears to be a courtship without a happy ending.

chapter 6
(1790-1792)

In 1790, Da leases 20 acres of better land in Glencarn townland. We build a stone cottage, thatch the roof, and plant oats, barley, and of course, potatoes. John and I live in the new cottage and take care of the crops. John is now 21 and I am 19. Seamus, his wife Mary McMenamin, and their children, they have two now, Patrick and Michael, stay at the hilltop farm with Da. The problem with the Glencarn location is that we are exposed to inspection by the authorities. The inspectors make a judgment as to how much profit our land can produce, and we are obliged to pay a tithe to the Church of Ireland on a percentage of that amount. There is also a tax on our single fireplace that we have to pay to the English government for the support of King George. Most of the Protestants have to pay more because their houses have more than one hearth. Fortunately, the successful harvests of our lands make payment of the rents, taxes, and tithes possible. The sale of barley is especially profitable. The buyers are mostly distillers of poteen, the illegal liquor made in the hillsides and inaccessible areas of Donegal and Tyrone. Our farm is close to roads that go to both Castlederg and Killygordon. Every illegal distiller within miles is aware that we have barley to sell.

Da and Seamus spend much time at the still. Seamus is active in poteen sales while Da takes care of the distilling. At no time is there any danger of revenue officers discovering the still. No one, especially the land agents, would think to turn in any illegal distiller. The sale of barley for poteen making assures that the rent will be paid on time.

The livestock we bought for our farm also produces profits. We are able to sell our pigs and wool at the markets and fairs in Castlefin, Ballybofey, and Castlederg.

I love going to Ballybofey on market days. It is a lively town with many shops and alehouses. There is constant movement of people on foot as well as in horse carriages of all types on the main street of Ballybofey. The principal reason for this activity is because Ballybofey is on the main road to Donegal Town, and the bridge across the River Finn at Ballybofey carries travellers north to roads that lead to Derry City, Lifford, and Letterkenny. On the other side of the bridge from Balleybofey, the north bank of the Finn, there is the quiet town of Stranorlar. Stranorlar differs from Ballybofey a wee bit. Whereas Ballybofey has the shops and alehouses, Stranorlar has the churches and inns. Together, they are known as the twin towns.

Every Thursday is market day in Ballybofey and there are cattle fairs in January, February, March, April, May, and December. Saturdays are market days in Stranorlar, and its fairs are in March, August, October, and December. The markets and fairs at Castlefin are nearer to us, but I greatly prefer going to the twin towns, especially Ballybofey, for its diversions.

My brother Seamus is an ambitious man with flexible morals. He frequently goes out in the middle of the night and returns with a cart full of manure which he adds to our pile in Glencarn. For certain, some neighbour's midden is a bit smaller in the morning. I worry about his soul. He seems to be accumulating years of punishment in Purgatory.

It is my week to see Anne. I visit her cottage and learn that she isn't home. Mrs. Kelly tells me that Anne is with Hugh McLaughlin at his father's place. This doesn't seem fair. I decide to see what is happening and walk to the McLaughlin farm in Mounthall. I spy Hugh talking to Anne who is sitting on the wall. I walk up to them both and give a hearty greeting. Hugh gives me an evil glance.

I say, "Anne, did you not remember that I was coming to see you today?"

She says, "Oh…it slipped my mind. I'm sorry, Patrick."

Hugh looks at me and says, "Why don't you get lost?"

I stare at him and don't know what to say.

Anne speaks up, "You don't have to be rude, Hugh."

I say, "Hugh, you are truly an ignorant man. Why do you think that you can get what you want by threatening people? The time has come for us to settle our differences. Meet me down the path."

Hugh says, "I can't be troubled, Paddy. Anne, I hope that you will come to your senses and leave this ugly runt."

Anne has heard enough. She jumps down from the wall and walks briskly away. I give Hugh my most menacing stare and join Anne walking back down the lane.

I say to her, "Ah then, that went pretty well, don't you think?"

I spoke too soon; I hear Hugh behind us. He is swearing and running toward us. I turn to face him. Anne looks shocked.

Hugh tells me, "Listen to me now…get out of our lives. Anne is to be my wife, and you will not interfere."

He grabs my shoulder and pushes me to the ground. I prepare myself for a kick in the ribs, but Anne steps in the front of him. Hugh pushes her out of the way, and she falls striking her head on a stone. He prepares to kick at my head, which I am protecting with my arms…then stops, realising that Anne is hurt. We both rush to Anne's side. She sits up; blood is trickling down her face from her hairline.

Hugh says, "I'm so sorry, Anne. I lost my head."

Anne refuses to look at Hugh. She asks me, "Take me home, Patrick."

I help her up, and we start walking the path to Monellan. Hugh is following us until Anne turns and tells him to go home. I feel sorry for Anne but am thinking to myself that this is turning out fine for me.

We walk in silence to her cottage where she meets her mother.

"What did you do to her?" her mother asks.

"Patrick did nothing to me. It was that bully Hugh who knocked me down."

Her mother looks at me and hustles Anne into the cottage leaving me standing there. I wait a few minutes...no one comes out, so I head back to Glencarn.

The next week is Hugh's turn to visit Anne. I don't know how that turned out, but I see Anne with her family after Mass on the following Sunday. I am standing on the road with my brother John. Anne leaves her parents and comes over to me. John mumbles something and leaves for home.

"Patrick, will you come to supper with us today? My mother will be cooking bacon. It will be delicious."

I am totally flabbergasted. "Of course I will. When should I arrive?"

"Come walk with me. We will discuss it."

We walk up the hill on a path I have never walked on before. It is lovely and passes near the rear wall of magnificent Monellan Castle.

I ask, "How has Hugh been treating you lately? Has he been holding his temper now?"

"I saw him last week, and he was alright."

"You do know that he can get violent when he doesn't get his way, don't you?"

"I do wonder about that. That is why I believe that I'll not marry him."

I am happy to hear that. "That is smart indeed. I hear of many women who are beaten by their husbands. Hugh does appear to be the sort for that."

She sits on the grass under a shady tree. I join her.

"When I am ready, I'm thinking of marrying a lad like yourself, kind and sensitive. What sort of lass would you care to marry?"

I smile at her and say, "I don't know, perhaps a fat lass with the knack for cooking delicious meals or maybe a rich Protestant with a grand house and servants."

She smiles back and slaps me hard on the shoulder. I fall back on the grass and she jumps on top of me.

I laugh and say, "Alright, a lass like yourself then. I want no one else but you. I'm not proposing marriage now, you know. I have to make sure that you know me better. I have to get your family to like me better, as well."

"Well, my parents like you better now after I told them about Hugh. Your farm in Glencarn is another thing that pleases them. They were appalled by your father's farm in Drumbeg."

"Ach, you know that it is not really my farm in Glencarn. It's my Da's, but he still lives up in Drumbeg."

"I know, but it gives them hope that I'll not starve if we marry."

"Speaking of that, when is supper?"

"Da has some chores to finish. Come in a couple of hours."

"I will. And you will be there and not with Hugh."

"There will be no more Hugh McLaughlin. What do you say to that?"

"I like what I am hearing. Shall we seal it with a kiss?"

We have kissed before, but never this long in duration. When we break off, we both are gasping for air. After our lungs are full again, we kiss once more. The birds sing, and the wind whistles through the trees. This is one of many romantic interludes I have with the lovely Anne Kelly.

Supper at the Kellys is a bit awkward. The conversation stops and starts many times with no resolution. Daniel Kelly is a fine tall man who today is wearing green galluses holding up his trousers. The sleeves of his clean white shirt are rolled up to show powerful hairy forearms. Anne's mother, Nelly Kelly, is short and thin. I can't say her name without chuckling. Mrs. Kelly is wearing a white blouse, a green skirt, and a white apron. Her dark brown hair is tied up in some manner and covered in a white bonnet tied around her chin. Anne has two brothers, one older and one younger. She has a sister, as well. They look at me with a bit of scorn. It is obvious that they prefer the company of Hugh McLaughlin.

The bacon and potatoes are delicious. Mrs. Kelly is a grand cook and I tell her so. When we are outside, I let Anne know how much I enjoyed the meal. Anne thanks me for coming, and we say goodbye with a kiss. This is one of many Sunday meals with the Kellys. I believe that they will get to like me someday.

Months go by, and I ask Anne to be my wife. She agrees and tells me to ask her father for his blessing. I dread this, but I must do it. Anne walks me into the cottage and tells her father that I want to have words with him. Surely he must know what is coming.

"Mr. Kelly, I wish to marry your daughter. We will be happy if you approve. I have full intentions of keeping Anne in comfort at our farm in Glencarn and treating her with the respect she deserves."

Mr. Kelly nervously runs his fingers through his hair and stares into the fire. He is thinking of what to say. I look at Anne who is wringing her hands. They are quite similar, Mr. Kelly and Anne. I just notice that they seem to have some of the same mannerisms.

"Well, Patrick. We had our doubts about your ability to support Anne, but it looks like, without your man Hugh in the picture, you could be alright. You have my blessing, but if you mistreat her, we're taking her back."

Is he serious, my man Hugh? Maybe he has a dry sense of humour that I didn't see before. Anyway, it looks as if Anne and I will be hitched, something that has been in my dreams since I met her.

Hugh McLaughlin learns of our upcoming wedding. He is not happy. While walking down to the Cross one day, I see him coming up the path. He blocks my way.

He sneers at me. "You are not marrying Anne. You don't deserve her, you piece of shite."

"What do you care, Hugh? She'll not marry you. You know that."

"Aye, I know that, but I'll not let you marry her."

"How are you going to stop me?"

A grin comes over his face. "Because I'll kill you if you do."

"It makes no sense for me to talk to you. Good day."

I try to walk past him, but he pushes me back. I try to push him aside, but he grabs my neck with both hands, and throws me to the ground. He pulls his leg back and kicks me in the knee. A sharp pain shoots through me. I wonder if he broke my leg or kneecap. Hugh spits on me and walks up the path saying, "Remember, I'll kill you."

I stand and try to walk. My right knee gives out on me, but I catch my balance. Because I can put a bit of weight on it, I don't believe that anything is broken. After practicing, I learn that I can walk on my leg if I hop a bit. I decide to head back home and give up my errand to buy salt and butter at the Cross. The Cross is too far. A fair size dead tree branch is alongside the path, and I use it to keep some of the weight off my knee. I start back up the hill, hoping that I won't run into Hugh again.

When I get home, John sees me.

"Why the gimp?"

"I fell. Sorry, I didn't get the salt you wanted."

"That's fine. Take care of yer leg."

Later, John asks again about my leg, and I repeat my lie about falling. John looks into my eyes and asks again. Finally I tell him about Hugh but ask him not to tell Seamus.

My leg wasn't much better the next day. John had Seamus come down from Drumbeg to help plant the potato seedlings in our plot. He caught me sitting on a chair when he came in for supper. "McLaughlin did that to ya, did he not?"

Damn that John. I asked him not to tell Seamus. "He did. Don't do anything now, it's my problem."

"Ya have me word on it. I'll not touch the lad."

Somehow, I'm not believing that.

Weeks later, I'm still walking with a gimp, but my leg seems to be getting better. Anne was shocked at seeing me at first. I lied again and told her that I fell. We continue going on walks and visiting friends. I suffer through them and pretend my leg is fine, although I wouldn't mind having a walking stick. Eventually the pain eases up, and I am back to normal.

"Did you hear about Hugh McLaughlin?" Anne's father asks me one day.

"I did not. What did he do now?"

"His horse kicked him and broke his kneecap."

"Ah no! That poor fella!" I say without sounding sarcastic.

"Aye, it is a bad break. He is now wearing a splint and can't walk at all. He is missing Mass, and his family has to do all of the planting this year. Hugh is getting fat sitting around all day, as well. His da says that he may never walk normal again."

Somehow I believe that Seamus is behind this. He will never tell me if he did break Hugh's knee. Hugh must be in fear of his life if he didn't tell anyone that it was Seamus and not his horse who broke it. Funny, I do not feel sorry for Hugh. He was a bully, and now he learned his lesson. I shall have nothing to fear from him again.

Anne and I are married shortly after the Beltane holiday in May 1791. We share the Glencarn cottage with my brother John and start our family the next year with a son. The Kellys arrange for Brigid McFaddin to be with Anne during the birth. Brigid is an experienced midwife, and she helped deliver most of the Catholic children born in the parish for the past 10 years. Since I was named Patrick and my father was a Patrick, it would be bad luck to name our son after his paternal grandfather. Three persons in a family would have the same name. Often when this occurs, one of those with the same name dies. We name him Daniel after Anne's father.

Wee Danny is not left alone a minute since he was born. Anne believes in the fairies and is afraid that they will swap Danny with one of their own. She thinks that some of the children in the lower townlands act unusually queer and she suspects they are fairy "changelings." I know intimately of changelings. My cousin Willie is one in fact, but Anne is not aware of this. Our child will not be alone without one of us watching him. Others believe that, if the baby must be left alone for a while, fireplace thongs placed across the cradle will keep the fairies from stealing the child.

Unfortunately, the naming plan for our first child doesn't work out. In November 1791, our father, Patrick Gallen, after developing a violent cough, dies at the age of 52. May he rest in peace. Secretly, I am glad that we didn't name our son Patrick. I would have been sure that it would have been the cause of Da's death.

There was no warning of his oncoming death, no banshee wail, no crowing hens, no frogs in the house, and no mysterious knocks on the window. His death appears to be a surprise to even the fairies of the underworld.

We have a wake at our home in Glencarn for only one night instead of two. The wake is a simple affair. Da had few close friends in the parish except his poteen customers. Aunt Mary comes up and helps our sister and Mary McMenamin prepare Da's body for the wake and fix some of the food. Da is laid out on a slab of wood supported by chairs in our best room. According to tradition, a candle is at his head, and the mirror in the room is covered with a cloth. When I ask why the mirror is covered, no one can give me an answer. They tell me that it has always been done. We greet the few mourners who show up to pay their respects. They solemnly say a quiet prayer over his body and gather outside. They return when Aunt Mary starts leading the prayers. Then the men gather again outside and have a drop of the poteen offered to them by Seamus. Snuff is offered to the women as well, and clay pipes stuffed with tobacco are available for the men who wish to partake. Inside, my sister starts wailing and speaking words I can't understand. Soon all of the women are wailing and sobbing, I think more for the memory of losses in their own families than for the loss of Da. Other than my aunt, sister, and sister-in-law, few of them knew Da well enough for them to carry on so. After a while, the mourners depart for home. My brothers and myself sit with Da through the night to keep his body from being stolen by the fairies. The night of the wake was a rather dignified affair with none of the drunkenness and rowdiness that I hear is more typical at wakes in our parish.

In the morning, Father O'Flaherty arrives at our home. Da is wrapped in a linen shroud and is placed in a coffin obtained through members of the church. Six of us are the pallbearers for the trip to the chapel. There is John and Seamus at the front, myself and Uncle Jimmy in the middle. Owen McCullough and Anne's father, Danny Kelly, are at the back. With the coffin on our shoulders, we follow Father O'Flaherty down the dirt path to the chapel. Our wives and a small group of relatives follow the coffin.

A Requiem Mass is said at the chapel. Father O'Flaherty gives a brief sermon about preparing ourselves for death by staying in a state of grace at all times. We then begin the long journey to the graveyard at the Church of Ireland in lower Donaghmore. This church land and graveyard once belonged to the Roman Catholic diocese. In fact, it was the land used by St. Patrick himself when he built his church and monastery there. When Queen Elizabeth made her religion the official religion of England and Ireland, the Protestant bishop of Derry installed a Protestant cleric there. Of course, the Catholics no longer attend Mass there, but because it is the only graveyard in Donaghmore, Catholics continue to bury their dead there with the blessing of the Protestant vicar. There is talk of getting land next to the chapel at the Cross for a cemetery, but until then we continue to use the Church of Ireland site.

The walk to the cemetery is a few miles over the bridge to Killygordon and down the Lifford post road to the graveyard. It is raining and only Father O'Flaherty and the pallbearers make the trip. Da is removed from the coffin which will be re-used by another deceased person someday. He is placed in the grave, dug earlier by Seamus's friends, in the men's section of the Gallen common gravesite. I always knew that the parish has many families with the name Gallen. I am not aware that any are related to me, and I never asked my Da if he knew any of them. I did learn that the church provided gravesites for people with Catholic family names, including Gallen, and now both of my parents have joined these strangers, who share our name, in the ground consecrated by countless Roman Catholic parish priests at this alien place. I believe that Da will soon join my mother in heaven if he hasn't done so already.

Our landlords agree to turn over the leases of Da's properties to his sons. Seamus takes the hilltop land and we subdivide the Glencarn land between John and myself. John builds a cabin on his land and appears happy to be free of Anne, wee Danny, and me.

chapter 7
(1792 - 1800)

More of our children follow each year, Ellen (named after Anne's mother), Patrick (after Da, finally), and Maggie (after my mother). We almost lose Maggie to a fever when she is a baby. She cries and cries, and the heat from her head worries us greatly. I walk from house to house asking if the women have a remedy. Many come to help, but it is now four days and there is no improvement coming. The word spreads down to the town, and on the fifth day my sister Mary arrives. She hurries Anne and wee Maggie outside into the rain, to my great concern, as I watch over the other children. They return in the early evening with the baby. The fever leaves the following day, and Anne tells me what happened. Mary took them up to the spring in the forest and bathed Maggie in the cold pool there. Anne says that Mary believes it to be a magic spring. Mary has seen many things at the spring that make her believe that the water has curative power. I was never one for believing in miracles, but I think I do now. Sure the next time anyone in my family has an illness, I'll be using the spring water first.

When I ask Mary about the spring she says, "Paddy, I have been lying to you for many years. Ever since I was a child, I've walked up to the forest each May to see the lady there at the spring. The lady never speaks to me but she gestures for me to take a drink. After I sip the water, she is gone. I believe she is the Blessed Mother. It seems that she wants me to know about the miracles that the spring can do. I never mention it to anyone because they'll think I'm mad."

"Did you speak of this to Father O'Flaherty?"

"I did. He doesn't know what to make of it. He told me that I should keep going to the spring until Our Lady speaks to me. When she does, I will be sure to tell him."

I reply, "I think that for now we should keep this a secret. If it is let out, the hills will be infested with pilgrims and our peace will be shattered. I believe that we should wait until Our Lady tells us what to do. Nevertheless, we must offer the cures to the sick whenever we hear of their need."

"Aye Paddy, that is a good plan but I am frightened of my duties in this regard."

I go to the spring often after this but see nothing out of the ordinary. Soon I lose my belief that there really is anything "miraculous" about it and start to doubt my sister's visions of "Our Lady". This doesn't mean that I won't be heading to the spring anytime someone in the family is sick.

My brother and sister are doing their best to populate the parish. Seamus and his Mary have five children, and Mary is again with child. Owen McCullough and our sister Mary have three children, and she is pregnant as well. John remains single, and it appears that he will stay that way.

Today is my newest son's baptism. He will be named James after my brother Seamus. Seamus will be godfather, and Anne's sister Rose will be godmother. I have my doubts that Seamus will raise James as a good Catholic if, God forbid, Anne and I suddenly die. He hasn't been to Mass for years and Da never gave him trouble for it. It would have been an insult if I didn't select Seamus as godfather for his namesake's baptism. We will have to rely on Rose who is a regular churchgoer. Seamus, who now prefers the name Jimmy, is well into leading a life of crime.

He often disappears for a few days and returns with money. It is well known that he hangs around the alehouse in Killeter with a rough group of lads. He has a horse now, and he is an excellent rider. I believe that Jimmy is one of the reasons that we are seeing more of the soldiers from the garrison in our hills.

Anne and I start early on the trip to bring the babies down to the Kelly's cottage where James's baptism will be performed by Father O'Flaherty. My son James will soon be a member of the true faith and will go to heaven if he dies in the state of grace.

Uncle Jimmy, Aunt Mary, and their son, Will, join us at the Kelly's home for the baptism. My sister Mary, her husband, and their children are there as well. The Dougherty girls couldn't come. They are now living in Strabane where they work in a linen shop.

"Jimmy, will Mary and the children be coming?" I ask my brother.

"Ah no. Mary isn't feelin' well today and can't come." He winks and says, "By the way, would that be whiskey you're drinkin'?"

I fill Jimmy's cup from a bottle that the Kellys provided.

Jimmy tells me, "I'll not be stayin'. I'm to join the lads in Lifford tomorrow. A new assize is startin' at the courthouse, and a few of me friends are being tried for minor infractions of the law. Perhaps I can be of help to them. Could y' call on Mary next week and see how she is doin'? I'll be busy in Lifford until Thursday."

Father Michael O'Flaherty is a friend of Danny and Nelly Kelly. Father brings us the latest news that he gets from visitors to his chapel from faraway places.

"I've got good news for you lads" he says. "The English have repealed the tax on homes with only one hearth."

"That is good news. And why do you think they did that?" replies Uncle Jimmy.

"It could be that King George is afraid of a revolution of the poor like they had in France" replies Father. "It seems that the lot of poor people in England is worse than our own. They have no food."

Mr. Kelly says, "It is a pity that we don't get the French to help us with our own rebellion like the Americans did."

"I believe that such a thing is possible. A parishioner who returned from Dublin says that members of United Ireland are in France now trying to get support for another rebellion here."

Uncle Jimmy replies, "We can hope that they will be successful, but they'll get no help here. It seems that there are many Protestants in the parish who like things just as they are."

"Aye. Although the United Ireland movement encourages Protestants and Catholics to join in their cause for an Independent Ireland, there are many Protestants in Ulster who want Ireland to stay British. Militant Presbyterians in County Armagh have formed a society to keep Ireland from being taken over by the likes of us. They call themselves Orangemen after the usurper, King William of Orange.

"There is more good news, nevertheless. Another link in the chain of penal laws has been broken. A Catholic seminary will be opening in County Kildare. We will no longer have to send our future priests to the continent. It is impossible to send them now anyway because of the war with France. Believe it or not, the seminary is being funded by the English government. I believe that they have given up trying to stamp out Catholicism here. They seem to think that a good Catholic is a less troublesome Catholic."

The discussion goes on for more than an hour. I find out that England has been at war with the new government of France for the last couple of years and that this is the reason that we are able to get such good prices for our crops. My brother Jimmy sneaks out later and rides away toward Lifford on his brown mare. Soon the party breaks up, and I return with my family to our farm up the hill.

On Monday, I stop by to see how Mary McMenamin and the children are doing.

"How are you getting along, Mary?"

"Ach. There is so much work to do here and Jimmy is gone most of the time."

"And what would be the reason for that?" I ask.

"I fear that Jimmy is up to mischief, Paddy. We always have plenty of money, and it isn't from the poteen. The still hasn't been touched in months. Jimmy has a pistol, and he takes it with him when he goes out. When I ask him about it, he doesn't tell me what he does. I'm afraid that he has been robbing people on the road to Castlederg. It is only a matter of time before he gets arrested."

I promise Mary that I'll talk to him when he returns.

Jimmy tells me to mind my own business when I see him next. All I can do is warn him of the consequences of his acts. He just laughs.

More and more, I am hearing about the adventures of my brother Jimmy. He is an active member of the Frank McHugh gang. The McHugh gang is a group of highwaymen who have been robbing travellers on the road from Castlederg to Enniskillen. Their favourite victims are the passengers on the coach from Derry. The redcoats have been patrolling the roads on a steady basis, but the lads can strike from anywhere.

The gang was named for Black Frank McHugh, a reparee who mostly robbed the homes of the rich. He was a gentleman who attended parties in the houses of landed gentry where he wandered from room to room studying the easiest way to steal their money and jewels. He would later return with his gang in the middle of the night to take their valuables. He was famous for never harming any of his victims if they came upon him when he was ransacking their homes. Frank was eventually caught by the redcoats during one robbery in 1782. He was tried and hanged at the jail in Enniskillen.

What connection Jimmy's gang has with Frank McHugh, I don't know. I just know that his gang is getting a reputation that is as famous as its namesake. Everyone in the parish knows how a widow in Tyrone had to sell her cow to get money for her rent payment. Jimmy and the lads waited until the agent of the landlord received his rent and then rode away. They ambushed him several miles from his home and took his money and his horse.

The money was returned to the widow who purchased a new cow at the next fair in Killeter. The landlord's agent suspected that the cow was purchased with his money, but he could not prove it.

Stories such as this ensure that the civil authorities get no cooperation from the local farmers in regard to information on the gang's whereabouts. The names of the members and where they meet is a well kept secret.

"What is the difference between a cow tick and a land agent?" Jimmy once asked me.

"I don't know," I replied.

"Well, one is a blood sucking parasite. The other is an insect," he laughed.

In 1797, the end comes for Jimmy Gallen. The authorities are making it difficult for Jimmy and his lads to make a living on the roads to Enniskillen. He now starts ambushing prosperous travellers at Barnesmore Gap on the road to Donegal Town. Soldiers lay in wait for him one night and catch him in the act of robbing a coach full of passengers near the alehouse at Barnesmore. There is gunfire and Jimmy is killed. The rest of his band escapes on horseback into the mountains. As a warning to other highway robbers who frequent Barnesmore, the soldiers tie Jimmy's body to a gallows erected in the old days at Barnesmore and easily visible from the road. One of Jimmy's gang passes by our farmland and tells me about it a few days later. I rush up to see Mary. She can tell by the look on my face that Jimmy is dead.

"Ah Paddy. We all knew that it would happen. I prayed every night for him."

John and I borrow a horse and cart to bring Jimmy home. When we arrive at Barnesmore, we see that his body is badly mutilated by the birds and rodents. We bring him back and arrange for a Requiem Mass to be said at the Cross. A wake is held at our home the night before the Mass, but none of Jimmy's outlaw friends manage to come. Thank God.

Jimmy is buried in the Gallen grave, alongside our deceased parents and all of the other strangers who share our name. Jimmy's widow moves into her parents' cottage with her six children. She keeps the lease of the hilltop farm and plans to return when her children get older. In the meantime, John and I take turns maintaining her farm. Any profits from the crops over the rent payment are split three ways between John, myself, and Jimmy's widow.

In May 1798, a rebellion breaks out. We hear of it from our parish priest. There is fighting throughout Ireland but nowhere near our parish. We learn that Lord Cornwallis is now the Lord-Lieutenant of Ireland. In August, French troops arrive in Mayo under General Humbert. He takes most of Mayo but Cornwallis traps him and he surrenders in September. We also learn that a French fleet tries to land troops in Donegal at Lough Swilly to support General Humbert, but seven of the ten French ships are captured. The French prisoners are brought to Buncrana in Inishowen. One of the prisoners is Theobald Wolfe Tone, the rebel who began the United Irishmen Society in Dublin. Wolfe is dressed in a French uniform and is not recognized as the Irish rebel and fugitive from English justice that he is. He had helped to plan the invasion while he was in France. The officers are taken to the hotel in Letterkenny. At the hotel, Wolfe is seen by a fellow graduate of Trinity College who remembers him and who turns him in. He is taken to Dublin Castle and tried for treason. At first he pleads that he is a French officer and only subject to international law, but he is convicted, nevertheless. His request for death by firing squad is refused, and he cuts his throat in prison with a small knife. The cut is not immediately fatal, and he dies the next day in considerable pain. We hear that he remarked before he died that he wished that he had studied anatomy while at Trinity College.

My daughter Maggie is the apple of my eye. She is a sweet four-year-old and clings to her mother much of the day. When I come in from work in the evening, her smile brightens the room, and when she hugs me about the neck, I feel that my heart will explode. Anne made a doll for her by cutting cloth bags into a human shape, sewing them together, and filling the doll with chaff. She stitched eyes and a mouth. Maggie beamed when her Ma gave it to her. She calls it Biddy and carries it wherever she goes. She holds long conversations with "Biddy" and it amuses me greatly. My other children are lovely as well, but Maggie has a special place in my heart.

Danny teases her about the doll almost every day. Maggie breaks into tears every time that Danny says something mean. We tell him to stop, but it seems as if he doesn't hear us. One day we hear Maggie screaming, and we run into the house to see Danny throwing the doll into the rafters.

"What is the matter with you?" I yell as I cuff him on the back of his head. "Why can't you leave your sister alone? Can you not see how much the doll means to her? "

"It's just a stupid rag. I'm just jokin' with her."

This time I lose control and slap him hard on the face. Too hard! I see Anne glare at me. Danny runs from the house and Anne runs to the door.

"He shouldn't speak to us that way," I say. "He must learn."

As I think about his proper punishment, Anne comes over and picks up the doll. She gently cradles it and gives it back to Maggie. Maggie tearfully hugs the doll and starts speaking softly to it.

Anne says, "Danny is only a young one too. He is only seven for God's sake. He doesn't know any better. He is used to playing roughly with the other boys."

"Well, he is going to learn proper behaviour with his younger brothers and sisters. I'll not raise a bully."

In the days following, I give Danny harder chores in the fields and make him go to bed earlier than the other children.

On another day, while gathering manure for the midden, I hear Maggie screaming again. Danny is running from the cabin and into the fields. Anne drops the potatoes she was gathering and runs into the house. When I go through the door, I see Anne trying unsuccessfully to console Maggie. Anne looks at me and says, "He threw Biddy into the fire."

I look and see the doll burning on the coals of the turf. The chaff is exploding into a bright orange display as ashes of blackened cloth fly up the chimney. Tears come to my eyes as my heart is breaking too. I can't understand how any child of mine could hurt a lovely wee angel like Maggie.

Danny doesn't return by nightfall. While Anne stays with the other children, I go looking for him with a torch and calling his name. He is too young to be out there alone. I call on my brother John and other neighbours to help in the search. After an hour or so, I hear my brother-in-law, Owen McCullough, calling my name. Owen came up from Ballinacor. He tells us that Danny is with them at their home. Danny told them that he is running away from home because he is afraid of me. I explain the situation and ask if he and Mary can keep him for a few days. He agrees and I return home to my family. Maggie is still crying.

I visit Owen and my sister Mary days later to take Danny home. He looks at me with fear in his eyes, and I try to smile. We have buttermilk and scone with Mary's family before we head home. At first, Danny and I don't speak to each other on the lane up the hill. Then Danny says, "I'm sorry, Da."

Apparently Mary and Owen have been talking to him and showing him the meanness of his actions. I resist the urge to lecture him, and I kneel down and hug him. He is only seven years old and I know now that he knew no better when he picked on Maggie. I pray that he knows better now. I vow not to bring the incident up unless something like it happens again. In my heart I was severely disappointed in him, and I am afraid that it will be a while before I can forget it. I hope that I cannot let it show.

Anne makes Maggie another doll and tells her that it should be called Gracie. Maggie takes it and plays with it for a day. She doesn't play with it after that.

We are expecting another child. It has been over four years since Jimmy was born. Anne had a few miscarriages over the past few years, and it looked as if Jimmy was going to be our last child.

On Sunday, Father O'Flaherty celebrates Mass in the rain at the Gleneely Mass rock. Normally it is the curate, Father

O'Donnell, who comes to the hills. I tell Father O'Flaherty that he is very welcome at our house for a bite to eat after Mass and he agrees to come. Back at the house, I tell him about our future child.

"Well then, congratulations are in order. We can certainly use more Catholics in this parish. Can I assume that the Kellys know of this?"

"They do," I answer. "Mr. Kelly called on us last Thursday. He seemed quite pleased."

Father says, "Did he tell you of the latest development with the parliament in Dublin?"

I answer, "He only mentioned that there was a petition taken at the Church of Ireland in Donaghmore but he didn't know what it was about."

"Well we know now what is happening. All over Ireland, many are trying to get us to join in the union with England and Scotland. The elected members of the Irish parliament seem to be for it. Of course, the appointed members would support it, including the Protestant bishops. They are English through and through."

"Ach! Once we are in the union, there'll be no more chances for our independence," I reply.

Father says, "Oddly enough, our Bishop O'Donnell is for it. He says that, with Irish sitting in English Parliament, the plight of the Irish will be heard. I've heard from others that emancipation for Catholics is perfectly assured once the union takes place."

I reply, "I can see no good coming from this. Our only hope is that France will somehow defeat England in the war. Any enemy of England is a friend of Ireland"

"It is highly unlikely that France will defeat England, Patrick. All of Europe has turned against General Napoleon."

"There is some good that comes from this war, Father. The prices for our grain at the markets are the highest I can remember. Finally I can afford to put meat on my table and still have money left over to buy farm tools. In another year, I may be able to buy a horse and cart."

Chapter 8
[1800 - 1806]

At the end of the century, our sixth child is born. It is a son, named Charles for Anne's older brother. The new century brings a lot of changes to Ireland although the changes matter little here in the Donegal outlands. The Act of Union is passed in Irish and English parliaments, joining Ireland with Scotland and England. The Irish Parliament is dissolved and English Parliament offers seats to Irish members. All of the Irish members of parliament are Protestant of course. No Catholic is allowed any political position. To assure this, all members of parliament must take a loyalty oath that includes remarks against the Pope and "idolatrous" papist behaviour (such as our praying to the Blessed Mother).

The new century brings us a change to our parish, as well. Father O'Flaherty passes on to his reward in heaven and Bishop O'Donnell of Derry assigns Father Charles McBride from Kilmacrennan as our parish priest. Father McBride is a burley, older man educated in France during the days of the penal laws. When I get the chance, I arrange to be a part of his conversations with other parishioners just to learn about what is going on in the world beyond our wee green farmland.

John and I sometimes visit the chapel in Aghyaran when we are working on the land of our sister-in-law, Mary McMenamin. Aghyaran is just over the hill from my sister-in-law's land. It is in County Tyrone and on the other side of the Mourne Beg River. The chapel was recently completed, and it has replaced an earlier chapel that may have been built when they were starting to ease up on the penal laws. The new chapel is larger than our chapel at the Cross, but it is still a simple thatched-roof building. Aghyaran's parish priest, Father James O'Mongan, was responsible for completion of the building.

The proper name of the Aghyaran parish is Termonamongan, named for the ancestral O'Mongan family who, for centuries, administered the parish lands there belonging to the diocese of Derry. Father O'Mongan is one of a long list of clerics from that distinguished family.

Shortly after the chapel is completed, the bishop transfers Father O'Mongan to a parish in Strabane and assigns Father Francis Duffy as the new priest in Aghyaran.

We learn that our Holy Father, Pope Pius VI, died last August. Pope Pius had been pope for my entire life. He is certain to become a saint someday, having died in captivity by the French. It seems that he protested the killing of King Louis XVI during the French revolution. Napoleon seized Papal Land and kept him prisoner in Valence.

After several months elapse, a new pope is elected. The new pope, an Italian of course, becomes Pope Pius VII. He negotiates with Napoleon for the return of the papacy to Rome.

We learn that James Napper Tandy is being held at the Lifford jail. Napper Tandy was one of the founders of the United Irishmen. During his years in Paris, Napoleon appointed him as a general in the French Army. In the 1798 invasion of Ireland, his ship, the Anacreon, entered Sheephaven Bay in County Donegal where he learned the ill fate of Wolfe Tone and the French fleet. He reportedly stepped ashore and made some sort of proclamation, got drunk, and was carried back to his ship. That seemed to be one of his main contributions to the 1798 rebellion. His ship left Ireland and put him ashore in Bergen, Norway. He was later captured in Hamburg and was returned to Ireland where he is imprisoned at Lifford.

Napper is tried as a traitor at the Lifford courthouse and condemned to death. Napoleon hears about his imprisonment and insists that Tandy is a French officer and must be returned to France. Because England is currently attempting a treaty with Napoleon, Napper is released from Lifford jail in 1801 and is exiled to France.

As I suspect, the rising prices for our crops bring an increase in our rent. Mr. Knox rides up to our cottage on a splendid chestnut-coloured horse in March and tells us about a large rent increase. Mr. Knox is the agent for our landlord, Sam Delap. Although Mr. Delap lives nearby in a manor house in Monellan, he employs a land agent in Killygordon to handle his business dealings. Mr. Knox is the agent for several other owners who lease land in Donaghmore, as well.

Our payment will be due in May. My thoughts of extra funds for improving our condition evaporate. He tells me that the value of our land has increased because of the price of the grain our farm can produce. I ask him if the rent will decrease when grain prices drop. He shrugs and gives me no answer.

Road construction is making travel about the parish easier for horse and cart. A bridge is built across the River Finn at Liscooley in 1801.

We have another child. Hugh is born in 1801. Anne is now pleading with me for mercy. She wants no more children. Hugh is a difficult birth and we almost lose both Anne and the wain. I will try to curtail my impulses and try to think of the consequences of my passion.

My son Danny is turning out fine. After the problems we had with his bullying Maggie, he has given us no trouble. Anne believes we have my sister Mary to thank for it. Mary and her husband Owen have a knack for turning out their own well behaved children. I'm thinking that we must not have that knack. We should have asked Mary and Owen to raise our children up to the age when they get some sense. The brief time that Danny spent with Mary and Owen seems to have straightened him out. Danny is my oldest and I think that he will grow to be a responsible man who can manage our farm when I get too old to handle it.

In 1806, Anne's cousin Denis sails from Derry to America where he plans to settle in Philadelphia. Denis lived near Castlefin and had managed to save money from his scutch mill for his journey with his wife and family. He was a secret partner in the mill with a Presbyterian neighbour; it is still somewhat prohibited for Catholics to become tradesmen and merchants. With his savings and the sale of his share in the mill, Denis and his family should do well in America.

Chapter 9
[1806 - 1808]

Since 1798, John and I have been farming my late brother Jimmy's place. With the work of taking care of our new land, we decide that we should terminate the lease. I mention it to Jimmy's widow, and she tells me that she would like to return there and take over the farm. Her son Patrick is now in his 18th year and with the other children's help, they should be able to manage. Mary and her children, Patrick, Michael, Brigid, Margaret, and Denis move up to the old farm to keep it going. Mary and Michael restore the ruined old still and plan to start selling poteen out of the shebeen in the old byre attached to her cottage. Our farms at Glencarn produce more barley this year which Mary hopes to turn into profit to pay us back. In just two years, she has a fair clientele of lads gathering at the shebeen to buy her alcoholic refreshment. Some stay around for drink and good craic on Saturday and Sunday nights. John and I frequently join them.

Uncle Jimmy dies in 1806. Anne and Mary McMenamin come down to join Aunt Mary in preparing for the wake. They are not needed, of course. Jimmy had many friends in the village, and Aunt Mary has plenty of help. The wake is crowded on each of the two nights. The death of Uncle Jimmy is like the death of my own father, and tears come into my eyes when the keening led by my sister Mary begins. I pray that he spends little time in Purgatory, and he receives his true reward in Heaven. He deserves it for his kindness and his saintly manner in all the years that I knew him.

I hadn't seen Uncle Jimmy's daughters for a long time. Cousins Mary and Teresa are solemn looking spinsters in their 30s. They smile guardedly when I talk with them. Cousin Lizzy is married to a man named Bradley, a foreman at the linen mill in Strabane. She has two children who are staying today with her husband's parents. Liz looks radiant and it is apparent that she loves her life away from Donaghmore.

After the prayers are said over Uncle Jimmy's body, I join the men in smoking pipes of tobacco provided by cousin Willie. Willie will now be the holder of Uncle Jimmy's farmland, and I am happy for him. I know that Aunt Mary will be well cared for because her son Willie has a fine disposition. A bottle is passed around and I have a drop of real whiskey supplied by Quinn's Alehouse at the Cross. Many of the men can't handle the whiskey and start acting stupidly by challenging each other to foot races on the road outside. The scene begins to seem disrespectful to me and I walk away to talk with my brother John.

John is sitting alone by the door. I say, "We'll miss Uncle Jimmy. Do you remember his stories by the fire?"

"I do indeed. I can still picture Cuchulan in battle sometimes when I look into the fireplace."

I consider bringing up Will's unusual ancestry.

"Uncle Jimmy told me something about Willie once that he wanted kept a secret," I suggest. "Did he tell you as well?"

John looks at me strangely. He laughs. "About Will being a changeling y' mean?"

"Aye. Then you know about it. Good. The secret has been eating at me for years."

John says, "The whole parish knows about it. The whole parish knows that it is rubbish as well."

"What do you mean?"

"Take a good long look at Willie's face. Do y' see anything queer?"

I say, "I can see him from here. His ears don't stick out as much as they did."

"Ach! His eyes! Look at his eyes for Christ's sake."

I walk over to see Willie closer. He is talking to some friends and doesn't notice me staring at him. I walk back to John.

"His eyes look grand."

"What colour are they?"

I try to think. I never paid attention to the colour of Will's eyes. I walk back over to see.

"They are brown, I think. What's the bloody difference what colour they are?" I ask John.

John says, "Aye. They are brown. Aunt Mary and Uncle Jimmy had blue eyes."

This is making no sense to me. So Will's eyes are different than his parents. Many children have different colour eyes than their parents. Sometimes dark-haired parents have red-haired children. No one thinks anything is queer about it.

John finally explains it, "Unlike brown-eyed parents, blue-eyed parents can have only blue-eyed children."

"Then Will really is a changeling."

"Ya eejit, ya! Think about it! Aunt Mary has sinful intercourse with a lad when Uncle Jimmy is out. She becomes pregnant and has the baby. Uncle Jimmy thinks that it is his. After a few days, the baby's eyes turn brown. Everyone knows but you, ya eejit, that it can't be Uncle Jimmy's baby. Aunt Mary leaves the baby alone for a few minutes and then tells everyone that the fairies took it and left one of their own. Everyone believes her. Years later, people figure it out that she could have been lying. No one tells her to her face."

I am shocked. First of all, John has never called me an idiot before. He must be drunk. Second, I can't believe my dear old Aunt Mary could do anything like that. She may have been pretty at one time, but even if she was the most desirable woman in the parish, she would never break her marriage vows. I would prefer to believe that Willie is a fairy changeling. Still,

I look at Aunt Mary differently now. I am sorry that I talked this over with my brother John.

After a long work day on Saturday, I walk over to Mary McMenamin's shebeen for a bit of relaxation. Tommy McGoldrick and Charley McGlinchy are already there talking with a few lads that I don't know. Ned and Andy are their names. They are already inebriated and are having a fierce argument about the quality of poteen over legally taxed whiskey.

The discussion turns to the increases of our rent. Ned and Andy are talking about assembling a group to meet the land agent with the hope of lowering their rent. It is apparent that they are having trouble earning enough money for rent with the poor harvests they have been having. Ned gets angry and talks about threatening his agent, Richard Clarke from Killygordon. I try to explain that it isn't Clarke's fault. He is under direction of the landowner, William Hanley. Clarke must do his duty by collecting the rent demanded by Mr. Hanley. The other lad says, "We must get him to convince Hanley to lower the rent. We just can't pay."

I sort of agree with this approach but his friend says, "Aye, and if he doesn't lower it we will kill the bugger to teach those blood sucking agents a lesson."

Andy says, "And what will ya kill him with, yer bare hands? He is half again as big as ya. By God, he'll wipe the lane with ya."

Ned says, "I can get a weapon. I know some people."

Andy answers, "Are ya thick? Think about it before ya do something stupid. Ya have a family to think about. Ya can't help them if you're transported to Botany Bay."

We spend more time trying to calm Ned down but can't seem to do it unless we appear to agree with him. I notice that my nephew Mickey, Mary McMenamin's son, is off to the side and taking all of the conversation in.

All of this is taking time, and soon my twelve year old son Jamie arrives and asks me to come home. My friends and the new lads at the shebeen laugh and one says, "Ach. It looks as if it is time for yer old lady to reel ya in. She'll be needin' ya to wash the supper dishes."

I reply, "It'll be no supper dishes for me. It looks like supper was an hour ago. I'll see you lads another day."

I return home with Jamie and get an angry look from Anne when I walk through the door. There is a cold dish of potatoes on the table for me. The others in the family have already eaten.

Anne isn't keen on me staying at my sister-in-law's shebeen after my work is finished. She feels that I should be home instructing the children. She asks me why I don't just buy a jar and bring it home. I tell her that I enjoy the company of the lads who stop by. It just isn't the same having a drop at home. We have many arguments in this regard, and she frequently stops talking to me for days. I still love her but I surely enjoy the feeling of good craic and poteen at Mary's.

We go to the Ballybofey fair to sell a pig we raised from birth. With our profits and some extra money, we buy our first donkey. It is a lovely looking animal, and it follows us back home with a few whacks on his backside with a switch. The animal, who we name Donal, will save us much work when we hitch him to the cart we have used for years and have had to pull ourselves.

Anne's father, Danny Kelly, dies in 1808. There is a big affair at his two-day wake that spills over into the street and down to Quinn's for pints of porter. The creamy liquid slips through my gullet and soon I am having a grand time with the lads on this sad occasion and feeling a wee bit guilty. A fight breaks out between two brothers. Charlie Quinn, with the help of a few burly lads, throws them into the street. I sheepishly return to the wake where there are prayers still being said for my poor father-in-law. Father McBride has arrived and is leading the prayers. He will celebrate the Requiem Mass tomorrow. I look forward to talking with him, but I think that I will wait until tomorrow when I am feeling more sober.

On the morning of the funeral, Father McBride walks to the Kelly home in his vestments. The pallbearers carry the coffin out of the cottage and follow the priest through the streets to the chapel. The Kelly family and friends form a solemn procession behind. After the gospel of the Mass, Father McBride turns from the altar and addresses the congregation. He tells many stories of his brief friendship with Danny and of the good works Danny has done for the parish. He tells of how Danny brought his family up in the true faith, and how he will surely see the face of God. Tears stream down the faces of Mr. Kelly's family members before Father McBride turns again to the altar and begins reciting the Latin words of the *Credo* in his loud but melodious voice.

After the funeral, I take our children up to the farm with me. Anne is staying with her widowed mother for a while. The Kelly farm will be left to Anne's brothers, Charley and Frankie. Things will soon return to normal and we will all be about the business of scraping a living out of the land.

As for the two unfortunate lads from the shebeen, Andy is able to make his rent payment in May, but Ned is unable to pay his. Because he already had one gale hanging, Mr. Clarke delivers a notice to Ned informing him that he will have to vacate his land. The notice is a formality. Like the rest of us poor farmers, none of Ned's family can read. His neighbours, including my sister-in-law, are helping to get his meagre possessions together when the land agent arrives with seven armed bailiffs. Many oaths are directed at the agent from the villagers, but no violence takes place. There is not a dry eye in the townland as Ned's neighbours watch him pull his cart down the road to Castlederg with his family trudging behind. Ned had told his neighbours that he will stay with his brother-in-law in County Tyrone until he can find work as a labourer. After Ned leaves, the bailiffs set up a high frame for the battering ram. They punch a hole in the side of the cabin and set fire to the roof just to make sure Ned does not return.

Chapter 10
(1808 - 1812)

The children are getting older now. My sons Danny and Patrick turned 18 and 16. They both are helping my brother John on his farm. My other sons are growing fast, but they are still a bit young. Jamie is 13 years old. He helps gathering potatoes, feeding the pigs, fetching milk from dairy farmers, bringing water from the well, and carrying in the turf for the fire. He has little time for play anymore. His brothers Charley and Hugh are still too young to work, and they spend a lot of time outdoors, watching their brothers in the fields and trying to help. Nellie and Maggie are young women now, being ages 17 and 15. They are learning the arts of sewing and mending clothes from Anne. The girls are the main reason I've been seeing many of the townland boys hanging around our farm on summer evenings before the midges get annoying. Whenever I turn around at Mass, I see Charley McGlinchy's boys, Owen and Paddy, looking at the girls. They quickly look away when they see me. I know that I have to get used to my girls marrying someday, but I sometimes wish that they would meet some of the farmers from better land in the valley. Anne and I are looking forward to the dance at the Cross in June where the girls can see some of the other lads.

Our nieces and nephews are becoming adults as well. Mary McMenamin's son Patrick is 21 and runs things at Mary's farm. He is big but gentle, and he is getting a bit fat. Mary is looking to rent another farm nearby that she hopes will be managed by her 19 year old son Mickey. Mickey is an outgoing and lively lad. He is lean and muscular from the hard work he did as a boy on Mary's farm. Mary's daughter Brigid is 18 years old and is often seen in the company of John Gallagher of Monellan. Mary has no problem with that match. John is a good farmer and will probably inherit his father's farm on good land. Mary's other daughter Maggie is 17 and unusually attractive. Her full lips and widely-spaced eyes give her an almost foreign appearance. Mary's other sons, Jimmy and Denis, are ages 16 and 14 and they look like they will be strongly built young men like their brother Mickey.

My sister Mary and her husband are happy and proud of their three sons and three daughters. All of their sons have attended the Protestant school in Killygordon and can read and write. Mary is hoping that their youngest son, Owen, will be accepted into the Catholic seminary at Maynooth.

There is a rent increase in the townland of Drumbeg. This sits poorly with the farmers there who can just barely make the payment as it is. They feel that they have no power to resist the demands of the landlords. Some believe that the landlords want the smaller farmers to vacate so that they can consolidate their lots for larger grain fields. Drumbeg, in the upper reaches of the parish, has some of the toughest lads in the parish, and it appears that they will be forming an organization to confront the landlords. I am aware that many violent acts have been committed elsewhere in Ireland by such groups who meet in secret.

Mary McMenamin is approached by one of the biggest trouble-makers in the townland. He asks her if he has her support and the support of her sons. Mary answers yes out of fear, and then she visits me to find out what to do. I tell her to find excuses for keeping her sons away from the meetings and to explain to her sons that little good will come from belonging to the group.

A few days later, the leader of the group, whom I will not name except to call "Mister Fox", comes to Glencarn and calls on me. He gives me the same story he told Mary and asks me to come to the meeting tonight after sundown at the old Mass rock in Meenluskeybane.

I attend out of curiosity. About 15 farmers are there. I recognize most of them, but I won't reveal their names. Mister Fox does a good job at stirring up the crowd and makes us take an oath. One by one, we recite the lengthy solemn oath while looking directly into the eyes of the leader. We pledge our lives in the support of fair treatment for Catholic tenants. We vow never to reveal what goes on at the meetings. All know the fate awaiting any informers in the group. Fox then gives us his plan to acquire weapons. I can see how this is going and decide then and there to stay away from future meetings. The secret organization is given the name "boley boys" by the leader.

It isn't long before word of boley boy activities reaches me. One of the soldiers from the garrison is ambushed and beaten. His musket, powder, and shot are taken. The home of one of the large landowners is invaded. No one is harmed, but all of the guns in the house are taken. A few nights later, the horse of land agent Richard Clarke is killed and mutilated. A threatening message to Clarke is found with the horse. Soon, Donaghmore is teaming with red-coated soldiers and things quiet down for a while.

June comes and the midsummer night ceilidh is held in a field at the Cross near the chapel. A bonfire is set, and fiddlers play for dancing. Almost all of the young people from the parish attend. Our daughters are there, but they are seen talking and dancing with the McGlinchy boys from my own townland. There seems to be very little mixing going on. The lads and lasses are standing around talking in groups of young people from their own townlands and villages. My dreams about my daughters meeting more prosperous suitors are for naught. A few Protestant lads show up but get a cold reception from the lasses and their parents. They soon depart.

The young people are not the only ones dancing. Most of the dancers are older women who dance with each other. The old widows seem to be having a grand time. They look in annoyance at the young couples swinging around the grounds at a reckless pace with little grace. Paddy McGlinchy seems to be the most rowdy and boisterous. He is well appreciated by the lasses there if you can judge by their laughter.

The adults are starting to feel the effects of the great quantities of whiskey and poteen drunk at the ceilidh. They start to stagger home before midnight, myself being one of them. Anne stays with her sisters to keep an eye on our girls. As I walk up the road I am surprised to run into a group of boley boys running down past me. I hear a "Hello Paddy" as they pass. They are all wearing uniforms of white shirts with black scarves covering their faces. I turn to see them run through the crowd by the bonfire shouting something I can't make out, and then they disappear into the darkness. I can't be sure, but I believe that my nephew Mickey is among them.

A few days later, we learn that some animals owned by Protestant farmers were killed that night. Also, a notice was nailed to the door of the Church of Ireland across the river stating that Catholic farmers will no longer pay the tithe. Trouble is about to start.

Within days, an Orange Society is established in Castlefin to protect Protestants. On July 12, Orange lodges from Antrim and Armagh march with the new Donegal members through the streets of Castlefin and Killygordon. Their parade shows the strength and dedication of the Protestant community. We can hear the sound of their drums even up here in the hills.

Tithes are collected this year by the land agents with the help of soldiers from the garrison. No one fails to pay. The only incident that occurs is when a soldier is shot in the leg on a side street of Killygordon. The assassin is seen running away, but no witness can identify him.

Few land agents are travelling alone in Donaghmore these days. They generally have a soldier or two with them. Nevertheless, today Alexander Knox rides his horse up to my cottage and knocks on my door.

"Hello, Patrick. May I have a few words with you?"

"Aye, what will you be wanting of me, another rent increase?"

"Patrick, I believe that you are one of the few sensible people here in Donaghmore. For the peace of the parish, I'm hoping that you will help us out. I know that you'll not be turning anyone in, but if you can get word to the leader of the despicable gang that is terrorizing the agents and landowners, I'll be mighty grateful to you. There is most likely a reduction in your rent as well."

I say, "I don't believe I like the sound of this. What do you want me to do?"

"Just arrange a meeting between the leader and myself. We want to negotiate a truce."

I tell him that I will try, and I ask him to come back tomorrow.

"I'm not wanting any reward for doing this. If there is a settlement in regard to the tenants, that will be reward enough."

Any other benefits will put me on the wrong side of this conflict. I walk to the leader's cabin a few townlands away and we talk in his cow byre.

"Paddy, you haven't been to our meetings. Are you not with us?"

I say, "I'm not for the methods you are using. They are going to cause some great problems for us here. I'm afraid you are already putting my nephews at risk. I'll not cause you any trouble, but I'm against your violent acts. I'm here at my estate agent's request to see if you will meet him. Perhaps he can arrange to meet your demands."

Fox laughs and tells me, "You know I cannot meet with him directly, Paddy. I'll be a dead man. You tell your man that we want the rents to drop at least to the amount they were two years ago, and we want no more rent increases for another five years, even if we improve our properties. This is reasonable, and if they come through, we will direct our efforts to other activities like convincing the Church of Ireland to get its funds from its Protestant parishioners only."

When Mr. Knox comes up the next day, I tell him what has to be done. He says that there is a meeting of land agents in Killygordon next week and he will let them know. He will also ask my landlord to lower his rents as requested.

The meeting of agents takes place; they correspond with the landlords, those in the parish and those far away. All of the landlords refuse to budge. Mr. Knox brings me the news which I relay to Fox. The brief peace ends, and the violence continues with an attempted attack on the home of my land agent. This gives me great sorrow. I believe Mr. Knox to be a decent and honourable man.

When I hear of the action against Mr. Knox, I walk up to Mr. Fox's farm and confront him.

"You have got to stop this. You may believe that you have justification for harming the agents, but it is immoral. They are just doing their job, man. It is the landlords you must threaten if you want action."

"I think that we will accomplish our purpose by killing one of the agents. They didn't try hard enough to get a rent reduction. We have to supply some motivation."

"You're mad if you think that is the answer. They will find you and hang you. You'll not get away with it."

Fox thinks a bit and says, "I admit that we shouldn't harm Knox. We should hit the agents responsible for past evictions, perhaps George Roberts or Richard Clarke. Aye, I'll feel better about that."

"I still believe that you'll hang."

Fox looks at me menacingly. "I won't hang unless someone turns me in. That won't be you, will it?"

I feel insulted that he would think that I would do that. Still, if I could save an innocent person's life....Ach, I couldn't do it.

For days after my meeting with Fox, I notice that I am being watched by young lads from Drumbeg. They must believe that I'll turn him in. One of them is standing next to a tree in the next farm. I sneak through the tall corn and get uphill of him. Quietly, I creep up and pin his neck to my chest with my forearm.

"Listen! Tell Fox that I'm not going to turn him in. There is no need for this. I don't want to see you or anyone else around here. Fox doesn't want me for an enemy."

The lad disappears up the hill after I let him go. I wonder if I made myself clear enough.

Late one night, six soldiers break into the cabin of Frankie Bonner, also known as the Fox, and arrest him. He is suspected of being the leader of the boley boys. Frankie is shackled and taken by coach to Lifford jail to await trial.

I am the person that the boley boys suspect to have turned Frankie in to the authorities. That night, a torch is thrown on our roof to start a fire. I hear the crackling of the thatch and get my family out of the cottage. With the help of my sons who run to get water from the nearby burn, I am able to quench and cut away the burning thatch. There is considerable damage to my roof, but when I think of the tragedy we avoided by hearing the fire start, I am thankful.

When morning comes, I go to the home of Frankie Bonner and talk with his wife. I express my sorrow of his arrest, and I tell her that I had nothing to do with it. After explaining how Frankie's gang tried to burn down my cottage, I ask her who she thinks was responsible.

"Ah, that is a terrible thing they did to you. It could have killed your whole family. I'm sorry, but Frankie never mentioned names when he talked about his boys. I wish I could help you, but I cannot."

I move on to Mary McMenamin's cottage.

"Mary, where can I find Michael?"

Mary tells me that my nephew is in the fields cutting barley. I hurry to where he is working.

"Michael, the boley boys tried to burn down my cottage last night. They believe that I informed on Frankie. Of course I did not. I know that you are a part of the gang. Were you in on it?"

"Ah Christ no, Uncle Patrick. I had nothin' to do with it. They had a meetin' last night, but I was busy at the still."

"Who can I talk to? Who is second in command?"

"Ach, there's Gimpy Doogan and Owen McGrath. I better take you to them. I should vouch for ya. I know that y'd never inform on us."

We both walk down to Gimpy Doogan's cottage. He is in the cow byre with a few lads. When we walk in, he looks startled. I believe that he knows of the fire that almost killed me and my family. I run over and grab his neck with both hands. The lads grab me by my arms and drag me off him.

Doogan yells at Michael, "Why in the name of God did you bring him here?"

Michael says, "Me uncle tells me ya tried to burn down his home with him and his family in it. Did ya?"

"We had a meeting at the rock last night. Some of the lads recalled that Frankie had suspicions about your uncle. A group of hot-heads must have acted on their own."

Michael glares at Doogan. "The man never got a chance to defend himself. What kind of organization do we have here now? Who is in charge?"

Finally I speak, "Gimpy, are you telling me that you had nothing to do with the fire?"

"Aye, I am"

"Well, I'm telling you that I had nothing to do with Frankie's arrest. I want that information given to the rest of the boys. Michael, will you vouch for me?"

"Aye, I will. I know that y'd never inform on our lads. I'll get some fellas to help ya fix yer roof."

Frankie's neighbour, Owen McGrath, and his family disappear from his land a few days later. Everyone believes that he was secretly arrested for his boley boys involvement. The truth comes out later.

The next assize in Lifford finds Frankie Bonner guilty of various crimes of assault based on testimony from Owen

McGrath. Frankie's sentence is transportation to Botany Bay for 10 years.

Of course, Owen, the witness against Frankie Bonner, never returns home to Drumbeg. When news of the sentence reaches Donaghmore, his cottage is burned. As far as the people of the parish are concerned, Owen is a dead man. Some say that he was given land in Leitrim. If this is true, for certain the lads will catch up with him some day.

With Frankie Bonner gone, the activities of the boley boys come to a temporary halt. The landlords and their estate agents breathe a sigh of relief. The tenants struggle to keep up their rental payments, and those families who can't succeed are evicted. Fortunately, those evictions are few.

No more acts of terror take place until the year 1812. Richard Clarke is the victim. He is attacked while coming home by carriage from church with his family. The assassins wait in Kiltown by the side of the post road. When Clarke's carriage approaches, one of them runs out into the road and frightens the horse to a stop. The other climbs into the carriage and shoots Mr. Clarke in the chest at close range with his pistol. Clarke's wife and children in the carriage are naturally horrified by the violence of the attack. The masked, white-shirted assassins run toward the river and get away.

Clarke's son, a 15 year old boy, is brave and smart enough to take the reins, and he drives to the physician in Killygordon. Mrs. Clarke presses on Richard's chest wound to stop the bleeding during the ride. The quick actions of the Clarkes and the skills of Doctor Babbington save the life of Richard Clarke.

Owen Dolan, a new landholder in County Leitrim, walks into his cottage in the townland of Clooneclare after working in the fields. He is surprised to find the cottage empty. Where are his wife and children? He places more turf on the fire. He should be eating supper soon. Where are they?

Four men come up the lane. Although he can't make out their faces, he sees that one has a gimpy leg. He recalls that limp. Owen walks to the door and looks at the unsmiling faces. He remembers them now, and fear overcomes him. His legs get weak, and he momentarily loses control of his bowels. He smells his own shite, but he doesn't care. He knows that it is the least of his worries.

"Hello Owen. Haven't seen you in a while," one man says.

"Ah fellas, yis haven't hurt me family, have yis?"

"We would not do such a thing. We are not savages."

The man with the limp says, "It's just you we want, Owen."

Owen kneels down and begs, "Is there not some way I can get out of this? I'll tell the court that I lied. Frankie is probably still in a prison in Dublin. I can get him out."

"It is too late for that. You have sinned grievously and must pay. I think that it is time for you to say some prayers. Do you know your act of contrition?"

Owen begins to babble his prayers. Tears are streaming down his face.

"Mickey, it is time."

A young man walks behind Owen. He wrinkles his nose at the stench. In a flash, he wraps a loop of twine around his victim's neck and tightens, pulling Owen up off his knees. Owen struggles and tries to stand. The struggle lasts what seems like minutes; then Owen falls limp. The young man stands there for a few minutes more and lets go of the twine. The four men walk back down the lane to their horses being held by another lad. They mount and ride north.

chapter 11
(1813-1815)

A young farmer by the name of Eddie Daly is arrested for the attempted murder of Richard Clarke. It has been one year since the ambush. On the day of the attack, a witness saw Eddie removing a white shirt near the bridge at Dromore. There is no one at the trial to remind the court that it was a Sunday, and Eddie probably only wore the shirt to Mass. The witness, whose identity is unknown because he testified behind a screen during the trial, recognized Eddie at market day in Castlefin and pointed him out to the soldiers who were keeping the peace there.

Incredibly, that testimony is enough to convict him of the crime. The judge, who has experienced some tenant violence of his own, wants to make an example of Eddie in order to stamp out what he calls "whiteboy" aggression. He sentences Eddie to death by hanging. The execution is scheduled for Castlefin on Saturday to show the boley boys an example of Crown justice. A scaffold is set up at the Castlefin diamond. Father McBride goes to Lifford to hear Eddie's confession, and Eddie is taken by carriage to the site of his impending death. A large crowd from the Orange Lodges are waiting for him. They jeer as he ascends the scaffold. A hood is placed over his head and a knotted rope is wrapped around his neck. The trapdoor drops and Eddie is gone from us.

On the night after the execution, the horses of several prominent residents of Killygordon are killed and some homes are set on fire. It appears that the boley boys have started again.

We now hear about the great man, Daniel O'Connell. He is a renowned lawyer in Dublin who defended many Irish causes in the past. In 1813, he defends the publisher of a Dublin newspaper who was accused of libel in his criticism of the government. O'Connell's speech, attacking the Orange jury, prosecutor, and judge, wins him the title "Defender of Ireland." Later that year, a bill is introduced in parliament called the Catholic Relief Bill. O'Connell vocally denounces it because it gives the English the right to appoint Catholic bishops and to supervise documents from Rome. The bill dies in parliament. Ireland needs a man like O'Connell.

After a long courtship, my eldest son Danny marries Nancy Callaghan from Cronalaghy. The marriage is performed at the Callaghan home by the new curate. There is a grand party with dancing to a fiddler and piper. The festivities last all day and late into the night. Everyone from the hills stop by. The party ends when we run out of drink, which is long after we run out of food. The happy couple runs off to their new cottage we built on the partition of land I gave Danny from my farm.

Danny and Nancy present me with my first grandchild the next year. It is a boy and is named Patrick after myself. He looks grand with a full head of jet-black hair like his grandmother's before it turned grey. I can't remember when I have been happier. We have a granddaughter after that. She is a wee red-head who will be named Brigid. Where in God's name she got her red hair, I don't know.

There are weddings in Drumbeg as well. My nephew, Mickey, who is my brother Jimmy's son, marries Agnes McMenamin from Bealalt. Agnes is remotely related to Mickey's mother but remote enough that Father McBride has no reservations about letting the wedding take place. Mickey and Agnes are renting land in Drumbeg from Andrew Devenny of Castlefin. In the years following, they have two sons, James and Patrick. There are several James and Patrick Gallens in the hills of Donaghmore now. Beside those in our family, the townlands of Meenreagh and Cronalaghy have quite a few as well. When they grow up, they will have to be identified by their townlands or their family nicknames. Mickey's sons are known as James and Patrick "Mickey" for their father. My Danny's son will be known as Patrick "Danny."

The war between England and France continues on and off through the years. Partly because of England's embargo of European ports, America declares war on England. All of this keeps the price of our grain fairly high which is helping the poor Irish farmer pay his bills. In late 1814, the war with America ends by treaty. In 1815, England and Prussia crush the army of Napoleon, ending the war with France. The ports of Europe are finally open to trade, and our crop prices fall again. Of course, the rents stay high.

At the nearby Killeter Fair in County Tyrone, suspected members of a secret defender society, possibly boley boys, are seen in the public house. Someone alerts the English garrison, and they surround the pub. When a sergeant enters the alehouse and attempts to arrest the alleged boley boys, gunfire breaks out. The soldiers rush in and fire into the crowd. Three men and one woman are killed, and twelve men are wounded, including two of the soldiers. No one knows who started the gunfight, and none of the people in the pub can be positively identified as belonging to an illegal secret organization. The only conviction after the "Killeter Massacre" is of one of the soldiers who is positively identified as firing into the crowd and killing Henry Gallagher, an innocent bystander. The soldier is found guilty of manslaughter and sentenced to only one year in jail.

The rheumatism is starting to bother me now and I am feeling a bit useless doing farm work. Fortunately, my sons are taking over. My walking is poor and I often use a stick. I am aware that I am now an old man. I am spending more time at the Cross talking with friends at Quinn's Alehouse. When I can't stagger home, I stay overnight with my Aunt Mary and her son Willie in Monellan.

Charley Quinn is about to sell his alehouse to Paddy Gallagher. I talk this over with Andy McGlinchy at the pub. Andy is the brother of my neighbour Charley McGlinchy. "Ach Andy, we have been drinking here together for many years now."

Andy jokes, "Aye and I am still hopin' you will buy your own pint someday."

"I will buy my own this moment and one for yourself as well, if you'll be civil about it. I can't believe that Quinn is leaving this place. It won't be the same without his evil temper and his filthy habits."

Andy whispers, "Shut your gob! Quinn can hear ya."

"He won't pay me any mind. He knows how I feel about him... Mister Quinn! If you please, a pint of porter for my old friend Andy here and one for myself. And one for yourself as well. Please let us have clean glasses this time."

I know that Quinn will not accept my offer of a free pint. He has been staying off the drink since he almost killed Mrs. Quinn after a night of drinking in his own pub. Father McBride gave him the scolding of his life. He also convinced Quinn that it is unwise for him to continue drinking in his establishment with the temptation of liquor about. Quinn agreed. A wise decision it was indeed because, on the nights when he became drunk, his patrons received many whiskeys and porters without paying for them. Mr. Quinn is a poor businessman and can ill afford to give away his wares for nothing. I believe that I was the beneficiary of Quinn's drunken benevolence on many a night. It is one of the reasons that I fancy Quinn's Alehouse.

Clean glasses we don't receive. Quinn waits until we finish our pints and he refills our cracked and filthy glasses with the black stout that arrives in barrels weekly from Dublin. Andy and I raise our glasses and sip the creamy liquid through the froth at the top of the glass. Lovely!

I ask, "Mr. Quinn, what will you be doing with yourself after the alehouse is sold?"

Quinn is a heavy set middle-aged man who seldom smiles. He is bald except for patches of wispy white hair above his ears. "I mean to join me brother in Tyrone. Our families plan to lease some land and raise cattle. It will get me away from this heathen business. Good riddance to this place."

I will miss Quinn.

Andy once told me in confidence that he, Andy, was a member of the Defenders and took part in the uprising for Irish freedom with United Ireland in 1798. I think he repeats his story every time I see him.

"Aye Paddy, when I was young, I took the oath at the Mass house in Aghyaran. Captain Caldwell was recruiting defenders in the parish."

I humour him by pretending I never heard his story before. "Ah, that was when I didn't know you, Andy. And did you see any action?"

"I did indeed. First, I received a pike for a weapon. There was a secret forge near Aghyaran where the pikes were made. Captain Caldwell marched us into County Antrim where we drilled and trained near Ballymoney. Other forces joined us there, and we then marched to Ballymena where we captured the Market House. While at Ballymena, we heard that Commander Henry McCracken's main forces in Antrim were defeated by the English, and that we should disband. My military career was over. While returning to our homes, many of the lads were captured by the army of Lord Murray. Almost all who were caught were hanged. Me and the lads from Donegal and Tyrone were able to make our way north to Coleraine and through Derry to home. I left me pike in Ballymena."

"Did you not kill anyone?"

"I did not. There was no struggle in Ballymena. We put the fear of God in them, and they surrendered. Actually, there were not many soldiers there to defend the town."

"Well. I'm proud to say that I know you. There are not many real Irish patriots with whom I have an acquaintance. Would you join me in another pint?"

Andy stares into his glass and sees the hardened greasy dirt at the bottom. "Mr. Quinn…If ya can't give me a clean glass, could ya please let me put me head under the tap? Me mouth holds about a half-glass. Just pour it in up to me lips."

I must say that, with all of the hard work I have done through the years, it has been worth it. Anne has been a good wife to me, and we had a lot of good years. The most rewarding part of my life has been seeing my children grow into young men and women. My hopes are that they will become more prosperous than myself and raise their own children, my grandchildren, to be proud citizens in a free Ireland and devout members of the Catholic Church.

Patrick Gallen 1815

BOOK 2 - JAMES

Chapter 1
(1795 - 1805)

My earliest memory of my mother is seeing her by the hearth in the front room of our cottage. She is either shifting the bricks of turf to keep the fire going or stirring food in big pots hanging from the crane in the fireplace. Her eyes are red and sore from the smoke of the fire. Mother was a frail woman with a lovely sense of humor. She would joke with me when she playfully gave me chores to do. My chores at the age of ten weren't terribly difficult. I would fetch things for her that she needed, such as turf from outside the door, potatoes from the storage shed, or water from the well.

My name is James. I am the fifth child of Patrick and Anne Gallen of Glencarn Townland in Donaghmore Parish.

My father was always outside working. If he wasn't laying manure or turning over the soil, he was whitewashing our stone cottage. I hardly ever saw him until he came in for his meals. On many a night he came late for supper. On those nights, it was a sure bet that he was on the drink. One night, my brother Danny made a smart remark about his inebriated state, and Da struck Danny with a punch that knocked him into our table. Both Danny and the table went down. Ma gave a scream and the other children ran to the corner. Danny got up, cursed Da, and left the house. Da just stood there staring at us. Later he went to the next room and fell asleep on the floor. Ma and my sisters put the table upright and quietly sat down to continue patching clothes. We could hear Da peacefully snoring on the floor. My brother Paddy took me outside and told me that Da was drunk, as if I didn't know that.

Unfortunately, Da was on the drink many nights. Paddy told us that Da used to beat him and Danny years ago for little provocation when he was drunk. He even saw Da hit Ma one night. Ma took us to stay with Granny for a few days. Da finally went to visit her and apologized. We returned with him, but Ma still had a bruise on her left cheek. As far as I know, he hasn't struck her since. He hardly hits us children anymore, but he still drinks too much whiskey on too many nights.

Our lives in the hills of Donegal are controlled by the seasons. The harvest starts in August. I try to help Da and my older brothers when they gather the crops in the field for delivery to market, but my main job is to gather the potatoes from our garden and place them in the storage shed in the yard.

Following harvest, the feast of Samhain comes. It is All Hallow's Eve, the evening before All Saints' Day. This is a happy time when Da brings cured bacon he purchases from other farmers in the townland. We have a lovely meal of meat and soda bread before sundown. At nightfall, we dress in outrageous fashion and head to the crossroads. A huge bonfire is lit and the young men and women dance to a piper or fiddler while others hit pans and buckets to the beat of the music.

Our meals following Samhain are pretty simple. We eat potatoes almost every day. I bring them in from storage, and Ma boils them in the big pot over the fire. She places them in a basket at the center of the table, and we simply pick them out of the basket, peel them with our knives, and cut off pieces to eat. When we have butter, we smear it on the pieces of potato and add some salt. It tastes lovely. The peelings are thrown in a bucket on the floor by our feet. I feed them to our pet pig later in the evening.

On Christmas, after Mass, we have eggs and bacon, both purchased from local farmers. Through most of the winter season, our meals are again boiled potatoes from our storage shed.

St. Bridget's Day, on February 1st, is a milepost on the way to spring. For several weeks before, Ma and my sisters plait rushes from the bogs into crosses that we hang in our home, in the byre, and in the storage shed. The crosses bless our buildings and assure good luck in maintaining our health, the health of our animals, and the preservation of our potatoes. Da tells us that St. Bridget's Day is really the old Pagan feast of Imbolc.

After Lent begins in February, we fast by eating only one meal a day. The richer Catholics also fast from meat. This is not a problem for us. For us, most of the year seems to be like Lent. St. Patrick's Feast Day falls within the Lenten season, and we treat it as a Sunday by attending Mass and eating as much as we want at supper. When Easter Sunday arrives, we go to Mass at the Cross and visit our grandparents for supper. Granny cooks a ham for the family.

Beltaine, May 1st, is the start of the growing season. We have sown many seeds prior to Beltaine, but this is when the family really goes to work on the crops that will support us for the year. We plant potatoes and cabbage for ourselves. My responsibility is the potatoes. It is easy. I place the potato seedlings along the ground on soft earth fertilized with manure. The seedlings are from the splittings Da cut from last year's potatoes. I dig long trenches with my spade and pile up the soil over the seedlings. What could be easier? By September, we will have enough potatoes to sustain us through another long winter. The cabbage grows faster. By summer, we are eating cabbage soup almost every day. I don't care for it. It gives me gas.

By the time St. Swithin's Day arrives on July 15, last year's potatoes from storage are typically rotten and inedible. This begins the summer hunger. The only food we can eat are the few newly grown vegetables, such as cabbage and turnips, that come from our garden. Oatmeal we have left from last year's harvest also keeps up our strength.

Lughnasa is another Pagan feast at the beginning of August. A bonfire is set and more drinking and dancing takes place. It signals the beginning of another harvest season.

Chapter 2
(1805)

I love Sundays. There are few Masses held at the Mass rocks these days, so we walk to church at the village we call the Cross. My older brothers and sisters go to the early Mass at nine o'clock. We go to the Mass at half eleven after Da completes his chores. The walk is several miles downhill and we start out early. Da and Ma seem to have a timepiece within their heads that tells them when to leave. If we wait until we hear the bells of the Protestant church, we will be late. Along the path at the bottom of the hill, we meet up with other families from the townland. The Doughertys, McGlinchys, and McGoldricks are churchgoers like ourselves and we pass the time of our journey with them. Ma gossips with their wives while Da talks about his farming and repair problems with the men.

Mrs. McGoldrick carries her 3 year old Tommy. Her 5 year old daughter Susan walks beside her, hanging on to her dress. I run ahead with the McGlinchy children. The McGlinchys have several children close to my age. There is lively Owen and Patrick, a bit older than myself. Nancy is my age. Nellie and Charlie are a bit younger. Their other children are babies, about the same age as my younger brothers.

As we approach the village, more families are on the road and it starts to appear like a procession. Finally we arrive and stand inside the chapel. There are seats in front of the altar, but they are only for the richer members of the parish. Father McBride says Mass and gives us Communion. We stand and kneel at the correct times during the holy Mass.

I now receive Communion with my parents. My First Holy Communion was three years ago. My present from my Da on that occasion was a wee crucifix that I carry with me everyday around my neck. Before my First Communion, I attended catechism classes after Mass every Sunday to learn the importance of the sacrament and how to get ready for it. There were over 20 children at the catechism classes given by Father McBride. My friends Owen and Paddy McGlinchy, as well as my cousins Owen and Maeve McCullough and Denis Gallen, made their First Communion that year as well.

Days before my First Holy Communion, those three years ago, my best clothes were washed, and I received a new shirt from my grandparents. On the night before, I was the first to bathe in the tub of hot water. We ate nothing on Sunday morning. The fast for receiving communion began at midnight on Saturday night.

When arriving at church on that day, we children stood in a queue in front of the confessional. We went, one at a time, into the dark cabinet to face Father McBride. When it was my turn, I said the required prayers to the priest and told him of all the sins I have ever committed in my life. Mostly I told him how many times I lied to my parents and how many times I disobeyed them. Of course I lied about the number of times I sinned. I didn't commit that many sins, but I had to have something to tell. I just included the sin of lying to the priest among the number of lies I confessed. I walked out with a clean soul, said my penance of three *Aves* and one *Pater Noster* kneeling on the floor in the front of the chapel with the other First Communion children, and waited for the Mass to start. At Communion, we stood and walked in pairs up to the altar where Father McBride put a piece of the body of Jesus, in the form of a wafer, on our tongues. After I received Our Lord, I walked back and knelt again with the other children. As hard as I tried, I couldn't swallow the hard piece of bread in my mouth. We were forbidden to chew it.

By the end of Mass, it was finally soft enough to swallow, and I did so without anyone seeing me. Granny and Granda had a party for me at their home near the church. It was a lovely day for me, especially after Da gave me the crucifix.

I receive Communion every month now, and I go to Confession within a week of any sin that I commit. On many Sundays, the weather is too bad to walk to the Cross and we miss Mass. Da talked with Father McBride and he said that it isn't a sin to miss on those foul days. We should try to go as often as we can, but if we can't go, we should say the rosary at home on Sunday morning. If we do go to Mass during bad weather, and offer our discomfort up to God, we will be blessed and spend fewer days in Purgatory when we die.

We also try to attend Mass on the holy days of obligation if we can. These are the Circumcision of Christ on January 1, the Epiphany on January 6, St. Patrick's Day on March 17, Ascension Thursday-40 days after Easter, Corpus Christi on the Thursday after Trinity Sunday, Saints Peter and Paul on June 29, the Assumption on August 15, All Saints' Day on November 1, and the Nativity on December 25.

On the night before the Nativity, we attend Mass in the field outside the chapel. Jesus was born at midnight, and it seems that the whole parish attends at that time. It is said that the Nativity Mass is worth twenty-one Masses and no one would consider missing Mass at the Nativity. It is a grand night. The families arrive bearing candles from their homes, and the candles stay lit during much of the Mass.

Most other Masses at the chapel are indoors. The altar is against the wall in the middle of the church. There are chairs in front of the sanctuary. The richer Catholics of the parish are escorted to these chairs by the church elders. The people who get the chairs are mostly freeholders with large farms and who employ labourers. Also in the chairs are the tradesmen who work for the mills and the creamery. The majority of the parishioners are poor tenant farmers like ourselves. We enter the chapel at the doors on the far sides of the altar and kneel on the bare flagstone floor on both sides of the chair seating. It is only fair that the richer people sit close because they support the priests and maintain the chapel with their donations. We tenant farmers donate little to the support of the priests except at baptisms, funerals, and weddings.

On many Sundays after Mass, we stop off at my grandparents' home to see how they are doing. We also like to break our Communion fast with some of Granny's food. Both Granda and Granny are old and move about their home slowly. They appear to be in pain most of the time. Our grandparents don't have to work hard anymore. The farm is cared for by their sons, Uncle Charley and Uncle Frankie. Granny offers our parents warm broth and buttered bread. We children are given cakes and cups of buttermilk.

On some Sundays, we visit Uncle Owen and Aunt Mary near the chapel. They have a large family and I like to play with my cousins Paddy and Owen. We like to run to the top of their hill where we can see the large farms across the River Finn.

Other Sundays, we visit Great-Uncle Jimmy and Great-Aunt Mary in Monellan. Monellan is just a short walk up from the chapel but just a bit out of our way back to Glencarn. Jimmy and Mary are as old as our grandparents. Da told us that they raised him when he was a wain. Only Uncle Will lives with them, and he minds their farm. It is boring there. I only have my brothers to play with. I am happy when Da and Ma finally leave after taking almost forever saying goodbye.

The walk home is mostly uphill, and we take our time. We stop at the stream that runs along the path at Meenahinnis and rest a bit. I show off for my younger brothers by leaping from rock to rock across the stream until I reach the other side. I spy a frog and make a grab for it, but it is too fast. Near our home, there is a disturbance in the high grass. Something runs across the path too quickly for me to see. Ma asks me, "Did you see the fairy running there?" I did not. It was too fast for me. I think perhaps that Ma is joking with me. It was probably a hare.

Da tells me some of the stories about Ireland he heard from Great-Uncle Jimmy. He tells me that at one time we weren't allowed to attend Mass, and our priests were hunted down and killed by English soldiers. The priests disguised themselves as farmers and came to say Mass here in Donaghmore anyway. Mass was celebrated at hidden locations in the hills. The Mass rock near us in Glencarn was one of those places. Another was in the forest in Meenluskeybane. Men stood watch in trees during the service to see if soldiers were about. As soon as Mass was completed, the priest was hurried out of the parish.

At my First Communion class, Father McBride told us about Father Cornelius O'Mongan from the old days when priests were persecuted. Father O'Mongan was from the ancient family who managed the church land in County Tyrone for the Diocese of Derry. His parish in County Tyrone was known as Termon O'Mongan in honour of his ancestors. At first, the Catholic Penal Laws allowed only one priest to say Mass in each parish. Father O'Mongan was the priest permitted to say Mass in Donaghmore, Castlederg, and Termonamongan parishes. He could do so only in people's homes or at outdoor locations. This was allowed for a few years before a law was passed that required him to take an oath that was against the beliefs of the Catholic Church. Only a few of the priests who were permitted to say Mass in Ireland took the oath. Father O'Mongan and many others refused and were ordered out of Ireland. Father O'Mongan stayed in Ireland and continued to say Mass in secret. He became known as the renegade priest.

Father O'Mongan was pursued constantly by English soldiers and by "priest hunters" who received a reward for turning in illegal clergymen. He was successful in outwitting the English for years until one day he was discovered by soldiers while saying Mass in County Tyrone. He outran the soldiers who were firing at him. When he reached the Mourne Beg River, the river was flooding and difficult to cross, but Father O'Mongan was familiar with the river. He jumped from stone to stone until he reached the other side. The soldiers arrived at the river bank, but no stones were to be seen. Some believe that God raised the level of the river to protect Father O'Mongan. After the soldiers finally found a ford to cross, they searched the mill and houses in the nearby townland but could not find their renegade priest. Father O'Mongan had disappeared into County Donegal.

Chapter 3
(1805)

Up in the hills of Donaghmore, we have experienced many supernatural events. When we walk about at night, we frequently see lanterns in the distance, supposedly carried by spirits who cannot leave the earth. They have been known to visit us on All Hallow's Eve.

When someone from the village dies, we hear the wailing of the banshees at night until the corpse is buried. Da tells me that he hears his own dead father outside in the fields on the nights of the full moon. He says that he searches for him and discovers him at the edge of the field next to Uncle John's land.

I ask, "Do you see him Da?"

"I do not, he hides in the high grass, but I can speak with him. He warns me about what I am doing wrong in my life. The last time, he told me that evil times are coming, and that I should make sure that I say my evening prayers every night so that our family will be spared."

I am not sure that I believe Da when he tells me this, but I believe that it is a good thing that Da says his prayers every night.

There is a fairy cairn and a fairy tree near Glencarn. Our townland is named for the cairn, which is a group of large rocks used long ago by ancient Irish people for burial of their kings and for worshipping their heathen gods. The land around the cairn was taken over by the fairies after the ancient Irish disappeared. They are sometimes seen at night on the eve of pagan holidays. We try not to disturb them by farming their land. The land is sacred, but the land around the fairy tree is often used to bury babies who are born dead. Fairies fancy young children, and we hope that they will accompany the souls of these unbaptised babies to a happy place, which could be the place we call Limbo.

Aunt Mary visits frequently from Ballinacor. As a rule, she comes alone and talks with Da. One day she takes me up to the spring in the mountain. She acts queer when we get there. She asks me to kneel down and say a prayer with her. After the prayer, an "Ave," she tells me to stare at the rocks where the water gushes out. "Do you see anything Jamie?"

I stare and stare but see nothing.

"What is it that I should be seeing, Auntie?" I ask.

"You'll know when you see it. It is truly wonderful."

We stay at the spring for a long time. I finally tell her that I can't see what she sees. She sighs and asks me to return here from time to time.

"Someday," she says, "you will see something here, and your life will be changed."

I often return to the spring, I love the place anyway, but I never see anything out of the ordinary, just birds, insects, and hares, but no fairies or saints.

Whenever I plan to go far from our home, Ma tells me to mind that the bogey man doesn't get me. Unlike the other spirits in Donegal that I hear about from adults, I have seen the bogey man. He is a big man with dusty grey clothes and with grey skin. He roams the hills looking to capture children. I believe that he takes them to his cave in the mountains and boils them for dinner. While playing with the McGlinchys one summer evening, I see him coming up the path toward the top of the hill. He looks at us, and we run away to our homes. I tell Ma, who hides us under the mattresses. She bolts the door and sits with a spade for a weapon to protect us if he tries to come in. She is still waiting on guard when Da tries to come in. Ma unlatches the door, and Da tells us that there is no bogey man about. He was out all evening and didn't see anyone. All I know is that I saw him and he was real flesh and blood.

I see him again when I go to help Uncle John and Da gather crops at Aunt Mary McMenamin's farm. Aunt Mary was widowed when her husband, Uncle Jimmy, my namesake and godfather, was killed. Uncle Jimmy was a highwayman. He was shot by soldiers during one of his robberies. I never knew him, but he is still remembered by almost everyone in our village.

While walking home alone down the lane from Drumbeg, I see the bogey man walking toward me in the distance. Before he sees me, I leap into the tall grass by the road and crawl into the bushes. I hide there, afraid to look out at the lane, until I hear his heavy breathing. He stops. I hold my breath. He doesn't move. I try to peek in his direction and am shocked to see him staring straight at me. He shuffles off the path toward where I am hiding. In a flash, I am up and running and falling down the hill. My ankle twists and I go down. When I look up, he is still stumbling toward me. Hideous black teeth between blue lips on his grey face are all I see. I get up and run again on my painful ankle until I reach a small stream. I never look back but continue stumbling and crawling along the side of the stream until I reach the path to Glencarn. From there, I finally make it home where I run inside and hide again under the mattress. Ma peers at me and asks what is wrong. I tell her and she goes outside to look for my pursuer. She comes back in and tells me there is no one there. That was a close call. I thought for certain that he would catch me.

Chapter 4
[1806]

My Aunt Mary McMcMenamin moved back to her farm in Drumbeg when I was 11. Her family, four sons and two daughters, are now living on the wee farm that Da and Uncle John used to mind for her. All of Aunt Mary's children are older than I am, except for Denis, who is my age. When I have the time, I visit Denis at the farm and we explore the countryside of County Tyrone around the Mourne Beg River. It is easier to fish on the Mourne Beg than the River Finn because there are fewer homes on the river bank. The owners of the homes on the River Finn are selfish and forbid us from fishing on their property. In Tyrone, we can fish almost everywhere, but the fishing is poorer there, except when the salmon return to Lough Mourne. Then, the banks of the river are filled with fishermen. Da fishes there at that time and frequently catches a few of the big delicious fish. Today we walk down to the river and jump from rock to rock across to the other side. Denis tells me stories about his trips to the river. He has seen weasels playing on the banks. He warns me to keep away from the nests of the animals. His brother told him that a young lass disturbed a nest many years ago, and the mother weasel leaped on her back and killed her by biting a hole in her neck. I think that I will leave alone any animal that I may see.

My Great-Uncle Jimmy dies. Jimmy was my Da's uncle who raised him after his mother died. Ma helps the women prepare for a proper wake. It is held at Uncle Jimmy's home in Monellan.

Uncle Jimmy is the first dead man that I have seen. His corpse looks peaceful but unoccupied by his soul. I know that Uncle Jimmy's spirit is nowhere about these lands. It is in Purgatory, perhaps, or wandering about in the nether-world waiting to get into heaven.

This is my first wake, and I am sorry to say that I enjoy it. After praying for Uncle Jimmy, I join my cousins and the other children outside where we play games all day and night. I never had so much fun. The older children gather near a fiddler and dance with each other. Some of the older lasses joke with each other about the lads at the wake. They play a game where they sit on the fellas' knees and recite nonsense rhymes like "Flimsy flamsy, who do you fancy?" Some pretend to get married to the young lads, where another lad plays the part of the priest. My cousins Denis and Owen and myself are racing each other and then hiding and trying to find each other. Only the adults are sombre for the occasion, and even they start to brighten up after a few jars of whiskey and clay pipes full of tobacco.

Denis and I join in a game of Horns with some other lads. We and the others put our right hand on our knee. A caller yells, "Horns, horns, cow horns." All of us raise our hand above our heads. If we don't, the caller's assistant will rub chimney soot on our faces. If the caller yells "Horns, horns, horse horns," we don't raise our hands or we will be sooted. We are only supposed to raise our hand for animals with horns. The caller speaks faster and faster until I raise my hand for "lamb horns" and get soot rubbed on my face. I believe that it was a trick question, but by this time half of the lads have sooty faces.

One rainy day, I am walking home from my cousin Denis's home when I see a grey pile of clothing in the high grass by the road. I walk through the grass to take a look. It is the body of a man. It is clear from the smell coming from him that he is dead. I poke him with a stick to make sure. He doesn't move. There is something familiar about him that I can't remember. I run back to my cousin Denis's home and get my Aunt Mary to come see. When we return, Aunt Mary turns him over, and I see his face for the first time. It is the bogey man. His grey face is distorted into a horrible expression. I tell Aunt Mary that I believe that he is the bogey man.

"Ah no, Jimmy. It is Neddy McCormack from our townland. Neddy took to drink a few years back, and his family drove him out of the house. He has been wandering the roads of Donegal and Tyrone since then, begging for food and money for drink. He sleeps on the side of the road like a wild animal. The drink has taken his voice from him and he just grunts. His sanitary habits have been getting worse lately. I don't blame yeh for thinking him to be the bogey man. He was a frightful sight even when he was living."

I look at him and suddenly feel sorry for him and wonder if he is seeing God now, or he is suffering in Purgatory for the pain he must have given to his family.

"What will you do now?" I ask my Aunt.

She says, "I'll send Michael to tell the McCormacks, but I don't think they'll have a wake for him. They disowned him and said that they hope they never see him again. We'll just cart his body to the chapel down at the Cross, and they'll decide what to do with him. We will possibly have to bury him in the McCormack lot at the Donaghmore graveyard without much of a ceremony."

I walk home in the rain, grateful that I'll never have to fear the bogey man again.

chapter 5
[1807]

I am now 12 years old and taking on more responsibility for work on my father's farm. I am also helping my brothers when they work with my Uncle John on his farm. A teacher has been staying in the parish with the Quinns and teaching some of the boys their numbers and how to read and write. For this, he receives his room and board. I ask Da if I could join the boys and become more educated.

"Ah Jamie," he says. "What will you be wanting to learn such things for? Are you after being a priest? If you're not, you won't be needing any such learning. You'll be a farmer like the rest of us."

I haven't given this much thought. Maybe I should become a priest. A priest's life is not as dreary as ours, and I will be sure of getting into heaven. I tell Da that maybe I should learn to read in case I decide to enter the priesthood.

He says, "Sure I can use you here for threshing, but if you want, I figure that we'll manage without you for a few hours. Mind that I don't have much to offer Mr. McLaughlin for his services."

I join the boys for Mr. McLaughlin's lessons the next morning. The teacher spends hours telling us about the numbers and how they represent quantities of animals and goods. Most of what he tells me, I already know from my years on the farm and going to market. For the next few days, he tries to get me to sound out the letters of the alphabet. I am getting nowhere. I feel like a baby learning to talk. I feel foolish as well, because most of the boys are younger than I am and seem to be grasping it faster. I drop out and return to Da's farm. Maybe the life of a priest isn't so wonderful anyway. Ma seems disappointed that I didn't continue with the studies. She would have liked to have someone in the family who could read. She considers sending my brother Owen, who is only 6 years old.

Bishop O'Donnell comes from Derry this year, and all the children of ages 11 and up who haven't been confirmed yet receive the sacrament of Confirmation. It is a special day in Donaghmore; unfortunately, the weather turns bad. The rain comes down in torrents, and we children are all damp in the confines of the chapel. The bishop seems to race through the ceremony. I chose Colm as a confirmation name in honour of St. Columbcille, the patron saint of the church in Derry. I thought that this would please the Bishop. After Mass, we depart quickly to my grandparents' home. Normally we would stay outside church and greet the bishop, but the weather doesn't permit it.

Next month Granda dies, and a wake is held at his home in Monellan. I will miss Granda, but I enjoy myself at his wake. I think that Da enjoys himself at the wake as well. After a respectful time praying at Granda's shrouded body, he disappears into the alehouse at the Cross with his friends. He tells me that he wants to try some of the new stout porter delivered from Dublin. He returns later to the wake in a relaxed state of mind. I note the disapproval in Ma's expression when he joins her at the coffin. My cousin Mickey nudges me and asks me with a smile, "What is the difference between a wedding and a wake?" I start to tell him, but he stops me and says, "They are the same except that there is one less drunk." I stare at him and he says, "I'm just jokin' with you, Jamie."

My Aunt Mary goes on a pilgrimage this year to the mountain of Croagh Patrick in County Mayo. She sets out on foot with about thirty other people from the parish in early July. It is a difficult trip for her at her age. Da says that she is almost 40. Her family can take care of themselves now, and she believes that this is the best year for her to accomplish her lifelong dream. Her gruelling hike takes her through the Barnesmore Gap to Donegal Town, then down the coast through Sligo and inland through County Mayo to Westport. They reach the base of the mountain on the last Sunday in July. Along the way they stop at homes of friends who offer basic accommodations to the many pilgrims who make this trip every year.

Aunt Mary is joined by hundreds of pilgrims at the base of Croagh Patrick. She walks behind them as they climb barefooted up the short rocky path to the shrine of Saint Patrick, just a few yards from the base. The pilgrims circle the shrine while praying and then begin the difficult climb to the top of the mountain. Aunt Mary offers prayers for her family and for everyone she knows, as she promised before leaving on the arduous trip. The climb takes hours. Croagh Patrick is much higher than any mountain here in Donegal. By the time she reaches the chapel at the top, her feet are bloody from the sharp rocks on the path. Aunt Mary kneels in the chapel and continues to pray for the souls of the living and dead parishioners from the Cross. The walk down the mountain is no less difficult than the walk up. She has to mind that she doesn't step on a loose stone and slip down the hill. Finally she makes it to the bottom and she offers another prayer of thanksgiving for the privilege of making this sacrifice to God.

Aunt Mary arrives back in Donaghmore well into harvest time. When we hear that she is back, we all walk down to see her. I am fascinated by the tale of her adventure and listen to her tell it over and over again to each new audience. Aunt Mary is positively glowing. I know that I will make the pilgrimage to Croagh Patrick someday, as well.

Aunt Mary walks with some difficulty after her pilgrimage. She must stay off her feet whenever she can. I believe that she is improving with each day.

She told me the story of Croagh Patrick before she left. It seems that St. Patrick went up the mountain sacred to the pagan god Crom for the 40 days of Lent. During that time, he battled Crom and banished him and all serpents from Ireland before he returned. This story has the ring of a fable to it. For one thing, we were taught that there are no other gods except the three persons of Almighty God. I may be young and stupid, but I can tell a false story when I hear one. I'm starting to doubt a lot of the stories that were told to me when I was a child.

Our family has planted quite a bit of flax this season and the harvest in September is difficult. Harvesting flax means pulling it out of the ground by hand, tying the flax into bundles, and taking the sheaves to the dam in the local burn. There we steep the flax by making sure that it is covered by water. The flax then starts to rot, and the smell is horrible. Nellie, my eldest sister, gets the job of pulling it out after a two week soak, and she lays the smelly mess out on the land to dry. The flax fibres are inside the woody stems of the dried plant. The soaking in the dam makes it possible to separate the stem from the fibres. Next we have to scutch the flax by beating the dried stems with a club to break them up, one of my jobs. Then we scrape the fibres with a knife to free them from the pieces of stalk. This is a long laborious process that no one in the family enjoys. The results are long flax fibres that my sisters spin into linen thread. We sell spools of the spun thread to linen brokers in Ballybofey. The linen fetches much more money than woollen yarn, but it seems unlikely that we will plant flax next year.

chapter 6
(1808 - 1809)

I am 14 years old now and aware that there are several beautiful lasses here in Donaghmore. There are the McGlinchys, Nancy and Nellie. Nancy is plump and rosy cheeked with light brown hair and is about my height and age. Nellie is her younger sister and is skinnier, has freckles, and is afraid to talk to me. Mary Dougherty is another cute lass who always talks to me when I pass her cottage. Sadie Bryson has flaming red hair, almost transparent skin, and eyes the colour of green. She is extremely buxom for her age. Katie Cassidy is my favourite. She has a different look about her. She has a perfect complexion of tan in the summer, and her face seems to glow when she smiles. Unlike most of the others, her eyes are dark brown, and they have a mysterious effect on me when she looks directly into my eyes.

I have beautiful cousins as well. Denis's sister Maggie has wonderful brown eyes as well, and her hair is jet black. Denis says that he thinks that they have some Spanish blood in them on the McMenamin side. He thinks that this is from the time the storm and the English fleet destroyed the Spanish Armada off the coast, and Irish families hid the ship-wrecked sailors from the authorities. Some of the Spanish sailors remained in Ireland and married Irish women. One of the reasons that I like to visit Denis is to be around his foreign-looking sister.

The daughters of Uncle Owen and Aunt Mary are lovely, as well. Margaret and Maeve are taller than I and have a graceful air about them. Grace is still a child but looks as if she will be a beauty in a few years, much like her sisters.

Aye, the only homely lass that I know of is my sister Maggie. She seems to have a mean look on her face at all times except when the McGlinchy boys are around. She teases me constantly about the lasses that seem to be attracted to me.

Truly, I do fancy being around the young women. It is hard getting them out of my mind. When I see them, I try to say a cheery word to them. I often dream of holding Katie Cassidy in my arms. I am hoping to accomplish this at the next wake or ceilidh. Unfortunately, no one is dying in our townland so the only way I'll get to touch Katie is when we waltz to the fiddlers at the next ceilidh at the Cross. I have never yet held a lass in my arms, but I know that it will feel wonderful when I do. I'm afraid that I can't dance well and I will have to ask my mother or, God forbid, my sister to teach me. I have to learn for sure before the mid-summer night bonfire at the Cross.

There seems to be some trouble up here in the hills of Donaghmore but no one will tell me what is happening. I see many adults and young people walking with great purpose and discussing things in secret. I also see men carrying weapons. When I ask Da about this, he tells me that we should mind our own business; this is not for us. Nevertheless, Da is having many talks with our land agent and with some of the angry men in the parish. He looks worried and I am getting concerned.

We have no weapons in the house. They are still forbidden to us Catholics by the penal laws. The only weapons owned by our neighbours are long ash poles, sharpened to a point. Now, some of the men are carrying muskets and blunderbusses after their meetings in the hills. A neighbour of Aunt Mary McMenamin is arrested and sent to trial in

Lifford. We hear that he was sentenced to exile in Botany Bay on the other side of the world and may never return to his wife and children.

One fine day, I visit my cousin Denis and propose an adventure to him. I have never been to Castlederg and ask if he would like to take a long walk to the town in County Tyrone. As he is telling me that he would indeed like to join me, I am looking past him into the cottage for a brief glimpse of his sister Maggie. She is nowhere to be seen today.

We walk down the hill into County Tyrone, and in a few hours we are in Castlederg. Our plan is to wait for the coach from Derry that stops to pick up passengers at the inn on the main street. There is one coach each way every day between Derry City and Enniskillen in County Fermanagh. It is my hope to be able to take that coach someday to see the faraway places along its route north through Strabane to Derry. I wish to see Lough Foyle, the lough that opens to the great never-ending ocean.

We gape at the many shops along the main street and visit the ruined castle on the River Derg. We were told that the castle was once owned by the O'Donnell chieftains until the English defeated the Irish. It was then occupied by Captain Davis who moved a large number of English and Scot settlers into the area. Irish rebels rose up shortly after that, massacred settlers, and destroyed the castle and the Castlederg Protestant church. The rising was short lived. The English retook Castlederg and rebuilt the church, but the castle was never restored.

We marvel at the number of merchants and shoppers in the town. We are a bit ashamed of our ragged appearance. The town people are all dressed in new or clean clothes. We must look like filthy animals to them, and we get disgusted looks. After we eat a sparse lunch of stale oat bread from home that we had stuffed in our pockets, the coach rattles into town. It stops at the diamond, and four passengers step out and walk over to the Castlederg Hotel. We stay until the horses are watered, and a man and woman come out of the hotel and enter the coach. Before long, the coach is on its way to County Fermanagh.

Our entertainment has come to an end, and we start off for home. We decide to take a different route home and take the horse path out of town that heads west into the hills. The path is straight, and we see many old standing stones and graves from the days of the ancient people who lived here in forgotten times. We reach Denis's home at sundown, and I hurry down the paths to my own cottage before it gets dark.

Chapter 7
[1810]

A most wonderful thing happens. Katie Cassidy calls on us to trade some milk from her family's cow for some of our eggs. When I hear her talking with my mother inside our cottage, I walk swiftly from the garden to greet her at the open half-door. She looks grand. Her hair is golden and her flawless skin glistens in the sunlight. "Hello Katie," I croak out when I get there.

"Ah, good afternoon, James," she sings. "Your mother and I have just completed a trade of goods to prepare for our supper tomorrow. I'll be off now for home."

Ma is smiling at my obvious discomfort at being in the presence of a goddess. I quickly stammer, "Would you mind if I accompany you up the path a ways? I must borrow a tool from Mr. McGoldrick."

"Not at all, James. I will quite enjoy your company."

Ach. What have I gotten into? My mind is racing, trying to think of things to say to Katie. The sweat is pouring out of my armpits and soaking the sides of my shirt. "Fine then," I bravely announce. "We might as well be off." I open the half-door for her, and Katie joins me outside.

I say, "Goodbye, Mother. Be sure to tell Father that I am going to see Mr. McGoldrick."

As soon as I say that, I am sorry that I said it. I never call my parents Mother and Father. I must have sounded like a pompous arse. I have to relax. Katie is nothing more than just another lass in the parish. If only she wasn't so damn beautiful! What am I going to tell Mr. McGoldrick when I get there? What do I say next to Katie?

She speaks to me first. "What would you be needing from Mr. McGoldrick, James?"

I have to think fast. "A slane, Katie. Aye, a slane. Ours is broken, and we are going to the bogs tomorrow to clamp turf. Tomorrow is the best day to get the lads together for clamping and spreading the turf." This, of course, is a lie.

"I see," she says.

We walk silently for a minute before I blurt out, "Will you be going to the bonfire next week at the Cross?"

"I will, of course. I adore it and wouldn't miss it for anything. I hope that the weather will stay this lovely."

I answer, "I'm sure that it will. I am looking forward to it as well. There will be music and dancing and maybe some games of chance."

"Music and dancing," she laughs. "Since when were you interested in music and dancing? I only remember you racing about with the McGlinchy boys and other lads."

I reply quickly, "Ah no, this year will be different. I am learning to dance, you see. I'm not good at the fast jigs and reels yet, but I hope that you will join me in a waltz or two this year."

"My, my, James! This is a change in you. I will certainly dance with you at the bonfire. This will be the first time I danced with anyone but my mother or cousins. I will be looking forward to seeing you there."

What in the name of God have I done? I must go home as soon as I leave Katie and get my mother to teach me to waltz. I walk Katie as far as Mr. McGoldrick's cottage and say goodbye to her. I sadly watch her as she walks up the hill, and I turn to knock at Mr. McGoldrick's door. Mrs. McGoldrick answers. I ask her how her family is; I tell her that we heard that they were ill. Mrs. McGoldrick lets me know that they are all fine and wonders why anyone would suspect otherwise. I say that my Ma will be greatly relieved to hear that, and that I'll be off to tell her.

I suffer the embarrassment of learning to dance from my mother while my brothers and sisters taunt me every time they pass by. Da doesn't say anything but smiles and shakes his head as he goes about his chores.

Although I lied to Katie about going to the bogs and cutting turf, we do go to the bogs on Thursday. There is Da, Uncle John, my brothers Danny and Paddy, and myself. We walk up to the swampy bogland that we share with the other families in our townland. Danny cuts the soggy turf with our slane and throws the bricks to Da and me. We take the bricks and spread them out on the heather to dry in the sun. Paddy is doing the same for Uncle John with my uncle's slane. I divide my time between the two clampers. When Danny and Paddy get tired, Da and Uncle John take their place. I try clamping for a while, but Da doesn't think that I'm good enough yet, and I return to spreading. After a hard day's labour, we have enough bricks for our fireplaces to last the rest of summer and through the autumn. We will have to come again before harvest to get our winter supply.

Next week we return to reckel the bricks. We will pile them up at angles to let the wind through to dry them thoroughly. We return again in a few days when they are bone dry, and pile them on our cart to take to our homes. We have Donal, our donkey, to pull the cart down to our cottage. Of course, there will be many trips required to bring down all the bricks that we cut this week.

The evening of the bonfire arrives, and we all walk down to the village of the Cross for the ceilidh. The fiddlers are already playing when we arrive, and the fire is just getting started. Katie and her family are not here yet. I wait by the fire with my cousin Denis. Soon other families from Glencarn show up, and I join the lads who are getting more wood to help build the fire.

A shock goes through me when I see Katie on the other side of the fire. She is staring at me. I don't know what to do. Should I stop what I am doing or wait until later to talk with her? I wait until later.

When it gets dark and the fiddlers begin a waltz, I walk over to her.

"Good evening to you, Katie. Would you like to dance?"

She gives me the most heart-warming smile I have ever seen and says, "I would indeed, James. I have waited over a week for this."

With my heart thumping, I walk with her, awkwardly, to the platform near the musicians. We join the other dancers, mostly old women, wait for the proper beat to begin and step off in my first dance with a lass. Not just any lass. It is Katie Cassidy. I am holding her hand and touching her shoulder. I am within inches of her beautiful face, her perfect nose, her deep brown eyes, her full moist lips. I glance around to see if any of my friends notice us. No one is paying attention. However, they will see us together sometime tonight.

The waltz ends and a reel begins. I quickly rush Katie off the platform as more old women are rushing on. I walk Katie to the table of drinks and get her a glass of cider.

"What do you think, Katie? Was I a horrible dancer?"

She laughs and says, "You were grand, James. I may not be able to walk tomorrow, but it was worth it. I enjoyed dancing with you very much. Your mother is a good teacher."

I am shocked. How did she know? She tells me that she hopes that we can dance the next waltz. This puts me finally at ease. I relax and soon I am talking to her as easily as I can talk to my cousins. She is truly wonderful.

Later in the evening, Ellen McGlinchy spies me and comes over to ask me to dance. I look at Katie and she nods. Ellen and I perform a careful but successful waltz together. She has my attention, but I am glad when the tune ends, and I can walk back to Katie. We spend the rest of the evening together, dancing when waltzes are played and sitting out the other tunes.

"James, I will be glad to teach you some of the reels and horn pipes," she says.

I tell her, "That will be lovely."

She asks me to come to her house for supper on Sunday, and we can practice afterwards. I gladly accept her invitation. A bit later, Charley, her older brother, comes looking for her. He tells her that the family is leaving, and she should go now. I offer to walk her home but get a long hard look from her brother.

"I guess you better go with them," I wisely reply.

Katie says, "James, I had a grand time tonight. I'll be looking for you on Sunday."

Charley gives me another look, and they both depart.

It seems that I'm walking on air when I ramble over to the lads wrestling in the field.

"Where were you all night?" asks Denis, who was being straddled by his brother Jimmy.

"I was with Katie Cassidy," I proudly answer.

"You were indeed?" asks Jimmy. "Did you buckle her yet?"

I feel my face turn hot and I jump in a rage on Jimmy. Jimmy is two years older than I am and almost three stone heavier. He gets to his feet and quickly throws me down. I get up and swing my fist at him, but he deflects my punch and whacks me on the left side of my head. I see a flash of light and go down in a heap.

"I was only joking with you, Jamie. I meant nothing by it."

What is it with Mary McMenamin's sons and their jokes?

When I lose my dizziness and get my legs back, Denis walks with me back to my family who are getting ready to head home. Da is fairly sober tonight and will join us on the long trip back.

Ma doesn't fancy me having supper at the Cassidy's on Sunday.

"Ah, those poor people, having another mouth to feed, and here it is the start of the summer hunger. We are as poor as church mice, but the Cassidys are poorer. Did you ever get a look at their ramshackled old cottage? You'll bring your own potatoes, and I'll bake some bread."

Our potato supply is surely dwindling, and soon we will be eating only oatmeal and cabbage. I am sorry I accepted Katie's invitation, and I am nervous about the reception I'll get at the

Cassidy home. When Sunday arrives, I walk up the hill to their home in Mulladoo with a sack of soda bread and four of our remaining lumper spuds. Katie meets me at the door and tells me to come in.

I give the traditional greeting, "God bless all in this house."

Katie introduces me. There is Mr. and Mrs. Cassidy, her older brother Charley, and two younger sisters, Elizabeth and Rose. I look around their cabin. It is much smaller than ours, the roof needs rethatching, and it appears that the whole family sleeps in the one main room. The back room of the cabin is used for their cow. The Cassidys have only a four acre farm with one acre dedicated to their cow and the rest used for corn and potatoes. Our meal is plain, just some cabbage and potatoes. I engage Mr. Cassidy in conversation about farming and learn that he is planning to sell the cow to increase his acreage for crops. The price is high for grain now, and Mr. Cassidy is losing money because the barter price for milk isn't too good. Charley doesn't say much and leaves the table when he finishes his supper. Katie talks with her mother as her sisters look at me and giggle. I help clean up after we finish, and Katie explains to her parents that we are going outside where she will teach me to dance. She obviously explained this to them before I arrived, so they nod, and I follow her through the door, blushing. We walk to a spot far from the cabin, and she starts showing me the basic steps of the reels. She is a good teacher, and soon I am whirling around the dusty ground humming a lively tune with Katie in my arms. I see Katie's younger sisters sneaking about in the fields watching us.

My lessons are over before it gets dark, and we sit down in the grass and talk. I keep telling her of the things that I would like to do and the places where I would like to go with her. She listens and tells me that she loves being in my company. I grin. It will probably take something tragic, like the death of my parents, to remove that smile from my face. I don't have the words to tell her what I am feeling now. Eventually, I say goodbye and head off for home. I was not bold enough to kiss her, and I don't believe that she expected it. I know that the time will come soon when such things will happen.

A week later, the word spreads through the hills that Dan Boyle of Drumbeg died. There will be a wake at his cottage, and the young people of Donaghmore are excited about demonstrating their deep sympathy to Mrs. Boyle and her sons. As soon as I hear about it, I tear up the hill to ask Katie if she would like to go with me to show our respects. Later that evening I return to take Katie to the wake. Her brother Charley is waiting with her.

"Mind if I join you?" he asks.

"It is grand you can come," I say, a bit too sarcastically.

The three of us head in the direction of Drumbeg and arrive after sunset. We enter the cabin one at a time and say a few prayers at the coffin. We didn't know Mr. Boyle, but he looks like he had a rough time of it in his final days. Mrs. Boyle could have used some help from the women in our townland when preparing the body. We say a few kind words to Mrs. Boyle and go outside. Charley is behind us, and we hear him say as we are leaving, "Mrs. Boyle, may your husband rest in peace until yis meet again." I'm sure that Mrs. Boyle was puzzled by that remark.

Outside, Charley isn't about to leave for home. He is looking for a drop of whiskey to drink. I show him where the men have gathered, and he leaves Katie and me for the company of the fellas in the byre in back of the home. We walk a few yards from the cabin and sit together in the dark on a low wall. We aren't alone. I see the silhouettes of other young couples embracing nearby.

"Katie, I have thought about you constantly since last Sunday. You are always on my mind. I want to tell you that I love you and want to be with you forever."

There, I said it. I wish I could see her expression in the dark.

Finally she speaks, "I love you too, James. I think of you always, as well. We are suited for each other; I know that we have many common interests. I think we should tell our parents that we are courting. I'm sure that they will approve."

I put my arms around her and we embrace. My ears are burning again. Our cheeks brush together and I kiss her. Her lips are warm and moist. I kiss her again, and we hold the kiss for as long as we can. As others are frolicking around us in the night, I hold Katie and tell her, over and over, how much I love her.

I walk Katie home alone. Charley is still sampling the Boyle's whiskey. Before she enters her home, I kiss her again and say goodnight. I fairly float down the path to Glencarn. I never felt so good before.

Katie is now a major part of my life. I see little of my cousins and go everywhere with her. Along with my other chores at home and at Uncle John's, I am helping Mr. Cassidy and Charley re-thatch their roof. In a few years, Katie and I will be married. Da says that he will split up the farm and give shares to all of his sons when the time comes. I am looking forward to the day when Katie and I will have our own cottage. It will be heaven.

Early in our courtship, Katie and I agree that we will be chaste until marriage. We know of other lads and lasses who are not. They are the shame of the parish, and we don't care to have their reputation. We are both young, and it will be years before marriage; but if we pray frequently to the Blessed Mother and the saints, I believe we can do it. Also, knowing Katie's feelings about this, I don't believe I have any other choice.

I have never had a fancy for whiskey. Maybe it is because I see how it changes the personality of my father. He doesn't get mean like some of the other men I've seen, but he does become more argumentative and difficult. Many a time, I had to bring him home from an alehouse or shebeen. So far, his love of drink hasn't caused us any hardships. He always manages to get up and work the day after one of his drunks. I don't think that he will become a bogey man like Neddy McCormack. As for myself, I have tried some of Aunt Mary's poteen, and I don't care for the taste of it or its effect on my body.

chapteR 8
(1811 - 1814)

Years go by and Katie and I are still sweethearts. We are the talk of the townland. There are other successful courtships as well. First, my cousin Mickey marries Agnes, a lass from Bealalt. Agnes is a McMenamin, a distant relation to Mickey's mother. The wedding at Agnes's parents' home is grand. Katie and I join some rowdy lads and lasses who arrive late and bang on the door of the house after Father McBride has performed the ceremony. Our group is made up of about twenty young people from the hills. We boisterously sing and dance throughout the rest of the day outside the front door of the main cottage. The lasses take turns dancing with Mickey, and the fellas take turns dancing with the bride. Later, we threaten to steal Agnes away from the party. Paddy McGlinchy and myself take Agnes by the arm and are leading her down the path when Mickey runs over and tells us that enough is enough. He appears quite serious, and we let him take his bride back to where he is sitting. When night falls, we get together in force and coax the couple into leaving us for their room in the cabin that the McMenamins have provided for their wedding night. We shout at them that it is time for them to consummate their marriage. They are aware of the custom, and they head toward the nuptial bedroom in the cabin. We follow them, shouting slightly indecent jests, until they enter the cabin. Throughout the night, we continue our noisy behaviour, encouraging Mickey and Agnes to enjoy their nuptial privileges. The party goes on as we shout and throw pebbles at the cabin window until almost morning.

Cousin Mickey's younger sister, Bridget, marries John Gallagher the following month. John has been courting her for as long as Katie and I have been together. The wedding is held at Aunt Mary McMenamin's cottage in Drumbeg. John and Bridget make a curious looking pair. Unlike her beautiful sister Maggie, Bridget is short and plump. John is tall, at least two feet taller than his new wife. Again, Katie and I join the other rowdies and make a racket at the wedding celebration. Because I am one of the few lads in town who can dance, I am popular with the other lasses. Katie doesn't seem to mind, knowing that she is the only one I care for.

I walk over to my cousin Mickey. He is usually good for some craic. He tells me, "I visited the Cross last Saturday, Jamie, to make me confession. I saw something there that I will never forget."

I had to admit that this was something that I thought I would never hear coming from Mickey. "What did you see, Mick?"

"It was the cripple, Danny Dolan, walking into the church with his crutches. He struggled to kneel at the altar, and he said a few prayers. Suddenly he shouted some words in Irish, stood up, and threw his crutches away."

"What happened then?"

"I ran as fast as I could to see Father McBride to tell him what happened. He told me that I just witnessed a miracle. He asked 'Where is Danny now?' I told him, 'He is over by the altar, flat on his arse!' "

Aye, Mickey always has a good story to tell.

As the queer tradition demands, we chase John and Bridget into their matrimonial bedroom in the rear of the house and continue harassing them from outside through their first night together. All I can think about is how I'll feel when Katie and I go through this strange experience.

Next it is my brother Danny's turn to marry. His bride is Anne Callaghan from Cronalaghy. Anne, who is the same age as myself, is the eldest daughter of the Callaghans. She is a slim brown haired lass with the same lovely big blue eyes as the other Callaghan girls. My brother Patrick is best man at the wedding, and Anne's 15-year-old sister is the maid of honour. Da buys a new hat for the joyous occasion and Ma wears her finest dress, one that she made herself five years ago. Da has a tall hat of soft felt, the latest style, at least for us farmers. He will make good use of it, wearing it proudly on market days.

The wedding is performed by Father McBride at the Callaghans, and the traditional festivities commence. When the happy couple leaves the party, they walk down the road to their new cottage in Glencarn. The young people of the town follow them, as customary, and entertain them outside their bedroom while Danny and Anne get acquainted on their first night, I believe, together.

Danny built the new cottage, with my help, on his own land. Da gave Danny four acres of the best land at the edge of his property. I think that I will be getting a similar share when Katie and I marry in a few years.

Now the babies start arriving, one at a time through the years. My cousin Mickey and his wife Agnes have two sons and my cousin Bridget and her tall husband John have two daughters. Thanks to my brother Danny and his wife Anne, I now have a nephew, Patrick, and a niece, Bridget. Danny and Anne have another child on the way. I see Danny and Anne's children every day and marvel at how they fast they are growing.

My great-aunt Mary Dougherty dies in 1814. She was my Da's aunt and sister to his mother. She raised him after his mother died. She is buried in the Dougherty grave with her husband in Lower Donaghmore. Only her son Willie is left at the farm in Monellan. Willie has yet to take a wife.

Chapter 9
(1815)

This year, my sister Nellie marries Jimmy Callaghan of Cronalaghy. Jimmy is the brother of Anne, the wife of my brother Danny. I guess this makes Jimmy a double brother-in-law to Danny. Their children will be double cousins. I'm not sure of this, but I think that the Church will not allow double cousins to marry each other.

Before the wedding, Da cleans up the farm as best he can and whitewashes the cottage. With our help, he purchases bacon for the wedding feast and arranges for plenty of poteen from Aunt Mary McMenamin. The wedding is another happy time for our family.

Katie's family, the Cassidys, are having a hard time of it. In the past, they barely made their rent payment on gale days. Partly it is Mr. Cassidy's fault. He has no skill in growing crops; he always preferred raising livestock. Now the war with Napoleon is over, and the farmers are seeing the end of wartime grain prices. The prices for our crops have dropped considerably, and we all are having trouble. The Cassidys have no chance of fully paying the rent to their tyrannical landlord, David Johnston, and they are in danger of eviction.

Agents are coming into the townland suggesting that there is work at the harvest in Scotland. They tell us that passage from Derry to Glasgow is free, and wages will be paid at the end of the harvest. Da asks if Patrick and I will go this summer to help make the autumn rent payment. A number of lads from the parish are going, and it sounds like it could be a brilliant adventure. Nevertheless, I will miss seeing Katie's pretty face for awhile.

I go to the Cassidy farm to tell her. She is standing by her cottage when I arrive.

"How are you today, love?" I ask. She doesn't look happy. She must have heard about Scotland.

"James, we must talk." I kiss her on the cheek and wait for her to tell me what's on her mind. She looks at me and says, "You must know how hard we are having it with our farm. We are sure to lose it unless a miracle happens. Our May gale is hanging, and Mr. Johnston is threatening to put us off the land."

"Aye, I know. I wish that we could help you, but it is impossible. What are you going to do?"

She replies, "Mr. Johnston, himself, has given us an answer. He is in need of a housekeeper. He suggested that he will accept our underpayment if I come to his home in Killygordon and work for him."

"That's grand", I answer. "Is it not?"

Katie looks into my eyes deeply. She says, "I don't like or trust him. He has a sinister look in his eyes when he watches me. I feel that I will be trapped in the lair of a wolf when I am in his home, but what choice have I?"

"Katie, I have known you for several years now. You can handle yourself well in difficult situations. I think that you must do this for your family. If Mr. Johnston treats you poorly, leave him and tell me or your brother. We will take care of Johnston and let the community know about him."

She sighs, "I'll come home on Sundays. I'll let you know how it is."

I then tell her about my going to Scotland.

I say, "I think that we can be married next year, if I save enough this summer."

She finally smiles and says, "I hope that maybe Daddy will finally get out of debt next year or the next. Then we can talk about it."

I'm not keen on waiting for the Cassidys to get out of debt before marrying Katie, but I don't want to bring it up. I return home; there is planting to be done tomorrow.

Katie is picked up in the Johnston's car on Monday and disappears down the road to Killygordon. I miss her and look forward to Sunday.

When I see her at Mass on Sunday, she smiles and my heart lightens. We walk home together, and she tells me that she hardly ever sees the master, and the other servants treat her well. Late Sunday night, I walk her all the way to the Johnston manor and watch her go through the massive front doors.

In late July, my brother Patrick, my cousin Denis, and I join the other lads and begin our walk to Derry. It is the first time I will be away from home. I haven't really been outside of Donaghmore, except for trips to Ballybofey and Castlederg. I see tears in Ma's eyes as I kiss her goodbye. It is silly, for I will be gone only two or three months. Still, there are tears in my eyes, as well.

There are ten of us. We walk down to the Cross through the rain until the sun finally shines again. We follow the road next to the River Finn, cross the river at Castlefin, and continue east toward Lifford. We reach the outskirts of Lifford by late afternoon. All of us brought bread from home, and we sit and eat it by the side of the road before lying down under the trees to rest in the open air. We walk through Lifford in the early evening. It is the biggest town I have ever seen, bigger than Castlederg even. Our leader, Sean Maguire, tells me that Derry is much larger. He was in Derry last year on his way to the Scottish harvest. Because of his experience, we depend on him to get us to Scotland. We follow the Letterkenny Road out of Lifford before turning on another road that leads us back to the river. The river is called the Foyle here, and it runs all the way to Derry. We are all weary by now, and we camp by the river for the night.

At daybreak, we wash on the bank of the river and finish what are left of the provisions we brought from home. Then we follow the road that leads to Derry along the river. The next big town is St. Johnstown. We walk through the town and realize that we are getting close to Derry. The road is now busy. We see many horsemen, coaches, and carriages on this road. If we were a smaller group, someone might give us a ride. As it is, we continue our rough walk on the side of the road and arrive at Derry in the afternoon.

Derry looks the way I pictured the castles of Ma's stories when I was young. There are many streets and houses on both sides of the broad river. A great wall surrounds the inner city and I see cannons on the top of it. Sean warns us not to enter the inner city through any of its gates. Catholics aren't welcome there. He also tells us to call the city Londonderry when speaking to people we don't know. Sean warns that it is important for us to behave in this Protestant-controlled city. During our long hike, he also told us much about the city's history.

He told us that St. Columbcille established his monastery here. He named it Derry after the oak grove that surrounded the church he built. It became an important Irish port because of the depth of the river and the entrance to the ocean farther downstream. When the English defeated the O'Donnells and O'Neills in the war that gave England complete control of Ireland, the city of Derry was given to the tradesmen of London. Many English moved here and set up businesses. They built the great wall to protect themselves from us Irish savages, and they called the city Londonderry.

When Catholic King James tried to occupy the city during his war with the usurper, King William of Orange, the great doors of the inner city were closed to James's troops. The city was defended by the Protestant militia inside, and King James laid siege to the city for many months. He blocked the river and surrounded the city to keep any supplies from getting to the people inside. English ships finally broke through, and James retreated. Today, the city celebrates the victories of King William several times a year with parades along the city walls. They commonly accompany their celebrations with abusive acts against the Catholics of the city. There have been many occasions when Protestant groups go into the Catholic neighbourhoods to beat, and sometimes kill, Catholic men and boys.

Sean has cousins in Derry. He leads us to an unused byre near his cousins' home just outside the city walls. The byre is in Creggan within the Catholic section of Derry. We will be staying there tonight. Although I am tired from walking for two days, I am excited by being in the city of St. Columbcille. And such a city! Tall buildings are everywhere, within the walls and outside the walls. Sean can see our excitement, and he takes us for a tour of the area.

First we visit the Catholic church at the hilltop on Long Tower Street. It is the Roman Catholic Cathedral for our diocese. Never have I seen a Catholic chapel such as this. It is more grand than the Church of Ireland in Donaghmore. Sean tells us that Bishop O'Donnell says Mass here every Sunday. His cousins call the bishop "Orange Charlie" because he supports the English parliament on most matters. Sean says, "Charlie was one of the reasons the Act of Union was passed. He and his fellow bishops from the archdiocese convinced enough members of the Irish parliament to vote for it. I think that they believed it would end the penal laws. Here it is 15 years later and we are still waiting for justice. He advocates the virtue of meekness in the face of abuse from the likes of the Orange Society, but his flock gets tired of it and plans revenge on them."

Sean doesn't believe that the Catholics of Derry have the same high opinion of Bishop O'Donnell that we of Donaghmore have.

Two years ago, a priest from Derry, Father Cornelius O'Mullen, was preaching against the government. Bishop O'Donnell ordered him to stop. Father O'Mullen refused and led a procession of anti-government Catholics to the cathedral when Bishop O'Donnell was saying Mass. There was almost a riot outside the church. Bishop O'Donnell would have no more of O'Mullen's tactics and had him excommunicated. Father O'Mullen left Derry for Dublin and joined the followers of Daniel O'Connell, the great Catholic orator.

I pray in the cool darkness of the Long Tower Church for my family and for the Cassidy family, as well. Later, we go outside and down the hill to the holy well of St. Columbcille. There, we stop and scoop up a few mouthfuls of the holy water to drink, and we pray some more.

We return to our lodgings in early evening. Most of the lads are tired and quickly fall asleep in the upper loft. Denis and I decide that we would not get a chance like this again, so we leave to see more of the city. Sean warns us again to stay outside the walls and to be careful of the gangs of rough youths that roam about at night. We assure him that we will try to be invisible to the people of the city. My brother Patrick tells me that he isn't interested in going with us.

We head immediately to the river. It is the widest river we have ever seen, and we wonder what class of monsters swim beneath its surface. We pass a few large ships at the docks. I'm certain that we will be on one of these in the morning. I'm also sure that some of them will be leaving for far away ports in America, Asia, and the European continent. It thrills me to be able to see such sights as these.

I just have to see what the city inside the walls looks like, and I convince Denis that, if we walk quickly, no one will bother us. We enter the walled city at Shipquay Street. Inside the wall, the street ascends a long hill with tall buildings running the length of it as far as we can see. Keeping our heads down, we walk up the street, furtively glancing at the variety of shops we pass. Every single person seems to be staring at us. We must look like lepers to them in the outdated style of our rags. At the town diamond, I look down a street to our right and spot a gate that probably leads to Creggan, and I advise Denis that we should be getting out of here. We walk quickly down the street past butcher shops and bakeries toward the gate. A group of seven young men is waiting there, apparently making sure that no Catholics from Creggan can enter the city.

Denis and I see them before they see us. We jump into an alley and discuss our options. We could rush past them; they won't be expecting us to be inside their precious city. Or, we could walk back to the diamond and leave through another gate. That would take us out of our way and would be cowardly. We choose the first option and look for anything in the alley that can be used for a weapon.

We find nothing except a few broken bricks. We bravely exit the alley and head toward the gate, a brick in each hand. As we near it, a lad on the top of the wall yells. He spied us. The others at the gate turn and run toward us. We have no other option now but to run for it. Behind us we hear, "Hey Paddy, where are you going? We just want to talk with ya." The Protestant lads can't catch us, and we reach the diamond and lose ourselves in the crowd. We look in every alley on the way toward the next gate on Bishop Street and finally find a couple of broken broom handles. We may need them if there are Protestant ruffians at the Bishop Street gate.

We didn't need them. There were no "sentries" there. Feeling a bit ashamed at having to run from the Protestants, we walk around outside of the wall to the Long Tower church where we get our bearings. From there, we find our way back to Creggan. On the way, Denis says that he would like to get even, somehow. I suggest a plan that might work if I could interest any of our lads to join us.

At midnight, Denis, Patrick, myself, and five other lads from Donaghmore go back to the Shipquay Street gate. We split up into four groups of two each. Some of the lads have weapons such as knives, broken hurley sticks, and axe handles that they have hidden under their clothes. Two of our boys engage the guard at the gate in conversation as the rest of us walk quickly inside the walls. The city is quiet, and we walk separately up to the diamond where we gather together. Our plan is for Denis and me to show our faces again, and lead the Protestant boys into an ambush. Again we walk down the street toward the guarded gate, and six of our lads hide in the alley. We approach the gate. There are only five there now, and they look as if they are ready to go home. We got here just in time.

Denis says to them, "How are yis doing, lads?"

All five of them stare at us. They can't believe their luck. From out of nowhere, knives and clubs with nails protruding, appear in their hands.

We let them approach us within a couple of yards before turning and running. The five are after us as we run up the street past the alley. Then, six of our lads jump out and begin beating the Prods before they know what is happening. I'm sure that they never expected any Papists to be the aggressors in a battle such as this. Denis and I turn and run back into the fight. The battle is over quickly, and the bloody Prods run away. We also run away in different directions before peace officers arrive.

The lot of us are laughing in the wee hours back at the loft in Creggan when we hear a commotion down the street. Since we can't sleep anyway, we go outside and see that a house is burning. A queue of people are already passing buckets of water to throw on the fire, and we join them. We learn that the family who lived there was able to get outside safely. Thank God! Our efforts and the efforts of the other residents are not enough to save the house, but they do protect the houses next to it. I think somehow that there is a connection between our actions last night and the fire. I feel ashamed.

Sean Maguire, who knew that we were up to mischief last night, walks over to me.

"I think that you had something to do with this, Jamie. The Orangemen don't tolerate acts of arrogance from us. Those poor people in the house fire had to sacrifice their home for whatever victory you had last night. They were lucky that they weren't burned alive. I hope that it was worth it to you."

I look at Sean and say, "Aye. We fought a few Prods at the city gate last night. I can't believe that they would do such a cowardly thing as this to get even."

Sean replies, "The Catholics here don't fight the Protestants for trivial reasons. The Protestants are too powerful, and

Catholics always come out as losers in confrontations. The Catholics of Derry choose their battles with more foresight."

"I am sorry. It was a stupid act of revenge that I arranged. I wish I could make it up to the poor people who suffered for my arrogance."

Sean says, "There are organizations here that will help them. Maybe we can leave them a donation from the wages we bring home from Scotland."

After walking to the docks in the morning with no sleep, we watch Sean discuss the terms of our employment with an agent who is using a barrel for a desk. Apparently they have reached an agreement because we see the agent and Sean shake hands.

The trip to Scotland is horrible. The sea is rough, and most of us are spilling our stomachs out over the rails of the sloop that is taking us to the rocky coast of Scotland. I have always wished to ride the open sea in a boat. It seemed to be exciting when I dreamed of it. The reality is different. It is quite pleasant at first, when we float away from the docks and speed down the river toward Lough Foyle. The city looks even more beautiful from the water, but at Lough Foyle the lurching and rolling of the deck makes my head spin. As soon as we are free of the land, my stomach is in open revolt.

Eventually, we enter another bay and are soon in another city where large open wagons are waiting to take us and the other Irish labourers who came with us to the countryside.

We work the land as we do in Ireland but with tools that allow us to gather the corn faster. Huge horses pull the wagons filled with crops to barns for storage. Our nights are spent in large unfurnished houses where we sleep on hay. A few men start the rosary, and soon others join in before bedtime. Others gamble using tokens for money they haven't earned yet. Others try to sneak up to the farm house to meet the girls who work there. I see little of my brother Patrick. He is one of the lads trying to charm the lasses in the farm house. I spend most of my free time with my cousin Denis, working out the financial aspects of farming in Ireland. I also think about Katie, and how things will be in our own cottage and our own farm. If I can work it, this will be my last trip to Scotland.

At my own farm, I will plant corn and flax. With a few animals to raise and Katie's help in sprigging and spinning for merchants in Ballybofey, I am sure that we can have a happy life together. When I go to bed at night, I close my eyes and I picture Katie's beautiful face, her deep brown eyes, her smooth complexion, and I hear her lilting voice. One of the last pictures in my head before falling asleep is of Katie lying with me in our own bed in our own cottage. Katie is in all of my dreams.

Even while cutting corn in the fields, I am thinking about Katie, her smile, her lively personality, and her sweet kindness. I would like to put her out of my mind during the day, but it can't be done. Thinking of her makes the days and weeks seem that much longer. However, the days do go by, one by one, and eventually October comes. We are on the boat that returns us to Ireland.

All I can think about on the long walk back to Donaghmore is Katie. I look at all of the lovely lasses I pass on the roads and realize that none of them can match Katie for beauty. I would like to stop in Killygordon to see her at the Johnston manor before going home, but Denis talks me out of it. He says that it might get her into trouble.

Patrick and I say goodbye to Denis at the crossroads. It starts raining hard as we walk up the path to our home in Glencarn. Da and my younger brothers are nowhere in sight. After pausing at the door, we walk in to see our mother at the hearth. She turns and sees us. A strange look is on her face. She breaks into tears and runs to hug Patrick and then me. "Thank God you are home! I have missed you so."

Tears swell in the eyes of both of us, as well. I tell her, "Ma! I never want to leave here again. It is mighty lonely outside of Donaghmore."

Ma is looking down. "I must get your father; he is over at Danny's. Paddy, would you please go to Danny's and bring him home? I have something to tell Jamie." Patrick looks puzzled but goes back out into the rain to find Da.

"What is it, Ma? Is there some bad news? "

Ma looks at me while biting her lip. "I have not the heart to tell you, Jamie. I would like it if your father tells you. It is about your Katie."

I am dumfounded and expect the worst. This is not the welcome that I expected. "Please tell me, Ma."

"Jamie, Katie Cassidy is dead."

chapter 10
(1815)

Suddenly, the room becomes a blur and starts to spin. I can't believe what I heard. As I stand there in shock, Ma sits on the stool by the fire and weeps. She says nothing more, nor can she. Some minutes later, my father and Patrick come through the door. Da is sombre and looks older than I remember.

"Jamie. I have bad news to tell you. It is about Katie Cassidy. It is shocking."

I sob and say, "Aye, Ma just told me. She is dead. How is that possible? When did she die?"

Da says, "It was in September. A fisherman found her body in the river near Castlefin. I'm sorry, Jamie."

I need to hear more. "I don't understand. How could it happen? Was Katie swimming?"

"Ah no, Jamie. Some of the lads around here think that it was foul play. Her brother Charley is still angry about it. He was so drunk at her wake that it was all the men could do to keep him from going to Killygordon and causing trouble."

My brothers, Charles and Hugh, and my sister Maggie, eventually arrive to welcome me home. It is a tragic homecoming indeed. All of my dreams are crushed. The most wonderful person in my life is gone. The fury rises in me. I need more answers.

I say to my family, "I must talk to Charley Cassidy. I am happy to see all of you, but I must go. Please don't wait for me at supper."

In the pouring rain, I rush up the hill to the Cassidy's farm, where I see Charley next to a shed.

"Charley," I yell. "What in the name of God happened, man?"

Charley invites me inside where his parents and sisters are gathered by the fire. They give me a mournful greeting, and I tell them how sorry I am for their loss, as tears begin to trickle down my cheeks. Katie's father looks at his wife, and soon both of them have tear-stained faces as well. Charley tells me what happened.

"Kate never came home that Sunday in September. I went to the Johnston Manor to find out why. The servants said that she was missing since the previous Thursday. The Johnstons told me that Kate was sick and went home during the week. I thought that she could be lying in a ditch somewhere, so I went to the barracks near the Cross and told them that Kate was missing. I asked them for help in finding her. An officer told me that a woman's body was found in the river near Castlefin by a fisherman just today. He rode me to the magistrate's office in Castlefin. The magistrate took me to the physician's home where Kate's body was kept. I saw that it was indeed Kate."

I ask, "How could it happen Charley?"

Charley's face is turning red. "It was no accident, Jamie. I'm sorry to tell you that Kate's body was in a sorry state being in the water so long, but I could see that there were bruises on her neck. I believe that it was David Johnston's work."

"Why do you think it was Johnston? It could have be any one of the low life scum that drifts about here in the summer, Charley. Katie should not have tried to walk home at night. I remember seeing plenty of travellers on the Ballybofey Road last year."

"It was not the travellers. Weeks before Kate died she told Mam that David Johnston was making indecent proposals to her. He told her that he would forgive our late rents if she would, as Kate said, comfort him some. No, Kate wasn't attacked when walking at night. It was that devil Johnston"

"Did you tell this to the magistrate?"

"I did. The magistrate and a peace officer questioned the Johnstons and their servants. When I asked the magistrate about it, he told me that he can find no reason to suspect the Johnstons. The investigation is still open, but they think it was a suicide."

"A suicide!" I shout. "My God...They are mad."

Charley says to me, "Could you join me outside before you go home?"

Outside in the rain Charley says to me, "I'm going to kill David Johnston. I am sure that he murdered my sister. He is an arrogant devil and a tyrant. He has evicted two poor families from here for missing only one gale, and he has stolen almost all of their property. He has plans to evict more. That in itself is almost enough to warrant his death. It is certain that he is terrorizing his women servants. He will die by my very own hands."

"Do you have enough proof."

"I have. I talked with one of the servants myself. She told me that David was making shocking requests to her before Kate started working there. She said that Johnston then gave all of his attention to Kate. The servant didn't tell the magistrate this because she feared for her life, and she was sure that Johnston would take revenge on her father, who was leasing land from him.

"Besides that, Johnston has been unusually kind to us lately because of Kate's death. That, in itself, is proof of his guilt."

"Charley," I say, "I believe you. Let me help you remove this filth from the earth."

Our harvest in October is poor because of terrible weather. Still we will be able to make our rent payment in November with the money made by Ma and Maggie from their sprigging work and with our wages from Scotland. The money from Scotland was reduced because Patrick and I made a tithing donation to the Catholic Beneficial Society in Derry to help make up for the destruction caused by Orangemen to the home in Creggan.

Da was still impressed with the money we made, and he wants us to go again next year. I am a bit less opposed to it now that Katie is no longer in my life.

I am still furious whenever I think of David Johnston. Every time I get a chance, I visit Charley Cassidy to plot our revenge.

"Jamie, how can we do this if we have no weapons? We need guns."

I reply, "Unfortunately, we must ask some of our friends about getting a gun, and that will throw suspicion on us when we set our trap. Many people hate David Johnston, but not all of them can be trusted. I have a feeling that my cousin Mickey may have some connections with former members of the old Boley Boys gang. I'll start with him."

I visit my cousin Mickey at his farm in Drumbeg. He and his wife Agnes now have a new daughter they named Grace after Agnes's mother. They have two lively sons as well.

He asks, "Will ya be havin' a jar of the best whiskey made in Donegal, Jamie?"

"Ah no. Not this time, Mick. I have a question to ask of you. Can we talk in private?"

"Very mysterious, Jamie. Let us go outside. It finally stopped raining."

I ask carefully so as not to cause suspicion, "I have a friend that would like to go hunting with me in County Tyrone. We are hoping to have some meat on the table this All Hallow's Eve. I am hoping that you would know where we can get a couple of muskets."

He looks at me intensely for a while. "Y'll be huntin' will ya? Ya wouldn't be huntin' pigs the likes of some that can be found in Killygordon would ya?"

I can see in his eyes that he knows my intentions.

"Aye. You know what I want. Charley Cassidy and I both want to teach that blaggard in Killygordon that he is not the Lord of Donaghmore, and he can't have his way with the daughters of his tenants."

"Jamie, up here we all believe that David killed your Katie. We were wonderin' when someone was going to do something about it. Aye, I can get ya some guns. I will be relyin' on yerself and Charley to tell no one. There is one condition on gettin' the guns."

"What is that?" I ask.

"That I will be joinin' ya. The lads I deal with want yer man in Killygordon to die, as well. There are many here and in Mulladoo who have experienced unpleasant dealin's with Johnston. The daughters of several tenants were abused by the tyrant. It is time to send him to hell where he belongs."

Charley Cassidy and I meet Mickey later in the week at his byre. He has two muskets and a pistol.

"Alright then, what is the plan," he asks.

We have none.

Charley says, "We could shoot him on his way to church on Sunday. He regularly attends the ten o'clock service at the Church of Ireland."

I quickly speak, "That will not do. His wife and children ride with him in his carriage. I cannot endanger his innocent family."

"Aye, y're right," says Charley.

Mickey asks, "Could we not get someone at his estate to give us his appointments for the week? If he has to go to Donegal Town or Lifford, we can wait for him alongside of the road and blast the bugger."

Charley tells of the servant he spoke to at the manor. He could talk to her when she comes home on Sunday. We agree to meet again in a week. For the first time, I begin to realise the seriousness of the business we are in. I am fully prepared for the consequences that can result from my anger. I imagine the worst, hanging from a rope at the Lifford jail. It will be worth it.

After meeting with David Johnston's servant for two Sundays in a row, Charley Cassidy is indeed able to get her to tell him of Johnston's travel plans. He has a meeting in Lifford to consult his legal councillors and is leaving early on Thursday morning. We have three days to prepare. First of all, we have no powder for our guns. We have ramrods and lead for scooping out musket balls but no powder. Buying gun powder in Ballybofey or Castlefin will cause suspicion, so Mickey travels to Castlederg where he is not at all known. He buys the powder at a shop just out of town on the Ardstraw road. Mickey is a friendly man with a face everyone trusts. He tells the shopkeeper that he is going hunting in the Killeter woods. After swapping a couple of jokes with the shopkeeper, he heads back to Drumbeg.

On Tuesday, the three of us head for far-away Killeter Woods for shooting practice. I have never fired a musket before, and my efforts at hitting a certain tree that we are using for a target leaves Mickey worried. Charley has never fired a gun before but is able to hit the tree fairly regularly. We are limited in the number of shots we can use for practice, so Michael tells me that he and Charley will use the muskets and take the first shots when we meet Johnston. I will have to use the pistol up close to finish him off.

I bring up what to do about David Johnston's driver. Charley says that we must kill him too. He will be able to identify us.

I say, "God no! We will be wearing masks. There is not a need to kill an innocent man."

Mickey says, "We will have to kill him to stop the car."

"Not if we run in front and seize the horse."

I am getting nervous about our murderous plan, but it is too late to abandon it.

Charley says, "Alright then. You will step out and point your pistol at the driver and get him to stop. We will shoot your man Johnston. You will threaten the driver that the Boley Boys will surely kill him if he gives any information about us to the magistrate or soldiers.

"Aye" says Mickey. "That is a good plan. It will be up to yerself, Jamie, if the driver is to live. He must be well convinced to keep his gob shut."

On Wednesday, we work as usual on our farms so as to cause no suspicion on us about tomorrow. I tell Da and Ma that I am spending the night with Denis. I meet Mickey in his byre that evening. Charley shows up there, as well. We have a drop of Mickey's poteen and then walk down in the dark through the heather to the River Finn with our guns wrapped in sheets made of flour sacks.

At the river, Mickey "borrows" a rowboat and rows us silently downstream past the Liscooly Bridge to a wooded area on the north bank of the river near Carrickcashel. We let the boat float away and wait.

Dawn comes. Charley sits in the bushes along the road to identify Johnston's car. Mickey and I are hidden farther east. About five carriages pass and a few farmers walk by. Then we hear a car moving at a good speed from the west and hear Charley's whistle. I put on my mask and jump out, levelling my pistol at the driver, who pulls on the reins and stops the car. Johnston is seated behind the driver. Charley runs down the road with his musket. Before anyone says a word, Mickey's musket booms, and Johnston slumps over on his seat. At this, the driver slaps his reins and begins to drive his horse forward. I fire at the driver just as Charley fires his musket. The driver is hit and his head is bleeding. I grab the horse's bridle and try to steady him. Johnston then stands up in the carriage, jumps down, and runs toward Charley who is reloading. Mickey fires again but misses. I release the horse and clumsily reload the pistol. Johnston grabs Charley, knocks him down, and tries to choke him. Johnston is a powerful big man. Mickey runs over and smashes Johnston in the head with the butt of his musket. He continues to beat him until Johnston's head is a gory mess. After Charley gets up, I rush over and fire into what's left of Johnston's head. Finally the monster is dead.

We see no sign of Johnston's car. I secretly hope that the driver will live through this horrible experience. We quickly grab the guns and run into the woods on the other side of the road and head up the hill into the northern part of the parish.

Our bloody deed didn't go the way I expected. Everything happened too fast. It was indeed a poor performance after all of our planning. I think we could have done better with the help of some of the lads who are still active in the old Boley Boys. Ach! We still accomplished our objective. The tyrant, who has ruined my life and the lives of many other families in Mulladoo, is dead.

We walk on hidden paths through North Donaghmore to a cottage in Cavan Townland belonging to one of the lads that Mickey knew from the Boley Boys. We leave the guns there and clean up at a burn nearby. Before we did that, we smelled of gun smoke. My hand was burned from my last shot, and I soak it in the stream. It hurts, but I am too excited to care.

There is not much said on our trip home. Mickey is sullen and Charley is exhausted. We walk all the way to Stranorlar where we cross the river into Ballybofey. In the afternoon, we arrive back at our homes and say nothing to anyone.

The gossip reaches our townland the next day. I am cleaning out the byre when a boy runs to our door and shouts the news. "Johnston was murdered!" There is much rejoicing throughout the parish. I wouldn't be surprised if there was going to be a bonfire up in Mulladoo this Saturday. At supper, Ma looks at me in a strange way and tells me that I must be relieved. She says it in a way that warns me that I shouldn't be if I had anything to do with the killing.

As I expected, there is a bonfire at the Mulladoo crossroads on Saturday. I am not in the mood for celebrating yet, but I wander up later as the fire starts to dwindle. I see Charley and walk to his side.

"Have you seen soldiers or any of the peace force about, Charley?"

"Not yet, but they will be here."

"I believe that they will be questioning you and your family. Get word to me if you need any help."

"You know that the driver was killed don't you, Jamie," he says quietly.

I shudder and gaze ahead. Finally I say, "Ach, the poor soul. It all went too fast. I guess that it had to happen."

"It did. The driver would have been able to point us out if he got away. It was bad luck on his part to be employed by that bastard. It is a pity though."

I do not feel like staying, and I walk away into the night. Uncomfortable thoughts spin in my head. I killed an innocent man. As much as I picture the tyrant dead at my feet, I feel no satisfaction. I am doomed to hell. Before going to sleep, I say many prayers for the soul of the driver, and I say an act of contrition as if that will save my immortal soul if I die tonight.

I miss Holy Communion at Mass the next day. I tell Ma that I forgot and broke my fast. We notice that most of the farmers from Mulladoo are not at church. After Mass, my brother Patrick and I walk up to see the Cassidys. Mrs. Cassidy meets us at her door and tells us, "Tommy and Charley were arrested this morning. Peace officers from Lifford were here and took most of the men. I think that they are being held now at the garrison."

I try to assure her that they will be released soon. "They cannot hold them long without evidence. Having a bonfire is not evidence."

Mrs. Cassidy looks me in the eye. "Jamie, did you and Charley have anything to do with the killing?"

I'm afraid that I can't look back at her. I say unconvincingly, "We did not. It must have been a group like the Boley Boys."

I am immediately ashamed. Not only did I lie, but I accused others. I feel like a coward as well as a murderer.

Every night I recite the Act of Contrition. On Saturday, I walk to Aghyaran for confessions at St. Patrick's. I am hoping the priest will not recognize me. I don't believe that either Father Higgins or his curate Father Porter knows me. Father Porter is hearing the confessions. I kneel next to the priest and pray, "Bless me father for I have sinned. It has been two months since my last confession."

Father Porter looks at me and says, "Are you of this parish?"

I say, "I attend Mass at the Cross, Father. I am embarrassed to confess my sins to Father McBride. He is a family friend."

Father tells me, "Very well, please continue."

"I have killed a man, Father. I may have killed another." I then ramble on quickly about my other sins. They seemed insignificant next to murder.

Father Porter waits a minute after I finish. He seems to be thinking of what to say. Finally he asks, "Were you forced to commit this sin by others?"

"No, Father. I agreed to take part in an ambush." I then rush into, "Father I am sorry for these sins and all the sins of my past life. May I please have absolution."

Father Porter then says, "This is a grievous sin. No man can take another's life. I will not tell you to turn yourself in to the authorities, but if any innocent man who did not participate in this is made to suffer for your actions, you must confess to the authorities. I will give you a penance and absolve you of this sin, but remember you must do what you can to prevent anyone else from suffering from it. Your penance is ten rosaries. This will allow you to take the sacraments. To stay in the state of grace, you must do good works and pray for the soul of your victim."

I say, "Thank you Father."

After an act of contrition, I spend more than an hour at the altar reciting the litanies of the rosary.

chapter 11
(1815 - 1816)

The Mulladoo men are taken to Lifford Jail where they are held until the week before Christmas. Most are released then, but Charley and Mr. Cassidy are held over Christmas. On one cold day in January, peace preservation officers arrive at our farm. An official looking document is shown to Da, and I am arrested and taken by horseback to the garrison. After hours locked in a cold room, I am brought outside where I am shackled, and a coach waits to take me to Lifford. During the ride, an officer tells me that I will be tried in the spring for the murder of David Johnston and John McCafferty. I say nothing.

At Lifford jail, I am taken past several barred rooms in the basement dungeon where various criminals are awaiting trial. I spy Charley and his father in one of the rooms, and I give them a greeting. I share a jail cell with a man from Castlefin who was arrested for stealing a horse. I am not there long before a guard takes me up to a room on the ground floor, where an armed bailiff and a handsomely dressed man are waiting for me. I take a seat across the table from them. The well dressed man, Mr. Wardlow, is wearing a black suit with a grey vest. His hair is trimmed quite immaculately and he is sporting a freshly shaven face. He asks me what I was doing on the day that David Johnston died. I tell him that I had to go to Ballybofey to buy boots. He asks the name of the vendor. I tell him that I returned without the boots, the price was too high. Mr. Wardlow looks disappointed that he can't check my story.

He then asks, "Mr. Gallen, what was your relationship with Miss Catherine Cassidy?"

Someone must have told him about my threat to kill Johnston. I hope it wasn't Charley.

"I was to marry Miss Cassidy."

"Do you believe that Mr. Johnston had something to do with Miss Cassidy's death?"

"Aye, I do."

"I wish to inform you otherwise. Miss Cassidy's murder was just one of several crimes against the women of County Donegal and County Tyrone. A Castlederg woman was raped in September. Miss Cassidy was raped and killed in October. A Stranorlar woman was missing in late October. We found her body in the Drumboe Woods in December. We arrested a filthy devil of a man named Tom Daly in November on the road to Letterkenny. He was identified by the Castlederg woman as the man who raped her. He was taken here, where he confessed to the other crimes. He hung himself in his jail cell on Christmas eve. Do you still think Mr. Johnston killed Miss Cassidy?"

I am dumbfounded and confused. I have nothing more to say to these people.

Mr. Wardlow says to me, "Mr. Gallen, we believe that you and others were in on the murder of David Johnston. We will prove it in the courts that convene here in May. Until then, you will be our guest. If you wish to confess to the crime in the meantime, I'm sure the court will be lenient with you and possibly spare your life. It is my understanding that hanging at the scaffold is not a pleasant experience. Our hangmen lack the practice necessary to perfect their craft. We are thinking of hiring a fiddler to play for the next execution. There is so much dancing at the end of the rope that the audience thinks us unkind for not supplying music. Please think about it."

They return me to my cell and to my thoughts.

My stay at Lifford jail is not as bad as I expected. The days go by quickly. The officers allow me no chance to talk with the Cassidys. My foul-smelling cellmate is a soft spoken man who keeps talking about wanting some whiskey. It is the only thing on his mind. He sleeps most of the day and night. I can't engage him in any meaningful conversation.

Some other lads from Donaghmore arrive and are placed in separate cells. Obviously, they are men suspected of being Boley Boys and responsible for the Johnston killing. My cousin Mickey is not with them.

The meals are better than at home. We have stir-about for breakfast, sometimes with a fried egg. Supper usually has some bacon along with boiled potatoes. It is quite good.

On Sunday evening, a priest of Clonleigh parish comes and says Mass. I take communion without fear of committing sacrilege, although I can't get rid of my feeling of guilt. On some days, one or two members of my family come to visit. The trip is too long for my parents, but Danny and my younger brothers visit when they can. They bring me cakes from home which I always appreciate. Danny tells me that Ma is doing more work with wool from the neighbours. She is carding and spinning, and Da is doing a bit of weaving on the long winter nights. He is hoping to sell some hand woven shawls at the Ballybofey and Castlefin fairs this spring. My brothers, Charley and Hugh, are still helping Uncle John on his farm. Crop prices are still low, so Danny and Da are thinking of buying some sheep and grazing them in the hills.

One day in March, Mr. Wardlow shows up in the hall outside our cells with a stranger. He takes him to my cell and asks him if he recognizes me. I don't know him, and he gives no sign that he knows me. Was there a witness to the killing that day? Wardlow takes him over to the Cassidy cell, and he again says that he doesn't remember either of them. He does the same with the other suspects from Donaghmore with no success. I hear the stranger mention that the man was a short lively lad with dark hair. He is probably describing my cousin Mickey. He, no doubt, is the shopkeeper who sold Mickey the gunpowder. We can see the look of frustration on Wardlow's face as he leaves with the stranger. Thank God neither of us was with Mickey when he bought the powder.

Mr. Cassidy is released with most of the other suspects in early April. By the middle of April, Charley, myself, and the remaining "Boley Boys" are set free. Apparently, the police can find no evidence to link us to the killing. We all begin a merry walk home on the Lifford-Stranorlar road. At Quinn's Alehouse at the Cross, we each have a pint of porter. Paddy Gallagher is the new proprietor of Quinn's Alehouse and is in the process of changing its name to Gallagher's. I ask Paddy to put the cost of the pints on my bill, and I will pay it at the end of the week. Paddy is a saint of a man and tells us that the drinks are on the house.

Chapter 12
[1816]

I am back to work now with Da on our farm. We now have our new sheep and are planting grass to make hay on land that used to be for corn. We are still planting corn but in last year's barley fields. Our barley crop will be sparse this year.

Many of our neighbours have purchased cows and have almost entirely shifted their farms to dairy and raising cattle for sale. This of course is the opposite of the Cassidys, who sold their cow and are attempting barley and oats. I fear that they will be in trouble with their landlord again this autumn. The new landlord is Mr. Johnston's son, Henry. No one knows how humane he will be with his tenants. My guilt for killing his father is still gnawing at me. I decide to see Father Porter in Aghyaran to try and talk it out.

One clear evening, bright with the light of the moon, I walk to Aghyaran and ask the housekeeper if I could have a word with Father Porter. She informs me that Father Porter is visiting a sick parishioner, but Father Higgins is available. I am troubled by this, but I don't want to make this trip again. I have rehearsed what I was going to say all the way up and down the hill to the chapel. Father Higgins, an elderly man with wild white hair, meets me at the door. He agrees to talk with me privately outside. He tells me that he doesn't know me from the parish, and I must repeat that I am too embarrassed to discuss what I am about to tell him with Father McBride of my own parish. Finally I get to tell him my problem.

"Father, a few months ago, I confessed a grievous sin to Father Porter and received absolution, but I still don't believe that my sin was completely forgiven. It is on my mind every day. I don't know how I can forget my guilt in this matter."

Father Higgins tells me, "Aye. It is often the case. It is not uncommon to feel this way. I believe that your feeling of guilt is a good thing. It means that you are truly contrite for your sin. Have no fear that you are forgiven."

"But how am I to get peace in my mind?"

"You should pray more often. Pray to Our Lord. Pray to the saints. Make sacrifices to ease the suffering of the souls in Purgatory. There are many ways. In time, you will find peace."

"Will I have to suffer for this sin in Purgatory, Father?"

"When Father Porter absolved your sin, it was forgiven by God. You may have to suffer in Purgatory, but not for that sin. You might wish to consider the stations or pilgrimages to holy sites to remain in a state of grace."

"Father, I have frequently thought about a pilgrimage to Croagh Patrick, but I will be in Scotland this summer."

"You know that you can make the pilgrimage anytime alone, but I have a suggestion. When are you going to Scotland?"

"We are leaving in late July, Father."

"Lovely. A group of pilgrims is going to Lough Derg from here on the first Monday of June. They will be staying three days at St. Patrick's Purgatory. I suggest that you join them. You will feel much better after you return, I can almost guarantee it."

I have known about Lough Derg since I was a child but never gave much thought to making the pilgrimage. I always thought that I should go to Croagh Patrick instead. I thank Father Higgins for his advice and tell him that I will try to make the pilgrimage in June.

My announcement that I will be going to Lough Derg brought admiration from Ma but few others. Da told me that he needed me on the farm until I was ready to go to Scotland.

I explained that I would be gone only three days and would work longer hours before and after my pilgrimage.

I work the extra hours before the time of my pilgrimage. Finally, the time comes for my trip to Lough Derg. I grab some extra clothes, a loaf of bread, and head over the hill to Aghyaran.

I arrive at St. Patrick's before dawn. I am too early, but early is always better than being late. Soon the other pilgrims start arriving. I strike up a conversation with a queer looking older man by the name of Francey McGuigan. He has wild red hair sticking out all over, and most of his teeth are gone. He speaks to me, and I have a hard time understanding his speech because of his lack of teeth. In a short time, I get the drift of what he is saying. Francey has been to Lough Derg many times before and tells me what to expect. To attend so many pilgrimages, he is either a repetitive sinner or a pious saintly man. He tells me that he is walking to the lough barefoot although I don't have to imitate him. I tell him that I will try to go barefoot, but I may change my mind up the road. Francey tells me that the priests require us to go barefoot at the Purgatory Island as part of our stations. Perhaps I should walk part of the way before removing my shoes.

Francey sees that I have a loaf of bread in my possession. He tells me that I should have fasted from the previous night and that no food or drink, except for water, is allowed on the pilgrimage. He tells me to give the bread to Father Higgins before we leave.

It appears that all of the pilgrims have arrived. There are ten women of mostly middle age and only one other man besides Francey and myself. I am the youngest in our group. Father Higgins arrives and gives Francey a letter to be delivered to the head cleric from Pettigo who oversees the stations at Lough Derg. We kneel as he leads us in one Our Father, a Hail Mary, and a Glory Be. Then he gives us his blessing and we are on our way after I present him the illicit loaf of bread that I had in my possession.

We will be walking along roads I never travelled before. First we cross the River Derg to the often travelled road used by the coaches that carry passengers and the post from Derry to Enniskillen. In less than an hour, we leave the road and take a path to a graveyard in Magherakeel. Here, the legendary priest from penal times is buried near the ruins of the parish's first church.

"Did ye ever hear of Father O'Mongan, Jamie" asks Francey.

"I did. My Da told us about the time Father O'Mongan escaped from the English soldiers."

Francey says, "I am shocked to learn that outsiders know of him. He is a hero to us from Aghyaran. Our parish church was once here in the grounds of the graveyard. The church was called St. Cairills. It was destroyed by the English before the penal times began. We had to pray at hidden Mass rocks until the chapel at Aghyaran was built."

We say some prayers at Father O'Mongan's grave and continue just a bit farther to a holy well near the side of the road.

"Aye. Saint Patrick stopped here himself on his way to Lough Derg. He blessed it, and the waters from it are mighty indeed. They will cure almost anything that harms ye. We gather here every year on the Saint's holy day."

The pilgrims take a drink from the well; more prayers are said as we walk in a circle around it, and we are off again. Soon we meet up at the post road again and begin the long walk to Lough Derg. I notice that Francey has no trouble walking barefoot, so I remove my shoes and throw them in my sack. About half of the pilgrims are barefoot. This is not surprising, because most of us went without shoes in the summer for a good part of our lives anyway.

We stop at another well. This is Saint Davog's well. Saint Davog was appointed by Saint Patrick to oversee his stations at Lough Derg. Miracles have occurred from the waters of this well also. Again we pray as we walk around the well, and then we resume our hike.

To pass time on the long trip, Francey tells me the story of St. Patrick's Purgatory. It seems that long ago, St. Patrick went to Lough Derg to offer penance. He crossed the water in a boat to an island in the lough and went into a cave. The cave provided him with the darkness to pray with no distractions. As he prayed, he asked to be shown the pains of Purgatory, and his prayers were answered. He saw millions of souls in human form being purified. Some souls in the fires of Purgatory were blackened by sin, and others were of a brighter colour. Over time, he understood that the fires were changing the colour of the souls as they were being purified. He saw some souls turn to a bright white glow and escape the fire to fly to their reward in heaven. After his vision in the cave, Patrick established the island as an earthly Purgatory, where sinners can go to ease their suffering and the suffering of others by days of prayer and fasting.

At first, there was just the cave on the island which became known as Saint's Island. Later, a church and friary were built there, and pilgrims were welcomed. A bridge was constructed to bring the visitors. The holy site became well known throughout Europe, and many knights from the continent made the pilgrimage. In the 16th century, the stations at Saint's Island were closed by the Pope for an unknown reason. A few years later, the stations were transferred to another remote island in the lough where the Franciscans built a friary and chapel. The remnants of monastic beehive cells and a magnificent high cross were brought over from Saint's Island. The centre of pilgrim activity then became a cave on the new island. Many believed that it was here that St. Patrick had his visions and not on Saint's Island. The new island was named Station Island.

Less than 30 years ago, the Franciscans left the island and it came under the control of the Diocese of Clogher. The pilgrims continued to come to Station Island in Lough Derg.

In the afternoon, we head off the main road and walk a dreary path through the bogs toward the lough. During this stretch of the trip, Francey tells me what to expect on the island. It doesn't sound too dreadful. It seems that lack of sleep is the major inconvenience.

Soon we arrive at the mighty lough. It gleams in the late afternoon sun. Station Island is off in the distance. A few stone buildings can be seen there in silhouette against the sun's glare. Boats are waiting at the dock where there are a few wee cottages. Other pilgrims are gathered here awaiting the voyage to the island. Most are older women.

We are greeted by a curate from the Clogher diocese at the dock. Francey hands him the letter from Father Higgins. It is my guess that it contains a promise of compensation for our accommodations. We join the other pilgrims waiting for the four boats shuttling passengers to and from the island.

Francey tells me that larger boats were used previously. In 1795, a great summer storm arose here and sank a number of boats carrying 93 passengers. Only three pilgrims survived. I seem to recall Ma telling me something about such a tragic event when I was young. It must have been the worst disaster that anyone in these parts can remember.

It is finally our turn, and most of our group from Aghyaran board one of the long row boats. One of the rowers reminds us to remove our shoes when we get to the island. He fails to notice that most of us are not wearing shoes anyway. At Station Island we go ashore and are welcomed by a lay person who directs us to a chapel just ahead. I can't fail to notice how tiny the island is. It is crowded with pilgrims who are gathered around every single monument erected on the grounds.

At St. Mary's Chapel, a cleric gives us our instructions. We will have a layman who will motion to us where and when we will go. Few words will be said. Our routine will be as follows: prayer around the "beds" of the saints; Mass and prayer vigils without sleep in newly rebuilt St. Mary's Chapel or the older St. Patrick's Chapel; Mass in the morning of the second day followed by confession; more prayer about the "beds" of the saints; a meagre meal of oatmeal; another Mass in the evening of the second day; sleep on an uncomfortable bed with no blanket on the second night followed by Mass in the morning of the third day; and more prayers about the "beds." The "beds" of the saints are stone monuments that are the remains of the cells of the abbots from Saint's Island. The "beds" are dedicated to Sts. Patrick, Catherine, Brigid, Columbcille, Adamnan, and Davog.

As we pass our prayer leader, he whispers to us the prayers we are to repeat over and over as we walk around the penitential beds. After circling each bed three times, kneeling, then circling the bed again three times, we move on to the next bed and do the same. There are other monuments and crosses on the island where we must kneel and pray, as well. After finishing this circuit, we have made one "station." Before leaving the island, we must complete at least nine of these stations.

I have walked barefoot most of my life, but I am unprepared for the sharp stones on which I will have to walk at Station Island. I see many pilgrims staring at their bloody feet as the rest of the day wears on. I am especially careful and have no cuts this day, but my feet are quite bruised.

There is a low hum around the penitential beds. It is the sound of many pilgrims repeating, over and over, their individual prayers and ejaculations. The effect on me is quite peaceful. After praying for hours around the beds, I begin to get hungry, but I know there will be no food until the next day. In the evening, the lot of us are led into St. Patrick's Chapel for Mass. St. Patrick's is called the Prison Chapel by the pilgrims. Francey had told me that the original cave where the pilgrims prayed was filled in, and St. Patrick's Chapel was built at the same site to replace the cave. He believes that pilgrims were locked in the chapel for 24 hours in the old days, and that is why it is called the Prison Chapel.

The actual vigil begins after Mass. We spend the rest of the night in prayer. There are prayers around the penitential beds outside until we are called into the chapel for night prayers and Benediction. I fight sleep by shifting my thoughts to the souls in Purgatory. I whisper my prayers, but noises from my stomach are making others look at me. I can't help it. Soon I feel myself falling asleep, but I get a poke and a dirty look from Francey. This is much harder than I thought. Following Benediction, it is back outside to complete another station.

During this vigil, I am starting to believe that I am helping myself and a few souls in Purgatory. I can visualize the souls of my grandparents and others flying out of the fire and winging toward heaven. I can feel my own soul being purified so that I can get back to living my life without guilt. One more day and maybe my soul will be free.

Finally the first night is over and the sun rises. We are led back for morning Mass celebrated by Father Murray, the prior of the island. After the recitation of the gospel, he launches into a fiery sermon on the evils of sin and its punishment. He screams at us and somehow touches upon a topic for which each of us feel guilty. Some of the women are crying. The men watch in fear that Father Murray knows their own private sins.

Following Mass, we queue up to confess our sins to a priest, in my case, Father Murray. Because I have confessed my sin of killing Mr. Johnston before, I only tell Father my sins of the past few weeks. Father Murray stares into my eyes as if he can see into my soul. After absolution, I move on to pray my penance.

Our prayer leader then takes a group of us to the hall for our meagre breakfast. Silently I accept the bowl of hot oatmeal and cup of water offered to me. This is the only food I have had for almost two days. After this unsatisfying meal, we leave to allow room for the next group of pilgrims who have finished confessing their sins.

Aside from fasting, we have had no sleep for over twenty-four hours, and there is still a long day ahead of us. I am dizzy and feeling chills. I look around me at the others in my group. They all look like they can put up with the suffering. I guess that I can too.

Our prayer leader takes us back to the "beds" for more stations and then leads us to the new St. Mary's Chapel for more prayers. This time, Father Murray leads us in the renewal of our baptismal promises. Then it is back to the "beds" and later back to St. Mary's for the Stations of the Cross. This is followed by Mass and another fierce sermon from Father Murray. The shuffling between the "beds" and chapel is a way to deal with the large number of pilgrims on the island. All facilities are in use at all times.

Later that night, the second night on the island, we have night prayers and Benediction in the chapel. This is considered the conclusion of our long vigil on Station Island. Our prayer leader comes and leads us to our sleeping accommodations. For me, it is an individual cell in a cold damp building. The only thing in the cell is a hard uncomfortable platform for my bed. There are no blankets. Nevertheless, I am grateful for the opportunity to finally get some rest after almost two days of staying awake.

I am awakened at dawn on the third day and join our group walking to St. Mary's Chapel. There are only men at this Mass. The women will get their turn later. After the gospel, we receive another lambasting from Father Murray. Father Murray has us squirming in the pews as he calls up every lustful action we may have performed, or even thought about performing. He makes us believe that we are disgracing our mothers and the Blessed Virgin every time we have such thoughts. Every one of us pledges to remain pure in spirit from this moment on. I receive Communion and feel that I am cleansed. I resolve to remain forever in a state of grace and never sin again. I give thoughts to joining a friary. I believe that I could devote my life to God.

After Mass, we follow our prayer leader outside to the saints' beds to resume our soothing prayers. The boats take us off the island at noon. The journey home is uneventful, except that we are frequently soaked by sudden rainfall. Francey scoffs at my ambition to be a monk. He says that, as soon as I am home and around the young lasses, I will return to my old desires. I am beginning to understand why he is such a frequent pilgrim to Lough Derg.

chapter 13
(1816 - 1817)

Francey was right. I gave up many of my bad habits, including the drink, but I still find the young women of my townland attractive. I could never be a monk. I remember Katie and my love for her, but I realise that I will have to get over it. On midsummer's eve, I dance the night away around the bonfire with every lass who is near to the age of myself.

In just a couple of weeks after the bonfire, Patrick and I join the group going to Scotland. The trip through Derry doesn't involve any fights with Protestants this time. We keep to ourselves in Creggan until the boat leaves for Scotland. I work hard during the Scotland harvest, and the days turn into weeks. Soon enough, I return home in time to finish the harvest on Da's land.

After another long winter the month of May arrives, and I remember to walk up to the holy spring as I promised my Aunt Mary. I plan to pray there for my innocent victims, David Johnston and his driver, as well as my own deceased kin. Especially wish to pray for the soul of my beloved Katie Cassidy.

It is a lovely day, and the walk is pleasant with birds singing in the trees and wild flowers growing among the heather.

When I push through the bushes that keep the spring hidden, I see a young woman standing there.

Throughout my life, I have been wishing to see the mysterious lady at the spring that my Aunt Mary saw and told me about. Aunt Mary said the lady could be the Blessed Mother, but she wasn't sure of it. Maybe this woman is her.

Ah, but not at all. She is flesh and blood, sure enough. She turns as I approach, and she is a short, plump, dark haired lass dressed in old everyday clothing. She is wearing a long brown dress with a white shawl. A dark coloured scarf covers her hair which is cut straight across her forehead. She looks at me as if to say, "What are you doing here at my spring?"

"I am Jamie from Glencarn," I say, introducing myself. "And who might you be?"

"I am Kate Gallen from Meenreagh," she says.

I stare at her when she tells me her name. I have never seen her before, and yet she has my last name. "I am a Gallen as well. My family has been in these parts for years, and I have cousins in Drumbeg."

Kate says, "I have relatives all over this parish and in County Tyrone. Did you think you were the only Gallens in Ireland?"

"I did not. I am only surprised to see you here. I didn't believe anyone else knew of this place."

"You are right, there. I love this place and keep it my secret. I come here often to meditate and pray."

"I do as well. Have you ever seen any saints or fairies here?"

I see the change in her eyes. She looks away from me and says, "Why do you ask that?"

"My aunt used to come here frequently and see strange things. Although I have not seen anything myself, I believe that the spring is holy or haunted, but I don't know which."

"I can tell you no more, but I have proof that this is a holy place. Please don't ask me anymore about it."

I can see that she wants to leave, and I tell her that it was a pleasure meeting her. I add that I want to pray here now if it doesn't bother her.

"It is fine with me. I must go now. Goodbye, Jamie Gallen. Perhaps we will see each other again."

I kneel and begin the rosary. Soon I am losing my place in the prayers, thinking of her. She is my age but not especially pretty. She never smiled once during the time we spoke. She seems a bit too grim, but what right have I to judge her? She means nothing to me. Isn't it queer that she has the same first name as my Katie, the lass that I shall never forget.

The lass I met at the well has me puzzled. What did she mean that she had proof that the spring was a holy place? That question gnaws at me. I must have some more words with her, but I have no reason to ever go to Meenreagh. It is too far away to travel and isn't especially pleasant there, but I decide to go after spending a Sunday visiting my new niece at the Callaghans in Cronalaghy. Meenreagh isn't too far from Cronalaghy.

My sister Nellie and her husband Jimmy have a nice cottage on about 100 acres of rocky land. Only 10 acres are cultivated. The rest is used by the sheep of the townland for grazing. Da plans to send his flock up here this summer. Their wee baby Annie is a beautiful doll-like creature when she is asleep, but she spikes the air with her screams when she is awake. Nellie is pregnant again and will have her second child a few weeks after All Hallow's Eve. I ask them if they know any Gallens from Meenreagh. They both laugh.

"Ach, Jamie. You can't throw a cow turd around here or Meenreagh without hitting a Gallen," replies Jimmy. "The hills up here are infested with the buggers."

"Are any related to my family?" I ask.

"Not that I am aware of. The Gallens have been here for centuries. Being from Cronalaghy, I probably have more Gallen relatives than you do," Jimmy answers. "Why are you interested in the Meenreagh Gallens?

I tell them about Kate, and how I met her at the spring. Nellie is surprised that anyone from Meenreagh knows about the spring. I ask why I never saw Kate at Mass at St. Patrick's.

My sister answers, "You know that many from Meenreagh go to a Mass rock at Lough Trusk. The curate from the Cross still says Mass there. Lough Trusk is closer to Meenreagh than the Cross is."

Before going home, I walk over to Meenreagh and keep my eyes open to look for someone to talk to. A young farmer is piling manure on his midden. I ask him if he knows Kate Gallen. He asks me which one? I describe her and that limits the number to two young lasses. One lives not far away. Her cottage is on the hill above the Mourne Beg River. I walk there and ask for Kate. A skinny brown-haired girl comes to the half-door. I ask her if another Kate lives nearby, and she directs me to the cottage on the next farm. She is her cousin.

Finally, I see Kate. She looks at me with apprehension when she comes to the door to meet me. I explain that I would like to have a talk with her sometime. I ask her if I could accompany her to Mass next Sunday. She replies seriously that she would have no objection, but I would have to come early. The Mass at the lough is an hour after sunrise.

With great difficulty, I arrive at Meenreagh the following Sunday. Kate's family is preparing for the walk down to Lough Trusk. They all knew I was coming. Kate introduces me to her parents and her brothers and sisters. She is the oldest of the children.

I walk with Kate alone as we lag behind her family. She doesn't say much, just looks ahead as I babble on. I ask her if she would like to join me at the Glencarn bonfire next month. I mention that we have a fine fiddler for dancing. She tells me that she doesn't dance.

"Well then, I can teach you."

No reaction from Kate. I talk and talk and apparently make no impression on her. Why am I bothering? Who the hell does she think she is?

Mass is celebrated by the curate from the Cross, Father McCafferty. After Mass, we start back up the hill to Meenreagh. I am talked out and say little going back. When I say goodbye at Kate's cottage, she says to my surprise, "I would like to join you at the bonfire."

I don't know if I am glad or what. She surprises me again by saying that I shouldn't come to Meenreagh, We should meet at the holy spring about two hours before sunset.

I am rightly confused by Kate. I have no idea what is going on inside her head. She is not the type of lass I would have chosen to take to the bonfire, but there is something about her that is mysterious and exciting. I just wish she would be a bit more attractive and less plump. I would like the other lads from my townland to envy me a bit when I accompany a lass to a ceilidh.

Midsummer is the longest day in the year, and it occurs in late June. The men meet in the field next to the road with wood and branches that will be used for the bonfire, which they hope will burn at least until midnight. All over Ireland, bonfires are being prepared for this festive night.

Kate wants to meet two hours before sunset. I decide to go to the spring early and wait for her. It is a peaceful place, and I can be alone with thoughts about my future. When I approach the wooded area, I hear Kate's voice. She sounds as if she is talking to someone. Has she brought a friend for the bonfire? When I push through the bushes, I see her alone facing the spring. No one is with her.

"Good evening Kate" says I. "Who are you talking to?"

"Hello Jamie. I was only praying to Saint Brigid. I didn't know that I was praying so loud."

"It was quite loud. You should be careful. Someone may think that you are daft."

I can see in Kate's face that she doesn't approve of my last statement. We are off to a poor start for the evening. We begin our walk down to the road in silence.

I ask her, "Is there a bonfire tonight in Meenreagh?"

"There is" she says. "Generally it is a brilliant fire that can be seen as far away as Killeter."

"You will let me know how our wee fire compares, won't you?"

The field is getting more crowded, even though the sun is still far from setting. Carts arrive with poteen to be sold. My cousin Mickey is there with the largest number of bottles. I have talked with Mickey many times since returning from the jail, but we never brought up our bloody deed. Most of my family is there, as well. First I introduce Kate to Mickey. I can see that Kate doesn't approve of my cousin's illicit enterprise. After leaving Mickey, I introduce Kate to my brother Danny and his family. Danny now has four children. I catch Kate smiling for the first time when she sees Willie, Danny's baby. Kate seems quite at home with Anne, Danny's wife.

Ma and Da haven't arrived yet, but the rest of my family is here. My younger brothers are racing about with the Bryson lads. My sister Maggie walks over to meet us. Maggie is beginning to look older now, and it appears that she has passed her prime. With no suitors in her future, she is starting to accept her fate as a spinster. Her main chore at home is carding and spinning the wool we are collecting from our sheep and those of a few neighbours. She and Kate also share a pleasant conversation. I believe Kate approves of my family so far, and they approve of her. The question is... do I approve of her?

Next, Ma, Da, and Uncle John arrive. Ma has a basket of cakes with her which she offers to us. She seems surprised that Kate is here with me; I forgot to tell her. Kate respectfully greets Uncle John and my parents, even though Da seems to have begun celebrating the evening early with a drop of whiskey or two.

My brother Patrick is with the McGoldricks and doesn't join us. He has been in the company of the McGoldrick's daughter, Susan, for the past few months. It appears to be a serious courtship.

The fiddlers begin to play, and some of the lasses start to dance in a flat area near the road. A few lads share a bottle of poteen near Mickey's cart. The festivities have officially started. I ask Kate if she would like to learn a few dance steps and she says, "Not yet, Jamie, perhaps when a waltz is played." I leave her talking with my family and walk over to Mickey's cart. Paddy Bonner and Owen McGlinchy are talking to Mickey. They are both well on their way to drunkenness, even before the fire is lit.

I haven't talked to Paddy in a while. I yell, "Hiya, Paddy. How's your wife?"

"Ah! Better than nothin' I guess."

Mickey greets me again, "How are ya, Jamie? Do ya have plans tonight for your lass from Meenreagh?"

"She is not my lass Mickey, just a friend."

Owen says, "Meenreagh? I have heard many things about the lads of Meenreagh. They are full of the devil. Last year, a group of men from Meenahinnis were bathing in the Mourne Beg without a stitch on. A Meenreagh man crept up and stole their clothes. They had to walk home naked."

"My God, man," roars Mickey. "That is shocking. Can ya believe that? I can't imagine it. Meenahinnis men bathing! It is beyond belief. From the way that they smell, y'd think they were born filthy."

The men began laughing loudly, and many heads turn toward us.

Paddy says, "Aye. We found Danny Slevin in a ditch last year. He was unconscious and bloody so we carried him home. The smell from him was mighty. Mam and me sisters tried to wash him before bandaging his chest. They took off his shirt and started scrubbing. They scrubbed and scrubbed, but his body remained black as soot. My sister tried to scrape the dirt from his skin with a spoon. Then they discovered that he was wearing another shirt."

There was more laughter. Owen asks, "Are you and Patrick going to Scotland with the lads this year, Jamie?"

"Not this year. I think that I should stay and help at home. Uncle John is getting a bit lame, and my brother Hugh and I will mind his farm. Patrick and Charley are helping Da. With a good harvest, we should make our gale."

Paddy says, "It was a sure enough sad year for corn last year. That and the prices in Ballybofey were the lowest I can remember. I'm not a religious man, but I will be on me knees prayin' for fair weather this year."

Mickey interrupts, "Will ya have a drop of me poteen, Jamie. It is some of the best I brewed."

"I am no longer a drinking man, Mickey. I thought you knew that."

Paddy looks at me and laughs. "Aye, It's the talk of Glencarn. What got into ya, Jamie? Ya had no reason to quit."

"It was a promise I made to God. I am hoping that our family's luck will change."

Owen says, "I would rather have bad luck than put up with my life without the drink. Whiskey is the only thing I have to look forward to in this life."

Paddy asks him, "What about women, Owen? Don't ya look forward to spendin' a cold night with a warm lass in yer bed?"

"Not at all. Not at all. I have no desire to share me life with a mean spirited woman. I can see how miserable my cousins are with their wives. I think that I would rather be dead."

I look at Mickey. He seems contented in his marriage. He now has three lovely children, and his wife Agnes is a good mother and a fine partner in his moonshine business. "Can you talk sense to Owen, Mickey? You don't have it bad."

Mickey sort of smirks, "It is fine, indeed. A marriage is what ya make of it. Ya must rule the homestead with a firm hand in the beginnin'. Agnes and me has an agreement. She pays no attention to my shenanigans as long as I keep the family well fed and reasonably prosperous."

It is starting to get dark and the fire is lit. I hurry back to Kate to rescue her from my family. She seems to be happy with them. I invite her to dance a waltz, and she joins me with the other dancers. She is clumsy, but we survive the tune. A reel begins, and I take her off to the side and try to teach her what she should do to stay in step with me. She picks it up more easily than I thought.

The other lasses I danced with at the last ceilidh are looking at us. I'm sure they expect me to dance with them, but I cannot. They dance with each other because none of the lads know how to dance or desire to learn how. I must concentrate on Kate this evening.

Instead of going back to my family, I sit with her near the fire. She asks me why I didn't have a drink with my friends, and I tell her about how I gave up the drink after my pilgrimage to Lough Derg. She seems surprised and pleased that I took the stations. She tells me that she had gone to Lough Derg a year ago. We discuss the effect that it had on us. I am truly impressed with her piety, and it is this quality that starts to endear her to me. I think that she is impressed that I am somewhat pious, as well. I will never tell her, however, about my bloody past.

After about an hour of darkness, the fire is still roaring with high flames. Other fires can be seen on the north side of the River Finn. Many townlands have bonfires. It is a contest to see which burns the longest, but most of us can't wait that long to see. The midges are getting annoying, and people are leaving for home. The fiddlers move closer to the flames for relief, but they must stop as well before being driven mad by the bothersome insects. A team of lads will remain to keep the fire going. Someone will tell us tomorrow how we did against the other townlands.

Kate and I begin the long walk to Meenreagh. I start to bring up the subject of the holy spring, but Kate stops me. "I'm sorry, Jamie. I must not speak of the spring. Let us discuss other topics."

"Very well. Can you tell me about yourself. I don't know you well. What chores do you have at home?"

"I milk the cows, churn butter, help Mam spin yarn, cook the meals."

"How do you get time to visit the spring?"

She seems annoyed that I brought up the spring again. "How do you have the time, Jamie?"

"I usually only visit it on Sundays. Besides, it is much closer to me than to you."

"I must tell you something else about me that you should know. It may explain things. I am a healer. I have found that I have the power to cure some illnesses and heal some wounds. Really, it is God who is doing the healing. For some reason, He chose me to help him perform the cures."

This admission stuns me. She is still a young woman, and yet she has this power. I now remember that someone told me that a woman in Meenreagh was a healer. I would never have believed it would be someone like Kate.

"Have you cured everyone who comes to you?"

"No. Most get well, but there are some who don't. I have seen several die, in fact. I don't know how God chooses which ones are helped."

"I am happy that you told me about yourself, Katie. I am happy to be your friend, as well. My hope is that I will deserve to be your friend in the future."

"It is my hope too. Of all the boys I have met in my life, you are the one I like best. I'm sure that you can meet more lively lasses than me, but I hope you will continue to call on me." She smiles at me, and my heart jumps a bit.

At her cottage, I pause and ask her if I can embrace her. She smiles and lifts her head to kiss me. I step in, and we kiss. Her lips are soft and warm. The embrace lasts a long time, and the tension in me leaves my body.

The trip back to Glencarn is one of wonder. Thoughts of beautiful Katie Cassidy alternate with those of short plump Kate Gallen. I know that I will continue to make this trip up to Meenreagh, but I don't know where our friendship will lead.

chapter 14
(1817)

The weather this summer is fine, and the crops are doing well. I have been visiting Kate in Meenreagh each Sunday and attending Mass down at Trusk. Kate's parents, Charles and Margaret, are a pleasure to talk with. Her father jokes that I will be hearing the beast of Lough Trusk if I come this winter. He claims that there is an animal as big as a bull that swims underwater in the lake. Only a few have seen it, but many have heard its screams under the ice when the lake freezes. I ask him if he has heard it, and he tells me, "Many times, many times." I don't believe him. Her father has a droll sense of humour.

Kate is the oldest of Charles and Margaret's children. She has two younger sisters, Anne and Mary. The youngest in the family is her brother, Murty.

I haven't completely given my heart to Kate yet. I have been visiting some of the Glencarn lasses during the week just for comparison purposes. Mary and Rose Gallagher are quite lively although both are rather tall for me. Nancy McGlinchy is too fat, and her sister Nellie seems too simple-minded to hold a conversation. Red-haired Sadie Bryson is just too talkative, and that scares me a bit. Susan McGoldrick is being courted by my brother Patrick, and lovely Mary Dougherty is being courted by

Paddy Bonner. I have a lot to think about. Maybe bachelorhood isn't that bad.

The Cassidys of Mulladoo, the family of my beloved but departed Katie, were finally evicted last year. They were too far overdue in their rent, and the charity of their landlord Henry Johnston, and son of the man we murdered, came to an end. Charley asked me to pray for his family. They headed off toward the farm of Mrs. Cassidy's brother in Fermanagh where they hope to get back on their feet again. God bless them.

The parish is saddened by the death of Father McBride. He will be buried on the grounds of our chapel at the Cross. The curate, Father William McCafferty, will be our new parish priest. Da is particularly morose about it. He considered Father McBride a close friend. We will attend the requiem Mass and burial. I decide to invite Kate and rush up to Meenreagh after I hear the arrangements.

Kate joins me and my family at the chapel. After the burial, we visit my Aunt Mary and Uncle Owen in Ballinacor. They have a nice farm there, run by Uncle Owen and two of his sons, Manus and Patrick. They have five daughters, each one a beauty. It is hard to believe that the lasses are still single. Their other son, Owen, will be ordained a priest next year at Maynooth.

I am anxious to have Kate talk with Aunt Mary. Aunt Mary has seen visions at the holy spring. Maybe today I will learn what is going on there. I corner Aunt Mary when she steps outside for more bricks of turf to throw on the fire. I tell her that I met Kate at the spring where she was praying.

"Did she tell you if she ever saw anything, James?"

"She won't tell me anything, Aunt Mary, but I believe she did and often does now."

"Could you ask her to step outside for a word with me?"

I don't know if Kate will be happy about this, but I go inside and say softly, "Do you remember me telling you that my Aunt

Mary has seen things at the spring? Well, she would like to speak to you outside for a minute."

Kate stares blankly at me for a minute and then gets up to go outside, showing no emotion. I follow. When we are outside, Aunt Mary says, "We would like to talk privately if it is alright with you, James."

I go back inside and wait. It is a good thing that Kate doesn't have the temper of the Glencarn lasses that I know, but I am expecting the worse.

Aunt Mary and Kate return in a few minutes like nothing has happened. Soon we are heading home. When we are walking alone back to Meenreagh, I ask the question that is on my mind.

"Did Aunt Mary have the same experiences as you at the spring?"

"Ah, you won't give up will you? Our experiences were similar but different. Did you not ever think to ask your aunt what she saw?"

I answer no.

She says, "I still am not going to reveal the secret of the spring. Maybe you'll have better luck with your Aunt."

After seeing Kate to her cottage, I race back to my aunt's farm.

When I see Aunt Mary, I say, "I am fond of Kate, Mary, but she will not tell me anything about the spring. Can you tell me what she said to you?"

"James, the spring is a spiritual place. Since I have been going there, I've had nothing but good luck in my life. There are supernatural things that occur there, but I'm not at all sure they are Christian. Kate would not tell me what she sees there. I can tell you what I see there. On some days, I see a young woman who beckons me to stay with her by the spring. She smiles but says nothing to me. At first, I believed that the woman was the Blessed Mother. I am not so sure now. The woman disappears before my eyes when I try to talk to her. When she goes, it is as if she wasn't there to begin with. Sometimes I feel as if I am mad and dreaming the whole thing. I told this to Kate. She didn't seem surprised. Perhaps she experiences the same thing."

This is all confusing. I want to tell Aunt Mary about Kate praying to Saint Brigid, but it would just confuse things. I thank my aunt and leave for home. I am going to have to forget about all this if I can. I will have to look beyond this mystery if I am to get along with Kate.

Chapter 15
(1818 - 1821)

After thinking it over this winter, I have decided to ask Kate if she will marry me. It is time. Of all the lasses in the parish, Kate seems to be the best of them. She is pious and will keep me on the path to heaven. Also, Kate is hardworking, charitable, and she will be a good mother.

First I ask her father if he wouldn't mind having me as a son-in-law. He says, "My God. Where will ya sleep? I have barely enough room here for me own family."

He is joking of course, but he raised a good question. Where will Kate and I sleep? Da's farm was divided when Danny married. It left Da with only six acres, and there are four more sons. How can he part with any land for me and my future family? Uncle John has ten acres, but we all work his land. We share the profits from grain sales among all of us, and we all share the rent and tithe payments on the same basis. Nevertheless, Uncle John is the lease holder for his ten acres, and it doesn't seem fair to ask him to part with any of it. It would be good to lease some other land in Glencarn.

I see Kate returning from visiting a sick resident of Meenagolan. I meet her outside on the path.

"How is Mrs. McGlinchy doing today?"

"Ah, she is grand, James. She just has a deep cough, and she worries about it too much."

"I must speak with you. It is important. Would you have time to walk with me to the spring?"

It is another grey day in the hills. The skies look as if they will be dropping a soft drizzle at any moment. On the way, we discuss the everyday problems of working the land. We talk about the tools that are broken, the animals that became ill, and the changing market prices for yarn and linen in Ballybofey. Finally, we reach the spring. As many times before, we kneel and say a decade of the rosary.

She rises and says, "I must be going home now, James. There are chores that must be done before nightfall."

I tell her that I love her and want to marry her. Tears come to her eyes, and she gives me one of her rare smiles. With the stormy skies above and the soft musical sound of the water falling into the pool at the base of the spring, she says that she would be happy to be my wife. The rain starts to fall, and we walk back to Kate's cottage, hand in hand, to get warm and dry by the fire.

I talk to Ma about our marriage and where we will live. She calls for Da to come in from the field. I ask if there is any land nearby to lease. Da tells me that he has been thinking about this for several years. He knows that there is not enough land for all of his sons. He believes that old Willie Maguire may be interested in sub-leasing his nine acres. His children have moved away, and his land is starting to look shabby. He lets our sheep graze on a part of it. We must talk to him.

Willie and his wife Anne are happy to let go of the land. We agree to let them live on a quarter-acre plot surrounding their cottage. Da will talk with Mr. Knox, the agent for Sam Delap, Willie's landlord who is our landlord, as well.

Sam Delap has been the landlord of Glencarn and surrounding townlands for many years now. He had inherited the land and moved from Dublin into the magnificent castle in

Monellan. He has been a fair man and hasn't raised the rent for several years because of past poor harvests.

Mr. Knox lets us know of Sam Delap's decision to let us take over Willie's lease for his nine acres. This will give us a total of 29 acres for all of our family. We all will share equally in the profits, rent, and taxes. Uncle John will farm his 10 acres with the help of Hugh and Charles, who will live with him. Danny will farm his four acres. This leaves five acres each for Da, myself, and Patrick, who is planning to marry Susan McGoldrick this year. Willie and Anne Maguire will live rent free on our land with their cottage and garden. All of us are happy with the arrangement.

The whole family helps Patrick and myself in building our two cottages on our plots of land. They are exact copies of Danny's cottage and easily constructed. It is happy work. Finally, Patrick and I will have our own farms and get started on our future lives.

Kate and I are married at the Gallen cottage in Meenreagh by Father McCafferty. My cousin Dennis and Kate's young sister Anne are witnesses. Never before was there such a large congregation of Gallens. I never dreamed there were so many of us. This is the largest wedding I have ever attended, and I am the bridegroom. There is drinking and dancing to a family fiddler, and there is food galore, contributed by Kate's many cousins. The children are racing about the paths and running down to the river to jump across the stepping stones into County Tyrone. The children are mostly filthy and sweaty now, and everyone is glad they are entertaining themselves and not being a bother to their parents.

My cousin Mickey is outside talking to Maurice, one of Kate's cousins. It is a shock seeing Mickey talk to a man. For most of the day, he was joking with many of Kate's women cousins and ignoring his wife, Agnes. Agnes, who is shy and who has a completely different personality than her husband, is speaking to Kate in a corner of the yard.

I walk over to talk with Mickey and Maurice.

"Jamie," says Mickey. "Maurice tells me that it is good luck to marry someone who has the same last name as yerself."

"Is that so? I haven't heard that."

"It is. Is it not, Maurice?"

"It is indeed. The...children...such marriage...unusual...power. Should... doubly so...since Kate...power."

Maurice speaks fast, without moving his lips, and I can only understand a word here and there. His speech sounds like the buzzing of bees. I just get the drift that it is his belief that it truly is good luck marrying someone with the same name.

I ask, "Kate and you are first cousins, are you not?"

"Aye. Me father...her father. Died...two years. Kate...help...drinker...care of...health."

I have no idea what he just told me. I excuse myself and leave him drinking and buzzing with Mickey.

Married life is quite pleasant. Kate seems contented with living away from her family. She is friendly with my family, and has made them her own. Kate is powerfully energetic and hustles about in her house-keeping duties while continuing her healing work when people call on her. The thing I like is that she remains affectionate to me and seems to take pleasure in our marital relationship. I made no mistake when I chose her to be my wife.

We both remain devout Catholics. Before retiring for the night, we say the rosary together. On some nights, I may feel too tired, but a cup of buttermilk helps me get through it.

Being closer to the spring and the chapel at the Cross, Kate frequently visits both. She has made friends with the clergy at the Cross and volunteers to help them with laundering the Mass vestments. The new curate, Father Neill O'Kane, calls on us when he visits other parishioners nearby. Having him join us for a bite of food gives me the opportunity to learn of the many happenings outside our wee world here in the hills. The talk of political change in Dublin especially interests me. He talks about a Catholic attorney by the name of Daniel O'Connell, who continues the fight for Irish home rule and for the equality of Irish Catholics. I learn of Mr. O'Connell's victories and defeats in court every time Father O'Kane stops by.

Kate is already pregnant when my brother Patrick and Susan marry. Susan has no sisters, so she chooses Kate as her witness, and Patrick chooses myself. Their wedding at the McGoldricks is another happy event for my parents. The Gallens are now fully occupying our corner of the world in Glencarn.

Our first son is named Patrick after Da. He is followed by a daughter, whom we name Margaret after Kate's mother. Next is our second son, Charles. So far, Patrick and Susan have no children. I have asked no questions about this. It is not my business. Kate is pregnant again but continues to work as hard as before the children were born. She is a bundle of energy. Her activities make me dizzy.

Willie Maguire passes on, leaving his widow alone in their cottage on our land. Willie's daughter Grace comes to stay with Mrs. Maguire until things are straightened out. We, of course, help dear old Mrs. Maguire as much as we can.

Our curate, Father O'Kane, stops by one day to tell us that he will be spending more time away from the Cross. He has been saying Mass in Castlefin and hearing from parishioners who want to build a chapel near the town. In asking around, he discovered a kind Protestant lady willing to donate the land. Many members of the parish are keen on helping build the chapel.

Father tells us that mad King George has died. His son, George IV, who has been ruling as regent for the past 10 years, was crowned king. George IV is planning to visit Ireland next year. Daniel O'Connell will be meeting with him to discuss his ideas for Catholic Emancipation.

Chapter 16
(1821 - 1822)

Ma drops by all of our homes to tell us that her cousin, Denis Kelly from America, is visiting. He is staying at the home of another cousin, Barney Kelly, in Ardnagannah. Denis's wife Mary and their child Bridget remain in America.

We are invited to meet Denis at a party in Gallagher's Alehouse on Thursday night. We are all excited and can hardly wait. Thursday comes and the whole lot of us, including our wains, head to Gallagher's. Drinks are free at the party, and Da manages to down two pints of stout before Ma notices.

Denis Kelly is a large gentleman, who speaks with a booming voice. He is a distinguished looking man, freshly shaven, and wearing a stylish woollen suit of a light tan colour with dark brown checks. His matching jacket and trousers set him apart from the rest of us in our rumpled, ill-fitting and ill-matched clothing. We are introduced to him and shake his hand. The women sit at the large table in the corner drinking cider or ale mixed with water. The men stand with their pints. Denis holds everyone's attention with the story of his life in America. With his booming voice, even those standing outside the pub can hear his tale.

"The voyage to America was horrible. The ship smelled bad, and the food was inedible. We were sick for our two months on the ocean. Once we landed in Philadelphia, we despised the squalor that existed in the city. I arranged for a coach to take us to Western Pennsylvania so that I could start an enterprise with the money I saved from my scutch mill here. Mary, wee Biddy, and I shared the coach with two men who spoke English with a foreign accent. They were not gentlemen, for one of them spoke profanity in the face of Mary and the baby. I told him that I would thump him if he didn't stop. He apologized and continued his conversation. A short time later, he used God's name in vain again. Mary insisted that we would go no further with this foul-mouthed person. I called to the driver to stop, and Mary took Biddy out of the coach. We were in a small village just west of Philadelphia. Mary wanted us to stay for one night at an inn nearby and take the next coach tomorrow. The driver took down our trunk as I was cuffing the foul individual inside the coach. I was able to berate him without using bad language myself. He cowered and was as glad to be rid of me as I was of him.

"The village's name was Oakmont, a clean and pleasant little place. Mary and I liked it immediately and arranged to stay at the inn until I acquired a room in a boarding house. By my wits, I was able to find work right away at a store that sold sundry goods. Within months, I was running the store for its owner. The next year, I found investors willing to start up a woollen mill on the creek that goes through the town. The mill was greatly successful, and we started enlarging the mill by adding looms for weaving. Later, I purchased other mills that were already operating on the same creek. In 1812, America went to war with England, and I arranged a contract for making uniforms for the American soldiers."

By this time, Da was draining his third pint. The rest of us were spellbound with Denis's story. He told of the riches he enjoyed as a woollen mill owner. He had a large house built in Oakmont and kept several servants. By means of letters he sent home, he was able to attract many single men and women from our parish to emigrate to his hometown and work in his mills.

"I believe there are more Irishmen living in Oakmont than Americans. America is a land of opportunity for anyone who wants to take the long voyage across the ocean. I give my word, here and now, there will always be a job at my mills for any lad or lass from Donaghmore."

Even I had to think about that one…but not for long. Life is good for me here. Also, I couldn't bear leaving my parents…or my brothers and sisters. To the friends and family left behind, going to America must be like dying. Denis Kelly is the only one that I know of who has ever returned to Ireland, even for a visit. The rest who left have almost been forgotten.

Denis brings his 20 year old nephew to the front of his audience. "For those who don't know him, this is Charley Kelly. He is the son of my brother Barney. Charley is joining me on my trip back to America. He is a bright lad with a brave heart. I'm certain that he will be an asset to my mill and he will enjoy, someday, the riches that I have."

The men at the gathering slap Denis and Charley on the back and wish them well. There is some weeping going on in the Kelly families. They probably know that, after a few days from now, they will not see Denis or Charley again for the rest of their lives.

In 1822, the Irish Constabulary is established in each county in Ireland. With a bit of training from the local army garrison, a group of Irish men, wearing dark green uniforms, begin serving as policemen. They enforce the laws regarding land leases, taxation, and crime, both petty and felonious. A constable stops at our cottage while Danny is visiting and introduces himself to us. "Good day gentlemen. My name is Tommy Ramsey. I will be serving in the parish as one of your constables. We will soon have a station house at Crossroads. Please feel free to call on us if you need us."

When he leaves, my brother Danny says, "Ah, this will be an improvement, won't it? We can finally get rid of those bloody arrogant Brit soldiers. An Irish constable is somebody who may understand our problems."

I am not as sure. We rarely saw the soldiers up here in the hills. I have a feeling that the constables will be paying us many visits in the future, friendly and otherwise.

Chapter 17
(1823 - 1829)

We haven't seen Father O'Kane in a good while. The last time was a year ago when he baptised our son Danny. His new chapel in Castlefin, St. Mary's, was built last year and Bishop O'Donnell appointed him Curate in Charge. The bishop also installed a young priest from Castlefin, Father John McLaughlin, as a second curate at the Cross.

Father O'Kane pays us a visit. He seems pleased to see us and has a lot to tell us. His hero, Daniel O'Connell, has founded the Catholic Association in Dublin. O'Connell plans to use the organisation to represent Catholics all over Ireland in their struggle for political rights and in their disputes with landlords. He hopes to propose another Catholic Emancipation Bill in parliament. Father O'Kane tells us that O'Connell believes that King George is sympathetic to Catholic causes. A Catholic Relief bill was introduced in the House of Commons which gave Catholics the right to serve in parliament, but it was defeated by the House of Lords.

There will be chapters of the Catholic Association here in Ulster. All Catholics are expected to become members, and each family is to contribute one penny per month. It will be collected at Mass on Sunday. There is often talk of re-organising secret agrarian societies here in Donegal, but the work of the Catholic Association has made such societies unnecessary. Tenants bring their complaints to the association, and an official tries to mediate between the landowner and the tenant. The payment of tithes is another sore point that the association is trying to correct in discussions with members of parliament.

On a sadder note, Father O'Kane tells us that Pope Pius VII has just died. Pope Pius has been the head of the church almost my entire life. I knew of no other. The Congress of Cardinals is meeting in Rome at this time, to select the next pontiff.

Because of Daniel O'Connell, there is an interest now in politics throughout the parish. My cousin, Manus McCullough, has the kindness to visit Da and Ma on Sundays. Manus learned to read at the Protestant school, and he carries the Londonderry Journal with him to bring us up to date on the progress Daniel O'Connell is making on our behalf. Our families gather at Da's cottage after Mass, and Manus reads the latest news. Being published in Derry City gives the newspaper a Protestant bias to its reports of O'Connell's actions, but Manus manages to see through it and gives us the facts we want to hear about the successes of the Catholic Association.

Kate continues to have people coming to our door asking for her help in curing the illness of a family member. Kate always goes with them, taking our children with her and dropping any household duties she is performing. One day, she tells me that she seems to be losing her gift of healing.

"Jamie, it has been a year since I have helped anyone. Just two days ago, Patrick Bonner's daughter, Ann, had a fever. I spent the night praying for her and holding her hand. There was no change in her. I visited the spring and brought her water to wash her forehead. She seems to be worse. If something doesn't happen soon, she will die. I feel so helpless. What have I done wrong?"

"I don't know what to tell you. There is old Doctor Babbington in Killygordon. Have they not tried to bring her there?"

"They have no money for that."

"Surely, the doctor will treat the baby without charge when he sees her. Talk to the Bonners."

Wee Annie Bonner does die. Her parents did not bring her to Doctor Babbington in time. Kate is having a hard time getting over it. She now believes that her healing powers have been taken from her for something she has done. I have no answer for her. She has done no wrong and remains as devout a Catholic as before. She will not tell me if things are different at the holy spring. It is something I never bring up. When people show up at our door, Kate tells them that she no longer has the power. She suggests another woman in Trusk who may be able to help them.

Pope Leo XII is our new pope. We have a new bishop as well. Orange Charley O'Donnell passed away, and Peter McLaughlin is appointed the Bishop of Derry.

In 1826, Daniel O'Connell runs against a popular candidate in County Clare. Catholics are allowed to vote in elections if they hold property worth 40 shillings. Normally, these Catholics vote according to the wishes of their landlords. If they vote otherwise, they stand to be evicted from their property. How they vote is no secret to the landlords. The priests urge the Catholic freeholders in their parishes to vote for O'Connell. They will be backed by the Catholic Association if anyone takes action against their freedom to vote as they wish. O'Connell wins, the first Catholic elected to English parliament. There are celebrations all over Ireland.

O'Connell cannot sit in parliament unless he takes an oath against the "worship" of Mary and against the other "idolatrous" practices of the Church of Rome. He goes to

London but refuses to take the oath against his religion and is, therefore, not permitted to participate in parliament. In the meantime, Robert Peel, the Prime Minister, is weakening on Catholic Emancipation. King George asks parliament to review the reasons for Irish unrest, especially the laws creating it. All of this we learn from the lips of Manus McCullough at his weekly recitations at Da's cottage.

Father O'Kane informs us that Bishop McLaughlin wishes for him to serve at the discussions in Derry on Catholic Emancipation. There will be members of parliament at the Guildhall to discuss what it is that Catholics want. It appears that we won't be seeing Father O'Kane for a while.

Ma tells us that she has heard from Barney and Sarah Kelly. Their son Charles is doing fine in America. His uncle has leased another textile mill in the town of Upper Darby, just outside Philadelphia. Charles is in charge of the mill, which they call the D and C Kelly Mill. Charles asked for his cousin Margaret to come to America to be his wife. The Kellys in America are getting wealthy beyond belief. At Charles's urging, several young men from Donaghmore are taking a schooner from Derry to work at the new mill in America.

Dr. Francis Rogan is a landowner in Castlefin and a surgeon at the hospital in Derry. In 1827, he acquires a ship and begins transporting grain to Derry from a dock and storage yard in Castlefin. On the return trip, he brings sundry goods and farming supplies back up from Derry. Dr. Rogan's ship makes one trip weekly to Derry.

This is a godsend for us and the local farmers. We have the choice of either selling our harvested corn to the local mills, or having it milled there and carting the grain to the market at Castlefin. The price we are now getting in Castlefin is much better than what we get at the Balleybofey and Stanorlar markets.

My sister Maggie marries our cousin, Jimmy Kelly. Jimmy is a shoemaker and the happy couple is satisfied to settle on just a quarter acre of Uncle John's land. We help them build a wee cottage there, and Jimmy agrees to pay John a rental fee for his land and garden.

My brother Patrick and his wife were slow starting a family but have five children now. It looks as if my brother Danny will have no more children. He and his wife have three sons and two daughters.

My son, Hugh, is born in 1827, and we now have five sons and two daughters. With all of these children, I am wondering if we will have enough land to support them when they grow up.

In 1828, a chapel is built in Sessiaghoneill for the Catholics in the western part of the parish. Kate's family in Meenreagh will now attend Mass indoors and no longer in the open air at Trusk. The Mass in Sessiaghoneill is attended by some Catholics from the town of Ballybofey, as well. Our Curate, Father John McLaughlin, is in charge of celebrating Mass at the new chapel.

More news reaches us through Manus McCullough. Although the Bishops in parliament are against it, the Lords promote a Catholic Emancipation Bill. The Fear of an Irish uprising and civil war is the main reason for the new bill. The bill passes both Houses, and the King signs it in 1829. All civil rights of Catholics are restored, including the permission for Catholics to sit in Parliament. Daniel O'Connell, now known as the "Father of Emancipation," sits proudly now in London as a Member of Parliament.

O'Connell continues working to repeal the Act of Union and proposing other reforms affecting the poor rural people of Ireland. He dissolves the Catholic Association. There will be no more collections for the association at Mass on Sundays.

There is much discontent in Drumbeg. Cousin Denis tells me that the lads are talking about uniting another whiteboy society to threaten their landlord into fairer rents. They want the Church of Ireland to stop collecting tithes, as well. Denis is considering joining them. His brother, Mickey, is one of their leaders, for certain.

It doesn't take long before the land agent's home is vandalized and some of his livestock slaughtered. The new constables are called upon to investigate, and they arrange for soldiers to protect the Clarkes. The constables visit each of Richard Clarke's tenants and search the homes. Unfortunately, they discover two muskets in one of Mickey's out buildings. Mickey isn't there; he has been visiting former neighbours in County Tyrone. Agnes tells the constables that she doesn't know where Mickey is, and she is telling the truth. No one has seen him for a week.

Cousin Mickey has been missing for over a month now. He must have received word that he is wanted by the constables. Rumours about his whereabouts drift back into Donaghmore.

Denis tells me in secret, "He is hiding out in Fermanagh. No one knows when he will return."

I am astonished. "How do you know, Denis?"

"He sent word to his friends at the alehouse in Killeter by means of a farmer bringing grain to Rogan's. The farmer doesn't know where Mickey lives, only that it is somewhere in his parish."

"Let me help, Denis. I will borrow Danny's horse and go to Fermanagh next week to see if I can find him. If you or anyone in his family leaves to look for him, it will look suspicious to the constables. In which parish is he hiding?"

"Thank you, Jamie. It will be a comfort to Agnes and ourselves to know he is doing well. God bless you. He is in Drumkeeran."

I leave on Monday for Fermanagh on horseback. It takes me most of the day to reach Drumkeeran, which is across the border near Lough Erne. I ask at several cottages if they know where he can be found but have no luck. Then I see an alehouse and ask inside. I should have thought of this earlier. Mickey is a lover of ale and alehouses. The publican tells me that a stranger named Mick is staying at the home of Willie and Teresa Burke. He says that Mick comes to the alehouse often; then he tells me how to get to the Burke's cottage.

I find the Burke's cottage on a farm not far from the pub. Sure enough, Mickey is whitewashing the walls. I call to him and he laughs. "Jamie, I hope to God that no one has followed ya."

He invites me into the cabin. "So ya heard about me from the publican. Ach, that alehouse is a terrible place, the cursin', the fightin', the drunkenness, the pissin' on the walls. The publican said that if I don't behave meself, he will stop me from drinkin' there."

We talk for awhile, and I find that Mickey has no immediate intention of returning to Donaghmore.

"If I come home, they'll be sendin' me to Botany Bay. I don't believe I'll care for that," he says. "Can ya get Denis and Paddy to help Agnes with the farm? When I get settled, I'll send for Agnes and me family to start a new life here."

Before I leave, he tells me that he changed his name to Mick Cullen. He says that he will visit Agnes and his children secretly when he is able. I embrace him and wish him good fortune. I have a bad feeling that I'll never see Mickey again. I am sorry to say that I believe Agnes and the children will never see him, either.

chapteR 18
[1830 - 1833]

Our parish priest, Father McCafferty, is transferred to a parish near Ardstraw in 1830. Father Francis Quinn becomes our new priest. Father Quinn is a big burly fellow who is feared by wayward parishioners. All it takes is a complaint from the wife of a drunken man to find Father Quinn showing up at their cottage door. He puts the fear of God in the man by threatening to thrash him within an inch of his life if he misbehaves again. The children at catechism school are the best behaved in the history of the chapel at the Cross.

Along with Father O'Kane at the Castlefin chapel, we have two other curates under Father Quinn. These are Father Edward O'Hagan and Father William Logue. With three chapels in the parish, and an expanding group of parishioners, there is plenty to keep the priests busy.

Kate tells me that the mysterious beast, known as the Dorhagh, has been seen in Lough Trusk. Neddie Byrne, a local farmer, was walking by the lake when he saw an odd looking animal, the size of a cow, swimming on the surface. The animal dove back under the water when it saw Neddie, who then reported the apparition to the constables. Boats were sent to the lough to try to find it. It was never seen again. Kate believes that the Dorhagh is real. As a child, she had heard it cry out several times when she was walking to the mill in Navenny.

Throughout my life I have often heard the cry of the banshee, but I have never heard it close to our home. That changes on one wintry night in 1832. We are getting ready to go to bed when I hear it. It sends chills up my spine. It is a low howl that grows louder as time goes by. Someone will die tonight. In my mind, I consider those in the family who are not well. I immediately think of Da and run to his cottage in my bare feet over the frozen ground. He is at the door when I get there. He heard it as well. We speak softly to each other and promise to pray the rosary before going to bed so that it will not be anyone in our families. When I return home, Kate has all of the children awake and praying. The wailing continues, and we try to sleep after our prayers. We close our eyes and hope that morning will come soon.

The banshee had cried for my Aunt Mary in Balinacor, who passed away during the night. She died just four years after her husband Owen. The wake and funeral for Mary is another main event for the parish and is well attended by all. Aunt Mary was a heroine of mine. She was the most saintly of all my relatives. She had a powerful connection with God and the Saints. Only my wife Kate really knows what went on between Aunt Mary and the mysterious lady she met at the holy spring, and Kate will not tell me.

The banshee cries again a month later. This time there is no mystery. Uncle John has been not feeling well lately and can hardly walk about our fields. We have talked him into staying at our home in the bed by the fire until he is well. Da worries about him and visits John often. Kate has been feeding John oatmeal mixed with pig's blood to give him back his strength, but he seems to be getting worse. Sure, we have been bringing him the water from the holy spring to drink. The whole family is concerned, especially Hugh and Charles, who live in his cottage. We move him into Da's cottage, where Ma can keep an eye on him. Today, we are worried about his colouring, a yellowness of his skin. When we hear the banshee tonight, we know that John will be leaving us.

Ma breaks the news to us in the morning. The men head out to notify our relatives and friends throughout the parish. My sisters and the Gallen wives gather at Ma's cottage to prepare for the wake. Word is passed to the Ballybofey and Castlefin markets. John had many friends there.

There is a surprising large number of mourners at the two day wake. John was well liked by all who met him. He was a quiet man with a kind and generous heart. I fear that my brothers and I didn't appreciate him as much as we should. The wake was typical for the parish, with much tobacco, snuff, and drink.

We had learned last year from the Sunday readings by Manus McCullough that there was a meeting of church leaders in Dublin. The subject of excesses at wakes was discussed, and there was a declaration made that forbids whiskey and tobacco at the wakes. Father Quinn failed to bring it to our attention at the time, so the ban is ignored throughout the parish.

As usual, Uncle John's wake is an occasion for many young people to meet others and enjoy themselves with the food and drink. Wakes are one of the times in our lives when we can put away our cares for a while and share pleasant conversations with our relatives and neighbours. Of course, we feel badly for the family of the deceased, but that doesn't stop us from laughing at the jokes and reminiscences of some of the clever lads among us. In Uncle John's case, he had no family except my Da, and his nieces and nephews. I walk over to see Da talking and laughing with his old friend, Andy McGlinchy.

Da yells to me, "Jamie, has Andy ever told you about his days during the rising of '98?"

I feel that I should have stayed where I was. I've heard Andy's stories a thousand times.

I say quickly, "I have. Hello Andy. How are you feeling?"

Andy is an old fellow. He has trouble moving now with his rheumatism. With some pain, he turns slowly to see me. He searches my face to see who I am.

"Is this yer son?"

"Aye, and a good help to me in me old age."

"Could I have a word with you, Da?" I ask.

We point Andy in Ma's direction, and he totters away with his stick and a drink in his hands.

I ask, "I know that this is a bad time to bring this up, but have you thought about John's land? Will Hugh and Charley take it over?"

"Aye, they will. They're good boys, they are. They have been a great help to John there."

I add, "And I guess you know that they are both courting the Bryson sisters. There will be a wedding or two sometime soon, no doubt."

Da has tears in his eyes. I think it is sadness for his brother, but he lets out a hoot and doubles up with laughter.

"I have to tell you what Hugh told me," he says. "It's about Rose Bryson."

He laughs heartily again and can't continue until I say, "What Da?"

He stops laughing for a minute and catches his breath.

He chuckles, "Rose told Hugh about her trip to the Cross in a horse car driven by old Mr. Muoy."

Da starts laughing uncontrollably again. Others at the wake are staring at him. When he gets hold of himself, he continues.

"The ride is rough, and Rose accidently farts quite loudly. She says nothing at first until the smell of it gets too awful. She thinks that perhaps she should say something. She says, 'Please excuse me,' and Old Mr. Muoy says to her, 'That's alright Miss, actually I thought it was the horse.' "

Da can barely get the last of his sentence finished before he has another fit of laughter. I really don't see the humour in the situation at all.

John is buried in Lower Donaghmore in the Church of Ireland graveyard. His land is split between Hugh and Charley, who are to marry Rose and Mary Bryson. Both weddings are performed by Father Quinn on the same day, three months after John's funeral. Another cottage is built on John's land. Each couple now holds five acres of land in Glencarn.

All over Ireland, tenants are protesting the paying of tithes to the Church of Ireland. Protestant churches are being vandalized by local whiteboy gangs, and Protestant priests are harassed in public. They are emboldened by Daniel O'Connell's gains in parliament. Fires are set at the Protestant Church at Lower Donaghmore, but no damage is done. Reverend Irving beseeches Father Quinn to let his parishioners know that the Church at Donaghmore contains relics from the time of St. Patrick, and the church should be sacred to all Christians. Father Quinn agrees and gives a bombastic sermon on Sunday, condemning anyone who desecrates any church. His sermon lasts a half hour, and his face is bright red at the end of it. God help anyone involved in the church vandalism if he catches them.

Our landlord, Sam Delap, lives in a castle-like manor in nearby Monellan. His son, Robert, studied at Trinity College in Dublin and became a lawyer and member of the Irish Bar. Robert made a radical change in his life later by abandoning law and entering the seminary of the Church of Ireland. After he was ordained a priest, he moved back to Monellan as curate of the Donaghmore Church of Ireland under Reverend Charles Irving.

In 1833, the Delaps fund the building of a small chapel of ease at the Cross, and Reverend Irving names Robert as Curate in Charge. The lovely chapel, close to our own, is known as St. Anne's.

Reverend Delap arrives in Donaghmore during the controversies about paying tithes. He is not harassed by the parish ruffians, however, because he gives the appearance of being a kind and pious gentleman. He can often be seen in public at the shops of Killygordon and the Cross.

chapter 19
(1834 - 1838)

Since Uncle John and Aunt Mary died, I have gotten overly sentimental about my parents. I see them in a new light, knowing that they will be with me for only a short amount of time now. Da and Ma are both 61 years of age. I try to be kind and understanding to them, even when Da is unreasonably critical of something I do. Actually, I feel blessed that they were such good parents. They were kind and loving and gave us all that they could to make our lives better. In the past, I have had a problem with Da's drinking, but I see now that it did us no harm. Other than a few events in my early years that I cannot forget no matter how hard I try, he led a good holy life. Their love for us has been passed on now down to their grandchildren. The grandchildren love them back. I only hope that they both will stay with us for many more years, and that their lives will be comfortable and happy during that time.

At a Sunday reading of the Londonderry Journal, we learn that there is still strife in many Irish counties in regards to the payment of tithes. Daniel O'Connell has asked that his countrymen pay the taxes until he can do something about it in parliament. Also, we learn that Ireland will start building schools to enable every Irish child to get an education. I am hoping that a school will be built near us soon to teach my children to read and write. If a school isn't coming soon, my children will be too old.

The first National School near us is built near the Mourne Beg River in Laught, County Tyrone. Families start sending their children there from as far away as Meenreagh in our parish. However, it is too far for us.

Soon other schools open, although not part of the government system. Reverend Delap opens a school for mostly Protestant children on his property in Monellan. A school for Catholic children opens near the chapel at Ballinacor with Denis McBrerty as its teacher. A hedge school starts in the month of November in nearby Gleneely. The teacher, Alex Craig, has taken over a vacant byre on the Bradley farm. We decide to send James and Hugh there. My brother Danny is sending two of his younger children, as well. We hope that this will be the start of a better life for our offspring. Alex Craig is a devout Catholic and plans to educate the children in their religious responsibilities, as well as giving them a secular education. Alex boards with the families of his students during the winter and will be staying with us for a few weeks as partial payment for his services. In spring, he plans to return to County Derry to help in the fields of his parents.

There is another change at our parish. Our burly parish priest is transferred to a chapel in Derry. Bishop McLaughlin sends us Father Charles McCafferty, a cousin of our former parish priest, Father William McCafferty. Our new Father McCafferty looks cheerful, pleasant, and seems quite different than Father Quinn. A lot of parishioners who have avoided going to confession with Father Quinn are now planning to get back into a state of grace. Our former parish priest was known for his explosions in the confessional when he heard the sins of some men. His penances were the most brutal of any priest we have ever had. It wasn't uncommon to see men of the parish, and some women, praying for hours at the altar after their visit with Father Quinn.

Our children are a great joy to us. My oldest, Patrick, is a hard worker and lightens my load in the fields considerably. Maggie helps with Kate's household duties. I have no trouble with the younger children; they will turn out fine. My only challenge is Charley. Charley is naturally lazy, and I have to keep after him to turn him into a responsible man. I know that he resents me harping on him, but I do it for his own good.

Ma is not well. Kate and Danny's wife are trying some common remedies to get her to keep her meals down. She is rapidly losing strength and appears to be in great pain. Da tries to comfort her, but Ma barely notices him. She has been in this condition for over a week. Kate sends for Rose McAnulty from Trusk to visit us. Rose has had some success at curing people. Rose arrives and spends a couple of hours with my mother with no one else present. She leaves Ma's bedside with tears in her eyes. "I'm sorry," she says to Kate, "Nothing seems to be working. Keep her warm and comfortable. Give her some whiskey if she can keep it down."

A few more days pass. I decide to walk to the hidden spring in the hills and pray for a miracle. In all the years that I have been there, I have never felt any spiritual presence like Aunt Mary and Kate have experienced, but this is a desperate time. I will give it just one more chance.

I walk up the hill and pass through the bushes that hide the spring. There is the sound of the wind and rustling leaves. The water gurgles into the wee pool, and birds chirp. I kneel at the pool and try to clear my mind. I recall events in my childhood when Ma spoke quietly to me. I recall her jokes and teasing. Then I pray to God the Father, the Son, and the Holy Ghost. I pray to Holy Mary, Mother of God, and to Saint Bridget, Saint Patrick, Saint Columbcille, Saint Eugene, Saint James, Saint John, and to all the saints that I can remember. I ask all the saints to make Ma well again. I close my eyes and remain silent for a few minutes.

I hear a rustling in the bushes. I look up but only see a fawn staring at me. Is this my apparition? Is this a sign? I think not. The fawn quickly runs into the thicket. I am alone again with my thoughts.

I start walking back to Glencarn when I suddenly remember the bucket that I brought. I return to fill it at the spring, but I am no longer sure that the water has any power. We will offer a drink of the spring water to Ma and hope that our prayers do some good.

Ma doesn't improve, and we have Father McCafferty come and give her the last rites of the church. One by one, her children stop by her bed and say a few words of thanks for her kindness. She can barely talk, nevertheless, she whispers words of her love for us. Then the grandchildren come in to say goodbye. She tries to smile and talk, but her words are difficult to make out. A few nights later, the banshee announces Ma's death. She passes during that night with some of her family by her side.

Our family greatly mourns her. Ma seemed to bind us all together. There is a well attended wake and a funeral.

We had all believed that Da would die first. He seems to be going strong now but appears to be on the drink more. He fell from his roof one day and is now barely able to walk without the stick he has been carrying with him for years. He does very little work in the fields; we do it all for him.

Although he must walk with a stick, he still manages to get to Gallagher's Alehouse at the Cross. He has been going there for as long as I can remember, even when Mr. Quinn was the proprietor. He tells us that he is discussing politics with the lads. Some nights he doesn't return, but we know he is fine and is spending the night at Willie Dougherty's cottage in Monellan. Sure enough, he shows up the next day. Not a one of us even asks him about it anymore.

Da also finds time to walk to Aunt Mary McMenamin's once in awhile. Mary is now in her 70s. Her son, Patrick, lives with her and they continue to make poteen. Da always liked Mary's poteen and always agrees to sample it anytime it is offered.

Mary's prodigal son, Mickey, also distilled poteen, but his family never kept up the business after he left them almost ten years ago.

In 1836, the various constables of each county are organized into the unified Royal Irish Constabulary. They are now better trained to enforce the laws of the king. The constables are an impressive looking group in their new black uniforms and peaked caps. Sergeant Ramsey is still in charge of protecting Donaghmore Parish.

Our Sunday readings at home are now performed by Patrick McCullough. His brother Manus has been too busy helping Father McCafferty at the chapel. Patrick is the one who informs us that King William died in London without issue. The next in turn of succession is his young niece, Victoria. Victoria is not yet in her 20th year. Imagine that, a child queen of mighty England.

From Patrick, we learn more about the politics of England. The collection of tithes is getting expensive because of the guards required to protect the collectors. Tithe reform is led by Daniel O'Connell in parliament. With the new Whig government, the Tithe Act is passed in 1838. The tithes are reduced 25 percent and are payable by landowners, not tenants. Of course, our rent will be increased to compensate the landlords. At least, it feels as if we are not supporting the Protestant churches directly.

Another act in 1838 extends the English Poor Laws to Ireland. What this means is that Work Houses will be built here to house sick and starving paupers. They will be living in those buildings and receiving food. If they are able, they must perform some practical work for their keep. More than 130 Poor Law Unions will be established in Ireland with a Work House built in each. The cost of building the Work Houses will come from a new tax on the landowners in each Poor Law Union. The Work Houses will be the responsibility of the Board of Governors selected from ratepayers in each Union.

We learn that there is a movement started by an Irish priest, Father Matthews, to encourage abstinence from alcohol. There will be pressure in each parish to vow membership in the Total Abstinence League. It will be interesting to see how Da takes to this when it comes to Donaghmore.

Work has begun on a new cathedral in Derry to replace the Long Tower Church as the mother church of our diocese. It is believed that it will be the grandest Catholic church in all of Ireland, and it will be known as St. Eugene's Cathedral.

chapter 20
(1839 - 1840)

Da has taken ill, and we all know that he may never come out of it. He moves in with us, and Kate is kept busy caring for his needs. He dies in the afternoon one autumn day after receiving the last rites from Father McCafferty. We hold the wake in his own cottage, and all of his friends and relatives visit us for one last toast to old Patrick. I myself have a drop of some good Irish whiskey, given to us by Paddy Gallagher from the Cross. There is little sadness because we all know Da had a full life and lived without much trouble. He was respected by the whole parish for his common sense and dignity. Even Father O'Kane manages to pay us a visit from Castlefin. Our family appreciates all of the sympathy shown to us by our friends.

My cousin Denis pays his respects on the second night of the wake. Denis finally married Nancy Floyd from Cronalaghy. They have two children. Denis tells me that his brother Mickey has never called on his family in over ten years. Agnes and her children have gotten over him and are doing fine with the family farm. Her sons, James and Patrick, are still single and running the farm for her. Her daughter Grace is married and living in County Tyrone. Denis asks me if I ever heard from Mickey.

"I'm sorry Denis. I never expected Mickey to come back to Donaghmore. He seemed to enjoy his freedom too much. He committed a despicable sin when he left Agnes."

Denis replies, "It is true of course. I cannot understand him. How could someone just leave his wife and children like that. Agnes wanted to visit him a year or two after he left, but I talked her out of it. Now she and the children just want to forget him. I would like to talk to him just one more time. Would you be free to join me in searching for him in a few weeks?"

"Aye. I can do that. I would like to see him again just to see what the devil looks like. I expect that he has horns and a tail by now."

Weeks go by after Da's funeral. We now use Da's cottage as a storage shed and share in the crops we have harvested from his fields. Denis calls on us one day. He wants to visit his brother Mickey in Fermanagh if he can find him. I have already committed to helping my brothers clamp turf today for the coming winter and can't go with Denis. I give him directions to the pub that may be a help in locating Mickey. I suggest that he takes my 19 year old son Charley with him. Denis can use the company, and Charley could get to see a little bit of the world beyond Donaghmore. Charley jumps with enthusiasm when he hears. He takes our horse, an old nag that we usually hitch to a cart when we have to travel distances. Denis rides his own mare. They head off south in the direction of County Tyrone and Fermanagh.

They return a day later. Denis tells me what they came across. They stopped at the public house in Drumkeeran. When they described who they were looking for, the proprietor said that Mick Cullen hadn't been seen at the pub for years. He married Neddie Quinn's daughter and is living on a plot of land that Neddie gave them.

I can't believe my ears.

Denis says, "Aye, Mickey married again, with Agnes very much alive in Drumbeg."

"Did you call on him at his home?"

"I did. He had a shocked look on his face when he saw me and was speechless for once in his life. He introduced me to his new young wife and quickly walked me outside. It was a stiff conversation we had then."

"How did my Charley react?"

"Charley stayed silent and glared at Mickey. He doesn't know Mickey well, but it is certain that he hates Mickey for what he did to his family."

I asked, "How did Mickey explain himself to you?"

"He just said that he met Nell and fell in love. He knew that it was wrong, but he couldn't help himself. He knows that he is weak."

"Shocking."

"Do you know that he and Nell, his new wife, have four children? All of them are under 10 years of age."

"Will you tell Agnes and the children?"

"I will tell them the truth, that Mickey is the lowest type of scoundrel that Ireland can produce. It will be well for them to forget him. Nell came outside asking questions. She is a lovely lass, and I didn't have the heart to tell her that her husband is a piece of shite and has another family. I just explained that we were kin from County Donegal and were passing through to Sligo. She offered to feed us and put us up for the night, but I told her that we had other arrangements."

"I will pray for them. Mickey will probably burn in hell for this sin. I don't know how he can live with himself."

"Mickey is weak and selfish. I will not give him another thought. I'm sorry that I even went looking for him. I would rather have not known about him."

As Denis rode away, I had many thoughts about my own evil dealings with Mickey, and how I should have known that his soul would be lost to the devil someday. I thought that he would eventually wind up in prison. I never dreamed that something like this would happen. I have a hard time thinking how he could condemn himself in the eyes of God. Does he believe in God? Does he think that God will forgive him if he stays in this relationship? I guess I should feel lucky that Da and Ma raised us to live responsibly. Ach! Enough of this! Mickey's soul is lost and I must forget it.

Lately, many interesting events have been happening in the parish and in Derry.

Bishop Peter McLaughlin of Derry Diocese dies. The late bishop's nephew, John McLaughlin, a native of Castlefin, will be our new bishop. The new Bishop was once a curate in our parish.

Father McCafferty of our parish is transferred to a parish in County Tyrone, and Father O' Kane, the curate in charge of St. Mary's in Castlefin, returns to become Parish Priest of Donaghmore. In his new position he has two curates, Father McKenna who has been here since 1833, and new Father John McKeag, to run the chapels in Castlefin and Sessiaghoneill.

As you well know, we are great friends of Father O'Kane, and we are happy to have him return. Our happiness turns to shock and grief when he is found dead with a broken skull on the Lifford Road, apparently thrown from his horse. His requiem Mass is said at the chapel that he built in Castlefin, and he is buried in the front of the chapel.

There are some in the parish who believe that Father O'Kane was murdered. Barney McGill from Carrick wanted to marry Elizabeth Watson, a Protestant girl from Castlefin. Elizabeth's family was dead set against the marriage. They didn't know which they hated more, Barney or his religion. Elizabeth loved Barney and saw that the only way they could marry would be in the Catholic faith. The couple met with Father O'Kane and they discussed their problem. Although Elizabeth would not convert to Catholicism, she agreed that she would raise her children as Catholics to please Barney. Father O'Kane agreed that the marriage could take place. When Elizabeth's father heard of this, he was furious. He met with Father O'Kane and told him to forbid the marriage. Father O'Kane said that there was no reason not to perform the ceremony. Elizabeth's father threatened bodily harm to the priest and the happy couple if the marriage should take place. The wedding was held at St. Mary's during an evening ceremony. The bride's parents did not attend.

Father O'Kane mentioned the argument between himself and Mr. Watson to my cousin, Manus McCullough. Manus, worried as usual, asked Father to mind himself when he was travelling around the parish. After Father O'Kane died, Manus met with Magistrate Mansfield in Killygordon to discuss the possibility of foul play. The magistrate told him that the constables found no gun or knife wounds on the body. Father's head was smashed. Manus pointed out that he could have been struck by a club. Magistrate Mansfield was satisfied that it was an accident, and no investigation was ordered.

After Father O'Kanes death, Edward Boyle is named as our new Parish Priest. Father Boyle was raised in our parish in the Daisy Hill area of Sessiaghoneill.

We seem to be getting by on our land in Glencarn although we all seem to be worried about the future. After subdividing Da's land over the past 35 years, we have little left to give to our children when they need it. My brothers and I have less than six acres each, of which we need at least an acre for potatoes to feed our families. Collectively, we have five cows, three horses, and one donkey.

We can pay our rent on the gale days even with the lower prices for crops, but it is getting more difficult. We now only get seven pence per stone for oats, 15 shillings a barrel for barley, and 23 shillings a barrel for wheat. We sell the clover hay that we don't use to feed our cattle for 35 shillings a ton, and the potatoes we don't keep for two pence a stone. Typically, we just have enough to pay our individual rents although we miss the May payment this year, but our landlord lets us catch up in November.

What will happen when our sons marry? Right now we are feeding forty-two people on a total of five acres of pratties. Kate and I have seven children, Danny and Anne have five, Paddy and Susan have five, Charley and Mary have four, and Hugh and Rose have five. My sister Maggie and her husband have four, but their quarter-acre of land is used for garden vegetables. Maggie's Jimmy works as a shoemaker at the Cross, where he makes enough to pay us for his rent and food. The land cannot provide for more mouths to feed. With our financial responsibilities, we cannot afford to lease more land, and there is no more available. We must arrange to return to the old system whereby the eldest son inherits the farm, and the others in the family must move on to fend for themselves.

I have the biggest problem, because with five sons and two daughters, I have the largest family. I could subdivide; there would be land enough for potatoes, but there would be no land for cash crops. I must talk this over with the family to prepare them. Already my three eldest sons are courting lasses from nearby townlands.

James Gallen 1840

BOOK 3 - CHARLES

chapter 1
(1835)

I hate my father. He is always criticising me. Either I don't work fast enough for him or I am doing something wrong. When I was young, I used to talk back to him. This would typically earn me a beating with his strap. Now, I just glare at him.

For some reason, my brothers get away with things that I can't. They can slack off on work or come home on the drink, and Da won't say a word. If I accidentally spill a cart or arrive at the fields late, he screams bloody murder at me.

Also, there is the sarcasm.

"Ach, what do you expect? Charley fixed this latch. Maybe it is supposed to catch only half the time."

I agree that I am not skilled at mechanical things; I am clumsy at handling tools. I try my best, but it never is good enough for Da.

"How do you expect me to bring this corn to the mill? I ask you that. Half of it is chaff. Should I bring wee Jimmy in from the fields to show you how to winnow it? Are you thick? "

"No Da. Let me try again. Could you not yell and try to shame me?"

"Not shame you? You need to improve, son. Why does it not sink into your head to think before you attempt anything there? How do you expect to go out on your own when you're older?"

"That's fine Da. I'll get the knack of these chores soon."
"Until you do, I'll keep yelling."

I live here on a five acre farm in Glencarn with my Da and Ma, my four brothers, Paddy, Danny, Jimmy, and Hugh, and my two sisters, Maggie and Nancy. Our grandparents, uncles, aunts, and cousins live nearby.

My mother is the sweetest and kindest woman on earth. She makes us believe that we are the finest children in the parish. Ma is short and round. When I was a child, I used to love it when she took me to her bosom to comfort me when I was hurt. Now, she gives me hope when I am criticized by Da. At times, Ma seems to be my best friend.

Granny dies after a long illness. She was loving and kind as well. Her smile made me feel wonderful. I will truly miss her.

Da tells us that he heard the banshee the night before she died. I heard no such thing. I sometimes wonder about Da. He could be a bit daft. When Granny was ill, he went up to the fairy spring to get the holy water that he believed to be a cure. Look at the good it did. He and Ma are awfully superstitious. I believe that it is all rubbish. I get an argument from my friend Paddy Carlin every time I bring up the subject. At Granny's wake, we get into another odd conversation.

"Do you think my Granny is in heaven right now, Paddy?" I ask.

"She could be in Purgatory." he answers.

"Jesus, what possible sins could she have committed to earn her Purgatory?"

"No one knows what happens after death. One of my uncles believes that we could spend some time in the underworld here on earth before entering God's kingdom. He says that he saw his granny every All Hallows Eve for three years."

"Aye. That was because she was still alive then."

"No, for Christ sake. She was dead and buried. He believed that God was not ready for her because she died too soon. He thinks that she was living in a fairy hill until God finally took her."

"I don't understand how you can believe that shite. We live; we die; we go to hell or maybe heaven after suffering in Purgatory for our venial sins."

"Charley, I don't think that it is as simple as that. There are a lot of unexplained things we see in our lives. There are the floating lights at night, the banshees, and the apparition of fairies."

"More rubbish. Have you ever seen any fairies?"

"No, but my uncle has. He was coming home late one night, and he saw his neighbour's piglet wandering the road. He picked it up and started home, planning to return it the next day. Then he heard the pig say, 'Put me down before I chew your hand off.' The pig was talking with a gruff voice. My uncle looked at the pig and saw that it had a set of vicious looking fangs like a wolf. He dropped the pig and ran home."

"And this was your Uncle Tommy no doubt."

"It was. If it wasn't a fairy, what was it?"

"It was your drunken uncle's imagination. That's what it was."

"Ach, you must surely believe there are supernatural beings like angels and demons."

"Well Paddy, I am starting to believe that a lot of what I've been taught is rubbish. Sometimes I'm not even sure of heaven and hell anymore. I only believe what I see. If it wasn't for Da and Ma, I wouldn't be going to Mass every week."

"It is shocking to hear you say that, but knowing your Da and Ma, you will be going to Mass at the Cross as long as they have you under their roof."

"That's likely true. Let's get some drink and relax. Talking to you is giving me a headache."

Paddy is my best friend. He lives up the hill in Baywood. He is skinny and taller than me and has light sandy hair. Mostly he has a vacant expression. Keeping his mouth open all the time makes him look more stupid than he really is.

When I met Paddy, I had believed that his name was Thomas. I was confused and asked him if his real name was Patrick or Thomas?

"It is Patrick. You must have misunderstood my Da. He often calls me 'dumb arse.' A lot of people think he is saying Thomas."

Paddy is frequently the butt of my brother Paddy's jokes. Da calls him a fool to his face which I feel is a bit too cruel. Paddy and I have good times when we get together. When we meet with the other lads of the townland, the craic is mighty.

Chapter 2
(1836)

I myself used to be the cure for mumps in our part of Donaghmore. My mother had the same last name as Da before they married. Superstition runs wild up here in the hills. The people here believe that the children of parents with the same last name have the power to cure mumps. Whenever a child feels the symptoms of the mumps, his parents come to our house and ask for the cure. Da, being as superstitious as the rest, has us perform the miracle that would free the child of the disease.

Before I was chosen as healer, my older brother Paddy had the chore. He would lead the afflicted child to the holy well in Meenahinnis. Horse blinders were tied on the child's head and Paddy would lead the child around the well as all were saying the rosary. Strangely enough, no one laughed as this mad performance was going on. Also, strangely enough, the cure sometimes worked.

I got the job of mumps healer when I turned 10. Unlike Paddy, I roared with laughter when I first saw the poor child wearing the strange headgear. Da led me a way off and gave me a stern warning that this was no laughing matter. He whacked me on the head to emphasize the fact. I carried out my duties after that with great dignity. My younger brother, Jimmy, now has the job.

I learned that Ma used to have healing powers when she was young. As far as I know, she has not the power now. I'm not sure what to think about that. I would like to believe that our family has or had some connection with God that can make miracles happen, but it is hard to have faith when our lives seem to be a mighty struggle every day.

At the midsummer night bonfire in Glencarn, Paddy Carlin and I meet Grace McCormack and her friend Mary Bradley from the next townland. Blond-haired Grace is taller than me, a perfect match for Paddy. Mary is a dark-haired lass. Both are younger than ourselves, and we know that their parents are closely watching us from the other side of the fire. Paddy is speechless, so I have to start the conversation.

"Did you enjoy the weather Saturday Mary? It finally turned sunny after all the rain we've been having."

"I did. We were able to do a bit of bathing in the river. Gracie and I went down to the Mourne Beg and found a lovely secluded pool where we could undress and splash about in the water."

I glance at Paddy. He looks nervous. I know he is picturing the lasses in the water. He is most likely picturing them naked although they were possibly swimming in their underclothes. I was picturing them naked as well. It looks as if I'll be confessing this sin to Father McCafferty soon.

Grace adds, "It was lovely. After our swim, we laid on a rock in the sun to dry off."

Paddy involuntarily lets out a sigh and turns away from the lasses to hide his embarrassment.

I say, "It does sound grand. It is a pity that we weren't with you."

The lasses giggle. I blush. It is fortunate that they can't see my face turn red in the glow of the bonfire.

Mary says, "I don't believe that my Mam would go for that. It is a rare day I can get from out of her sight much less swimming with you lads."

I say, "On the next fine Sunday, she might let us go to the river if I meet your family first. They may approve of me."

"You could be right Charley. Come over to our house some day and perhaps Mam and Da will let us go shopping at the Cross or the market at Ballybofey."

"Aye. I'll visit them this week."

The conversation continues between Grace, Mary, and myself into the twilight of the longest day of the year. Paddy makes a few dumb remarks that halt the talk briefly, but soon Grace has him in her spell. He opens up and tries to charm her with his knowledge of farming. Grace looks at Paddy as if every one of his words is golden.

Mary asks me about the other lads and lasses of Glencarn. Because most are my cousins, I tell her many details about them. She tells me about the young people in her townland of Coracreagh. We talk until we can endure the midges no longer. Mary and Grace get up to return to their parents. Mary says goodbye and walks off alone into the blue-grey twilight. I follow her, and she turns and kisses me on my lips. She then walks quickly to the other side of the fire where her parents are waiting. When I return to Paddy, he is alone. Grace has gone as well.

As the fire is still blazing, we get closer to the flames hoping that the heat will chase the midges.

"What do you think Paddy?" says I.

"About what?"

"The lasses, you eejit."

"I think that they are nice. Grace is beautiful and pleasant to talk to."

"I agree. I think that it is time for us to get to know more about the lasses of our parish. Jesus, we're old enough now. Mary Bradley is grand. Will you be seeing Grace again?"

"I believe so. She is going to the fair at Stranorlar in two weeks. I think that I will meet her there."

"I will see Mary again too, but I must meet her parents first. You should meet Grace's people as well. You should have their approval."

Paddy stammers, "I don't know about that. Sure, they won't approve of me. I don't make a good impression."

"Ach. Don't worry about it. They will be fond of you. Just don't say too much about yourself there. Let them do the talking."

I meet Mary's parents at their cottage the following week. Her parents are Ned and Bridget Bradley, who share a large farm with the McGlinchys and McCormacks. The Bradleys' eldest child is their son, Jimmy. They have five daughters, Ellen, Mary, Catherine, Bridey, and Elizabeth. Elizabeth is only four years of age. The Bradleys have two wains as well, twin sons Eddie and Charley. Mary's Da is a large powerful man with a pleasant round face. His arms are excessively hairy, but the hair on his head is severely lacking. His wife is a short, stout, black-haired woman with a face as friendly as her husband. Their eldest son is working in the fields and I don't meet him, but I have to suffer under the gaze of Mary's sisters as I ask her parents for permission to accompany Mary to the Ballybofey market this Thursday.

Mary is the prettiest of the sisters. Ellen, the eldest, is a bit taller than Mary but with her mother's straight black hair. Her face is round like her father, and she looks like she enjoys the potatoes more than her sisters. Catherine and Bridey look somewhat alike. They have freckles, light brown curly hair, and look as if they should eat more. The wains are wee babies.

Ned knows my Da and Ma, mostly from seeing us at Mass at the Cross. He asks how the sowing is going at our farm. I tell him that we are planting barley this year. He and his son are planting oats again although they should have rotated to a different class of corn. He believes that his field is well fertilized and can take another crop of oats. Soon he says goodbye to get back to work in the fields. Mrs. Bradley tells me to visit anytime, and I leave with Mary to make our plans for Thursday.

"Well, what do you think of them, Charley?" she asks.

"They are a lovely family, Mary. Do you think they like me?"

"Why would they not? You are a handsome farmer that they would be proud to have as a son-in-law."

I laugh, "Hold on. Not so fast. We are just getting acquainted. Let's see how Thursday goes. You will, perhaps, not care for me after getting to know me. My Da doesn't think I'm worth the trouble to talk to."

"Ah, don't worry. You're grand. Call on me Thursday morning."

Ah...Thursday arrives. I give a lively hello to Mrs. Bradley and escort Mary down the hill to the river road where we will walk west to Ballybofey. As soon as we are out of her mother's sight, Mary rushes up, jumps into my arms, and kisses me on the mouth. I am shocked but quite a bit excited.

"I missed you Charley. Thinking about you has kept me awake at night along with Ellen's snoring."

"I missed you as well," is all I could think of to say.

We walk along the road holding hands. At times she turns smartly, gives me a smile, and another kiss. Near the Navenny Mill, we sit for a while talking about how wonderful summer is. She embraces me again and we fall over into the heather. I can't believe that this is happening to me. My experience with lasses was almost non-existent before this, and now I am committing a litany of sins which my religious training tells me I will have to confess soon. A complete feeling of helplessness comes over me as I wrap my arms around her and feel her soft back through her clothing. My hands slide down to her waist and over her well cushioned backside. What am I doing? All the while, she is kissing me and rubbing my back. My hands finally reach the tops of her legs and I feel them moving as she tries to roll on top of me. I am getting a bit too excited now. Should I try to pull up her dress? Should I reach around to touch her breasts?

No. No. I shouldn't. I roll her off and stand up. I don't know what to say to her. She lies there smiling at me. Then she stands up brushing her dress.

"I think we should get along to Ballybofey now, Charley."

Her sly smile tells me that it is over for now but watch out.

The Ballybofey market is busy when we arrive. It is getting close to the summer hunger when most people's stores of potatoes are gone and the local mills are selling oatmeal as a substitute foodstuff. They have stalls set up alongside the merchants selling eggs, butter, salt, tea, and other sundries. There are merchants there selling tools, used clothes, and books as well. Mary purchases some clothes for her family and tries on boots while I wander fascinated with the activity. There is much noise from the alehouses on the main street. I peek in to see a fight starting between two patrons. I retreat as they come tumbling out of the doors and into the street. Soon a crowd gathers urging them on. I walk back to find Mary walking proudly with a pair of old but well polished brogues. Her old brogues are in her hand along with the clothes she had purchased.

"Do I look lovely in these?" she asks.

"They suit you. You are pretty enough barefooted, but these will keep the rough roads of Donegal from ruining your beautiful feet."

From Mary's apparent extravagance, it appears that the Bradleys are doing well. They have enough money to buy the goods they need at the market. It makes me realize that my family is not doing as well. We must barter everything we need from our neighbours. It is a rare day indeed when anyone in our family goes to Ballybofey.

The trip back is fairly uneventful until we reach the burn next to the path up to Coracreagh. She steps down the bank, reaches into the water and splashes her face. I reach down to help her back up to the path but she leads me into the rushes. We embrace once more but without the savage passion that we experienced at Navenny. This is more tender.

"When will I see you again?" she asks.

"Soon. Very soon." I reply.

In later weeks, I find myself wandering up to Coracreagh when I get the chance. Mary and I find the time to take walks through the townlands nearby and embrace whenever we are in a hidden area. I am prepared for Mary's passionate kisses and manage, by a strong will, to keep from committing any sinful actions. This amuses Mary. She knows that I am under her spell. Although I am not old enough, and I am not exactly ready for it, I am considering marriage to this hot blooded Bradley.

I meet my friend Paddy Carlin at the wake of one of Ma's friends. I ask him if he has been seeing Grace McCormick.

"I have. The first meeting wasn't good."

"How's that?"

"I met Grace's parents and they didn't seem to care for me much, but they let me go to the linen fair in Stranorlar with her."

I tell Paddy everything about Mary and me. His eyes are popping. I say that I will talk to Mary about having her and Grace join Paddy and myself at the ceilidh at the Cross next month. Paddy looks encouraged.

A week before the ceilidh, I introduce Mary to my parents. Ma is obviously charmed by Mary. Da is all smiles, and I wait for him to embarrass me. Finally he asks Mary if she would like a ride in our new horse and cart. Mary says that she would. I know what is coming. He tells me to hitch the horse to the cart while they are having some milk and biscuits. I have never learned to properly get the harness on our horse. Normally Da or my brother Paddy does it.

"Aye, Da," I say as I head outdoors.

We are keeping our horse in the byre while our cows are grazing in the hills above us. At the byre, the horse we call Donal looks at me as I wrestle the harness from the rails. I sigh and try to figure out how it goes on. It shouldn't be complicated, it's just that I have never done it. I throw it over Donal's head and walk to buckle the straps. Donal throws his head suddenly and the harness falls to the ground. I hear laughter behind me. Da and Mary are watching me.

"Are y' sure you want anything to do with this poor eejit, Mary?" Da says.

Mary doesn't answer. I walk away into the field. Mary runs after me with Da still laughing. She catches up and walks beside me.

"I have never been able to please him," I say. "Maybe you should find a handier lad."

"Ach. You are fine. I want no other. I see that he doesn't encourage you to learn. Belittling you is no way to treat a son."

"I promise you that I will be the man you want. I will be an excellent farmer someday for you."

We walk back and wave goodbye to Ma who is at the half-door. Da is in the byre attaching the cart to the horse.

"Do y' not want a ride, Mary?" he shouts.

Mary gives me her sly smile and shouts back, "Some other day perhaps. Charley promises that he will give me a ride."

The night of the ceilidh arrives and Paddy sits with Grace and I sit with Mary. Along with other young people, we are taught a four hand reel by a man and his wife from the parish. Brian McMenamin, a brilliant fiddler, provides the music. I constantly miss the steps, but I am not the only one. Like me, other lads stumble through the moves and are glad when the music stops. Mary and Grace have danced like this before, but I am astonished that Paddy is dancing like he has done it his whole lifetime. We walk home together after it is over. We all agree that we had a lovely time.

Paddy and Grace walk to her cottage which is not far from the Bradleys. Mary takes me behind her byre, and we embrace as we have many times before. Mary kisses me and holds me tightly. She slides her hand down to the front of my trousers and touches me.

"You can touch me if you wish," She says.

I do. It is the start of our fondling each other whenever we are together alone. I am not proud of it, but Mary seems to like it. She also wants us to go farther, but I have the willpower to resist. I know that nothing good can come of it. It will have to wait until Mary and I are married. God knows when that will be.

chapter 3
(1837)

Da asks me to help my great-aunt Mary McMenamin and her son Patrick with making poteen at their still in Drumbeg. I think he wants me out of his sight for awhile. I will be living with my cousins in Drumbeg while the brewing is going on and won't be seeing my Mary. I go to Coracreagh to tell her that I'll be gone.

"I'll be missing you greatly," she tells me. "When will you be back?"

"It will be soon. I think that it will only be a few weeks," I say.

"Can I visit you up there?"

"Ach! It is too far. I'll be home before you know it."

My great-aunt's late husband is a legend around these parts. He was a famous highwayman who was killed by the redcoats many years ago. Great-aunt Mary maintained her husband's still after he died and her poteen is well appreciated in the parish. She is old and moves slowly now, but her moist blue eyes are always looking about as if the revenue police are hiding outside her door. Her wariness has kept her from arrest of any kind during the many years she conducted her business.

Mary's son Patrick is older than my Da. He is short and stocky with not a hair upon his head except around his ears. He is the eldest of great-aunt Mary's family but has never married, so he takes care of his mother. His youngest brother, Denis, lives with them. Denis never married either but is courting a woman from Cronalaghy.

Mary's other children are married and live nearby but are busy with their farms. Her son Michael deserted his family a few years ago. His wife Agnes has three grown children who work their farm now. They seem to be getting along fine without Michael.

Barley is the major crop among great-Aunt Mary's family. She makes enough money with her poteen to buy their barley which helps them pay the rent to their hated landlords. She has been paying her children better than they can get at the grain market. I am to help my great-aunt and her sons in making a new batch of poteen. I hope to God that I don't make a mess of it.

The distilling of poteen is a complicated process. The first job Patrick gives me is to soak the sacks of barley in a wee pond near the shed that they use as the still-house. The pond was created by damming a fast running burn nearby. After a couple of days, I drag the sacks out of the pond and let them drain a bit. When the sacks are light enough, I drag them into the still-house and spread the barley out on the floor. The wet barley has been sprouting buds, and I can see that shoots are growing. It is my job to turn the barley over twice a day until it is reasonably dry and the shoots don't get too long. Denis helps me re-bag the barley after a few days, and we take the sacks to a crude kiln hidden in the woods for more drying and to keep the grain from further development.

Next, Denis and I take the sacks of grain, which Denis calls malt, to the mill at Navenny. He has bargained with the miller to grind the malt to a fine flour-like meal during the middle of the night in secret. The miller will receive kegs of our poteen when we finish.

While we are at the mill, Patrick gets the parts of the still from an empty grave hidden in the woods. The parts of the still: the body, the head, and the worm, are on the floor of the shed when we return. The body and head of the still are made of tin, but the worm is made from copper and it is valuable. We are finished for the night. Denis and I return to the cottage, and Patrick stays to guard the still.

In the morning, we return to the still-house with the sacks of malt from the mill. Then we help Patrick build a channel to divert water from the burn and bring it into the area near the shed. Great-aunt Mary brings our meals to us. Our meals are baskets of hot boiled potatoes. We peal them by hand and use our knives to cut off slices to eat. We are hungry and they taste lovely.

When nightfall comes, Denis and Patrick disappear into the woods. They return with buckets, kegs, barrels, and a large wooden vat that were hidden in secret places. They leave the vessels inside the shed. I help Denis bring the body of the still outside, and we place it on the firebox and fill it with water from the burn. Patrick starts the fire.

The first step in brewing the poteen is mixing the malt with boiling water from the still. This is done in a vat kept in the shed. My job is to keep the mixture, called mash, stirred. When the vat is full, we cover it.

Later, Denis removes the plug from the bung hole near the bottom of the vat. A barrel is placed under it to catch the thick greenish liquid, they call wort, that flows out. The cover is removed, and Denis resumes pouring hot water from the still into the vat. Barrel after barrel are filled with wort until the liquid coming out of the vat starts to lose its colour and thickness. No more barrels are filled. Patrick adds his special ingredients to the barrels now. He throws in handfuls of hops. They are the buds of some plant. He tells me that they give his whiskey its special flavour. He also adds a substance he calls barm.

The barrels sit and cool but begin to bubble and froth. I am told to sit and watch the barrels. If one looks like it is about to overflow, I am to stir the mixture until the froth subsides.

Two of Patrick's neighbours arrive. They must have sensed that the brewing was happening tonight. Maybe they saw the fire or smelled the smoke. Patrick gladly gives them each a stick and tells them to stir the barrels like I am doing. They are jovial and many jests are spoken. The atmosphere becomes less tense in the still-house, and Patrick and Denis start to relax and smile. I am relieved and joke with the men as well.

After a while, the barrels stop frothing and one can see that the liquid inside is now a golden brown. I see Mickey, one of the neighbours, put his head over the barrel. He breathes in.

"Ah. This is lovely."

Denis tells me that it is "pot-ale" at the top of the barrel. He takes a cup, scoops a bit off the top, and lets me have a taste. It is tasty and strong.

"Would ya spare a drop for me?" asks Conal, the tall, redheaded fellow.

Patrick, Denis, and the other lads have a taste.

Patrick says, "That'll be enough for ya now. We'll be needin' the rest of it."

It is comical to watch as the two lads quickly drop to their knees with their heads over the top of the nearest barrel, breathing in the rare aroma of the pot-ale before the next step of the brewing takes place.

Denis tells me that it would be best if the pot-ale could stay in the barrels a long time. The flavour of the whiskey it produces gets better with age. Nevertheless, the brewing must be completed tonight for the sake of secrecy. The pot-ale is only allowed to age about a half-hour before each barrel is poured back into the still.

The fire is relit. Before the ale comes to a boil, the head and worm are attached to the still. We seal the joints with clay to keep steam from escaping. The head has a long arm which leads the steam to the coils of the worm. The worm is immersed into a barrel filled with water from the burn. The cooling of the steam condenses it into a clear liquid that flows out of the worm and falls into a keg underneath. Patrick takes his cup and gets a few drops off the worm. He tastes it and smiles broadly.

I am amazed at how brilliant Patrick and Denis are to have built such a complicated contraption. When I congratulate them, they tell me that the still has been around for generations. They are using the same equipment their grandfather used many years before they were born.

The poteen continues to flow out of the worm and into kegs placed under it. Each time a keg is full, the output is tasted to make sure it is still strong. When Patrick feels that it is weakening, he asks Denis to shut down the still and we remove it from the fire.

Patrick washes down the insides of the still. I am believing that our work is done, but I am shocked to hear him ask us to put the still back on the fire and pour the kegs back into it. It seems that the poteen in the kegs is known as the singlings. To get a more refined drink, it should be doubly distilled. The water container is reassembled, the head and worm cemented to the still, the worm immersed in the cool water, and the doubling begins. I sigh. It has been a long night.

After this final distilling and after the kegs are refilled, we take the still apart again and empty the remains.

I wish I could say that I was a help to Patrick and Denis in this operation, but I can't. I knocked over the head once when attaching it and I spilled some of the pot-ale before adding it to the still. I felt a bit left out when some of the duties I should have performed were carried out by Patrick's friends. Patrick never scolded me, but I felt as though he did, and I know that Da will hear of it.

Now that the work is over, we all relax in the shed to sample the new poteen. The first shot is poured into a cup and given to Denis who takes it outside with him. Denis walks away into the darkness.

"Where is he going?" I ask Patrick.

"To give it to the fairies," Patrick replies.

I don't know if he is joking, but I learn later that it is the custom to pour the first shot of new poteen upon a fairy hill for good luck. Luck is what the poteen makers are always needing. When Denis returns, the cup is re-filled and passed to each of us.

"It never tasted better," says Michael.

"It takes me breath away, "says Conal.

I have my drink of the poteen. It tastes nothing like the pot-ale I had earlier. I preferred the taste of the ale, but I praise the quality of the poteen. Patrick's friends tell me that the Gallen poteen is the best in Donegal. By the looks of them, it is possible that they have tasted quite a bit of Donegal's poteen.

Because it is still dark, Patrick decides to go and hide the parts of the still. The rest of us straighten up the shed and carry the kegs to Aunt Mary's shebeen where they are hidden under bundles of clothing.

My brother Danny comes up to Drumbeg to see me late the following night. He asks if my Mary has visited me today. I tell him that of course she has not. Why does he ask? Danny tells me that Mr. Bradley is worried about her. She left their farm in the afternoon and hasn't returned yet. He assumed that she came up to see me. I assure Danny that I have not seen her since I left Glencarn.

"Should I return to look for her?" I ask.

"Ah no. The Bradleys have been calling at everyone's home looking for her. I don't see how you can aid in it."

I don't think that I can rest if I don't find her. I return home with Danny and join Jimmy Bradley in going from cottage to cottage around the parish. There is no sign of her. At midnight I go to my parents' home to get some sleep.

The next morning, I call on the Bradleys. Mary is home. She arrived at dawn with no explanation about where she spent the night. I can see that she has been crying and I see the rage in her Da's face.

"Can you tell me what is going on?" I ask her.

She says not a word, she just continues sobbing. He father speaks up.

"She is not worth talking to. I will not be raising a hoor. There will be no more leaving the farm for Mary. I'm sorry Charley, but that means she will not be keeping company with you anymore."

I feel that he thinks I am responsible for her poor behaviour, but Mr. Bradley adds, "Charley, this is for your own good. You deserve better than Mary."

I don't know what to think. I'd like to find out what Mary was up to last night, but I'll not find out today. Maybe her brother will let me know tomorrow. I tell Mister and Missus Bradley that I am sorry for their trouble and leave.

Da has some sharp words for me that I feel I don't deserve when I return to the cottage and tell my parents about the goings on at the Bradleys.

"What have you done to make Mary like that?" he asks. "What have you been telling her? A young lass does not disrespect her parents without influence from a bad companion."

"I have nothing to do with it. I haven't seen her in weeks. Why would you think I am involved?"

"She is too young for you, anyway. You are forbidden to see her again."

"I am forbidden? I'm old enough to make up my own mind about who I see."

"No you're not. You are still living in our home and you will follow our rules."

"We'll see about that then."

I storm out of the house with Da's booming voice following me. On the way back to Drumbeg, I consider my options. I could ask my great-aunt Mary if I could stay to help her family, but she, most certainly, wouldn't want me and wouldn't want to displease my father. Living there would be too far from my Mary as well. I could ask my uncles in Glencarn if I could stay with them and help, but they already know my reputation as a poor worker. I know I could improve if they let me, but it still wouldn't help. I guess I must stay with my Ma and Da for a while until I become more independent. I'll see Mary in secret until I can break out of my Da's control.

Back at Drumbeg, great-aunt Mary has been filling black bottles with the new poteen. Before pouring it into the bottles, she mixes two glasses of water with every five of poteen. It is still a potent drink. Women come to her shebeen to buy the bottles. Mary tells me that they cut it again with water before they sell it by the glass to drinkers in their own townlands. Mary's shebeen is well known in the parish, and men show up in the evenings to get a drop of her real mountain dew. Mary does a good business here.

My work is apparently over here in Drumbeg. Patrick sends me home and tells me that he'll ask Da for me again in a couple of months when they will begin brewing another batch of poteen. I head home and hope that Da has cooled off from this morning.

After a few weeks at home, I run into Jimmy Bradley on the lane between Coracreagh and Glencarn. I ask him how Mary is doing. Jimmy tells me that she has been giving her parents a rough time. She has been sneaking out of the house whenever she can and returning late at night. It is all that her parents can handle. Her Da hits her with a switch every time she misbehaves, but it does no good. He even struck her on the face once, but her Mam put a stop to that. Jimmy suspects that she has been visiting the cottage of a bachelor down in Drumfergus. With each word Jimmy speaks, I become less interested in seeing Mary again.

I visit my great-aunt with my friend Paddy Carlin after a few months. Aunt Mary tells me that there was another brewing a few weeks ago, but they didn't need me. I could have guessed that. She invites us to the shebeen and says that we can finish an open bottle of poteen if we want. I guess this is to make me feel better about being overlooked during the brewing. We follow her into the room where there is a half-filled bottle sitting on the counter. She tells us that we are welcome to it if we like.

Paddy's eyes are wide open with anticipation. I still haven't developed a taste for the drink like Paddy, but I am happy to keep him company while he finishes the bottle.

Paddy is still courting Gracie McCormack. I ask him if he heard anything about Mary Bradley.

"She doesn't live with her parents anymore. They couldn't control her. She is living with other relatives. Gracie doesn't know where she is. Her parents tell her nothing."

I explain that Mary was too bold for me. Paddy tells me that Grace stopped being friends with her for that reason. Paddy takes a few mouthfuls of poteen and hands the bottle over to me. I take a long drink of it myself. Soon we are forgetting our lasses and telling stories.

"Charley, I drank a lot of whiskey with me brother Owen last week. We were out in the byre with the cows. He was awfully drunk. I asked him if he saw any mice running about, and he said he didn't. He must have been really pissed because I could see that the floor was full of them."

Our stories now are getting silly.

"Paddy, have you ever seen a fairy?"

"No I haven't, but I believe that they exist." Paddy was slurring his words. "I know that you don't believe in them."

"I don't, but just suppose you see one someday and catch him. Suppose he offers to give you three wishes if you let him go free. What would be your wishes?"

Paddy thinks for a minute. His head is swaying a bit.

"I'd ask him for an everlasting bottle of whiskey. Every time I finish the bottle, it fills up again."

"And what would your next two wishes be?"

Paddy thinks and thinks. I am waiting for his answer. Finally he says, "I would wish for two more bottles of the same."

It is quite dark when we stagger out and walk home. I am starting to like the drink. It makes me feel mighty.

Chapter 4
(1839)

A letter from America is delivered to the post office in Killygordon. As usual, it is addressed to Barney Kelly of Ardnagannagh. The postmaster frequently sees American letters to the Kellys, so this one should be no great news to anyone, but he mentions it to Francie Nelson who is loitering in his office. Francie shoots out of the office and notifies everyone he meets on the street about the letter. In no time the word spreads to the other side of the river and up the hills throughout the parish. Barney Kelly hears of the letter early when a neighbour rushes to their door to give them the exciting information. Barney gets nervous with each letter he receives from his son Charley. There is always the chance that the news will be bad. Perhaps someone in the family is gravely ill or has died, but mostly the news is good. He summons his son John to ride his horse down to Killygordon to bring the letter home. Meanwhile as the news spreads uphill, friends of the Kellys prepare to walk to Ardnagannagh to learn of the letter's contents.

John ties up his horse at the post office and walks in to pick up the letter. There is a crowd gathered outside who are hopeful to learn what the letter contains. The postmaster recognizes John and doesn't require any identification. He passes the yellowed envelope through the bars of his window. John looks at it, places it carefully in his pocket, thanks the postmaster, and walks out through the throng of people to his horse.

Most of the crowd disperses after John rides off, but a few people start the long walk to Ardnagannagh.

By the time John arrives home, a crowd has congregated at the door of the Kelly's home. I am there with my mother and sister Margaret; we are related to the Kellys. Some of the Bradleys are there because they are related as well. Mrs. Bradley is not present, having to take care of her new baby, born just a few months ago.

John gives his mother the letter, and she stares at it for a minute. She waits for her husband to bring a knife for opening the envelope without damaging any of the contents. Dennis McBrerty, the teacher from the hedge school at Balinacor, is already there to help read the contents if any of the Kellys have difficulty with the words.

The envelope is carefully cut open and the letter removed with a firm grip. Sure enough, the envelope also contains a "ticket," sometimes called the "pearl" of an American letter. It falls gently to the floor when the letter is unfolded. The crowd gasps then breathes easier when Barney grasps it and takes it to another room for safety.

The "ticket" is a cheque in either American or Irish currency. We know now that the letter brings no bad news. It is simply another greeting from the Kelly's successful son Charley, who owns and operates a textile mill in America.

Barney tries to read the letter but passes it on to John, who takes a few minutes before handing it to the school teacher. Mr. McBrerty looks it over to see if he should read it in private to the Kellys or read it publicly to the crowd. He decides that it contains no sensitive material and proceeds to speak.

"It is from Barney's son Charley and his wife Margaret. It starts, 'Dear Mother and Father. I take this favourable opportunity to write a few lines to let you know that we are well and doing fine.'"

Mr. McBrerty continues reading. The letter contains a brief description of new products his factory is producing.

Then it speaks of the weather in America and the people from our parish he met over there. He ends with blessings on his father, mother, and siblings, as well as cousins, uncles, aunts, all of whom he mentions by name.

After the reading, we all offer our congratulations to the Kellys and depart knowing that at least someone from the parish is doing well.

I often think about going to America. My opportunities here in Ireland are limited. My family has little land and not much of it will be mine if I decide to start a family. I know of many lads from the parish who have emigrated to America to work for Charley Kelly at his mills. This is one reason I have been staying close to the Kellys. I believe that America and the Kelly mills are in my future. I dread the thoughts of leaving my friends and family, with perhaps the exception of my Da, but I see no other possibilities.

It is market day in Ballybofey and Ma asks me to buy some buttons for clothing she is either sewing or mending. She trusts me to choose the right kind after spending a half hour describing what she needs. I take the long walk down to the river road and westward to the town.

I see Mary Bradley and her sister Ellen when I reach Navenny. Mary had returned home with her family again. Both Mary and her sister are talking to some rough looking characters by the road. It appears that they are trying to walk away, but the lads keep pestering them. I approach them and ask the lasses, "Are these fellas bothering you?"

The shorter man with red hair growls, "Piss off laddie. We have business with these two hoors here."

I react and take a swing at him, but he easily blocks my arm and punches me square in the face with his other fist. It knocks me down and he proceeds to kick me in my ribs. I hear the lasses screaming, but I can see nothing. It is all a blur to me.

I hear the other lad yelling, "Kick 'im in the bollocks." He does and then kicks my head. I black out.

I wake up in a bed at the Bradleys. Mary's and Ellen's screams brought help from the town, and the lads ran off. Fortunately Tommy Floyd was on the road with his cart, and he and the lasses brought me up to the Bradleys. Mr. Bradley is standing over me.

He hands me a half glass of whiskey.

"Here, get this down ya. Y'll feel better."

I swallow and it burns all the way down. He tells me that my nose is broken but probably no other bones. I ache all over, especially my groin. They must have scored with that kick at my private parts. Ellen and Mary thank me for my good intentions and wish me well. They tell me that my Da is coming for me. Lovely, just what I need.

"I guess I'll be getting no work out of you until summer," is what Da says after he gets me home. I am too weak to respond. Ma gives me some brochan and buttermilk. I crawl into bed and sleep.

I don't wake until the next morning. I can hardly get out of bed from the pain, but I move to the main room where I can see the concern in Ma's eyes. I must look a wreck. She quietly mutters, "Oh my God."

Ma gives me a mirror so that I can see my new facial appearance. I can hardly recognize myself with my nose flattened and pushed to the side. I try to straighten it, but it is hopeless. I guess that I should have ducked. Ma always told me that I was handsome. That is in the past now.

The thought that I was so easily beaten embarrasses me. It is the only thing I can think about. I won't be able to face my friends. I go back to bed.

Later that day, Ellen Bradley comes to see how I am. Ma gets me up, and I walk out to the main room to find her sitting with Ma eating scone and drinking buttermilk.

Ellen says, "I was just telling your mother how brave you were to defend us from those two brutes."

"It was a poor job of it I did. I'm glad you were able to get away from them there."

"They were cowards. You were outnumbered."

"I'm sorry you had to experience rough men like that. They soon should be taught a lesson about treating women with respect."

We walk outside and it is like seeing Ellen for the first time. I never noticed how pretty she is. Her long soft raven hair frames a lovely round face with fair skin and a few freckles spaced attractively under her pale blue eyes. Her shape is a wee bit more stout than the other Bradley lasses, but she should have been the one I courted instead of Mary. Now look at me. I must look like a monster to her. Ellen most likely has a suitor already, and she is here to see me out of pity. I thank her for her concern and apologise for my appearance.

She smiles and says, "Ah, you look grand. Your face is more manly looking now."

We say goodbye and I return to the cottage. Ma looks at me and says, "Ellen is a nice lass. You should call on her sometime." Her smile tells me that she knows that Ellen wouldn't mind.

Every night when Da returns from the fields, he has some remark for me that makes me furious inside. "Oh, here is the terror of Glencarn." "If it isn't Mighty Charley, the defender of our women." I try to put it out of my mind, but it still bothers me and keeps me awake at night. I must somehow get even with those devils for my humiliation.

Paddy Carlin calls a few days after Ellen's visit. He laughs at my new face.

"I'd never know ya for yourself. Ya look more fierce."

"I'm not too fierce with my swollen bollocks Paddy. I walk like an old man."

He again laughs. "Ah, y'll be as good as new in a week."

I tell him about my constant silent rage and my need to get even with the lads who did this to me. He thinks about it for awhile and tells me that weapons, like a club or hurley, could give me an advantage in a future confrontation, but it could be considered a bit cowardly. He suggested that I practice fist fighting.

"How can I do that?"

"Do ya know Smasher Conaghan in Drumcannon?"

"I don't."

"Carney Conaghan is a lad of about our age who is a real scrapper. Carney enters the prize fights at the Killeter Fair and wins most of them. The payoffs are a big help to his family."

"I never heard of him."

"The lad's famous. The fights are staged in a field near the Derg River and the crowd who comes gets rowdy. The wagerin' is fierce. I'm thinkin' that he could give ya some tips on defending yourself and gettin' in a few licks on your own. "

I think it over. It can't hurt to talk to the lad. When I feel better, I'll get on it.

Old Willie Lungan passes away and his wake is held at his home in Rushy Hill. I decide to ask Ellen to accompany me. She smiles and accepts. My family will come up later.

Outside the Lungan home, I tell Ellen that I am feeling better each day and will be joining my Da in the fields soon. She says that she can tell that I'm getting my spirit back. Little does she know the fury that is in me to beat to a pulp those two animals who insulted her.

We ignore the lads playing games in the lane, but we sit on the wall talking. She teases me about how shy the fellas from Donegal are with women. I tell her that it is because of our rural mentality. The men are too practical and are definitely not romantic.

I say, "There is a joke that says a Donegal man proposes marriage by asking, 'Would you like to be buried with my people?' "

She smiles and says, "That sounds about right."

I tell her of the problems I have with my father. She sympathizes with me but asks me to tolerate it. She tells me that God wants us to honour our parents no matter what. "After all, you will have your own family someday. You can lead your own life away from him if you wish."

It gets me to thinking. I tell her about our problem with money and land. "Our family is too big, and we can afford no more land. I'll have to leave someday to America or England to work. Perhaps I can return with enough money to rent a decent farm here and then start a family. I should be thinking of doing so now."

"Why not work here. There are plenty of farmers who need labourers. You'll not return if you go to America…. I'll miss you."

I'm shocked to hear her say that. I have grown fond of Ellen. Even at this early stage in our courtship I believe I will miss her if I decide to emigrate.

"I hear that there are hiring fairs in Strabane. I could try my luck there."

"Why not work closer? My Da could use someone, even this year."

"I think that your Da wants someone handier than me."

Ellen says nothing. I consider my inadequacies in farm work. To be of any worth to anybody, I'd have to try to learn all the necessary farming methods from my Da this year. I'd have to swallow my pride and beg him to give me a chance.

On our walk back home, I ask about her family. She doesn't say much, just that they are well. I know that her family was embarrassed by Mary's behaviour, and they speak little of it. When I call on Ellen, Mary is frequently there, but she gives no indication that we were lovers at one time. From the way she acts, we might have been strangers.

Ellen gives me a tender kiss when we reach her cottage. I believe that our relationship is sealed. I will continue to call on her and see what the future brings.

At supper, I ask Da if he knows the Conaghans of Drumcannon.

"I do, and you should as well. Mr. Conaghan assists at Mass each Sunday."

"Could you introduce me to their son Carney? I'd like words with him."

"Smasher Conaghan? I will. Let's go tonight. Do you know that he is courting your cousin Bridget, Aunt Mary's granddaughter? He'll be pleased to see you."

So Da knows Smasher Conaghan. This is a surprise. As the sun heads toward the horizon, Da and I walk down to Drumcannon. I tell him that I want to learn to fight better. He agrees and thinks that it will do me some good.

We see Carney standing by his byre door.

"Hey, Smasher. I want you to meet my son Charley. He has something he wants to discuss with you."

"Sure, Jimmy. How are ya, Charley? Been through a few battles yerself recently, have ya?"

We shake hands and I say, "Could we talk in private. I've a proposition for you"

We walk out of earshot of Da, but I see Da knock at the Conaghan's door and be invited in by Mr. Conaghan.

I tell Carney what happened to me at Ballybofey and ask if he could give me a few tips about how to defend myself. I offer to work on the farm with him in payment.

He says, "No payment required. Just get here every morning after the six o'clock bell from St. Anne's and we can work out before field work. I'll be happy to help ya."

So begins my training as a fighter. At first we just do strengthening exercises. After a week, he shows me how to anticipate blows and how to deflect them. We practice throwing punches by jabbing a bag full of clay. Two lefts and a right, two rights and a left, each time stepping into each punch. Carney tells me to keep my fingers straight out and then curl my fist while twisting my hand just before landing the punch. He says that it does more damage to the opponent. He also reminds me not to admire any of my punches and to get into a defensive position after the last punch of a combination.

The training keeps up through the summer, along with working in the field alongside my brother Patrick. I am getting stronger with each day although it looks as if I have already stopped growing taller. I could use a bit more height if I am to beat the taller of the pair who injured me.

I only see Ellen on Sundays now. We will see more of each other when winter comes and the farm work is completed. I do take her to the Killeter Fair in County Tyrone at the end of September.

I had been to the July fair with my brother Patrick where I watched Carney Conaghan beat a man who was half again as big as him. The fight lasted almost ten minutes until Carney threw a savage right fist into the other man's face. Blood and spit flew out of the man's gob and down he went. I think his jaw was broken. The referee stopped the fight and Carney raised his arms in victory.

The September fair is just as lively. We drink cider as we stroll through the stalls of animals for sale and the festive booths of merchandise. Carney is fighting again outside the fairgrounds, but it isn't a place I'd want to bring Ellen.

It is a long walk back from Killeter but a pleasant one. The fields always seem greener on the Tyrone side of the hills. We stop at the Mourne Beg River on the way back and rest beside the bubbling waters. I bought a bag of apples at the fair and we wash one in the cool water of the river and cut pieces with my knife to eat. She sits and I lay my head in her lap. She leans over and I raise my head up to kiss her once more. We could stay here for hours. It is like heaven here.

When the evening gets cooler, we rise, wade through the shallow water, and start the climb past Garvagh to Carn Hill. At the top, next to the Graveyard of Giants, we take one last look at the green fields of Tyrone. One more tender kiss and then it is downhill to home.

My grandfather dies in early October. He had been living in his own cottage until he took ill. Then he moved into our cottage where Ma took care of him. The wake is held at his own cottage with what seems to be hundreds of mourners.

It would be a large affair even if only our family attends, but it seems that everyone from the parish shows up, at least on one of the nights. We offer some of great-aunt Mary's poteen, and Mr. Gallagher from the alehouse brings some whiskey. Mr. Kelly brings tobacco and snuff from his store at the Cross. Father McCafferty visits on both nights to pray the rosary over Granda, and the curates from Castlefin and Sessiaghoneill come to show their respect as well.

Over the years, we've had a lot of craic with Granda. We can't say that he didn't enjoy his life. He had many good times with his friends at Gallagher's Alehouse up to the time of his death. With his rheumatism, he couldn't work the fields at all. He didn't mind that a bit. We are all wishing that we will have as good a life as he had himself. I hope that he has a lovely time with Granny in heaven, if that is possible after death. May he rest in peace.

We will be needing some turf before the winter. The main bog field is in Tieveclogher, a townland west of Meenreagh. After a few days of dry weather, Da organizes a crew of himself, myself, and my brothers Patrick and Danny. We leave early in the morning and carry a slane, a spade, and two hand barrows up to the bogs. Many farmers now attach wheels to their barrows to require fewer helpers, but not us…maybe next year.

When we get to the bogs, Da starts spading the sod off the peat in one area. Patrick, who will have most of the hard work, rests as Danny and myself pile the sods of grass on the barrow. We carry them off a distance to spread on the ground where the bricks of turf will lie.

After a wide area is cleaned, the cutting begins. Da uses his slane to cut out a foot long brick of peat then moves to cut the one adjacent to it. Patrick grabs each brick with his hands as the next one is cut. He places it on the barrow and moves to the next one cut, making sure Da doesn't cut off his fingers. This takes a great deal of bending and lifting and is the main reason that only young lads do it. When the barrow is filled, Danny and I move it off a bit and place a second barrow where

Patrick is working. Our job begins now. We carry the turf to the spreading area and lay the bricks down to dry. By the time we return with the barrow, Danny has filled another barrow and we replace it with the empty one. We return to the spreading ground with the next barrow. This process is repeated over and over with no one stopping until lunch time.

Lunch is when Ma and my sister Maggie arrive with wood for a fire, a pot, a bucket of water, and another bucket full of potatoes. They start the fire and boil the potatoes. They shout, "praties" and we all stop. We eat our fill and get back to work.

In older times, cutting turf was a two man operation. One man cut and threw the bricks to another man for spreading. The method we are using today seems more efficient. Four men produce in one day what it would take two men a week.

At the end of the day, the cutting stops and we all are satisfied that it will keep our family in enough turf for at least half a year. We still have to foot the bricks. Danny and I have been turning the bricks every hour or so to help them dry, but now all of us go to the spreading field to stand the bricks up and lean them together in groups of three or more for further drying. The last ones cut are still wet so we "window" foot them by placing two bricks parallel on dry ground and stacking others, two by two, across the top of them.

Hopefully when we return in a couple of days, the bricks will be completely dry, and we can take them home. We will bring our horse and cart to carry most of the turf. Da says that he used to carry the turf home in side creels mounted on Granda's donkey. What wouldn't fit into the creels was carried in sacks on his and his brothers' backs.

I'm still working with Carney Conaghan on my fighting skills. We have been sparring with each other every morning. I know he could kill me with one of his blows, but he pulls his punches. I hope that he feels that I am helping himself as well by keeping him alert for some of my erratic swings. My combinations of punches are improving and soon I will be ready for my moment of revenge.

Paddy Carlin and I go up to my great-aunt Mary's shebeen for a wee drop of poteen. Mostly it is some craic we're after. The alehouse at the Cross would be more to our liking, but we can't afford the drink there. Some lads from Ballyarrel Mountain are already at Mary's having a drop or two of the poteen. Mary gives us each a jar and introduces us to Jimmy Gallagher and Sam Beaty. We get to talking about marriage.

Both Jimmy and Sam are older than ourselves and have wives. Jimmy says, "Every man should get married. If he doesn't, how else would he learn of his faults."

Sam jokes, "My wife tells me that our neighbour Kelly kisses his wife everyday at the door before going into the fields. She asks why I couldn't do that. I tell her that I don't know Mrs. Kelly that well."

As we all get a bit pissed, the jokes get dumber and dumber. I would like to tell one, but I can't think of any.

Sam has another one. He tells us that he was at the Killeter Fair with his wife when he passed the pens holding the pigs. He remarked to her, "Don't they remind ya of yer relatives?" She agreed, "Aye…me in-laws."

Soon the mood turns sombre and we start talking about the death of friends and relatives. There are tears in everyone's eyes when we recall recent wakes we have attended. I tell of my Granda's wake and Paddy talks about his brother who died four years ago. I ask Jimmy what he would like said about him at his wake when it comes.

Jimmy says, "I'd like them to say that I was a good husband and father. That I provided for my family so that they would never know hunger."

Sam says, "I'd like them to say the same and that I was a good son of Ireland, and if needed, willing to fight the injustice of English tyranny."

We all take a good look at Sam after that remark. I haven't experienced that kind of patriotism in my whole life up to now.

Paddy speaks up. "Do y' know what I'd like said at me wake?"

We all ask, "What?"

"I'd like them to say, 'Look. He's moving.'"

I get to thinking about Ellen and myself. As nice as Ellen is, I'm sure that the lasses in America are just as nice and that I could meet her equal. I continue to court Ellen even if it isn't fair to her. Truly I don't know how to tell her my plans, so I keep them to myself. I'll deal with any unpleasantness in the future.

I'm ready to find my attackers. I ask Ellen if she ever saw them before. She says no, and what in the name of God are you thinking of? I tell her that I plan to make them pay for their actions.

They both looked like Catholic lads, but I never saw them at the Cross, so I started attending Mass at the chapels near Ballybofey. First I go to St. Mary's in Sessiaghoneil, standing outside during the Mass and searching for their faces after the service. No luck. The next week, I go to the chapel in Stranorlar. No luck there either. Could the vermin be from far away, and I'll never see them again? I try to attend the market days at Ballybofey. Da really doesn't approve of me taking off every Thursday, but I try to make it up to him on Sundays before and after Mass. After the first month of me prowling about Ballybofey, I'm almost ready to call it quits, but finally I see the familiar red hair of the bastard who punched and kicked me.

Sure enough, his companion is with him. I see the taller one grab some merchandise from a table when the merchant is occupied by the red haired one. They both move off, and I follow them without them noticing me. After two hours or so, they start for their homes, crossing the bridge into Stranorlar and heading into Drumboe Woods. They divide their loot in the forest. I am right behind them. I must wait until they are separated. I hope that I can see where they both live so that I can get my revenge on the two of them without letting one go free.

Together they head north toward the road to Letterkenny. A lane leads to a group of cottages in what I believe is the townland of Creggan. The red haired one walks into the byre next to his cottage, and the taller fellow goes into another nearby cottage. Good. I know where they live. I believe that I'll take the advantage by working on Reds first. The tall piece of shite will have to wait.

I walk up to the byre, wrap leather straps around my hands to protect them, and I wait. Soon Mr. Reds walks out with a bottle of mountain dew in his hand.

I say, "Remember me?"

He just stares. I don't have to do any fancy dancing or getting into a fighting position. I just put all my weight into a right jab at his nose. Down he goes. He falls on the bottle and breaks it.

He feels his wet trousers and says, "Jesus. I hope this is blood."

The wetness is the poteen. The only blood I see is dripping from his nose. He looks at me in surprise. Finally recognition shows in his face. I stand in a boxing posture as he glares at me and tries to stand. I let him. He staggers to a fighting stance. He throws a punch at my face, but I block it and deliver two lefts and another mighty right to his jaw. Down he goes again. He stays down. I am finished with him and start to walk away. Then I remember something.

I go back and say, "I forgot to give you something to remember me by."

He is lying on his back with his legs askew. I take careful aim and deliver a kick to his bollocks. I think I connected. He gives a scream that brings a woman to the door of the cottage. I walk triumphantly down the lane and into the woods.

I possibly had the advantage of surprise in my fight with Reds. I won't have it with the taller bastard. That will be another day.

My hands hurt, but I don't believe I did any damage to them. The leather did its job. My workout with Carney was well worth it there. I can never repay him for what I have learned.

Later I start thinking about the fight. It really wasn't fair, with him holding the bottle with one hand. I will have to give him another chance to fight me.

I wait a couple of days and return to the cottages in Stranorlar where the two villains live. I show up at the taller one's cottage in early evening when I believe him to be home. I knock on the cottage door and sure enough he opens it.

"Who the hell are ya?" he asks.

I'm the lad you and your friend beat on the road out of Ballybofey many months ago. I'm here to get even."

He smiles and steps out. Jesus, he is a head taller than me.

"That's grand with me. Y' fancy another beating do ya?"

I get into my stance with my fists protecting my face. He removes his jumper and lays it across the rail next to the cottage. It is a handsome jumper. I wish I had the likes of it.

He laughs and takes a swing. I duck, but he catches me on the side of my head with his other fist. I jab with my left and catch him under the chin. My arms are too short to reach his nose or eyes. I try a right undercut into his belly. He grunts and swings a left that I fend off. He tries another right that I deflect with my left, and I drive my right fist into his belly again. I'm connecting but not doing much damage. He steps into me and wraps his arms around me, pinning my arms to my sides. So much for the London Rules of Prize Fighting. I stomp on his foot, and he releases me but returns with a hard right to my face. I see stars and taste blood in my mouth. I put my arms up, but he delivers another right to my face. I hit him with two left jabs and a right that staggers him a bit. He hugs me again and I am powerless. No more rules. I knee him in the bollocks, and he lets go, yelling bloody murder. I step in and finally connect solidly with his chin and down he goes. That's it. Fight's over. I spit on him, more blood than saliva, and walk away. I look back at him writhing in the dirt. A woman comes out of the cottage to help him.

As I walk home, I feel with my tongue that one of my bottom teeth is loose. Lovely! I feel it with my fingers and pull it out. With my crooked nose and missing tooth, Ma will never again call me the most handsome lad in the parish. Fortunately it isn't one of my front teeth. I notice that my right hand is swelling, and my face is sore. It wasn't an easy victory.

The fight didn't go as I planned, but at least I feel that I've gotten even. I think about a fair fight with Red again. I decide that I've had enough fighting. I see the effectiveness of dirty fighting, and I'll almost certainly consider it if I'm forced to fight again. To hell with fair play! Hopefully I'll not fight again unless my life depends on it.

Chapter 5
(1840)

At supper, Da finally tells us what we already knew anyway. Our property is too small to subdivide any further. This means that Patrick will inherit the farm, and the rest of us will have to find other ways to survive. Da encourages myself and my brothers to consider emigrating to Scotland or England as farm labour or maybe to consider the priesthood. We all get a laugh out of that last suggestion.

Patrick is courting Jane Maguire from Raws Lower. When he marries, he will stay on the farm and eventually be the primary tenant. It isn't feasible for the rest of us to marry until we find a place to live and enough work to pay for it. Both Danny and myself are courting lasses. Da says that he won't push us off the land if we marry, but he makes it clear that we'll have to go when the wains start coming. My sister Maggie doesn't share in our predicament. She is being courted by Packie Curran of Cornabrogue. Packie is well situated at his Da's farm, and Margaret will leave us when she marries. My younger siblings are not a problem at the present time, but their time will come.

I am now seriously considering going to America. It will be the best for all of us. I walk to Ardagannagh to visit the Kellys.

I humbly ask them if they think their son can use me at his mill in Philadelphia.

"Of course he can, Charley. He welcomes the lads from here," says Mr. Kelly.

"Do you think he can pay for my way there. I'll pay him back from my wages."

Mr. Kelly thinks and says, "When Charley opened his mill, he gave free passage to a large number of our lads to work there. He can't afford to take chances on advancing money anymore. Too many lads were disappearing at the Philadelphia docks and taking other jobs. I'm afraid that you'll have to earn the passage here before you go, but be assured that there will be a job waiting for you."

My immediate dreams of America are crushed. How can I afford passage to America? I'm lucky to find any work here. My thoughts go to Scotland. I can earn enough during the Scottish harvest to pay for my ticket to America. I thank Mr. Kelly and head home.

Mr. Kelly yells after me, "The town where the mill is located is named after my Charley. It's called Kellyville. Isn't that a corker?"

I talk to Da about Scotland. He worked there as a youth. He tells me that the cost of passage to Scotland is deducted from my wages after I work there, and I need nothing in advance. The money left over is likely enough to get me to America. He says that he will expect nothing from my wages, and I can keep it all for my grand trip there. The wonder of it all is that he is speaking to me with respect. I am not used to him treating me as an adult. I am getting a better opinion of him as a result of our talk.

Now I think about Ellen. We haven't seen much of each other since I have been working the fields and sparring with Carney. I'm afraid that our relationship will come to an end in August when I join the other lads for the Scottish harvest. I'll have to tell her at the Glencarn bonfire in June.

The Glencarn bonfire is an annual event anticipated by many in our townland and surrounding townlands. There are fiddlers, dancing, and many jars of poteen to signal the end of the sowing season. I escort Ellen to the field where a great fire is already raging. Paddy and Grace are here as well as almost everyone I know in the parish. It seems that everyone here is somehow related to everyone else. When the whiskey flows and conversation starts, people who don't know each other well become best of friends and discover that they have many relatives in common.

Paddy and Grace are getting married in October. Ellen and I wish them well, far in advance of their nuptials. They have had a fairly stormy courtship mostly because of Paddy's inability to keep his gob shut. He always utters the first thing that comes into his mind without thinking it may offend someone. Most of us know him by now and understand that he doesn't say anything out of meanness. Finally, Grace accepted his queer personality.

Traditionally, the June bonfire is a place where couples discuss their future romantic plans. Ellen is aware of this and begins such a discussion. She tells me about how lovely it will be when we marry and have a family. I have to stop this sort of talk.

I blurt out, "Ellen. I have made a serious decision about my future."

I have her complete attention. I tell her that I will have to move from Glencarn soon to begin my own life. There is no future for me here. I tell her about my working in Scotland and my plans to go to America.

"I could leave directly from Glasgow to America at the end of this year, but I won't. I'll return here to say goodbye and then leave from Derry."

Ellen looks shocked and then she begins to cry. Her sobs sound as if her heart is breaking. I feel terrible. Was I too blunt? It's true that I could have said it better, but I think that she is overreacting. After all, we haven't been together that long. Sure to God I'll miss her. She has been kind and loving to me, but I must move on. It seems that she doesn't know what to say to me now. She starts to speak but stops with a sob. I don't know what more to tell her. Maybe it would have been better to have considered what words to say before I said them.

Finally she utters softly, "I believed that we would spend our whole lives together. My dreams are gone. I feel so humiliated."

I try to hold her, but she pushes me away and runs off in tears. I try to follow her but give up. It is certain that I performed badly tonight. I walk over to some friends from Cornabrogue.

"Do you have any drink you can spare?"

Ma doesn't speak to me the next day. I know I deserve it, but I am in a poor situation. How can I support myself and a family here in Ireland where there is no new land and no work for unskilled labourers. Ma should understand my predicament. Da does. I work in the potato beds with Danny and tell him my troubles. It helps to put my thoughts into words. I want to see Ellen again and explain myself better. Later I walk to the Bradleys and ask to see Ellen. Mrs. Bradley is cool to me and tells me that Ellen is not interested in seeing me. I walk away, confused as ever.

It seems as if everyone thinks that I am a fool for breaking off with Ellen. My friend Paddy says that I was lucky to have her with a face like mine. His betrothed, Grace, asked him not to talk to me anymore, but this he wouldn't do. Paddy would like me to remain in Ireland as well.

"Ya could lease land in the upper townlands."

"Jesus," says I. "I'm a poor enough farmer as it is. Nothing grows up there until the rocks are removed and the land is fertilized. I'm not up to that."

"Did ya not think of takin' Ellen with ya to America?"

I considered that at one time, but I believe that it would burden me to have another mouth to feed while I was getting settled. I will miss Ellen, but I must go without her.

A week later, Paddy tells me that Ellen has been in the company of Willie Beaty of Drumfergus. I know Willie. He is a strapping lad of about 13 stone, but I believe that I could best him in a fair fight. He is a wee bit too stout. Ach, I have to stop thinking this way. Beating Willie will endear me to no one, especially Ellen. I'll have to forget Ellen. I have too many things on my mind right now.

Da tells us at supper that his hero, Daniel O'Connell, was elected Lord Mayor of Dublin, the first Catholic to reach such an exalted position. Also, O'Connell has founded the Association for Repeal of the Union. All of this interests me not at all. I think to myself, "Who gives a shite?" I must have been thinking too loud and maybe with my lips moving because Da gets up, walks over to me and claps me on the side of my head.

I yell,"Jesus, what was that for?"

Ma claps me on my ear.

"You'll not say the name of Our Lord in this house except in prayer."

Da says, "It sounds as if oul' Smasher here is gettin' too full of himself. He better learn some humility. He should remember that he is an Irishman too and should have some respect for those who are trying to improve our lot."

"And have some respect for God, as well," says Ma.

My face and ear, are red now. All eyes are on me. I swallow my pride and apologize, "I'm sorry for my outburst. Please forgive me."

Da and Ma return to their supper, and things are back to normal.

About ten of the lads from the parish are going to Scotland. Andy Quinn is our leader. Like me, most have never gone to the harvest before. Andy goes every year. He tells us to meet in front of Gallagher's Alehouse on Monday morning at dawn.

On Sunday, most of the lads attend Mass at the Cross. Our new priest, Father Boyle, invites us up to the rail in front of the sanctuary and gives us his blessing. That night, after packing my things for abroad, I join the family in the main room to say goodbye.

"I'll miss you Ma, Da. Take care of yourselves. I'll miss all of you, Maggie, Nancy, Patrick, Danny, Jimmy, and especially you Brian."

"Me name's Hugh."

"Oh, sorry, Hugh. I always get you mixed up with some other lad. I'll be thinking of you."

I never miss an opportunity for codding Hugh. He's a grand lad. Da is sending him to the hedge school in Gleneely. He wants at least someone in the family to be able to read.

The hedge school is run by schoolmaster Alex Craig in a converted outbuilding on Henry Bradley's farm. Compared to the other students, Hugh is a bit older, but he is coming along in his lessons. Da bought him used books at the Ballybofey market. One is a book on reading which everyone calls "Reddy-may-Daisy." It is really named "Reading Made Easy." The other is the "Universal Spelling Book." Hugh carries them to school proudly. If I ever have children, I will want them to attend school and learn their reading, writing, and numbers, as well.

We all meet at the Cross in the morning. Andy leads us across the Dromore Bridge and up to the post road where we walk to Castlefin. At Castlefin, we head back down to the river. Andy has made arrangements for us to load grain on the boat to Derry in return for free passage. The boat is owned by Doctor Francis Rogan who runs a shipping service between his dock at Castlefin and the quay in Derry.

Dr. Rogan is a surgeon at the hospital in Derry. His shipping enterprise is making himself a rich landholder in Castlefin, but it benefits us, as well. His efforts have helped keep the price of grain high for the farmers of Donaghmore.

All of us pitch in to load the barrels of grain into the hold of the boat. When we finish, we squeeze into all the available space onboard and then we're off to the big city of Derry, known to the Protestants as Londonderry.

Dr. Rogan's boat is a marvel. It has sails but also has a boiler over a fire box which makes steam. The steam turns a wheel on the side of the boat that can move the boat upwind. Mostly, the sails are not used. The smoke from the fire departs from a metal stack above the fire box. It is noisy, but the design is brilliant.

We travel the length of the River Finn to Lifford where we meet up with the River Mourne. The river is much wider now and the captain tells us that we are now on the River Foyle. The captain and his mate raise sail and continue at a greater speed to Derry. We see many other boats as we sail along, and we reach Derry in late afternoon. It is an experience I shall never forget.

At the quay, we unload the barrels of grain onto wagons standing by. Bags and boxes of other goods are waiting on the quay to be loaded on the boat. Part of the arrangement for our passage is to reload the boat with the shipment to Castlefin. It takes a bit more time to load the boat for its return trip, but we do so merrily. The boat will return to Castlefin tomorrow with just the captain and his mate.

Andy takes us to a loft in the village known as the Bogside, outside the magnificent walls of the city. He tells us that we shouldn't go within the walls of the city. Catholics are forbidden. Andy says that the gates are well patrolled by gangs of Orangemen. I am not in the mood for any conflict at this time, so I am content to stay with the rest of the lads in the loft. One of the lads has a bottle of poteen, which he generously passes around. I sleep soundly after a dinner of some praties that I boiled with those of my new friends in a pot over the fireplace. I had brought the praties from home in my pack.

In the morning, we queue up at the quay beside a sailing ship going to Scotland. We board and I spend the rest of the trip vomiting over the side. I learn quickly not to vomit on the windward side of the ship. In Scotland, we are taken by wagons to the fields, given scythes and sickles, and told to gather up the sheaves from an endless field of corn. It is hard work, but I do my best. At the end of the day, we are driven to our quarters where the lot of us are assigned beds with mattresses filled with chaff. Just like home.

Our days are filled with this sort of work. Our meals are of stir-about and bits of some kind of meat. Each day seems like the day before. Only when the weather turns fierce do we get time off.

I have lots of time to think about my future. I dream about a life in America even if I really don't know what to expect there. It could be hell on earth compared to Ireland. I feel comfortable in Ireland. I'm only going to America out of necessity. Is there a way I can stay in Ireland? I think and think about it but ordinarily fall asleep before reaching any solution.

In my dreams, I see the lasses that we used to mess with from Lough Shinnagh. The lads and I would get together and walk there to fish. The lasses would be there when we arrived. We did indecent things to them, but they seemed to like it. I never did confess those sins to our priest. I frequently wake up with the pleasures of those encounters fresh in my mind.

I dream sometimes about Ellen's sister Mary. We are doing indecent things as well. Is this what people dream about when they are bored? Isn't it funny that I never dream of Ellen like that?

In our quarters, there is one lad who starts bullying one of our lads. First, he starts taking our man's food. Then he begins talking unkindly about our man's mother. He gets away with it because he is well backed by his gang, and our lad is a bit timid. I have had enough. I go over to the bully, I don't know his name. He is a thick headed turd with curly blond hair. He is about my size which is fortunate. I speak quietly to him.

"You seem to be bothering our man there when you get a chance. I think you should be reasonable and leave him alone."

"Fook off, Paddy. It is none of yer business."

"He is a friend of mine. I look after my friends."

"Take it easy. I'm not hurtin' the lad."

"Just mind yourself. I'm watching you."

I walk away and hear laughter behind me. I turn and walk back.

"Something is funny?"

"Aye. You are. Go on now. I'm sick of lookin' at ya."

He is sitting on his bed. I give him a punch square in the face. Blood squirts from his nose. I remain standing there. He stands up and squares his stance. Two left jabs and a right cross spins his head around. He goes down and stays down. I walk away saying,

"Funny. I don't hear you laughing anymore."

I'm thinking that I'll be visited by some of the bully's gang. I do... by two of them.

"That was some fightin', laddie, " says one, a young man going bald too early in life.

"Do y' fight for sport?" asks the other, who looks somewhat like a weasel.

"No. Just when needed," I answer. "Are yis looking for trouble?"

"Not at all," the first laughs. "I'm thinkin' that the nights here are pretty boring. Maybe ya would be willin' to fight some of the other lads for sport. Y'll be paid if ya win."

"How can you pay me? We don't get our wages until we leave for home?"

"We'll give ya letters of promise. We'll pay ya at the end of the harvest."

"Let me think about it."

I think it over. It's not worth getting my face and hands hurt for money that is promised by strangers who may not pay up. I tell them of my decision. I tell them to let their own men fight for pay. Leave me out of it.

"If that's yer decision, I can't guarantee that ya won't be contested anyway by some of the fellas."

It sounds a bit like a threat. I squint my eyes and give him a menacing look.

"I think that you ought to warn your fellas not to test me. It'll be bad for them, and it'll be bad for you. This is a warning to you in particular."

A few days later, a big ugly man from the wrong side of our quarters visits me.

"Get up!"

I get up and prepare for the beating of my life. A large ring of lads gathers around me.

"Put up yer fists!"

I comply and he swings at me. I try to fend off, but he drives my arm into my face. He swings his other arm, but I duck and punch him in the belly. We trade punches, but he is landing harder shots. My hands and face are bleeding. I don't need this.

"You win. I give up. I have no problem with you."

"Y'll have a problem with this."

He knocks me down with a strong right to the side of my head. I stay down. I've had enough. He stands over me with his arms high in the air. His crowd cheers. He walks away.

My lads lead me outside to the well to wash up. I tell them that I can't beat ugly giants like him. They sympathize with me.

On the day after the fight, the weather prevents work, and I walk over to the bald young man who tried to get me to fight for sport. I ask him to get up. His friends gather.

"I warned you about anyone fighting me. Mind yourself."

He looks at his friends. They come closer. I quickly hit the fellow in the nose, and without hesitating, I punch the lad closest to me in the gob. An instant later, I smash another fellow in the belly and then pummel another, doing maximum damage to his face and nose. I kick another in the crotch and again smash my original target in the belly. I am like a madman. They are raining blows on me, but I hardly notice. Soon my lads become part of the brawl. A few cooler heads among the others in our quarters prevail, and they begin pulling everyone apart. The tall ugly giant who beat me yesterday comes over to me and hugs me.

"That was brilliant! Y're a man, me friend. I never seen anythin' like it. Thank ya for the entertainment. Forget what happened here today. Y'll have no trouble from us again."

Nothing more is said after that, and mutual respect between rivals finally prevails in our close quarters in Scotland.

After almost three months of repetitive work and monk-like isolation in Scotland, we are returning to Ireland. I receive my pay at the dock in Glasgow and it looks substantial. Andy warns me not to spend it until I get home. Many of the lads lose it in the alehouses of Derry. I make up my mind that I may have a wee drink at the Cross, but the rest will be saved for my future. What is my future? I've decided that I am not going to America. I'll marry Ellen, if she'll have me, and find work on some farm in Donegal or Tyrone. I miss my home on the green grassy hills there, and I will never leave again.

When I arrive home, following a day of travelling from Derry on the steamboat, I am warmly greeted by Ma and Da and the rest of my family including young Brian, I mean Hugh. Da tells me that there is still some harvesting to be done in his field, and I should help my brothers tomorrow. Patrick tells me the good news that he and Jane will marry next year. After the harvest, the men in the family will build a cabin next to ours for Patrick and Jane.

Da asks about when I plan to go to America. I tell him that I am not going. He looks stunned and then disappointed. I tell him that I will look for work next spring. I feel as if I am being put out of my home. I tell him that.

"You are, are you? Well that's exactly what is happening. Everyone in this family is welcome here, but the land is too small for yis. The sooner you get settled somewhere else, the better. The same goes for Danny."

This is all too clear. First I have to talk to Ellen.

I see Ellen after Mass. She is walking home with her family. I run up to her. The family acts a bit surprised, but they welcome me back to the parish. I ask Ellen to walk with me. She looks to her mother and says to me,

"Fine! You can tell me about all your plans."

We walk slowly behind the family until they are out of earshot.

"Ellen. I have made a grave mistake. I don't want to go to America. I want to stay here with you."

"She exclaims, "What!"

Her sisters turn around and stare. Her parents continue walking.

"Do you think that I have been waiting here for you to pick up where we left off. I am not your plaything."

"I'm sorry for being so self-centred. I understand your feelings."

Andy told me to say that. The lasses always fall for us trying to understand them.

I continue, "If you don't care for me anymore, I will accept that. I just don't see any future for me without you. Will you marry me?"

There! I've said it. There is no bigger commitment in life than asking a lass to marry. That should do it.

"Charley, you have been gone many months now. I guess that you have not heard that I'm to be married to Will Beaty next year. It is all settled. You can meet Will later at our house if you wish. I'll not be marrying the likes of you."

Shite!

chapter 6 (1841)

My thoughts are on stealing Ellen from Willie Beaty. Willie is too stout and has a face that looks like a frog's. A wide mouth and a wide space between his front teeth, he has. I find it hard to believe that Ellen is going to marry him. Ellen may be a bit on the plump side, but I think she has a lovely figure. Her face gets more beautiful each day, as well. Although my nose is misshapen and I have a couple of teeth missing, I still consider myself more handsome than Willie. I can see myself and Ellen as a couple. I just can't see the Frog Prince and Ellen together. It is a mismatch made in hell.

I'll try to get Willie's viewpoints on marriage with my Ellen. I drift on down to see him on his Da's farm. His Da has a good size plot.

"Hello Willie," say I.

"Hello Charley. Back from Scotland are y' not?"

A Brilliant lad! Extremely observant!

"I am. How is it going with your marriage plans? Be living on your Da's land, will you?"

"Aye. Da's goin' to give me a good size property to farm. We'll be livin' with the family in an extension of me parents' cottage. We'll be startin' that in the spring."

"Grand. You know that Ellen and I were courting a while ago. There's no hard feelings between us, are there?"

"Ah no. I know that y' have only the best wishes for us. Y'll be invited to the wedding, I hope."

"I don't think that is a good idea. Ellen still has feelings for me, you know."

"No. I didn't know."

I got in a good one there.

"Aye. We have had many intimate moments on our trips into County Tyrone. I guess that Ellen mentioned them to you."

"No. Can't say that she did. Intimate moments, do y' say?"

"Aye. It would not be kind of me to talk any more about that. Anyway, I'll be seeing you around. Good luck to you."

I don't know where this will lead. If Ellen learns of this conversation she will be angry with me. I don't know how Willie will bring this up, but I hope that it goes in my favour.

"What in the name of God did you say to Will?" Ellen yells at me in front of my cottage.

"Ah, nothing much. I just mentioned that you and I were lovers at one time. I wished him luck with his marriage."

"Will looks at me in a different way now. He says that he understands my past indiscretions. What indiscretions?"

"I didn't say anything about indiscretions. It could be that Will is a suspicious and jealous man. He probably thinks that you and Mary are somewhat alike."

"Holy hell, man! Mary and I are not alike. I don't know what went on between you and him, but I refuse to let you talk to him again."

"We are not married, not yet anyway. You can't tell me who I can or can't talk to."

"Unbelievable!"

She walks away muttering to herself. I think that I got in a couple more good points there. I'll bring her some flowers tomorrow to calm her down.

The flowers from Ma's garden that I left at her cottage door with a note written by Brian are found at my door later. I guess she didn't like them. Thank God for Brian, I mean Hugh, writing the note. Maybe I can get her family to support me in my quest to marry Ellen. I hope that there is someone in her family who can read and has read my note.

I try to enlist some support from Paddy Carlin.

"Paddy. I must get Ellen to love me again. Would you and Gracie help? Could you put in a good word for me? Tell her how much I love her."

"Ya must be mad. According to Grace, Ellen hates ya."

"All Grace has to do is tell Ellen that I'll never marry anyone else because I'm lovesick for her. A good word is all I ask."

"I still think that y're mad, but I'll do it."

Another month has gone by. I think of other devious ways to win her over and for her to see the light. I try another approach. I will ask her sister Mary about my chances. This will be awkward, but I have to do it.

I stop at the Bradley's and ask to see Mary. I know that all the Bradley lasses are there. It is time for them to card and spin yarn from the new wool. Mrs. Bradley doesn't glare at me this time. I almost detect a smile. Mary comes to the door and asks me what I want. I ask her to come out and have a few words with me. Mary looks at me like I'm mad, but she comes outside and walks a distance away from the door. This is awkward.

"How is it going there, Mary?"

"Grand, Charley. Is this what you're after, to check on my well being?"

"Mary, you know that I am in love with your sister Ellen. I just can't understand why she is marrying Willie and not me. Ellen is making a big mistake. Do you know why she is rejecting me and going through with the wedding?"

"Charley, we love you and would like you to be a part of the family, but Ellen was hurt when you said you were leaving. I personally dislike Will. He has a good future at his Da's farm, but there is something about him that disgusts me. I'm not sure what that is. Maybe it's the way he looks at me sometimes, like he fancies me. I wish that you had a chance with Ellen, but I think that she will not step out of her commitment at this point in the courtship. She never mentions you, so I think Will is going to be my new brother-in-law."

A brilliant idea comes into my head. Maybe Willie fancies Mary more than Ellen. If I could somehow get Mary to seduce him, Ellen would change her plans. Ach! How in the hell could I ask Mary to seduce him. For all I know, she has decided to act like she is a virgin again.

"Thanks, Mary. If you would, will you tell Ellen that I still love her? I'll not give up even after she makes her vows with Willie the Frog in front of the priest."

Mary laughs. "Sure and I will. And Charley, when Ellen and Will marry, remember that I'm still available. Mind yourself now, won't you?"

Awkward.

Paddy visits me later this day. I tell him that I'm still trying to break up Ellen's marriage plans. He says,

"I know a way to stop the marriage."

After all the trouble I've put myself through, I think that it is unlikely that stupid Paddy knows how to break up Will and Ellen, but I ask him how. He tells me, and it is brilliant. Good old Paddy.

Chapter 7
[1841]

Da, my brothers, and my cousins build a second cottage on our land. We haul rocks from near and far as well as timbers unearthed from nearby boglands. Da directs the construction. It is the same cottage design used for generations. When it is completed, Da whitewashes the walls, and one of my uncles thatches the roof and ties it down with rope. My brother Patrick and his Jane will move in after their wedding. May God bless them and give them a happy life here.

Da tells me to keep word of the new cottage a secret. I ask why? It is there as clear as day for all to see.

Da says, "It improves the property, Charley. It adds to the value. When Reverend Delap hears of it, he will increase our rent to cover the increase in his taxes and tithes due to the change in valuation."

Unbelievable! We work hard to improve our landlord's land and we are charged more because of it. What a world we live in!

Patrick is married at the cottage of Jane's parents in Raws Lower. Father Boyle performs the ceremony with myself and Jane's sister as witnesses. Jane's parents hold a party afterward in the buildings on their land. There is whiskey, fiddlers, dancing, and the good craic that generally accompanies such an affair. My brothers and sisters are here, of course, as well as many of our friends. Gracie and Ellen come with their intended spouses, Paddy Carlin and Willie Beaty. I have a lass by the name of Agnes accompany me. As the evening progresses, I notice that Paddy and Willie have left the women and they have been in conversation by the table that holds the whiskey bottles. Paddy looks fairly sober, but Willie is getting a bit under the weather, so to speak. My friend Agnes joins them. Agnes is well known to be able to handle the drink as well as any man. I leave them to their pursuit of intoxication and join my family by the fire.

"Where in the name of God did ya find the lass y're with," asks Da.

"Oh Agnes? I met her when I went fishing with Paddy over at Lough Shinnagh. She's quite a character."

"She is that. Doesn't she have proper clothes for an affair such as this?"

"Ah no. Her parents are dirt poor. They were nearly evicted by their landlord. I thought that a night like this would cheer her up, poor thing."

"I don't know what you're up to, Charley. I hope we don't see her kind too often around here."

Later, Paddy returns to Gracie and Ellen, who are dancing in the open area next to the fiddlers.

"I'm afraid that Will is not well. He fell down outside the cow byre. I hope that he isn't hurt," he tells them.

Gracie and Ellen rush to the cow shed. Willie is not there. Paddy staggers over to join them.

He says, "Maybe he crawled into the byre."

All of them enter the building and hear grunting that doesn't seem to be coming from the animals. It comes from an empty stall. They rush over, and in the moonlight they see Willie with his trousers off wrestling with Agnes who has her clothes awry. Ellen lets out a cry of shock and runs from the building with Gracie close behind. Paddy watches for awhile. The two in the hay don't acknowledge any spectators. Paddy ambles back to the fire and slaps me on the back. Gracie and Ellen are already gone from the party.

I wait a week and call on Ellen. She agrees to see me. Neither of us speak of the events at my brother's wedding. She tells me, indeed, her wedding to Willie is off. I ask no questions. We take a long walk down to the River Finn and stand on the bridge dropping pebbles into the water. I say,

"Ellen, I love you with all my heart. I didn't realize how much you meant to me before. I do now. Please, please marry me."

Ellen smiles slyly and says, "And be buried with your people?"

I laugh and say, "Aye, and be buried with my people."

"I will marry you."

Mr. Bradley directs the building of a cottage next to his own. It will be Ellen's and mine. We lack the number of labourers we had for my brother's home, so more than two months elapse before it is completed. My Da helps as well as some of my brothers. Mr. Bradley had a number of his relatives help as well. I never worked so hard in my life. When I look at it, I feel proud. Soon, Ellen and I will share a fire in its cosy main room. I can hardly wait.

We are married at the Bradley's by Father Boyle. My brother Patrick and Ellen's sister Mary are the witnesses. Ellen and I will live in the cottage next to her parents with a quarter acre of land just big enough for planting some potatoes. I will work for Mr. Bradley on his farm and pay him rent from the money he pays me. Mr. Bradley is happy to have me work for him because he only has one son old enough to work in the fields. He always had to hire outside workers, anyway. I still have the wages I saved from Scotland, minus the sum that I paid Agnes, the whore from Taughboy. Surprisingly, Da never asked me for any of the money earned in Scotland. I will save it for whatever emergency turns up in the future.

The Bradleys have as fine a wedding feast as the Maguires gave for my brother. It is a cool misty day, but the crowd that attends is large and boisterous. Brian McMenamin and Jimmy

McGranaghan are again the fiddlers. They play grand together and are the favourites of the parish, playing at practically every ceilidh around these hills.

Someone shouts, "Smasher Conaghan is here," which turns many a head. Some of the men cheer. Sure enough, my sparring partner has arrived. He walks over to us and gives us his best wishes.

I say, "You are getting to be a famous figure around here. That was some entrance you made there."

He says, "Aye, and it embarrasses me to have to yell out my name like that."

"So that's how you advertise yourself now. I'll have to learn your tricks."

Smasher is still fighting and winning at Killeter as well as other fairs in the surrounding counties. He must be earning much for it because he is the best dressed fellow at the wedding and that includes myself and Ellen's father.

It is a lovely party, but it ends early before Ellen and I retire to our cottage. We are happy that we don't have to deal with the usual indecent taunts that follow couples who spend their first night near where the party is held. We are surprised that our guests appear to be well mannered. The lovemaking between us in our own cabin is gentle and sweet. Ellen and I will indeed have a happy life together, even if it took a bit of deceit to accomplish it.

Before the year's end, my friend Paddy marries Gracie and they live in Baywood. My brother Danny and Bridget marry, and they move to a farm in Lislaird, near Castlederg in County Tyrone. Their farmland was previously leased to a member of Bridget's family. Packie Curran is still courting my sister Maggie. They have no wedding plans as of yet.

chapter 8
(1842 - 1845)

In 1842, Father Edward Boyle's brother, John, is assigned to the parish as curate. The Boyle brothers are both energetic priests who try to get all of the parishioners involved in parish affairs. I avoid them as much as possible, but Ma sometimes works tidying up the chapel. I hope she knows what she is in for. Once they draw you in, you can never get out.

To bring Ireland up to English standards, large workhouses are built in Strabane and in Stranorlar for paupers, of whom we have quite a few, generally in the villages. The buildings are clean and new and possibly look inviting to the single men and women who are penniless. For the families of the poor, they don't look so inviting. Husbands are separated from their wives and placed in different areas of the workhouse. The children remain with their mothers but rarely see their fathers. To qualify for entry, the paupers must hold no property nor have any possessions of value. Of course, the inmates must work for their food and lodging. We farmers all hope that this will mean there will be no more shabby looking beggars at our doors anymore.

The care for paupers at the workhouses is paid for by the landowners in the new geographical divisions of Ireland called

Poor Law Unions. Most of Donaghmore is in the Stranorlar Union. Some townlands in the east of the parish are in the Strabane Union. As you might suspect, the landowners are unhappy with the new poor tax being thrust on them. I guess we can expect higher rents in the future.

Our daughter Bridget, named for Ellen's mother, is born in 1842. She is the pride of the Bradleys. I am just happy to have a healthy wain who I hope will grow up to be as smart and as pretty as her mother.

I remark to Ellen about the small difference in age between Bridget and Ellen's youngest sister, Mary Alice.

"Imagine that, will you? She is only three years younger than her aunt."

Ellen gives me a queer look. She walks over to me and sits opposite where I'm sitting.

"Charley, I'm surprised that you say that. What do you know about Mary Alice?"

I have no idea what she is talking about.

"What do I know about Mary Alice? What should I know about her?"

"I thought that the whole parish knew about Mary Alice. She is not really Bridget's aunt. She is really Bridget's cousin. I trust that you will not be sharing that with anyone."

My head is spinning a bit. I try to figure it out, but Ellen beats me to the answer.

"Mary Alice is my sister Mary's child. Mary became pregnant, father unknown, and spent her pregnancy at my aunt's home in Glenfin. After the baby was born, Mam took her in as her own child. We were able to fool most of the neighbours except those whom Mam dealt with often, and who knew that Mam wasn't pregnant that year. We asked close neighbours to keep the identity of Mary Alice's real mother a secret. I don't believe many of them kept the secret for long, but I thought that your family knew."

"No, they didn't. Isn't that something? Mary has a child."

"Aye, and it is working out for all of us. Mary Alice is a beautiful child with a grand personality. I hope our baby turns out as lovely."

I do as well.

My sister Maggie finally marries Packie Curran and moves to Cornabrogue, not far from Glencarn. She has a son in 1843. My brothers Patrick and Danny have children as well. Both of my brothers have sons named James after my Da. It will soon be confusing with all the similar names because my first son, another James, is born in 1843. They will have to be known as Jimmy Patrick, Jimmy Danny, and Jimmy Hurley (Charley) when we all get together.

Having a son is a dream come true for me. My only wish is that I will have some land for Jimmy to farm when he gets of age.

I'm starting to enjoy working with Mr. Bradley, and I'm learning how to farm the grain crops that pay his rent. On our wee plot, we are only growing potatoes for our own consumption. We do have a pig which we bought at the fair. It was cute when it was piglet and a grand pet for the wains. It is getting big and fat now on pratie peelings. We will sell it at the next fair for a profit. Of course, we will buy another piglet at that time for the next year.

One day in 1843, Paddy Carlin calls at our door.

"Is himself home?" he asks Ellen.

"He's doin' the fire. Do you want to see him?"

"I do indeed."

By that time, I'm at the door asking him to come in.

"What are you doing calling at this time Paddy?"

"I'd like some words with ya. Can y' join me outside?"

"I can."

I tell him that I'm sorry that I haven't seen much of him lately with my work and playing with the children.

He says, "Do y' know that Grace is with child now? The baby should be born sometime next year."

"Congratulations Paddy. Best wishes to you. Welcome to the adult life with the rest of us."

"Ach, nothin' to it. It was my pleasure."

"We should celebrate. Let's go to Gallagher's for a glass of stout."

I tell Ellen about Paddy's good news, and we walk down to the Cross. Before leaving, I get some money from my Scotland wages. I've only been to Gallagher's a few times in my life because Gallagher is a dirty mercenary, and he wants too many coins for his drinks. I never thought that I should pay that much. In the past, I could afford only the poteen at Aunt Mary's, but now I have my wages from Scotland, and tonight is a great occasion. I think we can have a couple of pints at the alehouse.

Gallagher offers his sympathy again for the loss of my grandfather. I mostly think that he misses Granda's business. I introduce my friend Paddy to him and ask for a pint of stout for each of us. I tell him the reason for the celebration, and he congratulates Paddy on the good news.

There are other lads in the alehouse, and I offer them a drink, as well. Two of them accept my hospitality, and I worry that I didn't bring enough money.

The stout is a wonder to behold in a glass. It is jet black with a foamy white head on it. It is creamy and delicious. It goes smoothly down my throat and I feel grand.

Paddy Carlin starts telling us about his neighbours.

"Oul' Missus McGoldrick is something. I haven't spoken to her in a while. I asked how her husband was doin'. She told me that he passed on. I didn't know that. I said, 'He's dead is he?' and she says, 'I hope so. We buried him a week ago.' She's a hard woman. She and her husband never got along well."

The fellow standing next to me at the bar overhears and says,

"Aye, Missus McGoldrick is truly a hard woman. I heard that, after Father Boyle prayed over her dying husband, he came out and told her that her husband wanted a few words with her. She went in to hear his dying words. Her husband quietly asked her,

'Dear, what is that delicious aroma I smell from the fire?'

'It is only some bacon that I'm cookin',' she answered. Her husband then asked if he could have a piece of bacon. Mrs. McGoldrick says to him, 'Sorry love, I'm saving it for the wake.'"

All in Gallagher's establishment laugh at this. I believe that I'm being codded by this fellow. It is a joke. I have heard that story a dozen times in the past about other widows. I let it go and laugh with the rest.

Paddy and I drink two porters each and I pay out of my pocket for our drinks and the rounds we bought the lads. Then the other fellows start setting up rounds for us. We are having a good time with all the craic and fellowship when one lad takes a swing at another. He connects and they begin fighting in earnest. I grab one and Paddy grabs the other to break it up. I take my lad outside to cool him off, but when I let him go, he swings at me. I duck and crack him one in the jaw. Down he goes. He has trouble getting up as Gallagher comes through the door.

"That's all for you, Matthew. Go home now."

I walk back in and see Paddy calming the other fellow down. Paddy then rejoins me at the bar.

"Bushmills Whiskey for the two of ya," says Gallagher.

It is apparent that Gallagher is grateful that we stopped the fight. The others at the alehouse would have liked the fight to continue just for the entertainment, but they grudgingly accept that we did the right thing. Paddy and I drink the whiskey. It burns all the way down. I order another round of stout to calm my stomach. This is on Mr. Gallagher, as well. Good man, Mr. Gallagher. He is not such a bad fellow after all.

By the time I reach my cottage, Ellen and the wains are asleep. I quietly remove my clothes and slip into the bed beside Ellen. She murmurs and turns on her side facing me. I embrace her. She is warm and soft. She puts her arms around me and gives me a sleepy looking smile. I will remember this lovely night forever.

We have another son, Edward, born in 1844. The parish population is increased by other children born this year, as well.

A daughter is born to my brother Danny and another son is born to my sister Maggie. My friend Paddy Carlin and his wife Grace have a son named John. On top of all that, my sister Nancy is set to wed Matt Quinn this year.

Paddy and I find many occasions to return to Gallagher's for a few rounds of porter. My Scotland funds are shrinking accordingly, although Paddy manages to have enough coins for drink from the sales of his livestock and grain at the fairs and markets. We always have a good time with the lads at the alehouse. Peter Gallagher, no relation to the proprietor, and Andy Slevin always seem to be there when we arrive. They are both bachelors who live with their parents in the fields of Drumbeg owned by the tyrant James Hanley. They are constantly complaining about their evil landlord. Hanley has evicted several tenants lately for missing the spring gales, whereas other landlords frequently allow their tenants to pay it off in the autumn. Peter and Andy tell us that their parents just barely make the rent payments each time they are due, but they never know what will happen next time. We wonder how Peter and Andy have the money for porter and whiskey if they are in such difficulties, but we never ask.

Andy says, "James Hanley is a despicable villain, and I have the notion to beat the shite out of him."

I start codding him about this. "You know that the bible tells us to pray for our enemies."

"I do," says Andy. "I pray that he dies a horrible death and goes straight to hell."

On some days, Mickey Gallen and his brother Kevin come to the alehouse with Peter and Andy. They live with their parents in the same area of Drumbeg, and they are distant cousins of mine. Their granny is my great-aunt, Mary McMenamin. Instead of the usual craic when we are in the alehouse, we talk about how to help the old ones who are threatened by eviction by their landlord. Peter brings up starting a whiteboy group to intimidate the greedy landlords. The whiteboys were secret organisations in the last century that vandalized property and killed the livestock of landlords who threatened tenants with eviction. We had such a group in our parish many years ago called the Boley Boys. The Boley Boys have been inactive during my lifetime. Kevin silences Peter as soon as he starts talking. He warns Peter that this is not a matter to be discussed in public. The serious discussion ends. There is silence in the alehouse for a moment. Paddy Carlin breaks the silence with a story about a conversation he had with his wife.

"I was at a wake when me wife asked to taste the whiskey I was drinkin'. She took a swallow and made a terrible face.

'How can you drink this horrible swill?' she asked.

'See...Y' think I'm out enjoying meself when I'm at Gallagher's.'"

There is no more serious talk at Gallagher's. The jokes have begun.

The work of Father Mathew's Abstinence League has arrived at our parish. In the spring, Father Boyle tries to get everyone to take a pledge of abstinence at Sunday Mass. He gives an inspiring sermon revealing all of the evils of alcohol, how it ruins families and destroys souls. He is an effective speaker. When he asks everyone to stand and take the vow, the entire congregation gets up. I stand, but I keep my mouth shut during the first part of the pledge. I can see Ellen looking at me. For the remainder of the pledge, I mumble the words of the *Pater Noster* instead of repeating the words of the vow.

On the walk back home, I explain to Ellen that I'm for abstinence as long as it is practiced in moderation. She says that she doesn't think that I'm funny. I tell her that the pledge is going to ruin my great-aunt's poteen business that supports many of my Da's cousins. All I get is a stony silence for the rest of the day. I know that I'll not give up my nights at Gallagher's. They are the only chances I get to relax and have a good time.

In 1845, my sister Nancy marries Matt Quinn of Cronalaghy. Matt and Nancy are trying to make a go with Matt's farm there. My brother Patrick and I both have daughters whom we name Catherine after our mother. Patrick has three wains now, Danny has two, Maggie has two, and I have four. My friend Paddy has a daughter named Bridget. We are all doing our part to overpopulate the parish. I wonder how the land will be able to feed all the children filling the cottages on our hills.

Bishop McLaughlin died of his illness a number of days ago. We had often seen Bishop McLaughlin when he visited our parish to administer Confirmation. He visited us more frequently than other parishes because members of his family live in Castlefin. He was a saintly cleric who often ministered to the ill and dying in Derry City, especially those in the workhouse. He eventually became ill himself and resigned as bishop. Edward Maginn took his place as Bishop of Derry after his resignation.

There have been reports of a blight on potatoes in the southern counties and to the west in the Glenties of Donegal as well. It is widespread and it kills the potato plants for miles about. This news, of course, is a worry to all of us in the parish. What will we eat if not the potatoes we grow? We have had other blights in past years and have survived in famine conditions. During those years, we managed to live with no food except for a bit of brochan at breakfast and supper.

As soon as he hears of the potato failure, my father-in-law stops me in the field.

"We have to watch the potatoes every day now. If we see any discoloration of the leaves, we will have to dig up the potatoes early, even if they are not fully grown. They may be all we'll have to eat until next year."

This is quite serious. I go out and check the plants every morning. So far, all is well. Everyone prays that we will be spared the blight.

Paddy and I stop again at Gallagher's. A number of lads are there including Peter and Andy.

Mr. Gallagher brings me a pint of porter.

"Sure it's the Lord's work you're doin'," I tell him.

Gallagher grunts and walks away.

Andy yells, "Ya still haven't taken the pledge I see."

"Nor you," I answer.

We discuss briefly how Father Mathew's pledge has reduced the number of customers at Gallagher's. Only the brazen lads, such as ourselves, can openly walk in during daylight hours. Others slink in like rodents when they get the chance. The shame of being spotted by gossipy neighbours is too much for those lads.

"What are they afraid of?" I say. "Their own shadows is my guess. It is a man's right to have a pint when he wants it. If their women don't fancy it, let them run back to their mammys."

A fellow standing near me at the beer counter says, "Is that coming from a man who lives with his in-laws? It'll be yerself who runs back to yer mammy."

His words rub me the wrong way. I walk over to him. He is a good sized, swarthy man who is currently wearing a sneer on his face. He stares at his pint.

"And what do you mean by that?" I ask.

He takes his time, looking me over.

"I believe that yer wife deserves more consideration from ya. How she puts up with ya, I don't understand."

"What do you care? It is not your concern."

"I'm Ellen's cousin. I hear ya in here shooting off yer mouth too often. I think Ellen is mad puttin' up with the likes of ya."

The crowd at the bar moves away from us. I grab his shirt and turn him to face me. He pushes my hand away, and I punch him. He punches back aiming for my belly. Soon we are in the centre of the floor swinging with all our might. He lands a few good ones on my jaw. I get in close and rapidly hit him with alternate rights and lefts. He pulls me to the floor and we wrestle until Paddy and a couple of others pull us apart. Mr. Gallagher yells for them to drag us outside. We are outside in the mud gasping for air when Gallagher comes out and says,

"You both are banned from this establishment. I don't want to see either of you again around here." He goes back in.

"Ellen's cousin you say?"

"Aye. A good fighter y' are."

"Thanks."

"By the way, I was only messin' with ya in there."

"Alright now. I didn't think I was that bad a fella. Did I see you at my wedding?"

"Y' did. I was mostly drinkin' with the lads."

"Where will we drink now?"

"Wherever it is, I guess it won't be porter we'll be drinkin'. The Killygordon and Ballybofey alehouses are too far. Bottled whiskey isn't bad when ya get used to it."

Most of the crowd watching us finally go back inside. Paddy joins me and Ellen's cousin as we walk back in the direction of home in the pouring rain.

I get the silent treatment from Ellen when I get home. I didn't drink much, but the smell of it is on me. The bruises on my face tell her that I was rowdy again as she has been hearing from neighbours.

Ellen is still sweet to me and I give her every consideration. Her looks have changed a bit since we were married. Her eyes look slightly tired now, and her waist has plumped out a bit. It is to be expected when you have four wains in four years. When we are alone, I tell her what I feel about her.

"You know, I never regret for a minute staying here in Ireland with you. You are all I think about when I'm working in the fields. Have your feelings for me changed since we married?"

"No, I still love you, even when you act like an arse."

"What does that mean?"

"You are a good provider, but you still do stupid things… your fights and drinking for example."

"I swear that I'll improve. My spirit gets the best of me sometimes. I'll improve as of this minute."

I move closer and hold her. She kisses me softly; it gives me a lovely tingling sensation. I do love this woman.

What Ellen's cousin said to me at the alehouse bothers me. It is the truth. I am working for my father-in-law and practically live in his home. I have not really made a home of my own like a man should. Being dependant on the Bradleys makes me feel like I've failed in my life. It eats at me.

It is good that I am banned from Gallagher's. My Scotland wages are practically gone. No more porter for me. Paddy still visits the alehouse and keeps me informed of the happenings there. He somehow keeps the right balance in his life and is smarter than I once thought.

Through my own efforts, a bottle of poteen comes into my possession. I hide it in the back of the midden and take a swig of it when I have the opportunity. It is wise to keep it out of sight from Ellen. I took the abstinence pledge reluctantly in the spring to please her, but I don't keep it. I don't believe that God cares if I take an occasional drink, but Ellen might. The poteen puts me in a world where every day is sunny even if it is teaming rain. I do love the drink.

It's now after All Hallows and it looks as if the blight has missed us. The potato harvest was as good as any other year. We have been hearing of the hardships caused by the famine in the south. Many starved to death and others were evicted from their land for missing rent payments on the November gale day. Without food or housing, many were forced into the workhouses. Thank God we were spared these problems. It's a pity about those who died, but there is nothing that we can do but pray for them. I have many questions in my mind. Did God not help those poor people because they didn't pray hard enough? If God didn't help the hunger victims, why didn't the English government? Was there not enough food grown in Ireland to feed them? I just don't understand these things.

Chapter 9
(1846)

I have the feeling that my drinking is causing a problem for my family. I don't know how they know about it. I do take a wee swig before heading to the fields in the morning, but then I work as I always do. The smell of it on my breath is gone by the time I return home. As far as I can tell, it doesn't affect my work, but Mr. Bradley keeps telling me to cut down on the drink. His son Jimmy looks at me in distain. I believe that the drink gives me strength for the hard job of working in the fields. I do lie down in the afternoon and sleep a bit, but I work twice as hard when I awaken.

Ellen tells me that her Da is complaining about me. She says that she knows that there is drink about, and if she finds it she'll pour it out on the ground. I tell her that I am not drinking much, and she better not do anything rash. After we argue, I go out and have another. When I come back in, she ignores me and I go to bed. I sometimes stumble a bit, but that is the nature of the drink. I am doing no one any harm.

Sure enough, herself finds the bottle by the midden the next day and empties it. The empty bottle is sitting on the table when I return. I begin to roar. Biddy, who is now three years of age, runs behind Ellen's skirt.

"That whiskey was my property. It was mine, the master of this house. I'll have myself a drink whenever I want it."

I storm out and head up to Drumbeg for another bottle. Most of the work is done now for the winter, and I deserve a bit of relaxation. I deserve a good bottle of spirits.

I try to buy another bottle from Da's cousin Denis, but he tells me that he was instructed not sell it to me anymore.

"Who told you that," I ask.

"Your Da, for one." he says. "God knows we can use your business, but not if it is hurting your family."

"I'm not hurting anyone. I just want me bottle."

"Sorry Charley, we can't sell you anything."

Next, I visit Paddy in Baywood. At my request, he gives me a glass of whiskey and talks to me.

"Charley, people are worried about ya. Ya seem to be losing your common sense lately. Ya have to cut down on your drinking. Ellen will be puttin' ya out if ya continue."

"Ach. It's not that bad. I can quit the drink anytime I want. It's just that I don't want to quit this winter. In the spring I'll be right as rain."

"I'm worried about ya just as well."

I ask him to get me a bottle.

"I can't. Grace will kill me. There's a fella by the name of Carabin in Corgary sellin' poteen. Please don't tell anyone that I told ya."

The walk to Corgary is cold and damp. When I get there, I ask a lady at a dirty looking cottage where I can find Mister Carabin. She points to a cabin in the middle of a field. I walk quickly across the field without even thanking the woman.

"Are you Mister Carabin?" I ask the old fellow who comes to the door.

"I am."

"Can I purchase a bottle from you?"

"Who are yeh, and who sent yeh?"

I figured that they would be suspicious of any stranger asking for poteen, although I don't rightly appear to be an informer for the revenue police. I tell him that I am from Glencarn and was in the area. Many recommended the poteen from Corgary for its flavour, I tell him. He stares at me and sees no threat. He wants nine pence for a bottle. I tell him that I have a shilling. Would he give me two bottles for a shilling? He will. That shilling is the last of my funds from Scotland, but I need the drink badly. I take the bottles and leave for the long walk back. I take a mighty swig to sample it. My God! It smells and tastes like horse piss.

Where will I hide it? I think about various places around our cottage. I can think of nowhere safe. The Bradley field is no good either, nor is any location in Glencarn. The only really safe place that comes to mind is the fairy spring up the hill from Glencarn. It is too far from my cottage for a quick drink, but if I get some time alone it is a good place to relax. I head across country to the spring.

It is starting to snow when I arrive. There is a thin glaze of ice at the edge of the pond beneath the water falling from the rocks. It is a pleasant spot to get away from the cares of life. There are pine trees, small ones and tall ones. Attractive bushes and ferns grow here, and the air is ghostly quiet. It is no wonder that this place is considered to be home to the fairies. No one would think of using this land for anything as common as farming or pasture. I wonder about the rich landowner who holds ownership to this piece of paradise.

While I think of a place to hide my treasure, I uncork the bottle again and drink the horrible tasting liquid. Soon I am relaxed and sit on a rock surrounded by white fluffy snow with the bottle at my side. The poteen is taking hold of me, and I consider singing an old song that my mother taught me. It would be out of place here in this cathedral atmosphere, but the music is in my head. Lovely! All my bad thoughts disappear. All my aches and pains disappear. I am starting to think that Corgary whiskey is better than I first believed.

I dig a shallow pit in the gravel under a bush far from the path taken by visitors to the spring. I fill it with fern leaves and place the bottles reverently in the hole. Then, I build a cairn of rocks over the bottles. They will be safe here. I believe that I can find the spot whenever I return.

Sure I feel like I am floating on air as I return down the path. I walk through my door like a mighty man, but I trip on the flagstone and fall flat on my face. Looks of pity come from Ellen and Biddy. My son Jimmy looks surprised and confused to see me. Eddie and wee Katie must be asleep. I get up and stagger to my bed and lie down. Sleep comes to me quickly among the sounds of everyday life in a country cottage.

First Ma comes over to our home in the morning. My head is aching and I haven't left my bed yet. Ellen leads her into the room.

"Charley, we are all ashamed of you. We expected better. You're married now with four wains. You must get control of yourself. We can help you if you want, but you must promise that you will stop the drinking."

I just stare at her. I have nothing to say. She starts to cry. Ach! Please stop.

She leaves. I go back to sleep. Da arrives. Shite!

"What's the matter with ya? I was proud of ya for a few years there, but ya slipped back into your old ways. What are we goin' to do with ya?"

I stare at him. What can I say? I look away. He grabs me by the shirt and shakes me.

"Y're driving us mad, son. Do ya have no willpower? Can't ya see what y're doin' to your family? Stop the drinkin'! Do ya hear me? Stop the drinkin'!"

I push his hands away but lie there. He looks as if he wants to beat me senseless but then looks at Ellen. He storms out saying to Ellen,

"I don't blame ya if ya throw this piece of shite out."

I sober up for a few days and do some work for Mr. Bradley. Sunday arrives and I disappear after Mass. It is an unusually sunny day, and the splashing of water at the spring greets me. I panic at first but then remember where the bottle is hidden. The rest of my day is spent with my friend Mister Mountain Dew.

When I walk down the hill to home, I see my neighbours looking and pointing at me from the distance. Am I that much a menace?

I eat no supper but head into bed. Herself doesn't speak to me, but all things considered, it was a lovely day.

February arrives and soon the field must be prepared for spring planting. I don't know of what help I'm going to be to Mr. Bradley this month. I make frequent trips to the spring. The first bottle is gone and I start on the second. When I come home there is the constant nagging from Ellen and her family. I get visits from my family too, all warning me to stop drinking. Paddy Carlin begs me to stop, even Carney Conaghan stops by to talk to me. He warns me that I will have no friends unless I stay sober. I tell them that I'll try, even though I know I can't. Who needs friends when there is drink about?

After another trip to the spring, I return home after drinking most of the last bottle. I am greeted by Ellen's father in the front of my cottage.

"You can't come in. Ellen doesn't want you living here anymore."

"It's me home. You can't stop me."

"Oh but I can. This is my cottage. You just live here because you're married to Ellen. What a sad day it was when that match was made. Go home to your parents. Let them put up with you."

Ellen opens the half door.

"Please Charley. Go home to your parents. Come back after you've given up the drink. I can't stand living with you anymore."

"You're my wife. This is my home. Let me in."

I thrust out my chest and try to swagger up to the door. It was more stagger than swagger. Mr. Bradley stops me with his hand. I push it away. He pushes me to the ground. When I try to stand, he pushes me down again.

"You have only one choice here. Crawl to your parents. We don't want to see you again. Go!"

It is no use. I'm too drunk to fight even if I wanted to strike Ned. I crawl a distance away and stand up with my back to my cottage. I sway down the lane and make my way to Glencarn.

Ma is at the door.

"Mind if I spend the night here?" I ask.

She sighs and says, "Alright. Sleep in Jimmy's bed."

I walk through the door, but there is Da.

"What the hell is this? Y'll not stay here with us. Y're not good enough for us. Sleep in the byre with the other animals."

Ma and Da argue about where I'll stay. Da wins out, and I spend the night on a pile of hay in the byre.

I'm ashamed to see anyone the next day. I go out and try to help Patrick, but my head hurts so bad that I return to the byre. After a long nap, I visit Ma in the cottage. She gives me a bowl of stir-about and a cup of tea.

Tea is a new vice of the Irish. It was introduced into England from China and is now popular throughout the isles. We buy it at the markets and at Kelly's store. It tastes lovely with a bit of milk and some sugar.

"I guess we are stuck with you for awhile," she says. "Don't say we didn't warn you about your drinking."

"I don't know what to do now," I say as I sup the tea.

"Neither do I. Your Da won't put up with you for long. You'll be out even sooner if you start drinking again. He says that if you don't find work, he'll send you to the workhouse."

I can sense that Ma would put up with me a lot longer than Da. I am not thinking clear enough yet to decide my future plans. I return to the field to help Patrick, but I feel that my bottle up at the spring is calling me.

After an hour with Patrick, I excuse myself and walk away. Patrick shakes his head. I soon find myself at the fairy spring. There is about two inches of poteen left in the bottle. I quickly dispose of that and start feeling better. It is so peaceful here. I stare at the clouds and the trees. Not once do I think about Ellen, my children, or my parents. I get drowsy, pass out and dream of fairies and giants.

When I awake, it is morning. There is the gentle whistle of wind in the trees. I hear soft footsteps near where I am laying.

I look, and I see an old woman at the spring staring at me. She is wearing a clean, shining robe unlike any I have ever seen. Her long hair is white; her face is pale and lined with deep wrinkles.

"A good morning to you," I say.

She doesn't answer. She cups her hand and takes a drink of the water running from the rocks.

"Good morning," I repeat.

No response, but she is making a gesture that I should drink from the spring water as well. I feel too awake to believe that I am still dreaming. I get up and start walking closer to her, and she makes another quick gesture that I should drink the water. Then she walks between the branches of two pine trees and disappears into the forest. What just went on here? I walk between the branches, but she is nowhere to be seen. I return to the spring, and out of superstition, take a drink from the spring. No, it doesn't taste like poteen, just pure cool water. I am thirsty and drink some more. It is refreshing.

Back at Glencarn, Da and the boys are in the fields again. Ma can't believe that I came back home.

"Sure you're brave to be back here. It's a good thing that your Da isn't here to greet you."

"I'm sorry Ma, but I have a mad story to tell you."

She gives me the look that I'm about to cod her a bit. I tell her about spending the night at the fairy spring. She stops what she is doing and stares at me. I now have her full attention.

"I woke up and saw a banshee."

"A banshee?"

"Aye. She was old, but she wore a beautiful gown."

"You better tell me more. Tell me all that happened. Did she speak?"

"She did not. I expected to hear her wail like I was to die that minute. Instead, she bade me to drink from the spring."

"And did you?"

"I did. It was refreshing. I was quite thirsty."

Ma then told me astonishing things. She said that she often saw the woman at the spring. At first, she thought it was the Virgin Mary. Others have seen her there as well, but she hasn't been seen for years. Ma thinks that the strange woman is a saint or an angel who watches over us. Some think that she is one of the fairies from the ancient times. Few mention her anymore. They don't want people to think that they are daft.

"This is a good sign Charley. Maybe she will help you turn your life around."

Indeed she might. After a dish of boiled potatoes, I join Da and my brothers clearing the field for spring planting. Da looks at me and shakes his head. I do the best I can until I collapse in a heap. Da and Patrick carry me back to the cottage. I need some drink; it will give me strength. There must be a bottle here in the cottage. I try to get up, but my legs won't hold me. The room is blurry and starts spinning. Then everything goes black.

I awake in my brother Jimmy's bed feeling cold. Da and Ma are standing by my side. My body shakes and Ma gets blankets to throw over me. The mattress is soaked with my sweat. I can't lie still. Ma says to Da,

"He has a fever."

"It's the drink. He'll get over it."

Ma doesn't believe him. I cry out,

"Please get me some whiskey. I'll be fine then."

Da says, "Let him sweat it out. There'll be no more drink for him."

I turn my head and vomit on the floor.

Da says, "Ach. Look at that, will ya?"

He brings a bucket over next to my head. I vomit some more into the bucket. My head feels like it is ready to burst. My vision is still blurry. I look from side to side. I try to get up. Da holds me down.

"Get it out of ya. We'll stay with ya until y're well."

Hours go by. My head is feeling worse. I have nothing left in my stomach to spit up. I continue to sweat profusely and I shake all over. Ma stays busy cleaning up after me and bringing me tea. Da helps me to sit up and drink the tea. After that, he sits near me and offers encouragement that I'll be fine. I hear Ma tell him that I saw the lady up by the spring. Da laughs.

"He imagined that he saw the lady there. It was the drink that caused it."

"No, I believe he saw her. He described her. She was the same woman that I used to see. It is a sign."

Da doesn't believe. He just laughs at the thought that his drunken son would see such a vision when others couldn't.

I spend the entire night in hell thinking that I'll die at any moment. My parents are there with me for the whole time. When morning comes, I am feeling a bit better. Ma offers me some stir-about, but I am not hungry. I don't believe that I'll eat for a long time, maybe days.

Da says, "It's over Charley. I think that the poison is out of ya. It's lucky you had it so easy there."

"Easy? That was easy?"

"I knew of many who were on the drink longer than you. They ended up wandering like eejits and seeing ugly crawling things on themselves. After weeks of torment, they died. I don't think ya want that sort of trouble."

"I did see the woman at the spring."

"I'm sure that ya thought ya did. Y'll be fine in a couple of days. Rest up here. When you feel up to it, give us a hand in the fields."

The next day, I get my appetite back. I eat everything Ma puts before me and it all tastes lovely. Ma asks me if I still fancy the drink. I tell her I do. She asks me to give it up for Lent at least. I tell her that I am giving it up completely. I was weak and selfish. I want to get back with Ellen. I'll have to prove this to all who know me. I will never drink alcohol again. I know that it will be difficult, and I'll need support from my family and friends. Ma asks me to pray on it. Prayer is something that never occurred to me. I vow that I will ask God everyday to keep me from the temptation of alcohol.

Paddy visits me and tells me the goings on at the alehouse. I confess to him that I am off the drink forever. He looks sympathetic. I finally mention the lady at the spring.

"Aye. I've heard talk of her. Ya saw her, did ya?"
"I did. She was an old one with a shining yellow dress."
"And were ya drunk or sober?"
"I was sober. I saw her as I am seeing you now."
"I believe ya. What do y'think she was, an angel?"
"No. She was too old. I thought that she was a banshee. Ma thinks that she is a saint. Ma doesn't believe in banshees or fairies. She says that they aren't in the bible."

"Ah, just because they aren't in the bible doesn't mean they don't exist. The bible doesn't mention a lot of creatures. Does the bible say anything about elephants? No. Does it say anything about bats. I don't think so."

"You have me there. Do you think God would put up with other supernatural beings on earth like the fairies?"

"Why not? There is no conflict there. The fairies have their world and God has his. He is interested in our souls. The fairies are interested in…….ah….. music and playing tricks on people. No conflict there."

I now take more interest in the holy Mass and greet one of the Fathers Boyle each week at the Cross. Ellen and the children, along with her parents, see me at the chapel each week. I don't have the nerve to face them yet.

I confess my sins to the priest each week as well and continue to pray to the God who will keep me from destroying my life. It has been over a month since my last drunken episode, and I seem to be able to function without the drink. Every time I want a drink, I pray. I am a wonder to my parents and family. They say they don't know who I am. I feel, nevertheless, that they are anxious for me to leave their home. It is crowded in Da's home. They've gotten used to me being gone for the years I was at the Bradleys. I agree that I have to finally face Ellen.

That happens at Easter. It is at the chapel when I walk up to Ellen before she starts walking home with the Bradley clan. I see my wains there huddled around their granny. All of the Bradleys are staring at me. I smile at them and turn my attention to my wife.

"Happy Easter, Ellen. You're looking grand today."

Ellen has heard from her friends that I have now taken my abstinence vow seriously and have been off the drink for weeks. She knows as well that I have missed her and the children, and I will do anything to make amends.

"Happy Easter, Charley. You're looking well yourself there. When are you comin' home to us?"

My God. Could it be that easy? I had already begun a campaign to let Ellen know that I have changed. I let word out to all her friends about the new Charley. I specifically had Paddy and Grace visit the Bradleys to bring the subject up. I am shocked to find that all I had to do was talk to Ellen.

"I'll be home in less than an hour," I say.

She smiles. I remember something I wanted to say.

"Oh, by the way, I can't tell you how sorry I am for everything I've done. Thank you for forgiving me."

"You were a selfish arse for the past year, Charley. At least you never raised a hand to me. I guess I should be thankful for that. It was just your demons that made yourself a useless drunkard. I heard that you are a new man. Come home and prove it to us. I miss you. The wains miss you."

I return to our cabin in Coracreagh, the first time in many weeks. I knock at the door. Ellen opens it, and I walk in and embrace her. We stay in this embrace for minutes. Tears flow.

"I missed you. I'm thankful that you came to your senses," she says.

"I don't know how I'll be able to make it up to you. It was selfish of me."

My wains are here. Wee Katie is in her cradle, but Biddy, Jimmy, and Eddie are staring at me dumbfounded. Maybe Biddy remembers me when I was sober, but Jimmy and Eddie are too young to remember when I wasn't acting like a bloody fool. How will I get them to love me? It will take a lot of work. I'll be sure to make parenthood my first priority in life.

I stoop down and hold my arms open for Biddy. She is reluctant but eventually runs to me. I pick her up, hug her, and swing her around. She finally breaks into a smile and says, "Where were you, Da? I missed you."

"I was away for awhile, darlin'. I'm back to stay now. I promise."

Biddy is a tiny four year old copy of Ellen. She looks like an Ellen doll with her plump wee face, cupid lips, and black curly hair. My heart breaks when I look at her. How could I ever leave her again?

Jimmy and Eddie are still looking at me. They are not sure they want to have anything to do with me. Jimmy, at three years, decides to run away into the next room. Eddie, unsure of his walking, is left alone to face me. Eddie has a bit of my looks although he has quite a lot of growing to do. He turns from me when I put Biddy down. I walk slowly to him, crouched over and smiling. I say,

"Eddie. Do you want a horsey ride?"

"Noooo." He is ready to cry.

"Are you sure? It's fun."

He toddles away to the next room with Jimmy. What do I do now? I look at Ellen and shrug. She calls to them,

"Come on out, you two! Your Da wants to see yis! Do you hear me?"

Eddie looks out first and toddles over to me. I am on my hands and knees on the floor. He climbs up. Ellen holds him on while I take a painful crawl around the main room. Eddie starts giggling uncontrollably.

Ellen says to Eddie, "Your Da is good at crawling around here. He is well used to it."

I sigh. She thinks about it and says to me,

"Oh, Sorry. It slipped out. "

"Ach, I deserve it."

Biddy takes a turn on my back and finally Jimmy gets a turn. My knees are killing me, but I keep it up until I think everyone is satisfied.

We eat a lovely meal of ham and cabbage courtesy of the Bradleys. Mister Bradley bought a nice ham from the Doughertys, who live a few farms from here. He gave some of it to Ellen. The Bradley family is having their meal in the cottage next door about now. We will visit them when we finish.

Meat is an uncommon treat for us here in Donaghmore. It is expensive, so we have it only on special holidays like Christmas and Easter. After the long period of fasting during Lent, the large meal at Easter seems almost sinful in its extravagance.

I am not looking forward to calling on the Bradleys. I am quite a bit embarrassed for my past behaviour, and I believe the visit will be a bit chilly.

But go we must.

The Bradleys are finished their meal when we arrive.

"God bless all in this house," I say.

"Welcome, Gallens. We're happy to see you."

Of course they're happy. They love their daughter and adore their grandchildren. Me, they have to put up with.

The Bradley children have vast differences in age. A couple of the Bradley lasses seem to be heading for spinsterhood. Mary, mostly because of her past sins and reputation, seems to lack any suitors. Catherine is too tall and somewhat unattractive.

Bridget is a pretty lass of sixteen years of age. Sure, she will have suitors in a year or so. Elizabeth is a gawky fourteen year old now, but her future may also include fellas. Time is on her side. The girls contribute to the family income by preparing wool yarn for sale at the markets. They card and spin all day in the Bradley home.

Jimmy is twenty-eight years of age. He hasn't decided on a wife yet. He is so busy at the farm that he hasn't the time, or so he tells me. I'm sure that my father-in-law, Ned, will welcome a daughter-in-law and grandchildren bearing his name when the time comes. And it will come. I'm sure of it. Jimmy is a desirable catch for any young lass in the parish.

That brings us to the twin boys who are now eleven years of age. Ned will welcome them in the fields when they get a bit older. Now they attend the hedge school in Gleneeley. There is talk about the government building a new school house there in a couple of years.

Mary Alice is a precious nine year old now. She is loved and spoiled by everyone in the family.

Our visit isn't too horrible. Ned and Jimmy talk to me as if I was a civilized human being. We talk of the need for potato planting next week and of last year's potato blight in the south. Ned stays current with the news and says that the southern counties are still devastated with the effects of famine. People are dying of starvation on the roads there after being put off their land. I ask why they don't go to the workhouses. Ned says that it is the Irish pride. Also, some people believe that those who enter the workhouses will die of disease. There is no effort from the English to relieve this famine except that Indian meal from America was purchased by the Prime Minister. It is sitting in warehouses in case of emergency. To me, it seems that we have an emergency here now. Bloody England! I have images in my mind of the horror that would occur here if the blight strikes this year.

Later we return to our cabin. After the wains are asleep, we kneel at our own bed and say a decade of the rosary together. I now want to stay in the good graces of God. My mother would be proud if she could see me praying. Then we undress and get under the blanket. I feel Ellen's soft warm body next to me. I love her so much. She embraces me. It has been a long time since we were here like this. We are husband and wife again. I am so thankful to God for returning me to this wonderful life, a life that I almost threw away. If my mother could see me now...... Ach. I have to get rid of that thought if I am to perform now what I have been wanting to do all day.

The planting of potatoes goes well this year. I start in my own plot before helping Mr. Bradley and Jimmy. It begins with placing the seed potatoes from last year in the warm sun for a few days to get the buds to start sprouting. After this, I cut the potatoes into slices that contain the sprouting buds, let them sit a day, and then lay the slices on richly manured soil about a foot apart in the field. Then I dig a trench alongside the slices and pile up the earth on top of the potato sprouts. When I'm finished, my field is lined with ridges of dirt. We have been planting potatoes in lazy beds like these for generations. After a few weeks, the stems begin to grow. As they grow, I pile the soil higher on the plants to give the potatoes that much more room to fill out in the ground. Potatoes will be ready to harvest about two to three weeks after the flowers appear. We will dig out the large ones by hand and let the smaller ones continue growing. We are still eating the potatoes we grew last year. It was a good crop, but we will be running out of them before this year's crop is available.

When my plot is planted, I join Mr. Bradley and Jimmy. They are well on their way with their beds of potatoes. When we complete that task, we start on the cash crops to be planted this year. We will have oats, barley, and wheat. These crops will be the principal source of income for the Bradleys for paying their rent on the November gale day.

Ellen tells me that she is pregnant again. My family is growing faster than I wished, but who can plan these things? I guess that I am too fertile. Conception must have happened on Easter evening. After this child, I'll have to practice abstinence of a different kind for a while. Ellen seems pleased about her pregnancy. I don't know why. It means more work and pain for her. For me, it means providing more food at the table. It will be a good year. I just know it.

Pope Gregory XVI dies in June. He has been the head of the church for 15 years. In a little over two weeks, we have a new pontiff. He is named Pius IX. I assume that he is Italian. Aren't they all now? It is just as well. We had an English pope once long ago, and he was the one who gave our country to the English.

Paddy Carlin calls on me. Since I stopped drinking, I haven't seen much of him about. I miss him and I miss the craic we used to have.

"Are ya goin' to the midsummer night bonfire."

"I am, Paddy. What else would I do? This will be my first sober bonfire since I was a young lad."

"Still abstaining are ya? Fair enough."

"What is the talk at Gallagher's? Are there any more troubles with the landlord at Drumbeg."

"Aye. He is still a pain in the arse, but he hasn't evicted anyone lately."

"Good. Let the lads know that I am with them if there is any trouble."

"That is one reason I'm callin'. The Orange order is parading this year."

"They can't. The parade was banned a long time ago."

"They now have permission from Lifford. There will be a parade in Castlefin and another in Castlederg."

"Ach. There will be trouble. I don't think that the constables can protect them if we Catholics decide to put a stop to their arrogance."

"I am shocked to hear ya say that. 'We Catholics.' I thought I'd never get to hear ya say that in me lifetime. Charley, y've changed."

"If I'm not wrong, the parade will be on the twelfth of July. Count me in on visiting Castlefin or Castlederg on that day."

"Please mind yerself. We are not planning on kicking Protestant arse on Orangeman's Day. We are just hoping to make sure that the parade doesn't wander off into Catholic areas. If the parade is peaceful, there will be no trouble."

"Aye. Let's pray for peace, but I hope that there will be enough trouble that the ban on Protestant demonstrations will be reinstated."

We have a grand time at the midsummer night bonfire. I drink cider while my friends are getting pissed on whiskey and poteen. I stay for a while near the music and dancing with Ellen and the wains but later wander up to a noisy group of lads to get some details about Orangeman's Day. They tell me that some are going to join the Aghyaran lads at Castlederg, but more are needed at Castlefin where over fifteen Orange lodges are planning to participate. I agree to meet the lads at Gallagher's on the morning of July 12th and proceed to Castlefin to "protect" the population of Catholics there.

It is Orangeman's Day. Off we go, about forty strong, down the post road to Castlefin. We hear drums in the distance and hope that we aren't late for the festivities. We arrive at the Glebe House where the Orange Orders are assembling. There are bands of musicians and drummers rushing to queue up. Dignified gentlemen are there as well, dressed in their best suits and wearing sashes with Orange emblems on them. All are waiting for the parade to start.

We pass them by and go directly to the Castlefin diamond. There are too many people milling about. It looks as if the parade will march east on the Lifford road to the bridge road, turn right and walk through the town to the diamond. My guess is that the parade will continue to the Protestant church near the bridge. It appears that no Catholic areas will be "invaded."

I haven't seen this many people together in one place since…. since ever. There is no mistaking Protestant from Catholic. The Protestants are well dressed and the Catholics look like they are wearing their field clothes. There are other physical differences as well. The Protestants are well fed and look as if they belong a different race than ourselves. They are descended from Picts and Saxons; we are Gaels. The Protestants have a belligerent look in their eyes, their faces are redder than ours, and their necks are so thick that they seem to spill out over their collars. On the other hand, we look like we are all related to each other. I can't look at another Catholic and not see a facial feature: eyes, ears, nose, mouth, or teeth that I haven't seen in another of my kin. Our hair often looks alike, and we lose it in the same manner and pattern. It seems as if all of our grannys had the same granny. Aye, there is usually no trouble telling Protestants from Catholics except for the Catholics who changed faith to marry or improve their station in life. According to Da, they do this at the expense of burning in hell for eternity. Naturally, I can't distinguish these rascals from ourselves.

There are many people waiting along the streets of the town for the parade to begin. Many are Catholics hoping for a bit of diversion. It is exciting to be there. Constables patrol the streets looking for possible trouble, but everyone seems to be in a jolly mood. Andy Slevin seems to be in charge of the Donaghmore "brigade" … us. He tells us to spread out along the streets where the parade will be routed.

The parade begins. We can hear the bands. As they turn the corner at the top of the hill, we see tall men in top hats who are wearing colourful sashes. They strut down the hill to the diamond. They are sweating and the sweat is rolling off their faces and onto their sashes. Pity they didn't dress in lighter clothes. The bands follow. There will be 17 bands and groups of marching dignitaries from the lodges. I await their arrival at the south end of the diamond.

The first group finally arrives where I am standing. The band members stop the music, but the drummers continue. A fat lad with a big drum starts to bang it with much energy. It is deafening, and he relishes walking over to a group of Catholics who are looking on. His evil smile does annoy them, but they let it go. I stand next to the group in case another musician tries to harass them.

Another lodge goes by, the music is cacophonous, and sure enough another fat drummer goes by with an enormous bass drum. One of the Catholic lads curses him, but the drummer just relishes it and marches right up to the group. I step in and grab the drum and give it a spin. The fat drummer loses his smile and goes down in the street with his huge drum almost on top of him. The Catholic lads laugh and cheer as the band stops marching. A constable is heading my way. I duck into the crowd knowing I'm safe from being arrested, but I hear a riot going on behind me. I turn and see the Catholic lads being beaten by a larger group of Protestants. The constable is trying to create order but is not succeeding. I return, but it is no use. The Catholic lads are being driven off by the Protestants. I'm sorry that I started it. It was my fault.

I walk up the street and stand near the top of the diamond. No problems here. The crowd is solidly pro-Orange. I walk back up to the Lifford Road and try to find someone who needs protection. Most of the Catholics have left, feeling slightly disgusted with the demonstration after witnessing the arrogance of some members of the Orange Order. It is one thing being proud of one's heritage; it is another shoving it into people's faces.

Except for a few minor skirmishes, the parade is relatively peaceful without any of the lodges deciding to march through a Catholic area. If they really wanted that, it would have been a long walk; the march itself was tiring enough on such a warm day.

The Donaghmore Brigade reassembles, and we start our long walk back home. We look at each other. Something is wrong. We sense that something is out of the ordinary when we get just outside Castlefin.

It is the smell which gets stronger when we walk past the farms. It is somewhat like rotten eggs or decaying meat but not exactly. We all have the same thought. Are the potatoes spoiling? They are. The plants in the lazy beds have leaves of brown and black instead of green. We hadn't noticed them in the morning. Now we are running back to Killygordon, hoping that our fields have been spared the blight. All are exhausted when we reach the Cross. As we ascend the road to our farms, the smell is stronger than at Castlefin. We are doomed.

Chapter 10
[1846]

All the farms I pass are crowded with men digging frantically in the soil or cutting the potato stalks. I look at the Bradley plots and then my own. The leaves are black; yesterday they were green. Mr. Bradley and Jimmy are in the fields digging in the hope that the disease has not yet ruined all the potatoes. I rush up and try to help. The smell is overpowering. Jimmy reaches into the ground to see how the spuds are doing. He pulls up a slimy mess that was once a growing potato. I do the same. I pull up what looks like a potato, but it is full of water and collapses in my hand, another piece of slime.

There is panic in Mister Bradley's eyes when he says, "We have to save what we can. Pull out all of the spuds. See if any are edible."

We get to work choosing the brown leaved plants first. Some solid potatoes are found. They are tiny, only a tenth the size of a normal spud. I ask Mr. Bradley to spare some of the brown leaved plants. Just cut the stalk. Maybe, a new stalk will grow from the roots. He tells me that it didn't work last year during the blight in the south. Once the leaves turn, the plant is hopeless. We return to search for more solid spuds. After the Bradley plot is searched, we start on my plot. In all the acreage we planted, only two baskets of solid potatoes are harvested.

That will do us for less than one month of food. Mr. Bradley believes that we should not eat them. They should be our seed potatoes for next year. Even at that, it is not enough to plant plots large enough to feed our families next year. What will we do for our food for the coming year? Our potatoes from last year are already gone.

Up in Glencarn the potato fields are black as well. There are no potatoes worth saving. I walk into my parents' cottage. Da and Ma are just staring at the fire.

Da tells me, "It was a mist that came through our hills. It carried the disease from other parts of the country."

I don't doubt him. That could have been the problem, but it couldn't have been prevented.

"Do you know what we will do now?" I ask.

"Now is the time for England to come to our aid. There is plenty of food here. We don't have to eat only potatoes, y' know."

There is plenty of food. If we can last until the corn harvest, we can use our grain for food. We can mill the grain and make bread and brochan. The problem is that we need to sell the grain to pay our rent in November. For now, we will have to use our stores of oatmeal to last until the harvest.

At Mass on Sunday, Father Boyle speaks to us about the blight. He says that we must pray like we never prayed before to survive this famine. He asks everyone who has friends or relatives in America to write to them and explain our problem. They know how serious this is and will help. He says that he doesn't expect England to help us, at least not quickly enough to do any good. I wonder if Father Boyle will write to our new pope in Rome and ask for charity. Rome must have riches beyond imagination. I mention this to Mister Bradley.

"They'll not help us. Everyone thinks that we have plenty of food in our fields to feed ourselves. They don't know that the food that we harvest is not our own. It belongs to the landlords. Only our Irish emigrants in America can help us."

Although she well knows the answer, Ellen asks if there is any money left in the emergency funds I earned in Scotland. I sadly tell that I used it all for drink. She gives me a grim look and sighs.

"Well, do you know how we can get by?"

"Sadly to say, we are going to have to eat our chickens and our pig after the oatmeal is gone. After that, our parents may help. Maybe their landlords will allow them to miss the payment in November, and we can live on the meal from the harvest."

"And maybe the landlords will evict us."

"Don't be so pessimistic. God will find us a way."

Ma asks me to visit the fairy spring with her. We had visited soon after I recovered from the drink, but we saw no saint or banshee. Ma thinks that her saint will give us the help we need if we pray to her. We climb the hill and enter the lovely glade around the spring. No lady is to be found. No apparition. Ma kneels and I kneel, as well. She starts the rosary and I join in. When we finish she prays,

"Please dear saint, help us through this trying time. Please let my family survive the great hunger that is to come. I ask you this in the name of the Father, the Son, and the Holy Ghost."

"Amen," I add.

I talk my problem over with Da at his cottage. He is well aware that I have no crops of my own, and Ned Bradley will not be able to pay me for working his land. I am penniless. Da knows that I will have to rely on others for my family's survival, meaning himself and my father-in-law. He looks worried; he has his own problems meeting his rent and feeding his family. He says that he will help us and everyone in his family who needs it if he can. We will have to pool our resources. First, he says, we must sell any possession we can spare to buy food at the market in Ballybofey or at Kelly's store at the Cross. When the food from these sales is gone, we have to sell our livestock. We have to cut down on the food we eat to make it last. We will have to eat turnips and even the roots of wild plants. It will be hard, but there is no choice unless the government gives us relief.

We have few possessions to sell except our clothing. I bring what little we can spare to the Ballybofey market and get little in return. I try to see what our pig will fetch at the market. Although he has grown a bit since May when I bought him, the price of a pig his size isn't much more than the price I paid for him. It is hardly worth selling him, and I can't keep him because we have no peelings to feed him. We will have to slaughter our pig to feed the family.

I try to buy oatmeal at the market with the money I received for the clothes and two chairs I sold, but the price seems too high. I try Mack Kelly's store at the Cross; the cost is higher still. I am feeling that free trade is not working here in Ireland.

I have our pig and two hens. That is the sum of my livestock. We will eat them all and then decide what comes next. Mr. Bradley has two horses, one cow, one pig, and several chickens including a cock. I tell him of the poor sales price he will get for them in Ballybofey and Stranorlar, and he makes up his mind. He will keep his cow which provides milk, but his chickens and pig have a poor future ahead of them. They will be killed and eaten. We will have no feed for them, and they will starve anyway. The cow will be driven up to the pastures to graze during the day and driven home at night.

Da has several animals including sheep that he probably will sell, even at low prices. He will just keep the animals he believes he needs, such as the donkey and horses. Of course, his chickens and pig are to be tasty meals for his family. For the months of August and September, we all will be on a carnivorous diet, one that we are not used to. The hunger will be worse when the meat is gone.

With chickens and pigs gone, the hills are strangely quiet in the mornings. There are no pigs grunting, cocks crowing, or hens quarrelling. The only livestock we hear are occasional cows lowing and horses neighing. We live in unusual times.

We try fishing. The river is full of trout and salmon at this time of year. Our problem is that the landowners allow no one to fish on their property without purchasing a permit. There is no free fishing along the entire length of the Finn, but I sneak down east of the Dromore Bridge with my brother and give it a go. We are there for less than an hour when a constable tells us to leave. We return home with plans to fish the pools along the Mourne Beg instead. The main classes of fish there are perches and eels. A salmon would be grand, but we would have to walk to the River Derg to have any chance for them.

Mr. Bradley asks his land agent about the November rent. The agent tells him that the landlord is sympathetic with his tenants in this time of trouble. He will reduce the rent by a quarter. This will give us extra grain at the time of harvest. We hope that we will have a good harvest with enough meal to eat through the winter.

The harvest at the Bradleys is successful. Ned had planted oats, barley, and wheat on his 22 acres. After cutting, stooking, stacking, thatching, threshing, and riddling, we load the barrels of grain on our cart and take them to the mill at Navenny. The miller is wise to the free trade system in times of hunger and takes a larger percentage of the meal in payment for drying and grinding the grain. We accept. What can we do? Days later we barrel up the meal and take it to market to sell. So far, there is still a good market for oatmeal. We only sell what the landlord requires and take the rest home for ourselves. We have no idea how long it will last because we never had to subsist on oatmeal alone.

Out of charity, Da's landlord, Reverend Delap, also decreases the rent on his land by half for a year. Many of Reverend Delap's tenants visit him in Monellan after hearing of this, and loudly cheer him when he leaves for St. Anne's on Sunday. News of his benevolence travels widely through the parish.

In Drumbeg, there is no such charity for the tenants of James Hanley. He expects full payment in November.

Andy Slevin is forming a secret whiteboy group in anticipation of trouble after the November gale. Many of the same lads who protected the Catholics at the Orange parade have joined. James Hanley is their main target, as well as some of the merchants who are unfairly profiting from the panic selling of personal property. Paddy Carlin tells me that Andy will ask me to participate. I don't know. My feelings about it at this time are not strong.

Except for my Da's cousin James and his family, who live on Hanley land, the family of my great-aunt Mary McMenamin live in the part of Drumbeg owned by Alex Devenny. Mr. Devenny is lowering his rent by a quarter like the majority of Donaghmore landlords. He wants to give his tenants a chance to survive the winter, unlike the despicable James Hanley.

Gallagher's Alehouse is empty most days. Paddy Gallagher is feeling the poverty of the farmers as much as the lot of us. There is inexpensive moonshine still available in Drumbeg thanks to my great-aunt Mary McMenamin. Mary is now 81 years of age and is no longer taking an active part in the distilling, but her sons still manage to produce a few kegs. In general, the amount of poteen consumed in our parish is down considerably, as much because of Father Mathew's Abstinence Association as the poverty created by the potato blight.

In September, news of starvation deaths throughout Ireland reaches Donaghmore. Most of the deaths are of the people who have little or no land. There is no work and therefore no wages for them. They can't afford the food prices, and they refuse to enter the workhouses which they believe will tear apart their families, and where they suspect that disease is rampant. Even our own workhouse in Stranorlar, which can hold 400 paupers, has only 125 living there at the present time.

Normally my family and I would be considered good candidates for the workhouse because we only have a quarter acre of land with no cash crops, but I am fortunate to have relatives nearby who can feed us. This makes me feel a bit ashamed of my dependency on them. I should be able to carry my own weight. Other than working hard on the Bradley land, I don't know what to do to improve our situation.

Although it appears that we will have enough oatmeal to get by for a few months, I hear that the meal available at Kelly's store at the Cross is getting scarce. What he does have is sold at a higher price. When I ask Mack if he is doing this just to make a bigger profit, he tells me that it is the millers who are raising the prices, not himself. They are holding on to most of their flour and meal to drive prices up. The local millers in Donegal and Tyrone have made a secret pact to keep most of their stock for winter when demand will be greatest, and then they will sell it for enormous profit.

I believe that these greedy merchants are other appropriate targets for the Drumbeg whiteboys.

The Bradleys pay their rent in November. Through the generosity of their landlord, Mr. Bradley saved enough meal from the miller to feed us for the next four or five months, as long as we can stretch it. We must find simple ways of serving it. Ellen plans on making oatmeal cakes by roasting the meal between leaves of cabbage on the fire. It is a simple meal and one that requires no other ingredients.

My uncle Charley has a plot of turnips this year. He is willing to share them with his relatives. I have never eaten turnips, but I believe that I am going to start this year and learn to love them.

Ma tells us that nettles make a fine soup. These are the weeds that grow around abandoned buildings and on uncultivated soil. They are everywhere, but they have to be picked carefully because they have stinging hairs that irritate the skin. Ma says that they can be boiled without removing the stinging hairs. They are fine in the soup. Who would have believed that stinging nettles would become a large part of our diet?

Word is getting out that a group of landlords is visiting America looking for donations of food and money. We wish them great success.

Only one tenant of James Hanley, Rory McCabe, fails to pay his November rent even after selling his animals. McCabe built an outhouse for those same animals earlier in the summer. Hanley found out about it and raised the rent. Hanley's other tenants manage to avoid eviction again, possibly because their families pooled all their funds to make sure they made their gale. The McCabes have no family nearby and have no choice but to enter the workhouse after eviction. The bailiffs arrive to batter in the door and tear down the roof of the McCabe cottage. Later the home will be levelled. Hanley has plans to turn this part of the townland into pasture for his cattle. The destruction is watched sullenly by the other families in the townland. I know that Andy Slevin is there, silently planning revenge.

Andy calls on me soon after the eviction.

"Charley, will ya help us punish Hanley for what he's done to the poor McCabes? Those unfortunate people are now in the workhouse for just comin' up a bit short of full payment for their rent."

"Did they pay their rent in May?"

"They did not, but that still doesn't excuse Hanley for his lack of consideration for the times we are in. He has to show some sympathy for the poor farmer."

"What would you like me to do, Andy?"

"I need ya to deliver a message to Hanley at his estate in Mullingar."

"I don't know where that is. Why don't you lads do it?"

"He has private guards at his estate. They know us all too well from past evictions. Y'll be able to get close to the property."

"I hate getting mixed up in this, but I'll do it for you. Who is going to write the letter?"

"Pete can write; he went to the National School at Laught. He will deliver it to ya tonight and tell you how to find the manor. Thank you, Charley."

I leave my cottage in the morning while it is still dark and walk through Killygordon and up the hill to Mullingar. I can't miss seeing the manor with the wall around his estate. As the sun is starting to lighten the sky, I walk to the front gate and ring the bell there. Soon a guard comes to the gate.

"Another piece of shite from the hills." he says. "What the fook do ya want?"

"I have a letter for the master of the house."

"Shove it through the gate, ya eejit."

I don't fancy his attitude. I must teach him some manners.

"The judge wants me to get a signature to prove that the letter was delivered."

The guard is an illiterate Irishman like myself. I'm certain that he can't write his own name.

"Judge? Wha' fookin' judge?"

"Judge Fairfax of Lifford."

He reluctantly unlocks the gate and pushes it open muttering, "Ya could have pushed the receipt through the gate, as well. Ya fookin' eejit."

I take the letter and hand it to him as I smash his fat face with a quick punch with my left fist. The letter falls from his hand as he hits the earth with a thump. He reaches for his pistol, but I am almost out of his sight as I run like hell down the road to Killygordon.

I tell Andy what had happened. The message was delivered but not as elegantly as he wished. I ask what the letter said. He says,

"To the tyrant of Donaghmore,

This is to notify you that you will be punished for your hateful acts against your tenants. Your punishment will fit the nature of your crimes and will include your death if anyone else suffers from your cruelty."

It is signed, "The Black Hand of Donaghmore"

I thought that the letter was poorly written. The Black Hand of Donaghmore? Jesus, how bloody stupid does that sound?

December arrives, and we have only a bit of meal left from the Bradley harvest. Our pigs and chickens have been killed and eaten. We are eating some turnips and cabbage from my Uncles' farms to supplement the brochan we make from the cornmeal. Obviously, we go hungry most of the time. With Ellen pregnant, she gets most of my share of the food along with the children. We all are getting thinner. It shows mostly in our faces, the tightness around the jaws and the darkness around the eyes.

I go to Ballybofey to see if there is any work available. There is nothing there. The town is a depressing sight. Most of the shops are closed. There are beggars up and down the street looking like skeletons; some look near death. There are families in rags walking through the town to the workhouse in Stranorlar. After seeing the hopelessness there, I return home passing other beggars heading up lanes to cottages to beg for whatever scraps the farmers can part with. Occasionally one will call at our cottage, and Ellen will part with one of our precious turnips. These are sad times.

Ellen is almost ready to deliver. Her mother and sister Mary stay with her on Christmas eve when the rest of us walk to the Cross for midnight Mass. As always, Christmas Mass is celebrated outdoors; the chapel can't contain the large numbers of worshippers at this Mass. We stand in the cold night air as Father Boyle prays loudly to God in the Latin words we almost know by heart. Many parishioners shouldn't be there. Weakened by hunger, some of the old ones fall to the hard ground and are aided by their families. I say prayers that they live through the night. God doesn't expect their sacrifice. Living through this hell on earth is sacrifice enough.

I arrive home to find that Ellen has delivered our baby. Born on Christmas Day! She and the baby are fine. I am warmly congratulated by her mother and Mary. Ellen is smiling at me when I go to see her. The baby is squirming in her arms when I lean over to kiss her; then I kiss the baby. It looks healthy enough.

"This is a fine evening for you to have a baby. Did you have a hard time of it?"

"I did not. The angels brought the baby to me."

She looks a bit weak. I don't believe her.

I ask, "I guess you'll soon be telling me if it is a caudie or a cutty. I haven't all night, you know. I need my sleep."

She laughs, "It is a wee boy. We will name him Jesus."

I laugh. "We will not. He will be Patrick, named after my brother. It was long ago decided."

"I know. Jesus will be his confirmation name."

We are up the rest of the night anyway. Mr. Bradley offers me a glass of whiskey. I refuse, of course. That night and next day are a break from the horror of the great hunger we are going through. Patrick will be the only one fat and happy for the next year or so as long as his mother can produce his milk. I, along with the whole Bradley family, will continue to sacrifice our rations so that Ellen is fed and stays healthy until Patrick is weaned.

We bring Patrick to the Cross to be baptised two days after Christmas. Carney and Bridget Conaghan are the godparents. Carney is still fighting at the fairs where he makes some money, but not as much as he did in the past. His family is suffering like the rest of us.

As Parish Priest, Father Boyle is privy to the rumours and facts about whatever action the government is taking about the famine. He tells us that there are grain depots in some of the larger cities which are selling Indian meal at low prices to the public, but none are anywhere near here. He says that the government has begun some public work projects. They are building broad roads a few miles north of Stranorlar. He tells us to apply to the Board of Works inspector near the Stranorlar workhouse.

"The inspector will have your name from the Relief Commission's list of eligible labourers. He will give you a ticket to work on the road project. Bring the ticket and a spade with you and come here in the morning before dawn. A man from the parish will walk you to the work site. It is a long walk. The wages are 10 pence a day if you get there early enough."

The road project is about seven miles from here. I consider my options. I have none. I will work on the road project.

The Christening celebration for my son Patrick is small. The refreshments are meagre. There is a famine going on, for God's sake. Ned Bradley and Carney finish Ned's bottle of whiskey. There will be no more whiskey around this place for a long time.

I walk to the inspector's office in Stranorlar the next day. The clerk there asks my name and townland. I wait as he looks up my name in a ledger. He finally marks his book and gives me a work ticket. I ask how my name got there. He tells me that the landlords gave the commission the information. I marvel at their efficiency.

I show up at the chapel the next morning in the cold darkness. About thirty men are there with their spades. Carney is among them. He must have gone to the inspector's office yesterday as well. We start the long walk to the work site at Meenavoy. It is getting light when we arrive and show our tickets to a crew leader. There are hundreds here. We are assigned a location where another crew leader tells us what we are to do. We follow his orders and join the rest in digging out rocks and levelling an area for the proposed road. A number of women are there who are breaking rocks with small hammers. All is madness here.

At noon, we stop for supper. Our meal is a full potato, boiled in a cauldron by the side of the work site. Where did they find potatoes in Ireland? It is lovely. It puts a warm feeling in my stomach that brings back memories of never being hungry. It could have used a bit of salt and butter, but I am grateful for the taste of it.

Work stops at sunset and we queue up for our wages. I finally stand before the paymaster, and I am given ten pennies. During the walk back to Donaghmore, every one of us is pleased that at least we can buy a bit of food for our families. The potato supper was a surprise to us. We will all be back tomorrow.

I stop at the Bradleys before going home, and tell them about my day. Mr. Bradley and Jimmy say that they will apply for a work ticket tomorrow. I walk to Glencarn and tell Da about the job. He says that he will advise his nephews to apply for work as well.

And so it goes. Every day, more and more of my friends and kin are walking the road through Stranorlar to Meenavoy. There are at least a hundred of us. We work hard all day and receive our supper; supper is a bowl of stir-about and a biscuit now, no more potatoes. If it isn't for Carney telling the new workers about the potatoes, my relatives would think that I lied to them about our delicious meal.

One afternoon on the job, Carney walks over to me and says,
"Do y' notice the men sitting in the cars over there and the men talking to them?"
"Aye. What about them?"
"They haven't done a lick of work all day, but watch them at supper and at pay time. They receive their meal and wages just like the rest of us."

I do notice them. Carney is right. There are about fifteen men who just get paid for showing up at the job. They play cards and dice all day. It does not seem fair.

Carney asks the crew boss about the men. He tells them that they are friends of the supervisors. No one questions why they are here. Anyone who objects to them gets thrown off the job.

Carney gets more angry about the freeloaders each day. Finally he explodes when he sees one of them getting a bowl of stir-about.

"This man gets no food. He did not a lick of work all day," he tells the kitchen worker.

The man spooning out the stir-about appears nervous. He looks around for support. Carney takes matters in his own hands. He knocks the bowl from the freeloader's hands. The man just stands there and sneers at Carney. Carney brings him to the ground with a right hook to his head. Whistles blow and constables rush to the site. I and some of our lads try to block their way, but we are clubbed by the constables. It takes three constables to pin Carney to the ground. A foreman comes over.

"Send this man away. Get a good look at him. He will never work on this project again."

Carney struggles, but the burly constables drag him off the work site and give him a shove. Carney falls down but gets up and charges into the nearest constable. He is clubbed unconscious by one of the other constables. They leave him there by the road. When we are done for the day, he isn't there. I feel bad that I couldn't have helped him more, but my family will suffer for it if I am banned from the works project.

chapter 11
(1847)

I am earning three shillings a week which buys one stone of oatmeal at Kelly's store. With Indian cornmeal being sold at the markets, the price for oatmeal has dropped a bit. The millers' control on the grain market is over. In two months, the price for one stone of meal had dropped from almost five shillings to three.

A stone, 14 pounds, of meal a week is only two pounds of food a day. This is just barely enough to feed my family. Before the famine, I was eating about two pounds of potatoes a day myself. Now all of us have to live on two pounds of food. No wonder we are getting skinnier. Ellen is still nursing Paddy, so I give her some of my share of the brochan she heats over the fire. Even so, her face is getting leaner and dark circles are forming around her eyes. There is one good thing, however. Ellen has lost weight in her belly and arse. Before the potatoes failed, she had been porking it up a bit. I must admit that now she has a lovely figure. It is hard for me to say something like this with all the starvation and death around us, but it seems as if the famine has been kind to Ellen's appearance.

The money I earn is justification for my long tiresome days. I leave home at four in the morning and arrive home at eight at night. I am barely getting enough sleep.

The snow in February keeps us from earning full wages. No work can be done with snow on the ground. We walk to the job site anyway. A paymaster is there, and after checking our tickets, he pays us five pennies each and sends us home. With no supper for us and the lower wages, we will be experiencing the hunger that we had back in December. Fortunately before we finish the last of our cornmeal, the ground clears, and we return to work at full pay.

It is time to start preparing the fields for the summer crops. Our problem is that there is no seed. We consumed our seed corn in November. Naturally, this worries us all. I understand that it worries the British government, as well. England depends on the grain imports from Ireland to survive. Maybe England will go hungry like the rest of us.

Ash Wednesday comes and Lent begins. I remember the fasting and abstaining from meat that we had to do in the past. God has made it easy for us to fast this year. Frequently, I visit the fairy spring on Sundays, the only day of the week that I don't have to work. As usual, there is no saint or banshee there. I am starting to wonder if the lady I saw last year was an illusion.

The Quaker religion, of which I am not familiar, has opened a soup kitchen in Stranorlar near the workhouse. God bless them. Anyone can stand in a queue and enter a formerly abandoned building where there is a cauldron boiling some stir-about. The soup kitchen has arrived at the right moment. There had been deaths from starvation almost every day in the twin towns of Stranorlar and Ballybofey. The soup is available to everyone. It is nice to know there is some chance that we can survive if I can no longer earn wages at Meenavoy.

Word has it that the work projects will close. In its place, soup kitchens will be set up at more convenient locations throughout the country. Anyone in need will be eligible for the free food. Until then, I report everyday at Meenavoy.

Apparently the project at Meenavoy is continuing on its own momentum although there was never a need for the road. It was just a meaningless government relief project. Nevertheless, the Relief Commission rules to limit the workers on road projects to only those living on less than ten acres of land. This requires us to get new tickets from the works inspector, who has the records of the amount of land each applicant holds. This new order excludes the Bradleys from the project. It also excludes many residents of Drumbeg who were working on the project. The main purpose of this rule is to encourage people with large farms to till the land for this year's crops. Rumours tell us that the government will somehow supply seeds to distressed farmers.

Mister Bradley sells one of his horses at the March fair in Stranorlar. He will live on the proceeds of that sale until he has to sell the other. His landlord, Reverend Hemmings, has provided him with seed potatoes from America and seed corn from Europe to plant this year. Of course, the quantity of seed is quite a bit less than we planted in previous years. The sowing will be started soon. With me working on the road project, Mister Bradley and Jimmy have to do the planting by themselves this year. After they start, they get some help from the McCormick and McGlinchy families.

Reverend Delap gives seed to his tenants as well, including my father. The British treasury lent these landlords money for the seed to encourage them to help their tenants in these distressing times. The government motto that applies here is, "property has its duties as well as its rights." A problem with this responsibility is that the landlords are getting hit with much debt. They are financing almost all of the relief, the workhouse, the public works, and future government soup kitchens. It is hard to be sympathetic to the landlords, but we have some fine ones here in Donaghmore, and we certainly don't wish them ruin.

There is one exception. The landlord James Hanley has resisted helping any of his tenants. He turned down the purchase of seed. He knows that if they can't plant their fields this year he will have the right to evict them all in November. One gale can be left hanging but not two. He sees that his dreams of cattle pasturage in Drumbeg will come to pass in just a few months. I know there will be trouble. Andy Slevin and the lads will not be evicted without a struggle. I wonder if Mr. Hanley knows that he is putting his life and the lives of his family in jeopardy with his actions.

With famine fever rampant in the workhouse and among the beggars in the streets, a fever hospital is added to the Stranorlar workhouse. Famine fever seems to be extremely contagious, and even though we know of no one in the hills who are afflicted, all of us are warned to stay away from anyone who appears ill. Many who come into Ballybofey on the Glenfin road are suspected of being from the Glenties where the disease is widespread.

In May, the soup kitchens open in Donaghmore. The one at the Cross is in a building near the alehouse. It has come at the right time. The public works in Meenavoy closed, and I have no money. At first, only destitute people are eligible. I am considered destitute because I hold so little land.

We must first stand in a queue outside the kitchen until a number of us are let in. The whole family must be there, including the wains. Soup is poured into the quart cups we bring from home. We have cups for the wains which Ellen and I hand to the kitchen worker. The wains receive a half cup of the hot liquid. We all receive a piece of bread as well. After exiting the back of the building, we sit on the ground and consume our day's provisions. We come here every day but Sunday when the kitchen is closed. On Saturday, two rations are given. There must be a better way. We borrow the extra cups we need on Saturday from the Bradleys.

What is in the soup? I am not sure; but it seems to be rice, cornmeal, and water. Sometimes I detect a bit of meat and some cabbage. On some days there is no soup; a loaf of bread is substituted.

I ask one of the workers why they don't just give us meal to take to our homes. It would be easier for everyone. He tells me that there are healthier ingredients in the soup besides cornmeal. He also tells me that the government suspects that if they just give out the meal, many would just sell it to buy tobacco, tea, or even whiskey. They just may have a point there.

At first, the Bradleys are not eligible for the free soup. How does the government expect them to survive until harvest? This rule changes in a few weeks. Almost all the farmers in Donaghmore are now in the soup queue every day. A second kitchen opens at the school in Ballinacor.

Of course, we pay no rent in May. Few of the farmers have any income, and this is understood by the landlords. We hope to pay something in November after the harvest, but as of now, we leave one gale hanging.

I'll not be able to pay rent to my father-in-law now or in November. Mister Bradley is officially my landlord, and this is how I am able to pass the test for destitution when relief is being passed out. I hold only a quarter acre of land. As long as my family is able to get outdoor relief at the soup kitchen, we are no longer a burden to my father-in-law. Maybe I can help my in-laws later, when I harvest the green vegetables we planted on my wee plot of land.

Most of our fields have now been sown, but a member of the Society of Friends calls on us and gives us some Swedish turnip seeds. Again, I say God bless them. We plant them in the unsown areas of the Bradley farm. If the blight returns, at least we will have the turnips.

News comes that the government is building a National School in Gleneely. Some surveyors are coming to the farm of Henry Bradley, a cousin of my father-in-law. Word of their coming spreads quickly through the parish, and there is a big crowd of men waiting for the surveyors when they arrive. They say that it will be a good-sized building with two fireplaces, one at each end. A work boss arrives with the surveyors, and he hires about ten men on the spot to do the work. Andy Moss from Aghyaran Parish known for his fine stonework is among them.

Work begins and the building is finished in just a couple of weeks. Some of the stones came from Drumbeg where James Hanley graciously gave them to the school from houses he had tumbled. The roofing was done by a tradesman in Killygordon who installs slate roofs. The finished school is grand. There are two sets of long desks facing each of the fireplaces so that classes of older and younger children can be instructed together. The schooling will begin after harvest in October. Perhaps my children can attend in a couple of years, God willing.

Mister Bradley tells me that Daniel O'Connell died. O'Connell was on a pilgrimage to Rome when he passed away. I know nothing about the man, but I nod my head gravely when he tells me. What he did for the Irish people, I have no idea. I can see no benefits here, but he must have been well loved by people of my Da's age.

While standing in the queue at the soup kitchens, we hear astounding things. We all know that there are paupers starving and dying in the Glenties. It seems that the workhouses there are full, and the relief commissioners are paying passage to British America to qualified paupers. The landlords there believe that it is cheaper to pay for the people to emigrate than it is to support them in the workhouses. I don't believe we are that much of a burden here. The workhouse in Stranorlar is only half full. Most of us should be off relief when the fall harvest comes in.

We hear of a tragedy that occurred along the Donegal road near Lough Mourne. A number of men from Taughboy were gathering their sheep when they came upon a family of five who died in a ditch. They must have been travelling to Stranorlar from the south when they had to spend the night there. They probably died of famine fever and exposure to the weather. The men went home and returned with spades to bury them in the ditch where they died. We hear such sad stories almost every day.

My great-aunt, Mary McMenamin, dies in July. She was 82 years of age. Her family holds a two day wake in Drumbeg with none of the usual drinking that goes on at such wakes. Most poteen production ended with the start of the famine. It is even unlawful for anyone to distil legal and taxable whiskey now because of the grain shortage.

Word of her death spreads throughout the area. Hundreds attend her wake. She was well loved.

On the second night of the wake, everyone is shocked when her prodigal son, Mickey, arrives. All remember that Mickey abandoned his family long ago. He is living in Fermanagh with a second wife and a second family. How he heard of his mother's death is a mystery. There is much whispering as he walks into the cottage to pray over the body. He walks out, talks to no one, and disappears into the night.

There is a rumble of mutterings both outside the cottage and within. I walk over to his brother Denis.

"Was that who I thought it was?"

"Aye. I can't believe that he would have the gall to come here after all these years... and with Agnes and his children standing there in the same room. Wouldn't you think that he would speak to someone in the family, at least?"

"He's the devil, that one," says his brother, Patrick.

"Maybe it is better he left without a row," I say. "I'm sure that it was uncomfortable enough for himself as well as for his family."

The next day, Mickey stops at our cottage. He knows me from the trip I took to Fermanagh with his brother when I was younger. He must have asked about my whereabouts. I despise the man, but I take some pity on him when I see his shrunken appearance. The famine has been hard on him.

He says, "I heard of Mam's death from the Kellys. I'm on the way to America with me family."

"What happened? Did you lose your farm?"

"Aye. Me landlord gave me tickets for a ship out of Derry if I gave up me lease. Me family was too much of a burden on him."

"Where is your family?"

He laughs sadly.

"They are living in a ditch by the Derry road. I left them there so that I could ask the Kellys about finding their son Charles in America. We must have been passing Ballybofey when Mam died. It is a queer coincidence. The Lord works in mysterious ways."

I ask him about his children. He tells me that he had five, but the youngest died. He stopped at our home now to ask if I had any food to give them. He had been begging through the towns, and he was able to get soup from the Quakers at Stranorlar. I tell him that we only have a wee bit of cornmeal and some turnips.

"I don't have any cooking utensils, but the turnips will be lovely. Thank ya. Sorry to trouble ya."

He leaves. I now pity him and his innocent family. I hope that they make it to America, but I have my doubts about it.

It is September. The potato plants had flowered and look fine. They have already produced edible spuds. Some turnips have been picked, and the wheat we planted is looking grand, as well. Because we had only enough seed to plant about a third of the Bradley land this year, it will not be enough to pay our rent. We are hoping that our landlord will give us another discount, and we expect that he will. This will benefit him in the long run because the poor law requires him to support his tenants in some fashion. If all the potatoes survive, we can live through most of the winter.

We harvest all of our crops in October. Reverend Hemmings asks us to give him half of the grain for our rent. With the potatoes and money from the grain, we have high hopes for the future. It is a good thing because the soup kitchens will close at the end of the month.

With a poor harvest, James Hanley's tenants can't pay their rent in November. They haven't paid rent since the May of a year ago. Every one of his tenants in Drumbeg are evicted in a show of force under the direction of the sheriff and Hanley's land agent. The agent, the sheriff, and a few constables arrive on horseback with bailiffs following in a wagon bearing the equipment to destroy the cabins. The occupants were warned by an eviction notice earlier in the week. Some remain in their cabins, but most have taken their belongings outside and are waiting for a last minute miracle that the landlord has changed his mind.

A large number of men of the parish, including myself, have shown up to show support and help for the poor people of Drumbeg. A man shouts out to the land agent,

"Don't do it. You'll meet death if you evict these unfortunate people."

Everyone looks at the angry man. He is another resident of Drumbeg but not of Hanley's. A constable writes something down in a book he has with him.

The sheriff reads the notice of eviction, calls the names of the residents, and officially offers them admission to the workhouse. After that he hands the notice to the agent who turns to the bailiffs. He says grimly,

"Get on with it then."

The occupants of the first cabin are standing outside, except they failed to remove their possessions. Some ragged looking men hired for the day go into the cabin and take out beds, chairs, and other furniture. There is keening and shrieking from the people as these house wreckers climb the thatched roof and saw down the main beam across the roof. The roof collapses as others use crowbars to tear the door off its hinges and to rip the windows from their sills.

With the first cabin out of the way, the group moves on to the home of Andy Slevin's family. Andy knows that it is useless fighting the armed group that is advancing on his place. He believes that he will get his revenge later, and it is not worth dying for a hopeless cause. He just stands cursing the agent in the most vile language imaginable. When his roof is collapsed, he switches his language to a more threatening nature, calling out the misfortunes that will come on the landlord, his agent, and their families.

Eight cabins are tumbled. Four families will enter the workhouse. The other families will stay temporarily with relatives in the parish. My friend Andy and his family will stay with his brother's family in Gortichar. My friend Peter's family will stay with kin in Ballyarrel. The parents of my distant cousins Kevin and Mickey are staying in Drumbeg, except they are moving in with their uncle Patrick. I don't know the other families, but they are staying with relatives in the parish. Most of the families have young single adults in the household who will have to find work somewhere or emigrate from Ireland.

Andy comes to me during one of the house tumblings and asks if I will help him in his revenge against his landlord. I think about it and say,

"Aye. It will be my pleasure."

The first meeting of the "Black Hand" is held late one night in one of the deserted, tumbled houses in Drumbeg. About fifteen young lads are there. Andy has taken leadership and has given himself the name, "Captain Midnight." The "Black Hand" and now "Captain Midnight." I am starting to wonder if I want to be a part of this organization. Captain Midnight asks if I would like a secret name.

"Wha? Ah no..no."

I know that there is hatred boiling inside each of these lads. They have suffered at the hand of an evil landlord. I don't have the hate, but I want the justice.

Andy tells us that it is not only Hanley that is the problem. There are tyrannical landlords in Stranorlar and Glenfin as well. We must strike terror in their hearts and take back what has been taken from us.

I don't know what he means about taking things back, although I am for spreading the terror. The guilty landlords should not get away with the suffering they cause.

Andy asks, "Are ya with us?"

I think about what can come from this; the years away from my family at the Lifford jail, or God forbid, at Botany Bay. I know that I shouldn't be here. My family should come first, but there is something here that is more important than my own welfare. The welfare of many families is at stake here.

"I'm with yis, but I'll take no part in murder or in harming innocent people."

"I respect that," says the Captain. "If there is any killing, I want to do it meself. First comes the terror. Will ya help me by bringin' another letter to Hanley?"

"Aye. I can do that."

Pete Gallagher, alias the Bishop, writes a threatening note like the one we delivered last year.

It says,

"You have been warned and now you must pay. Death to you and your family...... The Black Hand."

"That is a bit severe isn't it?" I ask. "Hanley's family?"

"I won't harm his family. It is only to frighten him."

Both Andy and I go to Hanley's estate in the dark of night. There will be no walking up to the house this time. We walk to the rear of the property, we cover our faces with scarves that conceal everything except our eyes, and we climb the wall. Our plan is to nail the letter to Hanley's back door. We drop to the ground on the inside of the compound and creep up to the house. All too soon, dogs start barking. The barks turn into growls and we see two great vicious dogs running at us. We can't climb the wall fast enough; the dogs grab and tear our trousers. Finally we shake them off and get over the wall and into the fields.

"Do you still have the letter?" I ask.

"I do. We need a better plan."

The Black Hand stations a member outside the Hanley estate. When Hanley's carriage leaves the estate, he is to jump on the carriage and thrust the letter into the passenger's hands, whether it is Hanley or not. There is a great amount of snow in December, and the carriage doesn't leave for days. The unfortunate Black Hander has to stand around in the cold every day until a thaw occurs that allows the occupants of the manor to leave by carriage. Finally one day, the gates open. The carriage appears with a male and female occupant. The Black Hander puts on his scarf and runs to the coach with the letter in his hand. He slips on some melting ice and falls. The letter flutters out of his hand, and the wind takes it into the fields. He watches it fly away until it is no longer in sight.

chapter 12
(1848)

"Maybe we should just post it at the Killygordon post office," says Captain Midnight.

We are now meeting in the snow at a different abandoned cottage in Drumbeg. It has been two months since we proposed threatening James Hanley. As far as we know, he is still happy with his takeover of the land and knows nothing of the hatred boiling in the hearts of his former tenants. The land we are meeting in tonight will soon be grazing land for herds of Hanley's cattle in the spring. We agree to take a different approach. We'll nail the letter to the door of Hanley's manor house, but we will do it with numbers on our side. Our society is now twenty lads. All of us will storm the manor in the dead of night. Mickey Gallen, who has his father's musket, will shoot one of the dogs. The rest of us will bring clubs to kill the other. Once inside the manor's walls, Mickey will go into the stables and kill Hanley's horses.

At midnight, we walk to Mullingar by a roundabout way through fields covered in snow. Peter, the Bishop, carries the new letter. Carney Conaghan is with us as well. It didn't take much for me to convince him of the need to put an end to landlord cruelty.

We arrive at the wall. Andy and I climb to the top first. The others then climb it and crouch along the top. Someone remarks that we look like gargoyles. I don't understand what he is talking about. The wall is lined with masked men waiting for the chance to cause mayhem. Andy and I drop to the ground, and as expected, the dogs run from the house growling. When one jumps at me, I swing my club and smash him in the head. He cries out and comes back at me. Mickey shoots him and reloads as other Black Hand members drop and beat the second dog to death. Andy and I rush the house with clubs in our hands. Just then, two guards appear from the house and begin shooting. This is not in our plans. We stop and retreat. We are the last of the lads climbing back over the wall. Fortunately no one was hit during the shooting. We didn't figure on Hanley having guards on duty at this hour. Still no letter is delivered, although I believe that Hanley is aware of our intentions now.

All of the homes in Drumbeg, as well as other homes nearby, are visited by the constables the following day. One of Hanley's guards is with them. He can identify no one. Not only were we all masked last night, but it was too dark to see. The constables know that the evicted tenants of Hanley were the responsible parties. They warn the people that the eyes of the law are on each and every one of them.

Ellen tells me that she is pregnant again. Now I believe that I am being totally irresponsible in joining the mad lads of the Black Hand. I decide that I will attend no more meetings.

The Black Hand continues without me. They finally deliver the letter. It is nailed on the office door of Hanley's land agent, John Harrison. Why didn't we think of that before?

A week later, a horse that was pulling a car and driver is killed by musket fire in an ambush on the road to Lifford. I know that the Black Hand is behind it. The only problem is that the horse and car belonged to Magistrate Mansfield of Killygordon. Magistrate Mansfield has been a decent landlord, and there was no reason for the killing. My guess is that someone believed it was Hanley's car. It was another stupid action by the "Hand." I am happy that I am not a part of this careless group any longer.

My cousin Mickey stops by on a snowy afternoon in March. He tells me that they have captured one of the bailiffs from the Drumbeg tumbling. They are keeping him prisoner in a deserted cow byre in Cronalaghy. I feel that I should at least go to make sure that Andy does no more mischief. Mickey and I walk up to the byre and are greeted by Peter and Andy as well as a few others from the "Hand." They are masked and they tell us to cover our faces before entering to see the bailiff. The prisoner is tied securely and seated on the floor. He looks like he was beaten and mistreated, but there is a more serious problem here. He doesn't look like any of the bailiffs at the Drumbeg tumblings. As a matter of fact, he is one of the lads who worked on the Meenavoy road project with me. I don't recall seeing him at the cottage tumblings.

"Jesus An... I mean Captain. He isn't guilty of anything. I'm not sure he is even a bailiff."

The prisoner answers, "I am a farmer from Carnowen. I'm no bailiff. I've been tellin' ya that."

Andy slaps him. The prisoner's face is already bruised badly.

"Jimmy and Paddy say that they remember him at Drumbeg. They are sure that he was there. They saw him yesterday leaving the store at the Cross and took him at the Dromore bridge."

Privately, I ask, "Captain, did you see him at Drumbeg?"

"I think so. There was a man who looked just like him who cut down me roof."

"Just like him? This is a joke. I worked alongside this man for months on the Meenavoy road project. I didn't see him at Drumbeg. You're giving the "Hand" a reputation for incompetence. This is the same mistake as Mansfield's horse. How are you going to get any support from the people if you keep fookin' up?"

Andy stares at the man, whose name turns out to be Sam Ewing. He asks the two masked lads in the room,

"Are ya sure this is our man?"

The silence and hesitation is all Andy needs.

"Take him to Dromore and let him go. I'm gettin' tired of this shite. We'll have to get Hanley and Harrison. We know them well."

We sow our seed potatoes and grain in the spring. The Quakers give us more turnip seed which we plant as well. Although most of us believe that the potato blight is past history, there are still many poor people begging on the streets and the workhouse is almost full. The partial harvest of last year was not enough for some to get out of their poverty even after selling their possessions and the lease rights to the land where they were living.

Our potatoes from the last harvest are almost gone. Mister Bradley sells his cow and his remaining horse, named Shelly, at the fair to buy cornmeal for the summer hunger. Ned's horse was a sleek brown mare, and the whole family was fond of it. Ned isn't embarrassed to tell us that he cried when his horse's new owner walked it away from him. He chokes up when he tells us that Shelly looked back at him with sad eyes as he was led away as if to ask, "What did I do to displease you?" Ned now uses a donkey he bought cheaply at the fair for carting the grain to the miller and to market.

Da and my uncles sold off livestock for cornmeal, as well. After shearing season, Da will probably sell his sheep.

Carney stops by in May and tells me that the Black Hand has finally captured a bailiff from the Drumbeg tumbling. They followed him to his home in Stranorlar from an eviction in Teevickmoy. Fifteen men took him from his home in the middle of the night and now have him at the byre in Cronalaghy.

"Not again. Are they sure they have the right man?"

"Aye. They were careful this time. At least ten of the Drumbeg men say they are willing to swear on it."

I must make sure. Carney and I walk up to Cronalaghy, cover our faces, and enter the byre. I will never forget what I see.

The poor man's mouth is bloody; in fact, blood is still gushing out as I stand there.

"What in the name of God have you done to him?"

Andy answers, "The lads cut out his tongue. He won't let them use the hot poker to stop the bleedin'."

One of the lads is waving tongs holding a bloody piece of flesh. He is smiling as he waves it in the poor man's face. The bailiff's bellowing is disturbing, at the least.

I am speechless. What class of animals have we become? I can bear it no longer and leave the byre. I am ashamed and will never face any of these lads again.

The constables show up in great numbers a few days later and arrest all of the males evicted in the November tumblings. This is a considerable number of persons and includes my Da's cousin James and his sons. Of course, Andy Slevin and Peter Gallagher are among them as well.

The poor bailiff survives his attack and we find out his name. He is Hugh Doherty from Stranorlar. He was associated with the Drumbeg tumblings; nevertheless, I don't believe that he deserved such brutal treatment.

After a few days at the garrison house, many of those arrested are released. Only about twenty young lads are charged and walked under guard to the Lifford Jail. Andy and Peter are among them as are Mickey and Kevin Gallen.

I see more of Paddy Carlin now that the Black Hand is inactive. He tells me that he and his family are surviving nicely now that the crops seem to be growing well. Worries about the potato fields are fading. He does mention that there was a riot between Catholics and Protestants at the Raphoe Fair in June. There is a Catholic group that calls itself the Repealers who were making speeches at the fair. Some Protestants took exception and a brawl broke out. Peace didn't come about until the constables drove the Repealers out of town. Paddy says that he would like to join me if we want to police the Castlefin Orange parade this year. I hadn't planned on it. There was no parade last year because of the famine.

"I don't see why not, Paddy, except there won't be many of us this year. Most of the lads are in jail. I'll get Carney and some of my cousins."

"I believe I can persuade some of the lads from Lismullyduff and Meenreagh. We should be there in numbers to prevent another Raphoe from happenin'."

"Grand," I say.

"Let's meet at the Cross on July 15."

"The parade is July 12."

"So it is."

I still don't know how Paddy gets by as well as he does. He should have careful supervision.

The Orange parade goes on without any serious troubles. Only coarse words are thrown about between the Orangemen and the Catholics. The constables are well represented to keep it going smoothly. During the walk back home, many talk about the parade in '46 when we first discovered the potato blight. This year the fields look fine with acres of green potato plants.

Our optimism is crushed when the leaves turn black again, almost overnight, in August. We all rush into the fields to check on the bulbs and roots. The blight is here once more. This time we will be better prepared. We remove all moisture laden bulbs and dry them to make cakes from the paste that can be wrung out of them. Ellen bakes them on the fire. The women call it boxty.

We will have no potatoes for the coming year. This much we know. We will have to eat meal again along with the turnips and nettle soup. To get meal, we need money. Some relief will come from the landlords who relax the rent. We will have some grain crops and the money we can earn from them.

There is also the Scottish harvest. They need Irish labour again. The Scots never depended on potatoes as their main source of food; they prefer bread and meat. Who wouldn't? The Scottish harvest will begin again soon, and I must go to earn money for my family. A problem is that my child will be born while I'm away. Ellen assures me that she has her family there to help her.

I join many of the lads who can be spared from their parents' farms. We walk to Castlefin where, again, we have arranged to load cargo into the small steamship for our passage to Derry. We reach Castlefin by noon.

Unfortunately we arrive the day of the Castlefin Fair and are met by a large body of Orangemen who recognise us from the July parade. As we walk down the hill past the diamond to Rogan's dock, we are followed by a large mob. One of the men in the mob throws a rock, and it hits one of our lads. Other rocks follow. We spot one of the rock throwers and wade into the crowd to get at him. A few constables are present at the fair as usual to prevent theft. They rush over to separate us from the angry crowd. They are attacked by both sides. One of the constables pulls out his gun. Jimmy Gallagher, one of our lads, sees the gun and takes it from him. All is chaos until Jimmy fires the gun into the air to establish order. The fighting stops as the constables rush Jimmy and pin him to the ground. They take him away as the Orangemen cheer. Jimmy's brother, Paul, follows the constables up the street pleading with them to let him go.

We can't wait for them. Our schedule is tight. We continue down to the docks where the cargo is waiting to be loaded on the boat. Good luck to the Gallaghers. We all expect Jimmy to be taken to Lifford where he will be charged with starting a riot. There will be no witnesses except his brother to tell the court that Jimmy actually stopped the riot. No help can be expected from the Orangemen or the constables. We wish him well and hope that he will be released when the circumstances of his arrest are brought out.

I return home in October after two months in Scotland. I find that Ellen has given me another son. He was named after myself and baptised in September. My youngest brother Hugh was the godfather. Wee Charley's godmother was Mary Doherty, the fiancé of my brother-in-law, Jimmy Bradley. Jimmy and Mary plan to marry in the spring.

With the money I earned in Scotland and a decent harvest of wheat and oats, we, the Gallens and Bradleys, make it through the winter without the need for outdoor relief. A significant reduction of our rent by our landlord was a large contributor to our survival.

Chapter 13
(1849)

In the spring, all the Black Hand members are released from Lifford jail; there is no evidence to convict any of them. I talk with Andy Slevin. He still has the rage in him against Hanley, his former landlord.

"Hanley will get no profits from his land in Drumbeg. As long as I'm alive, he will suffer for his greed."

"Please think about it, Andy. It isn't worth anymore trouble. You know that the eyes of the law are on you. Don't you have kin in some other parish where you can start over?"

"Donaghmore is my home. I'll not run like a frightened hare. My life is now dedicated to doin' away with the likes of tyrants like Hanley. Just wait and see."

Many of the landlords in the parish go to America to collect donations from Irish communities in the cities. Their cause is the support of poor families in Donaghmore. Little do the Irish in America know that they are really contributing to the welfare of the landlords and not the people who need it. I'm sure that the landlords feel differently. Many of them are suffering from low rent payments and high poor law taxes. They believe that the money they collect will eventually trickle down to their tenants.

In a way, it does. Several of them use the money they collect to hire their tenants for building roads and making other improvements to their estates. Some hire women to work at their manors sewing clothes for sale in England. Women who have talents in embroidery can make a decent wage. My younger sister Anne is working at the manor of Reverend Delap with other women from the parish. My mother taught Anne the art of sprigging, and Anne brings home some wages to help buy food for our parents and siblings in Glencarn. My younger brothers, Jimmy and Hugh, are working with myself to build a wall around the Delap estate. Reverend Delap pays us a decent wage which helps us get through the summer. While we are working for Delap, the planting of grain and potatoes is carried on by Da and Paddy at Glencarn, and by my father-in-law and his son Jimmy at Coracreagh. The seed was provided again by our landlords. We all pray that the potatoes will not suffer the blight again this year.

There are many men working on the wall. Reverend Delap has a lovely stone manor in Monellan that looks like a castle. The stones of the wall are brought from a quarry to match the stone of the manor house. Some of the men carrying the stones look too feeble to do so. Frankie Logan is one of them. He comes all the way from Meenreagh to help pay for missing his rental payments to Delap. His farm is small, and he has been hit hard by the famine. It is decent of Reverend Delap to allow Frankie to keep his land. I don't believe that Frankie has paid rent for the past three years.

One day, we see a number of lads gathered around a body lying in the road. We expect the worst. Sure enough, it is Frankie. He looks like a skeleton lying there with his grey face and with the life out of him. He most likely hadn't eaten in days. His neighbours carry his body back to Meenreagh. The Meenreagh lads he worked with look fairly robust. I don't understand why they didn't look out for him while he was alive. There must have been some spare oatmeal or turnips that they could have given him.

"Frankie was a proud man," someone remarks. "He never had it in him to beg."

"Ach, you could see he was eating nothing," I say. "Why did no one just give him a meal once and a while?"

"He would refuse it if he had no way to repay the kindness. His pride caused him to lose his oul' one last year. Maybe he wanted this cursed land to take him like it took his wife."

I am glad that most of us have the lack of pride that lets us rely on others to help us through the hard times. I blame both God and England for our troubles, but I am thankful that others, some decent landlords and our churches, both Protestant and Catholic, have helped us survive this mess.

This struggle to exist is not over yet. Perhaps it will never be over. I still believe that getting my family out of Ireland is the best solution to improve our way of life.

Hanley hires men to build a cattle wall around his pasture land in Drumbeg. He insists that none of his former tenants are among the workers, although a few of them manage to get on the crew by giving false names. These men still have hate in their hearts for Hanley, but they need the money he is paying them, most of which was collected from American donors. To add to their sorrow, many of the stones used in the wall are collected from the tumbled cottages from which they were evicted.

The walls are completed, and Hanley's cattle arrive from the port at Moville. The county is impressed by the size of the herd as it is driven through Inishowen and into Donaghmore. The cattle are beautiful. They are stout, black as night, and have curved horns different than most of the other cattle in the parish. The rumour has it that they were purchased in Wales. Once they settle in their roomy Drumbeg pasture, they are visited almost daily by well dressed spectators. Whereas most of our cattle are raised for their milk, these are beef cattle. Hanley is seen frequently admiring the herd. He expects to become rich from introducing the beef industry to this part of Donegal.

One sunny day, Hanley visits his pasture. His carriage climbs the hill from the Cross, and he encounters a shocking sight.

The fields are sprinkled with the black carcasses of his beautiful cattle. They were all killed overnight. The flies are abundant as he stares in horror. Who could have performed this slaughter? How many were involved? All twenty-six of his beloved animals are dead. He climbs the wall to check on the nearest carcass. Its throat is cut. He checks another. It was shot in the head. Hanley walks back to his carriage and driver in bewilderment.

"'Tis a pity, sir," says the driver.

"Take me to the constables," Hanley answers. "The bastards who've done this will all hang."

Strangely, there are no immediate arrests. Everyone knows who did the deed, but again there is no evidence. Finally, two ex-tenants of Hanley, Will Callaghan and Tommy Shane, are rounded up and carried off to Lifford. This action puzzles many in the parish because, although they are known members of the Black Hand, they were just insignificant followers of the real leaders, Andy Slevin and Peter Gallagher. Months go by and there is no news from Lifford. Then the Donegal constables arrive in the hills and arrest twenty of the Black Hand, including Slevin, Gallagher, and even Carney Conaghan. All are taken to the Lifford jail, where they are kept in a crowded dungeon cell.

There is a trial that is attended by the families of the prisoners. Not all can get into the courtroom, and so, family members take turns between the sessions. The county is prepared for possible violence and has a good contingent of soldiers both inside the courthouse and outside. Because my friend Carney is being charged, I attend a few of the sessions. It doesn't take long to figure out the prosecutors' strategy. They have a witness to the crime. It is Tommy Shane.

When questioned by the lead prosecutor, Tommy reluctantly names many of the prisoners as being there at the slaughter of Hanley's cattle. Fortunately, Carney isn't named and is released.

Apparently, Tommy was tricked into testifying by the prosecution. They told him that Will Callaghan identified him as one of the members of the Black Hand who participated in the cattle slaughter. I am sure that Callaghan did no such thing;

nevertheless, Shane was convinced that he would be accused of the crime. He was offered his freedom from prosecution if he became the Crown's witness. Tommy has a new wife and a baby. I'm sure that he thought that he would be sent to New South Wales if he didn't cooperate. He apparently relented. Although I understand his reasons for testifying, I wouldn't have the heart to turn in all of my friends.

The prisoners have no defence. Everyone is certain that they killed the cattle. They are all sentenced to twenty years transportation to Van Diemen's Land. There are gasps from their families in the courtroom. I think about my past actions with the Hand. It could be me on those dreadful ships. What would have become of my family? I hate to think of it.

The judge announces that the prisoners will be sent to a jail in Dublin until a ship becomes available to take them to Van Diemen's Land, an island that is part of New South Wales. They will be given hard work for at least two years. They can never return to Ireland.

Tommy Shane is a walking dead man, but the Crown does its best to get him out of Ireland. His wife and wain had been missing from the parish since the trial began. All believe that the Crown has given Tommy a farm in England. Recent Irish emigrants to England are asked to look for a new family who moved there and who have a Donegal accent. A good description Tommy is given to them. We believe that he will be found someday and will pay for his cowardice.

Once again, I go to Scotland to work the harvest. While passing through Derry, I learn that our beloved bishop, Edward Maginn, died of famine fever. Bishop Maginn, a native of County Tyrone, spent most of his life in Inishowen. As bishop during the famine, he raised many donations to aid victims of the great hunger. Many of our priests have died of the disease while administering to the paupers of their parishes. It is only to be expected that Bishop Maginn, known for his kindness to those dying in the workhouses, should contract the deadly disease. He will be missed by all in the diocese. He is succeeded by Bishop Francis Kelly.

In Scotland, I spend many nights talking with Matt McGlinchey of Meenagolan about how to survive our poor existence in Ireland. Matt is a young bachelor who works with me in the fields. He is the youngest of four brothers and lives on his father's land with little chance of ever getting his own farm. Matt also has a young lass he wishes to marry someday. The subject of our discussions often runs to emigrating to America. I tell him that it has always been my dream. He knows of several lads from Meenagolan who are living in America and working at the Kelly textile mill in Philadelphia. We decide that our destiny is in America. There is no future for us in Ireland.

"That's what we must do," I say. "We will have enough money to take a ship to Philadelphia and get a job with Mr. Kelly. You can send for your intended bride, and I can send for my family after we earn enough over there."

"By God, that is what we'll do. We'll go together. I've had enough of this shite. My belly is always empty, and my head hurts from thinking how to raise a family without a farm of my own. When will we go?"

"I believe that late spring will be best. We'll spend the winter in Ireland and help with the spring planting. Next year at this time, we will be in Philadelphia. What do you think?"

"I think that you give me hope. Thank you. I won't be able to sleep tonight with this in my head."

We return home to Donaghmore in late autumn. We have saved enough, we believe, for passage on a ship to America. If all goes well, our future is sealed.

Ellen and the children welcome me warmly on my return. My children are growing so fast. Jimmy and Eddie are running all over the cottage, and Bridget is starting to look like the princess of the house. Katie is a wee doll and the two boys, Paddy and Charley, are toddling about and keeping each other amused.

When I was in Scotland, I hardly thought about my family. Now that I see them again, my heart aches for them. Ellen looks especially lovely to me. We hug and kiss for several minutes after I arrive, until the boys try to pull us apart. If I go to America, I don't know how I will get along for the year or two that we are parted. I dread telling Ellen about my plans. I will put off telling her until winter.

The harvest this year was excellent. There was no potato blight and the fields were well grown with turnips, oats, and barley. It looks as if our landlords will be getting a bit of rent from us this year.

Chapter 14
(1850)

It is time to discuss going to America with Ellen. She knows that I have saved enough money for my passage, and it really is no surprise to her that I am planning for us to go. Matt McGlinchey has been coming down to our home often, but we only talk outside. Ellen has noticed Matt's visits but hasn't asked me about our conversations. I believe that Matt has told his intended bride, Sally McGoldrick, about going, and the news has probably reached Ellen's ears by now.

After Matt leaves one day for Meenagolan, Ellen says, "Well, when are we leaving?"

"Ah Ellen, you know it has to happen. I can't work for your Da forever. There's a lovely future for us all in America."

"Don't I know that? Can't we have just one more year here with our families? It'll surely kill them if we leave now."

I have to correct her misunderstanding of my plan.

"I have no money to take yis all, you know. What I have to do is go to America and earn enough for you and the children to join me there. Matt will travel with me. He will send for his Sally when he earns enough."

Ellen thinks about this for a moment and says, "When the time comes for us to go, I just hope that I'll want to."

I never gave that a thought. I can't force her to leave her folks and go to a strange land.

I say, "If you love me, you'll come."

She turns her head. We have gone through a lot in the past few years. I can understand her feelings.

"I'll come," she says finally. "If we don't like it there, we can come home, can we not?"

I don't know of anyone who went to America and returned home, but I say, "Of course we can."

She hesitates and then asks, "So, when will you be leaving us?"

"I'll help your Da through spring planting. Matt and I will leave for Derry after that."

Finally she starts weeping. I hope it is because she will miss me, but it could be because she will miss her family. I walk outside into the brisk winter air and see the green hills across the Finn in the misty distance. Will I regret leaving Ireland? Perhaps…nevertheless, after the last three years of hunger and hardship, America is calling me.

I have finished the spring planting at the Bradleys. No one knows of my plan to sail for America except Ellen and perhaps her parents. I notice some concern in her Da's face when we are working together. I want to talk with him. After all, I am leaving him with his daughter and a large family to support in my absence. I want to leave him some of my wages from Scotland as compensation, although I hope that he doesn't accept them. I'll need all the money I have saved to survive until I am receiving wages in America. Finally, I have a word with him.

Mr. Bradley tells me that he knows my plans already. I am sure that he has mixed emotions. He'll not miss me, but he will miss his daughter and grandchildren.

"How will you make a living there? Are there farms you can work at?"

"I'm sure there are farms, except I'll work for the Kellys at their factories. First, I'll be a common labourer, but maybe I can, you know, learn a trade there."

"Well I wish you the best of luck. When are you going?"
"The lads are planning to leave in about a week there."
"Who are going with you?"
"First it was just me and Matt McGlinchy. Now three others from Drumbeg are going."
"You'll be needing a hooley to see yis off. I have the room here for it. Just give me the word when you want it."
"Thank you, Ned. I'll always be in debt to you for your kindness."

I must move fast. There are many people to notify of my trip. First are my parents, then there are my friends. I walk up to Glencarn first. I can see my mother inside the cottage when I arrive. I dread the reaction I'll get from her alone. I walk past the door and head to the fields to meet Da who is talking with my brothers, Patrick, Jimmy, and Hugh.

"I have something important to tell yis. Can yis come to the cabin with me?"

"Why not tell us here now," Da asks.

"I need to have yis all with Ma when I say it."

They all look at each other.

"Alright then. This better be worth our time."

Jimmy and Hugh are still single men with no lasses. Although they are a help to Da in the fields, Da and Paddy can handle the work themselves on their land without them. I'm sure that Da would like Jimmy and Hugh to be the ones who leave for America.

When we get to the cottage, Ma and my sister Anne are waiting in front of the door.

"And what's this, a holiday in the middle of the day?" Ma asks.

"I have something to tell you Ma. I'd like yis all to hear it at the same time."

"Go to it then, son." says Da.

"Well it is this way. You know that I've been wanting to go to America for quite awhile there. Well…. I'm going next week with some lads from Drumbeg and Meenagolan. Ellen and the wains are staying here until I send for them."

"They're staying here?" Da asks. "Here in this house?"

"Ah no...no! They are staying with the Bradleys for Christ's sake."

My brothers laugh.

"There's no need for that kind of language, son," says Ma. Then it sinks in. She understands what I'm telling them.

"You're leaving us for good?" asks Ma.

"I am. I had enough of poverty and hunger. I had enough of hard work and having nothing to show for it."

My brothers laugh at the hard work part.

The tears start running down Ma's cheeks. I look at Da. His eyes are moist, as well. Finally they get it. They are losing one of their sons forever. Tears moisten my eyes too when Ma breaks out into heavy sobs. Anne comforts her and Da says to me,

"Well.... We will miss you son. These are hard times for the Irish, and you aren't the first to leave home because of them."

He places his hand tentatively on my back, thinks about it, and finally hugs me gently. I am touched, although most likely I will just remember the smell of his sweaty clothing when I think of this tender moment years from now.

Paddy offers his hand and wishes me good luck. My younger brothers, Jimmy and Hugh, ask me if they can go with me. Ma hears this and cries uncontrollably. I shrug my shoulders at this and go to embrace Anne and finally kneel at Ma's side. She is sitting on a stool beside the door. I lie and say,

"It'll be alright, Ma. Maybe I'll become rich and return to Ireland with gifts galore for yis all from America. Maybe you'll come to America with me and live in a big manor house with all your children and grandchildren."

She knows that will never happen. She says between her sobs, "I do wish you a good life, Charley, and this is possibly the best for you. I'll miss you terribly, and I'll miss your lovely children when they leave, as well."

"And you'll miss Ellen as well, won't you."

"Oh, aye. I'll miss Ellen."

"When is the convoy party?" asks Jimmy.

"Mr. Bradley will have it at his farm. It'll be grand." I tell him.

"It'll be like a wake we'll be havin' for ya, y' know. We've been to a few in Cronalaghy. There will be some nice lasses there, I'll wager."

"Aye, there will." I hope that he has stopped thinking about America. I don't have enough money to take care of him and Hugh. I believe that maybe he has forgotten already.

The word spreads around Donaghmore quickly. There will be a convoy party at the Bradley's on the night before we leave for Derry. That information gets spread even beyond the parish. I hope that the Bradleys are ready.

I visit Paddy Carlin next. I stop at his lovely cottage in Baywood. As I suspected, Paddy heard the news about me and will surely attend my American wake.

"I'm back to visiting Gallagher's, ya know," he tells me.

"And I am still free from the drink, you know," I say.

"Thank God for that. Ya were a proper mess for the years that ya were on the drink. How do ya stay sober?"

"I think about my wains and my wife. I well know that I can't handle the spirits."

"Herself reminds you of it as well I guess."

"She does and she should. You know that I'll be the only sober lad at the wake there."

"Ya can be sure of it."

Next, I visit Carney. He doesn't prize fight anymore, and he is starting to look a bit out of shape. His hips are now wider than his shoulders. Nevertheless, I still don't think that I could beat him in a match.

"Christ, I'll miss you, Charley. We had some good times, didn't we?"

"Aye. Remember me when you're teaching some new lad the tricks of fighting."

"I'm through with the fights, Charley. I lost too many times. The younger lads are better than I ever was. I'm saving myself for one last brawl. Most likely, it'll be at yer bottle night next week. I still get belligerent when I drink."

"Please, no rough-housing at the convoy. I want it to be a peaceful, thoughtful night. I have enough to think about without you tearing the Bradley house down."

"I'll try, Charley, but I can't promise y' anything."

Ma asks me to visit the holy spring on the day of the American wake. I am busy getting my pack together for my trip, nevertheless I agree to take the walk up to the spring. I haven't been there very often since those unfortunate days when I was on the drink.

The wooded area around the spring is void of any sound when I arrive. I am apprehensive of what I might see when the spring comes into view. My steps slow as I enter the clearing around the rocks. Finally I hear the sound of the falling water as it splashes into the pool below. I reach the clearing. No one is there.

I walk over to take one last drink from the spring. The area looks different to me since I was here last. There are religious articles left by other visitors here. Rosary beads and scapulars are hanging in the bushes. A few wee statues of Mary and the saints are standing on the ground. The spring water is cool and delicious. I kneel and say a prayer. Then I see something in the pool.

It looks metallic, but it is not shiny, possibly a religious metal left by a pilgrim. I scoop it up and look. It isn't a religious metal but a coin. I rub it on my trousers and some silver highlights appear. It is about the size of a pound sterling coin, except that there is no picture of the queen or any other person on its face. Instead, the outline of a wagon wheel is engraved on one side. The other side is worn smooth. I believe it is of some value, and I don't intend to leave it here even if a pilgrim left it as an offering. I'll need every coin I can get my hands on to settle in America. I drop it in my pocket and return home for the last day with my family.

My wake is held early in the evening. Mr. Bradley decided to hold it at the Gleneely schoolhouse. The other four lads going with me to America are standing outside at the four corners of the building greeting their friends and relatives. I am standing near the door of the school. It seems as if the entire parish is attending. The grounds are shoulder to shoulder with chattering people as more are coming up the hill from the Cross and down the hill from Baywood and Coradooey. My friends and relatives form a queue to shake my hand, wish me well, and shed a tear over losing me forever. My parents are standing next to me and are consoled by each party that passes us.

Each one I meet shares a story they heard of the wonders of America. All tell of how Americans eat meat almost every day. One tells me of the abundant fish that can be caught in every American stream. Another tells me of the equality of life in America.

"There is no difference between the lowest servant and the highest aristocrat. If ya take off your hat to the lord mayor of New York, the people will laugh at ya."

My cousins have supplied several jars of poteen, and the liquor and the craic are flowing freely. There are games being played in the road, and there is music playing in the school where a number of lasses are dancing. My brothers move through the crowd with a cup to try to collect some money for my trip. There are a few who contribute, but in these times there are few who can afford more than a couple of pennies to help a lad they will never see again.

At sunset, a number of torches are lit. We try to hush the crowd so that our parish priest can give me and the other lads a blessing. After a couple of minutes, the crowd does become silent, and Father Boyle starts his prayers. The Latin words send chills up my spine. When he finishes, he does call us by name and says in his perfect enunciation,

"Charles, Matthew, Patrick, John, and Francis. May you have success in America, but may you never forget your family, your people, or your church. Remember where you came from. We will still be here trying to survive the hardships of a difficult land and its cruel government. Help us if you can when you enjoy the fruits of your freedom. Take care of your parents here in Donaghmore. Any success you enjoy there is likely because of their prayers.

"When you are in America, be sure to avoid the temptations of Satan in that foreign land. There will be many. Find a good Catholic church to attend there and obey our laws and teachings. You may be far from here, but you are still in the eyes of God.

"And, don't drink too much… nomine Patri, et Filio, et Spiritui Sancto."

"Amen," says the multitude. The party continues, although I break away to talk to my Da.

He speaks first.

"You know son, I have been rough on you through the years there. I hope that you don't resent me for it. I meant it for your own good."

"I know Da. I did hate you for a while there. I was immature then. I hope that you will forget anything I may have said that hurt you. I do love you and I will never forget you."

Da can say nothing. He is too emotionally overcome, and there are tears in his eyes. He turns his head away for a minute. I tell him that I'll be back later, but he says,

"Don't go yet. I'm not finished saying what is in my heart."

I wait until he recovers.

He says, "You've given me much happiness lately. You've given up the drink that was hurting your family, and you've helped us through the hunger years. You've raised, with the help of Ellen, six lovely children. I don't want to lose you. I want you to go to America; make a lot of money there, and then come back home here and buy some good land. Don't tell us that you'll be gone forever. You belong here with your people."

"I'm sorry Da. I am going, and I'll not be returning. America is the place for me to be. It's the place for my family as well. Please accept that fact."

I embrace him for the second time in my life. I can feel his body shudder as he sobs. It will be the last time I embrace him. I leave him standing alone in the field.

The worst is to come.....Ma. I search her out among the crowd of relatives. She is talking with her sister Anne.

I say, "Hello Aunt Annie. Could I have some words with my mother?"

"Sure Charley. Are y' not having any drink with your friends?"

"I don't drink anymore, Annie. I can't handle it well."

Ma says, "I'll be back in a few minutes, Anne."

She walks with me to a spot where we can talk quietly.

"Are you still leaving tomorrow, Charley?"

"I am. I'm packed already. The lads will stop by in the morning for our walk to Derry. This will be the last time I see you. I want to talk with Ellen and the children tonight after I take them home."

I can see that Ma is shocked and distressed. She knew that this final meeting would take place tonight. She was dreading it as much as I was. How can two people as close as we were say a final farewell? Calling this a wake is fairly accurate. Effectively, we will be dead to each other after tonight. What makes it doubly tragic is that I am threatening to take her grandchildren away someday. I'm glad that I won't be here when that happens.

"Well….. I'll miss you terribly. Will you find someone to write to us when you get to America?"

She is holding up well. There are no hysterics.

"I will. I'm sorry that I never learned to write, Ma. I'll make sure that my children will go to school when they get to America. In the meantime, I'll find someone to write. You'll be getting American letters regularly from the Killygordon post office just like the Kellys."

"I think that Ellen will be sending Bridey, Jimmy, and maybe Eddie to Gleneely school next year. That will be nice. Oh….. Did you visit the spring today?"

"I did, except I saw no one. I just had a drink and said a few prayers."

I didn't mention the coin I found. Ma would consider it a sacrilege to take it.

"Well…" I say smiling. "Will you miss me?"

She cannot talk. The tears begin, and now she is openly crying. What did I expect? My smile disappears immediately, and the tears well up in my eyes. Neither of us can speak. Finally she says,

"I had hoped that this day would never come. When you were a baby, we almost lost you from some evil ailment. I felt like I do now. I am losing you forever. I know that it is best for you, and I know that I can't change your mind. I'm just so sorry, sorry for myself. Time goes on, and I lose the people I love, like my parents and friends. I never thought that I'd lose a child. Please forgive me. I'm making it hard for you. I'm just too emotional. I'm just an emotional old woman."

I am speechless for a moment. Her saying that has made it easier for me.

"I understand your feelings. I hope that you will feel better when you know that I am in a better place and not suffering through another famine like we did. There should be food on our table and a better life for me there. I'm only sorry that you will not be joining me. Maybe someday you will. Maybe all my loved ones will join me there and never suffer again."

"Sorry, Charley. I can never leave Ireland, the land your father worked, the people I know, and my other kin. Me and your father are just too old. I'm happy for you, just sad for myself. I'll be alright. There are many things between us unsaid. We'll have to say them on pieces of paper we send across the ocean."

I embrace her and kiss her on her lips like I did when I was child. Instant visions of our loving moments flash through my mind as we stand in this embrace. Neither of us want to let go. The night wind breathes through the trees and the tall grass sways. All of a sudden, we both relax our embrace. That is it. We are finished with this difficult moment in our lives. We will go on with our lives independently and with new strength.

The party is still going on. I have said goodbyes to my brothers, sisters, cousins, in-laws and everyone I ever met. It is time to walk my family back home and say goodbye to them before bedtime.

Once again, I tell my children what will happen. I'll be going away for a year or so, just like I went to Scotland.

Only this time, they will go too, but later and with their mother. They seem to understand this, and my goodnight and goodbye to them is not so traumatic. Bridget and Jimmy are alright with it completely. Eddie and Kate are six and five years old. They are less understanding, although they accept what I'm doing. The problem is that I will miss them terribly. They are just so damn cute. Cute is another word that applies to Paddy and Charley, my toddlers. They will be much older when I see them again. My children will be older by a year or more when I see them get off the boat in America.

Then there is Ellen. There is no formal goodbye for her. It is more like snuggling together in our bed and tender caresses. We have gone over our separation many times now. It is just that tonight is our last night together for a long time. Ellen doesn't want me to do anything tonight that could make her pregnant, although I am heartily for it. Tonight is the last time for a year or more I'll be with a woman, especially if Father Boyle has anything to do with it. Ellen doesn't want to have another child, especially one born when I'm away. People will talk although it is perfectly clear that the child's father is me. She wants to avoid any misunderstanding. So we cuddle, and I tell her how beautiful she is, how kind she is, and what a wonderful mother she is. She purrs like a 28 year old, 10 stone kitten. I enjoy touching her soft body. I'll remember this night for the many months I'll be alone, or God forbid, sharing a bed with another man in a boarding house.

Just before the sun rises in the morning, I kiss Ellen and leave her in the bed. The children are still sleeping. I make a cup of tea and heat up some stir-about over the fire. It is getting light out as I head outside with my leather pack to wait for my fellow emigrants. There are only three of them coming down the hill. When they arrive, I see that Francey is missing.

"He lost his nerve at the convoy party," says Matt. "His parents cried so much that he told them he would stay. When his uncle from Stranorlar told him that he would hire him to work in his fields, he was convinced he was doing the right thing."

"His loss," I say. "At least he didn't miss this morning because he was drunk."

The four of us start down the hill to the Cross. I look back and see a lone figure standing in the lane uphill from Coracreagh. The lone figure is my mother. She waves to me. I wave back. This will be the scene embedded in my mind for many years after I arrive in America.

chapter 15
[1850]

The four of us, myself, Matt McGlinchy, John Callaghan, and Paddy McMenamen, arrive just before dark in the Bogside, Derry. We lodge at the same house where we stayed when we took our trips to the harvests in Scotland. Mrs. O'Connor welcomes us and gives us some stir-about and tea before showing us the upper loft we will share with other lads who are also going to America. After our meal, we talk with our roommates about the chances of getting on a ship leaving for Philadelphia. The other lads are going to British America, to a city called Quebec. They have passage booked on a ship of the J & J Cooke Line that leaves tomorrow. They seem quite excited. Their ship arrived weeks ago from Philadelphia laden with coal for Ireland. The ship has been cleaned and refitted for passengers to Quebec, where it will again be refitted for a cargo of lumber to return to Derry. The lads don't know of any ships going to Philadelphia. We don't worry. When we walked past the quay today, there were more than six sailing vessels there. Agents were moving about quickly among throngs of passengers, selling tickets for the ships that they represented. We learned that the principal ports the ships were headed were New York, Philadelphia, Baltimore, and Quebec. I don't know why our fellow roommates are going to Quebec. It is still ruled by England. We are going to America to get away from England. I learn later that passage to Canada in British America is much cheaper than to the United States. I guess that if I couldn't afford passage to Philadelphia, I would be going to Canada as well.

The next day, we roam among the throng at the Derry quay. We find two ships that are sailing to Philadelphia. Both are barks, huge ships with three high masts, two of which will be rigged with square sails when out in the ocean. Both ships are magnificent and look quite complicated to handle when under sail. The *Barbara* is to sail on the third of the month, about 4 days from today. The *Creole* is leaving a week later. Another option is for us to take a steamer ferry to Liverpool. There are several ships leaving from there, and the passage is a bit cheaper. Also, there is no fare for the ferry, and the ship company will pay for lodging in Liverpool until the ships sail. That is only if we pay full fare here in Derry.

We decide to take the *Barbara* if it is available. Although the lodging at Mrs. O'Connor's is only pennies per day, we are in a hurry to get to America. Liverpool is out. We never want to set foot in England.

We find a shipping agent roaming about the quay. He is a short man with sharp features and a long narrow nose. He is wearing a top hat, striped trousers, and a vest. His name is Mr. Boylan, and he represents the J&J Cooke Line. We ask him about the cost of passage on the *Barbara*. He tells us that the *Barbara* has no more berths available. We ask about the *Creole*. Yes, he says. There are berths there, but we should pay him now. We ask him how much it costs. He tells us that the passage costs 5 pounds apiece. We are unprepared for that response.

"It's not first class we're after," I say.

We expected to board a ship for about 2 pounds. Although I have enough to cover my passage with a bit left over for expenses in America, the other lads look worried. We leave the agent and discuss it privately.

"I have exactly five pounds on me," says Paddy.

The others have less.

"Let's pool our money and see what we have," I say.

With my eight pounds and what the others possess, we have a total of twenty-one pounds plus a few shillings, enough for the passage but barely enough to survive in Derry until boarding. I still have my silver coin from the holy spring, but I will save that for America.

"Maybe we should leave from Liverpool," says Paddy. "We can split up. There is no need for all of us to take the same ship. Charley, you take your money and sail on the *Creole*. We can go to Liverpool or sail from here to Canada. It is only one pound for Canada."

I say, "We are all going to Philadelphia to work for the Kellys. God knows what waits for you in Canada. Let's bargain with Mr. Boylan on the price for the *Creole*. The cost to America from Liverpool is still about 4 pounds. Let's get Boylan to compromise."

There is much whining from the agent about the cost of passage. We tell him that the four of us can share two berths. We tell him that we will gladly pay fifteen pounds for the passage. He tells us that is impossible and walks away. We follow him.

"We can work onboard for half-price," says Paddy.

Mr. Boylan squints at him and says, "Can y'climb shrouds up to t' top of the masts, clamber over t'ose yardarms, furl sails from way up t'ere in t' heavens? T'ere is no farmin' and plantin' on a sailing ship. Y' need sailin' experience."

Paddy says, "We can learn. All of us are strong lads and can do the work."

I look up at the top of the masts. There is no way I can work up there.

Mr. Boylan tells us that the crew is set, and there are no half-price tickets. He thinks and then says,

"Alright. Fifteen pounds, and one of yeh is invisible. He'll get no meals aboard, and he'll sleep on the floor after t' lanterns are out. I'll get him on board and hidden during roll call. "

We select John as our invisible passenger and sign up for the *Creole*. We give Boylan fifteen pounds and receive a receipt. Only Callaghan can read, and he has poor reading skills. We all see the amount of the passage indicated by the number 15.

John sees the three names on the contract, and he can barely make out the name of the ship. We accept the receipt as proof that we have passage on the *Creole* leaving May 12. He says to meet him at the J&J Cooke office on Shipquay Street tomorrow for our actual boarding tickets.

Three of us go to Cooke's office the next day. There is no Mr. Boylan there. A man at the front desk asks if he can help us.

"Aye, we're here to see Mr. Boylan and get our boarding tickets for the *Creole* sailing to America."

"Sorry gents. We have no Mr. Boylan here, and the *Creole* is a ship of the McCorkell line. Their office is on Foyle Street."

We don't know why Boylan would tell us to meet him at the Cooke office if the ship was of a different line, but we believe that he will be here. We wait outside the office on Shipquay Street and get a lot of stares from the people passing by.

After a while Paddy says, "Let's go to the McCorkell office. Boylan probably made a mistake."

We don't quite understand why he would say to meet him here if he worked for the McCorkells, but we set out to look for the McCorkell office on Foyle Street. We enter the office and meet the man on the front desk. I ask to see Mr. Boylan.

"Sorry. We have no Mr. Boylan working here."

I am getting concerned now.

"We have this receipt for sailing on the *Creole,* and we would like to pick up our tickets."

The agent looks at our receipt and takes it to another man working at a big desk by the wall. They look at the receipt and talk about it for several minutes. Finally, the agent comes over.

"I believe that you have been swindled by a scoundrel who works the waterfront. This receipt is worthless. You have been robbed of your money. I suggest that you find a constable and tell him your story. Maybe the villain can be found, and you can get your money back."

After we leave, we set out to the quay in great haste to find Mr. Boylan. Our spirits are as low as they can be. All that hard earned money gone.

"How can he think he can get away with it?" asks Matt. "He must know that we will stay here at the quay until he shows his face again."

"He must be off on another crime," I say. "He may never work this dock until we have tired of waiting for him."

We see a constable and tell him how we were swindled.

"Ah! 'Tis a pity you weren't aware of all the criminals who prey on ignorant culchies like yourselves who are looking to leave our fair island. Some of them'd steal the buttons from yer trousers. There are a thousand swindles a year in Londonderry alone. It isn't likely that we'll find your man."

I don't like being called ignorant; nevertheless, we give the constable a description of our Mr. Boylan. We tell him that he had a different accent. He didn't speak like he was from Ulster. Maybe he was from the south or from Dublin. The constable tells us that he has seen such a man in the past few weeks but couldn't figure out what his business was. He says that he will give the description to his people, although he says that we shouldn't get our hopes up. The thief is, most likely, long gone from Londonderry.

I am not convinced that we will never find him. We stop back at Mrs. O'Connor's and get John. We then split up and visit the pubs in the Bogside telling our story and describing the man who robbed us. We ask if anyone has information on the man, to give it to Mrs. O'Connor. We do the same at businesses on Foyle Street and Shipquay Street. I prowl the quay frequently for a couple of days.

Then, a thought struck me. Why did Boylan not sell me a ticket on the *Bark Barbara*? Is it because he will be on it? That must be it. I must get the lads to watch the boarding of passengers tomorrow when the ship is leaving.

All is pandemonium the next day on the quay. Foodstuffs are loaded onto the ship, and passengers are milling about, most with chests and trunks that contain all they believe that they will need in their new home. We eye each of them, looking for the weasel who took our money.

I see him. A wagon pulls up at the quay with a driver and Mr. Boylan, who now is wearing the clothes of a peasant farmer. Instead of the top hat and fine clothes, he wears a wool cap, a vest, and thread-worn shirt and trousers. He gets out of the cart and quickly rushes to the back to unload his chest. He glances about nervously. I am on him immediately.

"Don't cry out or say a word. The constables are looking for you. Just come along peaceably, and you may not have to spend any time in jail."

He shakes his head in the affirmative. The lads with me unload his chest and drag it behind them as they follow us to nearby O'Donnell's pub. The driver sees us and assumes his work is done.

Few patrons pay us any attention as we all walk to the private backroom of O'Donnell's.

The proprietor asks, "Is it the thief himself?"

"It is," I answer.

In the dingy backroom Boylan asks, "What are y' goin' to do to me?"

"We will each have a punch at your face, and then we'll break your right arm. How's that?"

He shudders.

"I would have been better off in jail t'en, wouldn't I?"

"We're just joking with you. What we do with you depends on what we find in your possession. Let's open the trunk there."

He takes a key from his pocket and opens the lock. Inside are some of the finest clothes I've ever seen. There is a metal box on the top of the clothes. He opens it and there are jewels and gold and silver coins. It looks as if some of the silver coins are American. The Queen isn't embossed on them, just a lady in a long gown on one side and a fierce bird on the other.

"We won't be breakin' your arm then. Today is your lucky day unless you fancy keepin' your treasure there. Now empty your pockets."

He takes several silver coins, a handkerchief, and a leather wallet from his pockets. A boarding ticket for the *Barbara* is in the front of the wallet.

I say, "You'll not be heading for America today, lad. You'll be getting all of your fine clothes back, but the rest of it belongs to us poor victims of your cruel crime. Is that understood?"

"You must leave me some of t' money. T'at is all I got."

I look at the lads; they shake their heads no.

"Sorry, Boylan, if that is your name. You'll have to sell some of your clothes."

While keeping an eye on Boylan, I join the lads in the corner of the room. We discuss our next move.

Matt says, "This is enough to get us all to America on the Creole, except that it would be a sin to waste the *Barbara* ticket, wouldn't it? Why don't you take it, Charley, and go now."

John says, "Aye, and take some of the American coins. We'll take care of Boylan until the ship sails. We'll see you at the Kelly Mill in Philadelphia. Go now."

I like this idea. I tell them, "Keep him at Mrs. O'Connor's for a few days; then let him go. I don't think that he'll report us to the constables. If he does, one of yis kill him!" I say it loud enough for Boylan to hear. "And no harming him unless he tries to flee."

Boylan looks meek and helpless. I snatch the ticket and some of the coins. As I leave the backroom, I say,

"God bless you all. I'll see you in America."

I run to the O'Connor house, grab my pack, and sprint to the quay where the *Barbara* is still loading passengers. I ask a fellow there if my ticket is proper for boarding the *Barbara*.

"It is, Mr Bailey."

So, Mr. Boylan is really Mr. Bailey. The queue for boarding is moving slowly, but when I reach the gangplank and the official asks my name, I answer, "John Bailey." He hands me back my ticket and allows me to pass up the gangplank to the deck of the ship. Another fellow there is hollering for the passengers to come to a stairway that leads to the area between decks where the sleeping berths are located. Down the dim stairway I go and find a large open area where boxy partitions for sleeping have been installed. They cover most of the floor, leaving narrow passages between them. Some berths have been constructed on the ship's sides just above the lower berths. They managed to use almost every inch of the ship for its 150 passengers. I choose the first berth I see open. It is a bottom berth on the side of the ship and I throw my pack on the hard mattress-free boards.

There are many on board who had come to see their family members off to America. They are spending their last minutes with their kinfolk, who are embarking on this long journey. They will never see each other again in all probability. There are others as well, who helped the passengers carry their belongings aboard. I believe that it would have been easy to smuggle at least one of my friends on board. He could hide in any number of places within the dark recesses of the hold or even in this crowded community area.

Finally a horn sounds, signalling that the ship is ready to leave. A fellow comes down the stairway and yells that everyone without a ticket must depart. There is much sobbing as families split apart. They say goodbye for the last time. Some of the passengers follow them up the companionway and wave as their families descend the gangplank. I go up as well. I wish to see the ship depart Ireland.

Another horn sounds. Crewmen are shouting that it is time for roll call, and all passengers must come up to the main deck. There is grumbling as we all assemble in front of a raised deck where two distinguished gentlemen have arrived. They call out the names of the passengers, one by one. Each one whose name they call shouts, "Aye." The person named must show himself or herself to a man who appears to be the captain of the vessel. The captain collects the boarding ticket, asks the passenger something, and then inspects his or her face and hair. A few are asked to open their mouths as the captain looks for God knows what inside. Once satisfied that the he or she is not harbouring some dreaded disease, the passenger is asked to join a group of previously inspected persons to the right of the captain.

When they come to the name Bailey, there is silence. They repeat the name just as I remember who I am supposed to be on this voyage. "Aye," I shout. I walk up to the front, hand in my ticket, and receive my brief inspection. The captain asks me nothing.

As this is going on, I see all of the crew running about, but they are not working on the ship or preparing to sail. They are checking every square inch of the ship for stowaways. I guess my idea of smuggling another lad aboard wouldn't have been successful. Although I can't see them, I know that they are below doing a thorough job. The captain is still systematically inspecting the passengers as everyone sees two young lads being roughly escorted off the ship by crew members. They are practically thrown down the gangway.

During roll call, one lad tries to move into the inspected group before his name is called. A sharp-eyed crew member sees him and pushes him back into the crowd not yet called. The last name is called and he is left standing alone. The captain asks the crewmember to check his ticket. The lad just shrugs and walks himself to the gangplank and off the ship. Apparently, stowing away aboard this vessel is not easy to accomplish, and the crew knows all of the tricks.

The crew readies the ship to leave port. I manage to stay in the roped off portion of the deck allowed for passengers to watch the ship get underway. The sailors scurry about and men onshore release the huge ropes holding the ship to the quay. A triangular sail is raised on the rear mast. The ship slowly pulls away from the dock and settles in the middle of the Foyle. Slowly it drifts, propelled by a gentle breeze from the city side of the river. I am on my way to America. No one can stop me now.

After we are into the open water of Lough Foyle, I watch the sailors climb like squirrels up the rigging and walk out on the "branches" of the front two masts. They drop some of the sails that give the ship more power and life.

Down below, the living quarters are dark and smelly. What will it be like in a few days? A few are seasick already, and the stink of vomit fills the air. Lovely.

I sit in my bunk and look about. There is a mixture of people in partitions around me. Most are young men like myself. There is a young married couple a few feet away. Another couple with wains are nearby as well. There are many young women who are travelling together in groups near the bulkhead. Only a few old ones are on board. Everyone seems to be arranging their possessions for this presumably unpleasant voyage.

I have nothing with me save for the clothing I packed. I will have to rely on the ship providing my meals. I wonder what the meals will be like. Others are better prepared and have packages of food with them. I guess that they believe the captain will permit them to cook during the voyage.

"Do y' know if we are in the ocean yet?" the lad in the next bunk asks me.

"I think you'll know when we are," I reply. "I'm Charley from Donegal."

I give him my real name and wonder if I should have. Ach, the ship is already on its way. What will they do, throw me overboard?

"Pleased to meet you, Charley. My name is Willie Reilly. I'm from Strabane, damn close to Donegal. There are a lot of folks from Donegal on this fookin' boat, except most are from Derry."

"Are you staying in Philadelphia when we get there."

"Aye. Me brother is there already. We'll be makin' beer at a large brewery. Ain't that a corker!"

"Did he give you any suggestions about the trip across the ocean?"

"He said that I'll hate it, but it'll be over eventually."

Willie is about my age and height. He is strongly built and with red hair and a freckled red face. I believe that he has been in a few scraps during his lifetime. We decide to wander up to the main deck to see what is going on.

We can still see land on the left side of the ship. The area on deck for passengers is still clearly marked off with ropes. There isn't enough room for everyone, although it is unlikely that everyone will want to be up here. I see two structures in the front of the ship that are called privies. I believe that they are for taking a shite. I was wondering about that very thing this minute. I go and try it out. I sit inside the closet and my excrement drops below into the ocean. Brilliant.

I say to Willie afterwards, "It seems a shame to waste the shite; nevertheless, I believe they don't need it on board this vessel. I don't see any gardens here."

He asks, "Do y' think two shithouses are enough for all of the passengers onboard?"

I didn't think of that. "Ah no," I say. "What will they do? What about the ladies?"

"I guess we will find out soon, won't we?"

There is no meal on the first day. On the morning of the next day, the ship is rocking. We are now past Moville and out into the ocean. A bell is rung and the passengers assemble in a queue in front of a barrel containing loaves of bread. A loaf is handed to each passenger. Water for drinking, washing, and maybe cooking, is passed out from another barrel. There are gallon buckets available. Me and Willie grab one each and go below. Apparently, this is our ration for the day. We will have to conserve. As the days roll by, we find that we are given oatmeal on some days, bread or biscuits on others. We must heat our water for stir-about on the days we get meal. This means standing in the queue in front of the caboose, a fireplace on the foredeck, as each passenger cooks his own supper or the supper for his family. This all takes time and tempers flare. The fire goes from morning until sundown.

The queue to the privies lasts all day as well. Only a few men make use of the facility. Most of them wander down to the hold of the ship and find a filthy corner. So far, the smell of shite hasn't penetrated the sleeping quarters.

Many women and men already knew of the sanitary conditions onboard a sailing vessel. They were smart enough to bring a chamber pot with them. After using their precious device, selected crew members empty it and wash it with sea water. These crew members expect a reward for their services.

The crew is starting to get my goat. I frequently discuss it with Willie. When they aren't working, several crew members stand around near the queue at the privies, making dirty remarks to the women there. I can see that the women are uncomfortable. They have to go through this treatment every day. I suggest that we should talk to the offending crewmen about it.

Willie and I wait near the head of the queue where we can hear what is being said. I overhear laughter from one particularly dirty and ugly gentleman with stringy brown hair and an obvious lack of front teeth.

"What is so funny?" I ask him.

He stares at me and spits. "What do you care, Paddy?"

"I just want to be in on the joke. What did your friend say to you that was so funny?"

"We're comparing the arses of the lassies here. We're going to award the best of 'em with a pat from our hands."

"You disgusting jackasses had better get away from here. Surely your captain doesn't approve this class of behaviour."

The ugly one looks at his friend. "This piece of shite just called me a jackass. And him, a filthy Irish pig wearin' shabby, odd-looking clothing. Watch yourself, Paddy. Ya may find yerself swimmin' in the middle of the ocean some night. I'll remember ya."

The two men get up and move away. I see grateful glances from the women.

"I guess we better stay alert now when we're on deck," says Willie. "I don't think they like us spoilin' their fun."

"Grand. It'll give me something to think about during the boring hours. I sort of hope that they'll be back here tomorrow."

Later that day, we receive applause from the ladies when we go below.

"Thank you for getting rid of those awful men," says one.

I say, "Just let us know if they bother you again. It'll be no trouble to run them off."

She comes over to me, bends down a bit, and kisses my cheek. I turn red in the face, redder than Willie. She is a beauty, a tall, blond lass with lovely pink cheeks.

"Watch yerself, Charley. Maybe she'll let you pat her on the arse if y' ask her."

She overheard. "Maybe I will," she says.

I turn redder. For the first time since I left home, I picture Ellen standing behind me. I don't know what to say. It seems as if all eyes are on me. I mumble something to the lass and walk back up to the main deck. She follows me.

"I'm Sarah Dougherty. I'd like to know you better."

"How are you? I'm Charley Bailey." I know enough not to use my real name.

"Where are you staying in Philadelphia, Charley?"

"I'll not be staying in Philadelphia. I'm going west to work on the railroad. Chicago, I believe."

"Ah. 'Tis a pity. There is plenty of work in Philadelphia, you know. If you were working there, we could get together."

Why did I not tell her that I am married? I feel Ellen's eyes burning into my neck.

Sarah says, "I would love to see you there. We would have fun together. Can you dance?"

"No…not at all. I'm a poor dancer. Sorry."

She moves closer to me. She takes my face in her hands and kisses me on my lips. Her mouth is open when she kisses me.

"Hey Charley! Could ya help me down here."

It is Willie. He is breaking up my wee romance. I say goodbye to Sarah and hurry down the stairwell to the middle deck.

"Thanks," I say.

"I thought that y' needed my help. Sarah seems a bit forceful."

"She is. I didn't know how to get away."

"Her friend tells me that she needs a man badly. I hope that doesn't upset ya. I know that y' think that y're every lass's dream."

"Ah no. I never thought that. I'm married you know."

"Ya are? When were y' goin' to tell her?"

"I'd have gotten to it."

"I hear that she's pregnant."

"My wife isn't pregnant."

"I mean your lady friend up there."

"Ah Christ."

Now I realise why I am so popular with Sarah. It is definitely not my undeniable wit and charm.

Truly, being on the main deck is grand. The ship is a wonder. The sails on the front two masts are massive and billow out like clouds. Square rigged, I believe they call it. The ocean is a deep blue, marvellous to behold. When I can elbow my way to the rails through the passengers vomiting over the side, I see the creatures called porpoises. The porpoises travel together in packs alongside the ship, jumping through the blue waves. It is a grand time they seem to be having.

There isn't much privacy in the berths below decks. Most people sleep in their clothes, nevertheless some undress a bit before retiring. I try not to look at the ladies when they are removing their petticoats and things except that it is hard not to notice. I think that Sarah is trying to tempt me by removing more than she needs to, and I see her attempting to catch me peeking.

More and more passengers are sneaking below into the hold to perform their toilet functions instead of waiting for an open privy on the main deck. Day by day, the smell gets worse. It has been only three weeks. What in God's name will it be a month from now?

During the night, some of the married couples feel the need to satisfy their lust for each other. Their rutting results in the sighs and grunts I typically associate with farm animals. It is difficult to sleep when such activities are going on. Many images pass through my mind. I think of warm nights with Ellen. I try not to think of what it would be like with Sarah, although that passes through my mind as well. I hear a loud cry coming from a woman just a few bunks from my own; then I hear a loud chuckle coming from Willie. He isn't asleep either. As I say, there is no privacy here.

They're back. The crew members are back harassing the ladies at the privies. Willie and I stroll up to them.

"Did I not tell you to stay away from the ladies here?"

"Go to hell, Paddy. I work on this ship. It's me time off, and I'll spend it where I want."

"Do you want me to have words with the captain?"

"Go ahead. He doesn't care as long as we does our work."

"Fine then. Stay here and I'll be back."

"Wait. Let's settle this another way."

Willie gets into the conversation. "And what way would that be?"

"Come with me to the foc's'l. I have something for ya there."

I smile at Willie. It has been a while since I had any physical entertainment. I politely gesture for the two crewmembers to lead the way. The four of us head for the hatch to the foc's'l and when we get there, I spin the ugly gent around and smash him in the nose with a hard right fist. His friend, the larger one with a barrel chest, looks shocked. He gets his from Willie. Both are down on the deck as other crewmen stop what they are doing to rush us. A riot starts as we try to fight all of them, and we are not doing that well. The captain and an officer come out of their cabin on the quarter deck. They shout to the men, and the fighting stops.

The captain yells, "What caused this? Someone tell me!"

I speak with a bloody mouth to the troublemaking crew member who is still down on the deck.

"Do you want me to tell him?"

He shakes his head and yells up to the captain, "Just a bit of misunderstanding, sir."

The captain asks, "Are these passengers causing trouble? Should they be locked up?"

"Ah no, sir. We just had a l'il disagreement. They must have taken offence to our sailors's wit."

"Very well. Back to your stations."

The crew breaks up. The man I hit gets up and warns me again. "Y'll be very sorry for this me friend. We still have a long voyage ahead of us."

"Just stay away from the women passengers," I hiss at him.

It has been a relatively smooth voyage so far. There are only a few days when the boat rocks violently, and few passengers venture on deck except to use the privies. Those who use the privies, describe their experience to friends as they return soaked to the skin. Apparently, sitting in the privy is like riding a wild horse and water gushes through the seat as the ship crashes down on every wave. The ship's hold again becomes the passenger's place of refuge for performing certain bodily functions.

It is worse today. A storm is taking place, and the hatches to the steerage deck are bolted, and no one is allowed out. We spend the day rocking to and fro, and nearly everyone is sick and vomiting. Hour after hour, we wonder if the crew can keep the ship in one piece and afloat. Personal items are thrown about. The steerage deck is a mess with all manners of disgusting liquids underfoot. Besides all that, we miss our meal. Maybe that is just as well because it is unlikely that any food would stay down.

A day later, that storm is still battering the ship. There are prayers now, one constant series of litanies of the rosary. I promise God that I will stop thinking about Sarah if he will calm the storm.

Because there was no sleep the previous night, we are all weary. By late afternoon, the rocking settles down, and we stop worrying that we all will die. The hatches open and sunlight comes in. I look over and see a ghastly looking Sarah with her hair a mess. I will have no problem keeping my vow with God now.

All in all, except for some lovely moments on the main deck, the voyage is a vision of hell on earth. We don't get bread to eat anymore. We must be satisfied with hard biscuits with bugs in them or with oatmeal that we have to boil at the caboose. Soon we should be seeing land. Thank God for that.

We do see land far off in the distance. Some of my fellow passengers haven't been on the main deck since they boarded the ship. Now they are crowded to the right side of the ship staring at the misty edge of America. Some believe that they see a city in the grey mass at the horizon. It could be New York they say. I can see nothing of the sort. When asked, a crew member tells a passenger that we are still many days from reaching our port.

We sail on and on down the side of America, never getting close enough to see anything of interest. Nevertheless, we do see many sea birds which seem to be following us, and we see an occasional fishing boat. The spirits of all are improved. We know now that we will survive this trip and start life soon in a new country.

In a few days, we see land on both sides of the ship. We must be in a bay or a great river. We continue for hours, and a small ship comes alongside. A middle-aged man wearing a dark suit comes aboard from the other boat. The captain greets him and they both go into the wheelhouse. Things are getting exciting. What awaits us now?

We must be close to Philadelphia. The crew is going through the steerage deck and cargo decks, washing things down. They are also taking old smelly blankets and mattresses up to the main deck and throwing them overboard. Apparently, they want the ship to look, and smell, presentable for our arrival. The owners of the sleeping materials don't seem to mind losing their possessions. They were planning to leave them on board anyway.

As we sail up the river, we see towns and villages on the left side of the ship. That is the Pennsylvania side they tell me. Nothing seems to be on the right side except marshes. That would be the New Jersey side.

Later on, we see a group of buildings on the Pennsylvania side in the middle of marshland. The ship lowers most of its sails and seems to be heading for it. I don't think that it is Philadelphia. It looks nothing like a decent city.

The ship anchors next to an island with several buildings. Another sailing ship is already tied up to their only dock. After a time, a well dressed official comes out to the ship in a boat rowed by a labourer. He comes onboard and disappears into the wheelhouse with the captain.

Soon, a crewman announces that we are at the Lazaretto quarantine station and must come on deck for inspection by the doctor. All who can, report on the main deck. A few remain below, too sick to leave their bunks.

As our name is called, we walk forward to the doctor. He inspects our open mouths and checks our shirtless chests for signs of contagious diseases. The women are checked as well but only have to open their blouses a bit. I spy my lecherous friends among the crew enjoying the show. The doctor doesn't appear to have any concern about our health, although some of our lads appear next to death's door. I guess the doctor is only interested in infectious diseases such as famine fever, which I believe we have avoided. After looking at the passengers on the main deck, the doctor goes below to see how poorly the others are. He returns later and talks quietly with the captain. I see the captain shaking his head in the affirmative. I believe that we have all passed the test, even the sickly ones below, and will be allowed to go on to Philadelphia.

In the afternoon after leaving the quarantine station, we are towed by a paddle-wheel steam-ship up the river to our dock in Philadelphia. The city appears quite large with three and four storied buildings queued up next to each other down every visible street. A few churches with tall white steeples break up the rows of brick buildings. The ship crunches into a dock beside many other large ships with tall masts. Everyone is a bit apprehensive of what to expect when we disembark, although the process turns out to be swift and painless. Officials from the port are there with the captain as we come forward in answer to our names. An American official asks us our age, occupation, and where we will be staying in America. I give labourer as my occupation. I don't believe there are many jobs for farmers in these parts. He also asks if we intend to become American citizens. I answer in the affirmative. Another official, the customs inspector, briefly examines our possessions, a wee sack of clothes in my case. After that, we walk down the gangplank and stand on solid land for the first time in many weeks. The land seems to sway beneath my feet.

I'm in America. It doesn't look that much different than Derry except that the assortment of humans seems quite varied. There are black people, brown people, and white people, some of whom don't look either English or Irish.

The ship will be fitted for cargo on the trip back to England or Ireland. It is my understanding that coal will be the loaded on the ship at a different dock. Coal and lumber are the main exports from Philadelphia.

This is a busy waterfront. Many of the passengers have relatives waiting for them at the dock. Apparently, there is a journal published that lists all of the ship arrivals. Willie's brother meets him as he comes down the gangplank. Willie sees me and asks if I have a place to stay for the evening. His brother will be glad to put me up for the night. I thank him but say that I'll find an inn close by so that I can get an early start for Kellyville in the morning. We say our goodbyes. Willie was a good friend and a comfort on this horrendous voyage.

Behind me, a riot is taking place with each passenger disembarking. Local lads are fighting to take their trunk or trunks to the establishments or rooming houses that they represent. Most of the passengers are screaming at the lads to leave their luggage alone; they know where they are going, and they don't need any help. As for myself, I only have my sack of clothes, and they don't bother me except to ask if they can escort me to a fine waterfront inn. I ask each of them how much the inn will cost me, and I get no straight answer. These lads can talk around in circles. Eventually, they tire of me and move on to a different passenger.

Finally, a young lad comes over and tells me about an inn nearby with lovely rooms where they would charge very little for an Irishman, at least for the first night. He has an American accent with a touch of Donegal in it. After I question him a bit, he asks me if I am from Donegal. I tell him yes, and he says that he thought so. His granda, who lives at the inn, is from Donegal, and I have the brogue like himself. He tells me that the inn is called Gallagher's and it is located nearby on Front Street in the Dock Ward. The familiar name Gallagher convinces me to give it a try. The lad tells me that his Da will not be charging a greenhorn Donegal man like myself much money.

Eddie is only 12 years old. Even at his young age, his father sends him to the wharves on arrival day to try his luck at attracting some new tenants. He is skinny and frail but not shy. I guess that he will be taking over his father's business in later years. He and I walk the hard cobble-stone streets of Philadelphia up from the fantastic waterfront with its rows and rows of tall ships, past a dismal alley named Water Street, to Front Street. There we turn left and walk a few squares past tall lovely brick houses. We finally come to Gallagher's Inn. It is another good looking building that blends in nicely with the rich looking neighbourhood. It has a stable next to it with several fine horses and carriages.

Eddie's father, Charles, is sweeping the floor of the lobby when we arrive. He is a tall gentleman with sparse greying hair. Mr. Gallagher is well dressed, with a brown suit and vest. It looks a bit strange to me; nevertheless, his clothing seems to be cut in the latest American style.

Eddie says, "Da, this is a fellow from Donegal, just off the boat that arrived today."

Charles smiles and says, "Thank you, Eddie. Now get back to the wharf and see if there are others interested in spending money at our place here."

I say, "I'm pleased to meet you, Mr. Gallagher. My name is Charley Gallen from Donaghmore Parish."

"Donaghmore. I'm from there as well, Castlefin in fact. I came over here with my parents about 20 years ago. My Da ran this inn after we arrived. I took it over when he became too old. I'm happy to offer my place for you to stay until you get on your feet."

"I'm sorry, but I'll only be staying this evening. I'll be on my way tomorrow for Kellyville where I'll be working at the mill."

"Ah, another Donaghmore lad for the Kellyville mills. Many of you have passed through these doors in recent years. Incidentally, we have a few from Donaghmore living here now.

There is Rose Floyd from Cronalaghy and Jimmy Gallen from Meenreagh. Is Jimmy a relative of yours?"

"Not that I know of, except that it is possible. I was born in Glencarn, but my mother was a Gallen from Meenreagh."

"Well, Charley, welcome to my inn. I'll not be charging you, a fellow Donaghmore man, for tonight. Good luck to you tomorrow on your long trip to Kellyville."

"Thank you. Thank you. Would you, by any chance, know the way to Kellyville from here."

Mr. Gallagher stopped to think.

"Charley, let me convince you to stay another day here. You should get accustomed to the peculiarities of America. Rest up here for the night, and we will teach you some things tomorrow that you should know about this grand country. Also, the coach for Kellyville leaves early in the morning and it is some distance from here."

"I was hoping that I could walk to Kellyville. I don't think I have enough money for coach fare."

"Ach. It is many miles from here. It would take you all day to walk there. Are you sure that you haven't the money. I'll lend it to you."

"You don't have to do that. I'll get there somehow. You've been kind enough as it is."

"Very well, then. Go into the bar and have a drink. The bartender is Jimmy Murphy. Tell him that your first is on me."

"Once again I have to decline your hospitality, sir. I gave up drinking a few years back, but thank you anyway."

"Have a cup of tea then. I'll be in to see you again in a few minutes. We can talk about getting to Kellyville."

I walk through the door into the bar and see a couple of patrons drinking beer in the soft darkness. A few tables and chairs are there as well, but they are unoccupied. The room is immaculate with first class wooden furnishings. I introduce myself to the bartender. Murphy is a tall, strongly built man with light brown hair and a long, droopy moustache. He makes me a cup of tea and tells me about his past life in County Mayo and how he was lucky to meet Mr. Gallagher when he arrived here in 1845. Most of the tenants of the inn are Irish who work in the homes and businesses nearby.

"We have coachmen, butlers, and housekeepers living here. They are all lovely people."

I tell him of my plans to leave for Kellyville tomorrow where I have a job waiting.

"Ach. Stay with us awhile. What is one more day out of your life? God knows you'll only have this one opportunity to see what an American city is like."

"I'd like that, except I don't have much money to get by on, you know."

"Don't worry about that. Mr. Gallagher will take care of you."

I am starting to like the idea of refreshing myself before starting on my new adventure of travelling to Kellyville. Murphy tells me more about the inn. Mr. Gallagher runs it with his wife Rose whom he met when she arrived here from County Tyrone. They now have four children. Mr. Gallagher's father, who used to run the inn, is elderly and seldom leaves his room. The inn is three stories high and has six bedrooms, all but two occupied. Murphy thinks that I will be sharing the room with himself and two of the fellows who work at the carriage house next door. My guess is that I'll be sharing the bed with Murphy.

Mr. Gallagher enters the bar and confirms that Mr. Murphy will be my bed mate. He asks if he could speak with me privately at one of the tables. I join him at the table in the corner.

"Charley, the first thing I want to speak to you about is a difficult issue."

Not knowing what comes next, I am all ears.

"You will have to understand that Americans differ from us Irish. For one thing, they have a more sensitive sense of smell. They bathe quite often and detest the way our people smell. I am telling you this because I'd like you to take a bath as soon as possible. You probably have not bathed since you left home several months ago. I know that you couldn't help that, but you shouldn't leave for Kellyville without bathing. I suggest that you do it soon. We will have supper for you when you're done.

"Second, there is another reason Americans dislike the Irish. We are overwhelming them with our numbers. In many districts, we are the majority. We will work for less than the Americans, and therefore we are taking their jobs. The Americans also object to us sending our children to their schools. We greatly outnumber the American children in some schools, and the bishop is asking the schools to stop using the Protestant bible during classes. There was an uprising of Americans a few years ago when mobs of Protestants set fire to two of our churches. Another riot broke out just south of here a couple of months later which would have destroyed another church if it wasn't for the local militia. The police have the anti-Irish bigotry under control now. Good thing too. In the years since the riots, the Irish are now streaming into the city. Many Americans have already left the neighbourhoods where we settle."

He continues. "You will see that there are many Americans here who hate the Irish. They hate our religion, our dirty habits, and our drunkenness and boisterous behaviour. Please be aware that you could run into hostile people on the road to Kellyville."

I say, "I'll try to be as much like an American as I can. I'll blend in so that they won't notice me."

Mr. Gallagher laughs. "I don't think that is possible. If your brogue doesn't give you away, your clothes will. I think if you are polite enough, some reasonable Americans will accept you." He adds, "I hope that you will stay with us for another night. It'll cost you nothing."

"I will. Thank you, Mr. Gallagher. I hope Mr. Murphy doesn't mind."

There is no charge for me using the bath. I spend a reasonable time scrubbing myself in the tub in the luxurious downstairs bathroom, as Mr. Gallagher suggested, and then dress in some clean clothes. I am ready for supper and walk into the dining room where many of my fellow guests have already started eating. The food smells delicious. There is meat of some kind mixed in a stew with carrots and potatoes. I am in heaven. I talk with the guests after supper and later walk about the waterfront of the city until bedtime.

The next day, when everyone else is working, I walk up to Market Street. Market Street is a broad, straight road running from the docks through the city as far as I can see. It has tall buildings on each side and a row of covered sheds running down the middle of the street for the sale of food and sundry articles. Obviously, that is why the street is so named. The row of sheds in the middle of the street seems to stretch to the horizon. Many of the stalls in the sheds are unoccupied, but the others are doing a lively business. I am astounded by the number of large passenger coaches being pulled by teams of horses as well. Many of the buildings on both sides of the street have pane windows exhibiting wares for sale. Well dressed women are coming and going in great haste in and out of each. I notice that they go out of their way to avoid walking near me, and I get the feeling that a person like myself is out of place in the nicer parts of the city.

At sunrise the next morning, I say goodbye to Mr. Gallagher and my new Philadelphia friends and follow their directions to the stage coaches at the bridge over the Schuylkill River. They tell me that the coach to Kellyville leaves at about 9 o'clock, and I should be there long before that. They also warn me that I should only take the coach for the Baltimore Turnpike and not the one to the town of Darby on the Woodlands Road. I walk up Front Street and left on Market Street to the edge of the city at the Schuylkill River. I could have ridden the passenger coaches down Market Street to the bridge, but I need to be careful with my money.

On the far side of the Market Street Bridge, stage coaches are queued up and passengers are waiting. I walk to the stand located there and ask about the fare to Kellyville. The agent tells me that it is one dollar. I had changed some of my money to American currency; nevertheless, this fare will greatly reduce my remaining funds. I'm sure that I could walk to Kellyville; I have walked much farther distances in Ireland. I decided to take the coach because I feared getting lost or maybe attacked by Indians or anti-Irish Americans. I ask the agent if he would accept the silver coin that I found at the holy spring. He asks to see it. I remove it from my pocket and show him. It gleams in the morning sun, almost blinding him. He takes it in his hand, looks at me, and tells me that it is too valuable to trade for a dollar. I agree and give him one of the dollars from my other pocket. I admire the agent for his honesty. He could have taken the coin and sold it for much more money. Maybe these Americans aren't so bad after all.

The other passengers scheduled to leave on my coach seem to be looking at me with distaste, afraid to share their seats with me. I am smiling at them and trying to appear as friendly as I can. I don't think that I smell bad. It has only been a day since I bathed. I walk up to the driver and ask if I can ride on the top of the stage coach with him.

"Sure Mister. It'll be dusty up there, but you're welcome to join me."

Actually, I think that it will be more enjoyable than riding in the cramped passenger compartment.

A team of horses are hitched to the coach and away we go. I am excited. The wind is blowing through my hair as we rumble through the streets between the houses of Philadelphia and then through the patches of farms located in the open country. I'll remember this ride for the rest of my life. The driver tells me that we should be in Kellyville in about two hours. So soon! I'll be talking with Charles Kelly this very day.

The road we travel is an excellent road. It should be. We have to stop at toll stations where the driver has to pay to use the road. After he pays, a barrier is lifted, and we drive on to the next station.

The driver tells me, "This road has been in operation for over forty years. It was called the Philadelphia-Brandywine-New London Turnpike when it opened. In Philadelphia, we now call it the Baltimore Turnpike because it eventually continues to the city of Baltimore in Maryland. We are now on the portion called the Delaware County Turnpike because we are out of the city. The road is more travelled now that it goes through the town of Media. As of this year, Media is the new county seat of Delaware County. Chester City used to be the county seat."

"Does this coach go all the way to Baltimore?"

"No. That is too far. The passengers make stops at inns along the way where they change coaches. I'll be stopping at the Black Horse Inn past Media where I'll get fresh horses before turning back to Philadelphia. Any passengers going farther south will change coaches at the Black Horse."

The land I am passing looks much like Donegal except for the forests. There is wide open land as well, with farms much larger than you'll see in Donegal. The driver stops the coach at a crossroad he calls the Darby Road. Two passengers, a man and a woman, get out. The driver hauls their trunk down from the top of the coach. It was secured just in back of me.

He tells me, "There is room for you now in the coach, but you'll be getting off soon. Might as well stay up there."

I agree. The driver climbs back up and we are on our way again. In just a few minutes, we are down a hill, crossing a bridge over a creek where he pulls on the reins and stops the coach again.

"This is it. This is where you get off. That's the Kellyville Mill on the right. Good luck to you."

I grab my pack and descend from the coach.

"Thank you very much. This has been a new experience for me. I never rode in such luxury."

The driver laughs. "Well, you're very welcome. You're the first Irishman I've taken here. In the past, I've passed many on their way here, walking on the dusty road. I guess that you are a little richer than the other folks from your country."

I start thinking that maybe I should have walked. I could have saved some money for food and lodging here. Ach, I wouldn't have missed the thrill of the ride here for any amount that I could afford.

The coach rides off up the hill toward Media. I stare at the mill. It is a huge brick building with many windows. The water from a mill-race runs next to the building, obviously turning powerful machinery that transforms cotton picked from American bushes into material for trousers, stockings, coats, and shirts. There is a noise from the building unlike anything I have ever heard before, and I see people coming and going in and out of the massive structure. I walk toward the entrance of the mill and prepare my story for when I meet Charles Kelly.

I walk through a door, except that I am rudely stopped by a rather large gentleman who asks what I want. I tell him that I am here to work for Mr. Kelly. I tell him that I have just arrived from Ireland.

"Y' have, have ya? What makes you think that Mr. Kelly is after hiring you? We have enough people here now, you know."

"I'd like to see Mr. Kelly. He is an uncle of mine, and he told me that he had a job for me. That is the only reason I came here."

The large man considers that a bit and tells me that Mr. Kelly isn't in today. He sends me into a room where a number of men and women are working at desks. Not a sliver of cotton do I see there.

"Can I help you?" asks a young lad.

I explain that I am a relative of Mr. Kelly and that he offered me a job at his mill when I came to America. I am fibbing a bit. I never really talked with Mr. Kelly. It was a general offer of work to anyone in Donaghmore who emigrated, except that it seems to ring a bell with the lad who is speaking to me.

"I see. Mr. Kelly will be in tomorrow. Would you come back then? I'll arrange an interview with Charles."

I find myself in the street next to the factory. What now? I might as well wait until the workers are leaving for the day and look for someone I know from Donaghmore. I don't really know anyone who actually works here, but maybe I'll get lucky and see a familiar face.

It is early evening and I hear the angelus bell from the church on the hill across the creek. Immediately after that, a whistle from the mill signals the end of the workers' day. I see them leaving the mill. Most of them stare at me as they walk past heading for their homes in the lands next to the mill. There are more women than men. Some of their faces look familiar to me, except that I see no one whose name I remember from the parish.

Then I see a face from the old days. Jesus. It is my Da's cousin Mickey. Mickey is the black sheep who left his family and settled in Fermanagh with a new wife. We met again after his mother's wake before he left for America. I guess that I shouldn't have been surprised to see him here in Kellyville.

Mickey is walking up the road with a definite limp. He has two lads with him and a lass. From the way they are talking, I can see that they are likely his children, and they work with him at the mill. I run up to him before he can disappear into the cluster of homes next to the mill.

"Mickey!" I holler.

He looks at me strangely. He doesn't know me.

"Who the hell are ya?"

His daughter gives him a disapproving look.

"I'm Charley Gallen, just off the boat from Ireland. How'ya doing?"

He studies my face and then breaks into a smile.

"Ach, Charley. It is a surprise seein' ya. Are y' here for work at the mill?"

"I am. I'll be seeing Mr. Kelly in the morning."

"Where are y' stayin'?"

"Well. I was hoping to see a friendly face from the parish. Could you put me up for a couple of days?"

"Aye, I can, if y' don't mind sleepin' on the floor of me home. Oh, by the way, these here are me children. There's Eddie here and Jimmy. The lovely lass here is me daughter Mary."

The three young people are attractive and seem intelligent. They also show no interest in meeting me.

Mickey takes me aside and tells me that he is still using the name Cullen and not Gallen. He never told his wife of his previous life in Donaghmore and never will. I follow Mickey and his children home to one of several homes connected together in a row. There is a porch in the front of the house, and when we pass through his door, we are standing in the room he calls the parlour. The kitchen is in the rear of the house.

Mickey introduces me to his wife, Nell, a kind lady who welcomes me warmly. He introduces me to a younger daughter, Margaret, as well. Margaret will work at the mill next year when she finishes school. Mickey explains that I am a distant relative of his from Donegal. I go along with his story. Why should I not?

Morning comes and I go to the mill with the Cullens. They enter through a wide gate past the Kelly Mill guards. I go to the front door and tell the guard there that I am to see Mr. Kelly. After waiting on an uncomfortable bench for an hour, a young lad invites me into the throne room of Mr. Charles Kelly. He is sitting with his back toward me, reading a large bound book of handwritten figures. Finally, he turns to face me. He smiles, stands, and walks around his desk to shake my hand.

"Charles Gallen. Are you from Meenreagh?"

"Ah no, sir. I'm a Glencarn Gallen. In fact, I'm married now and my family is living in Coracreagh. I hope to bring them over someday. You may remember my granny, Anne. She was a Kelly and a cousin of your uncle Denis."

"I do. She was a lovely woman. I heard that she passed on. How are your parents?"

"They are fine, sir. We had a hard time of it during the hunger, but we managed to survive. I'm hoping to work here with you, sir. 'Tis a fine country, and I want to be a part of it."

"You will, don't you worry. You won't make much money at first, but with training, you'll learn a trade that entitles you to more pay. The hours are long, but you are a strong lad. You'll do fine here."

Well… Mr. Kelly is a fine gentleman. He leads me out to one of his clerks and tells him to bring me to a Mr. Miller. Mr. Miller is foreman of the crew that unloads the bales of cotton that arrive on most days. Miller introduces me to the other workers, and soon I am sweating with the rest of them.

One of the first things I must do is to write a letter to my family. Mickey Cullen's daughter Margaret said that she would write it for me. The Cullen children attended the school on the Springfield Road, about a mile away up the pike, and they know how to read and write. Margaret and I sit in the Cullen kitchen, and she asks what I want to say. This is quite awkward. I clear my throat and think.

"Dear Family," I say. "I am here in Kellyville after a long, hard, sea voyage. I am well. I am working for Mr. Charles Kelly at his mill. When I get a chance, I'll send some money to yis, but I am sorry that I have none to send in this letter. I miss yis all and hope that I can earn enough for yis to join me in a year or two when I can save enough for your passage. Your husband or father, Charles Gallen."

Margaret is writing furiously as I am speaking. When I finish, she stops writing and then starts on a new page. As she writes, she asks me questions as to the names of my family members. She finishes the letter and looks at me.

"See if you like this letter, Mr. Gallen." She reads to me what she wrote.

"My Dear Wife,

"I take this favourable opportunity of writing these few lines to let you know that I am well after an exhausting journey to America. I hope that you and the children are well, also. My blessings to you and blessings to our children: Bridget, James, Edward, Catherine, Patrick, and Charles. I long to see you again when I can earn enough to pay for your passage to this wonderful country.

"I have been engaged in the employment of Mr. Charles Kelly at his mill in the quaint village of Kellyville. I hope that I soon will be able to send for you to join me here.

"The best of wishes to your delightful parents, Edward and Bridget and your brothers and lovely sisters as well. Please give my regards to my father and mother, James and Catherine, as well as my brothers and sisters. Also give my regards to our cousins when you see them. They are in my thoughts as well.

"I am sorry that I cannot send you any money at this time. Perhaps I can do so in the future.

"Cordially, your loving husband, Charles."

A bit wordy I think, but I thank Margaret. The letter will be sent from the new post office in Kellyville.

chapter 16
(1851 - 1852)

I have been working at the mill for a year now. My workday is from 6 o'clock in the morning to 6 o'clock at night. I reach the gate at the mill when the morning Angelus bell rings at St. Charles Church on top of the hill above the Darby Creek. At the same minute the bell sounds, a whistle from the mill blows for us to stand at roll call. There is a duplication of sounds that tells us when work starts and stops. The whistle for a lunch break follows the noon Angelus bell. We have a few minutes to eat the lunches we bring from home before a whistle announces that it is time to go back to work. The Angelus bell ordinarily precedes the quitting time whistle at night. We work six days a week, and my wages are twelve dollars a month. My expenses are low, especially because I don't join my fellow workers at the local pub on Saturday night. Of my twelve dollars pay, a half-dollar is deducted for my bed in the bachelor quarters of the mill housing village. Many of my fellow workers often spend much of their pay at the Kellyville Bar, up the street from the mill. The married ones get holy hell from their wives when they get home, drunk from porter and whiskey. Most of their pay is gone to drink. It is wise of the mill to deduct the rent for housing from their pay. Otherwise, their families would have to live in the fields.

My three friends from Donaghmore arrived in Kellyville about two weeks after I did. Their voyage on the *Bark Creole* was as horrible as my experience. They work with me at the mill and live with me in the bachelor quarters. Mr. Kelly was true to his word about hiring men from his old parish.

My work at the mill involves the initial process of making fabric. After unloading the bales of cotton, I break them open and feed the cotton into the willowing machinery. All of the machinery in the mill is run from the two main water wheels by means of shafts and belts. It is brilliant. The willowing frame has spiked cylinders that rotate rapidly to loosen the cotton fibres. I also run the lap-frame that presses the fibres together to make flat sheets of cotton.

The laps of cotton are then carded into slivers by machines, generally run by women. Back home in Ireland, women also did the carding with stiff brushes. Here in America, the machinery does the carding. The machine has spikes on rotating drums that form slivers, long ropes of cotton. From this point on, I don't often see the machines that spin the slivers of cotton into thread except when I am cleaning up the floors where they are located. The next process is weaving the thread into cloth. I have never seen this process. I only assume that the weaving machinery is complicated and intricate. The men who run the weaving machines are the most highly paid workers at the mill.

I am saving most of my wages, although I have no idea when I can buy passage for my family to America. Perhaps I can learn to weave and get a better wage. I must ask my foreman how I can develop this skill.

I rarely see Mr. Kelly. He comes and goes from the mill as he pleases. From the other workers, I learn that Mr. Kelly is one of the richest men in Pennsylvania, and he owns most, if not all, of the land in Kellyville. He donated the land for St. Charles Catholic Church and was instrumental in having it built. Mr. Kelly is active in a group that is building a railroad from Philadelphia to the town of West Chester. There will be a Kellyville passenger station when the railroad is finished.

Mr. Kelly opened a post office here as well. He has been chosen by the United States government as Kellyville's first postmaster.

This mill has been here since 1820. Charles and his uncle Denis rented it in 1826 and later purchased it. Charles bought out his uncle shortly after that and improved the mill. He purchased land for himself and built homes for the workers. The mill grew larger and the number of workers increased to more than 200 today. Most of the workers come from Ireland, Donegal mainly. Some of the skilled workers were born in America, but others were born in Germany and England.

In the early days, there was no way that the Irish who worked and lived in Kellyville could attend Mass, so Charles Kelly established a mission here, and Mass was celebrated in the mill office by a priest from St. Denis Church in the village of Havertown. St. Denis was built by Charles's uncle near his mill in that village. In 1847, Charles donated the land and raised money for a church in Kellyville.

The church was completed in 1849, the year before I arrived here. It was named St. Charles Borromeo, who was Charles Kelly's patron saint. I guess that Borromeo must be my patron saint as well. The first pastor of the parish was Father James McGinniss who was the pastor of St. Denis. He was assigned by the bishop to both parishes. Father McGinniss is no longer our pastor here, as he was reassigned recently to a church in Manyunk, near Philadelphia. Our present pastor is Father John Shiels. Father Shiels is also pastor of St. Denis and lives next to the church in Havertown. On Sunday, I join the other mill workers as we cross Darby Creek and climb the hill to hear Father Shiels say Mass in the beautiful church that Mr. Kelly has provided for us.

St. Charles Church is a wonder. It would impress anyone, even those who attend the fine churches of Derry. It is constructed of stone by master American stone masons. The outside view of it would put to shame any of the churches in Donaghmore, either Protestant or Catholic. Inside, the ceiling reaches to heaven and the walls are painted with lovely pictures of Jesus and the saints. The altar is located in an alcove decorated with other religious paintings. Pews of the finest wood enable more than 400 people to attend Mass. When I enter the great doors of St. Charles, it almost takes my breath away.

Sunday is the only day we have for leisure. I can sleep late, typically until 8 o'clock. The bells from the tower at St. Charles ring at a quarter before ten to let everyone know that they should be on their way to Mass. Father Shiels arrives early on Sunday so that he can hear confessions during the half hour before Mass. He then dons his vestments and starts the Mass at ten. The Mass is about 45 minutes long. The ringing of three bells at the Sanctus signals that the body of Christ will soon be present at the altar. Many who are in a state of grace, those who went to confession earlier, receive the body of Christ from the priest at the communion. Although I feel that I am probably in a state of grace, I rarely go to the communion rail. I don't like telling the priest my sins. Also, I don't like fasting from food and drink after midnight of the night before in order to be able to receive. When my family arrives, I'll change my ways.

The parishioners at St. Denis have it a bit easier. Father says Mass there earlier on Sunday and therefore the fasting is shorter. He hears confession there on Saturday night as well. The only problem with St. Denis is that their parishioners don't get as much sleep as I do on Sunday.

All of Sunday is free to us lads from the bachelor quarters. We play football in the field or fish in the high water above the dam. There are not many fish in Darby Creek. I think that the dye dumped into the water from upstream mills kills them. There are no salmon here. Sometimes we catch catfish and a fish known as a suckerfish. They taste poorly when fried. Nevertheless, they are free food.

I finally agree to join the lads at the Kellyville Pub. They have been joking with me all day that I shouldn't miss the celebration of Tommy Maloney's birthday. They tell me that I don't have to drink alcohol if I don't want. It is a Friday and we have to work tomorrow, so I don't believe that the lads will stay at the pub too long.

The pub is loud and rowdy when I arrive after work. I believe that some had left work early to get started on the celebration. I walk in with Matt McGlinchy and John Callaghan to a great cheer.

"Charley is here. Howya doin' Charley. Come and have a pint with us."

I think about it. I haven't had a drink in years now. I believe that one pint can do me no harm if I drink it slowly. I join the lads who ask Mary, the barmaid, to draw me a glass of the amber stuff that Americans seem to like. The beer does look weak. It should harm me none.

It tastes like water. Shite. I am missing nothing by abstaining from drinking this weak liquid. I heartily start joking with the lads there, and in no time Tommy comes in to more loud cheers. I look at my glass. It is empty.

I don't remember much about the rest of the night. I wake up in my bed and stumble outside to take a piss. I have a great thirst and wonder how I can satisfy it with another drink. I walk to Callaghan's bed. He is asleep. I shake him. He wakes and stares at me.

"Johnnie, do you have any whiskey here. I need a drink. My head is going to burst."

"OK Charley. It's in me closet. Help yerself. Just don't drink all of it."

I didn't get up for work the next day. My wages will be docked for the time missed. Many of the other lads didn't go to the mill that day as well and will earn less at their next payday. I spend the morning in bed and the rest of the day wanting the drink but afraid to beg anyone for it.

Sunday comes and I go to Mass. In the afternoon, I wander over to the field to watch the lads play football. One of the men defending the goal is a tall fellow named George Palmer. He is an American who works with me at the willowing frame. George is a serious lad and has plans to move up to weaving when a position opens. After the game is finished, he comes over to me.

"Charley, the fellas tell me that you were drinking with them on Friday."

"Aye, I was. No harm done."

"Didn't you tell me that you had a problem in Ireland with drinking? Do you think that it is wise to start again?"

"I believe that I can handle it now."

I have my own doubts about that statement. I crave a drop of whiskey at this very minute.

George says, "I like you, Charley. I don't want to see you ruin your life. You have the responsibility of getting your family over here. If you feel the need for drinking, please see me. I can help you, perhaps."

George is a good man, and I want to have his respect. I believe that I will try to stay off the drink.

"I'll do that. Thank you."

There has been a series of letters between my family and myself over the months. Margaret Cullen has been writing mine, and I have been able to include a few bank notes in them. What they do with them over there, I have no idea. The letters from Ellen in Ireland are well written. Someone must be writing hers, as well. All have been good news. Today is the exception... an especially serious exception.

Margaret reads, "I have sad news to relate to you. Your father has taken ill and has passed away."

Those are shocking words. My head is spinning. He was the picture of health when I saw him last. I knew that I would hear of his death someday but never this soon. The letter tells nothing of the nature of his illness.

"His wake was beautiful and well attended. He is buried in a new plot in the graveyard at the Cross where there is room for your mother and others of your family when the time comes. May he rest in peace."

Short words...short letter. Margaret looks at me with sympathy as does the rest of her family. She gives me the letter. I take it and walk to my quarters. I haven't gotten over the way my father and I had made amends in the recent past. I finally realised that he was a loving parent and not the monster that I originally imagined. It will take some time for me to grasp that

I missed his wake and burial. I'll not see him again until I join him in heaven.

Mr. Kelly hears the news and arranges a Mass to be said for my father at St. Charles. It is kind of him.

I notice that George Palmer is keeping an eye on me, so that I don't have an excuse to raise a glass to Da at the local taproom. George always knows the right words to say to me. He keeps me occupied at work and invites me for dinner at his parent's home. I have to say that this American is the best friend I have here in Kellyville.

I have Margaret write to my mother. It takes an hour to put the right words into the ink on the paper. I am sympathetic and hopefully say the proper things to her. I get a letter from Ellen a month later. She tells me that my mother is still in mourning, but her outlook is improving. Almost everyone in Donaghmore has visited her and given her comfort. My brother Patrick and his wife take care of her every need. The next part of the letter puzzles me. Ellen tells me that my mother asks why I haven't sold the silver coin to pay for my family's passage to America. No one knew of the coin. I told nobody about it except the man at the coach station in Philadelphia. I realize that my mother is right. Why haven't I sold the coin? It must be of a good value, especially because it is seems so rare. I must talk to George about this. I can trust him. I am not sure I can truly trust anyone else here, not even Mickey and his family.

I believe now that I know how my mother knew of the coin. When my father was sick, she went to the holy spring and talked to the lady there. The lady knew of the coin because she placed it there for me to find.

When George hears of my silver coin, he asks to see it. I take it from the hiding place in the ragged sack I brought with me from Ireland. He holds it, feels its weight, and examines the unusual design on its face.

He tells me, "Charley, I think that this is some ancient coin from Ireland and worth much more than its silver content. It could be a rare Roman coin."

"I don't believe that. The Romans never set foot in Ireland."

"Maybe it is a Viking coin or a Roman coin brought to Ireland by merchants. We should have someone look at it."

It is unlikely that anyone in Kellyville would know anything about my coin. George suggested that I should ask Mr. Kelly what he would do.

Mr. Kelly knows of a teacher in Philadelphia who might tell me the value of a rare coin. I am afraid that the search for the right man to help me will take too much of my time. Mr. Kelly says that he will show this person my coin on his next trip to Philadelphia, but I don't want the coin to leave my possession. I tell him to never mind. I'll just keep it as a memento of Ireland.

After a month passes, Mr. Kelly walks over to me at the receiving area of the mill. He has a distinguished looking gentleman with him. Apparently, Mr. Kelly contacted a professor at the university, and there was some interest in what sort of ancient artefact I could possibly have in my possession. The gentleman asks to see the coin. Mr. Kelly gives me the time off work to go to my quarters and bring it back. I return with the coin and show it to him. I can see the excitement the sight of it brings to the professor. You would think it was a piece of silver from Judas's own purse.

"This is very interesting. I believe that it is a Celtic coin of some kind, possibly from Germany or France. How much do you want for it?"

I have no idea. I ask Mr. Kelly how much it would cost to transport seven people from Ireland to Philadelphia.

Mr. Kelly has no idea either. He tells me that whatever it is, Professor Broadbent will pay it.

I agree to sell it for passage to America for my family from Ireland. The contract is sealed with a handshake.

The Thomas P. Cope Company is located in Philadelphia. It is a steamship line that carries passengers from Liverpool to Philadelphia and returns with lumber and coal. Mr. Kelly arranges to purchase the tickets for my family and transfers them to the post office in Killygordon. The cost of the tickets is unknown to me. George tells me that it was most likely more than a hundred dollars. I don't know how I could have ever have saved that much money. The silver coin was truly a gift from the spirit of the holy spring.

My family will soon be here with me. I can hardly wait for them.

chapter 17
(1853)

Many letters are now crossing the ocean in connection with my family's emigration. I worry about the dangers of travel with Ellen and our six children, the oldest who is only eleven years of age. I warn her of the villains who prey on immigrants. Ellen informs me that her younger sister Elizabeth will be coming with her. This comforts me greatly, although I know that only seven passenger tickets were sent to her.

I'm not sure how I will find out when my family arrives in Philadelphia. The ships of the Cope Line will be listed in the city newspapers when they arrive, but I don't know of anyone who reads the newspapers except Mr. Kelly. I ask him if he will read the ship arrivals and let me know of any Cope ship that docks in Philadelphia. He eases my mind by assuring me that it was always his intention to do so.

In my letters home, I ask Ellen to go to the Gallagher's Inn after they arrive. Knowing Mr. Gallagher's kindness, I am sure that he will put them up until I arrive to take them to Kellyville. I will now wait until spring when I hope to see Ellen, Elizabeth, and my children.

Mr. Kelly seems to be taking a personal interest in reuniting me with my family. Not only does he tell me when a Cope ship arrives, he has one of his friends in the city look at the passenger list. So far, there have been no Gallens in the lists for the spring arrivals.

One day in late May, I see Mr. Kelly walking toward the loading platform. The workers see him as well and start working harder. I look at him in anticipation. He has a smile on his face.

"Well Charley, here is good news. Your family has arrived. My friends at the port tell me that they are staying at the Gallagher Hotel on Front Street. I believe that you are familiar with that establishment."

My fellow workers slap my back and congratulate me.

"I don't know how to thank you, sir."

"You'll be needing a house now in the Kelly village. Please check at the office with Sarah. You'll also be needing a few days off to bring your family home. You're free to go as of now."

I run to the weaving floor to tell George Palmer of my good fortune. He is as happy for me as I am for myself. I think about the next thing to do. I'll start walking now to Philadelphia on the turnpike. I should arrive at Gallagher's by night fall. I run home and pack a sack with some clothes, money, and food. I'm on my way.

It is a long walk, but I walked just as far in Ireland. I hurry when I spy Gallagher's Hotel on the cobble-stone streets of Philadelphia. Soon I am at the door and enter the front room. I see Mr. Gallagher behind the desk; he stares at me as I walk up to him. He doesn't remember me.

Breathlessly I say, "Mr. Gallagher, you don't remember me, but I was here three years ago. I'm Charley Gallen and I've come to bring my family home.

I see the recognition in his eyes.

"Certainly, Charley. Your family is in one of our rooms on the second floor. I'll bring you to them."

I rush ahead of Mr. Gallagher. I believe that I hear the sound of children. Mr. Gallagher catches up and knocks on the door. My heart is pounding when I hear footsteps and the door unlatching.

"I'll leave you alone now," he says as he walks back toward the stairs.

The door opens. It is Elizabeth. She is an attractive young woman now with long brown hair and a clear, unblemished complexion. I see my children playing on the floor, except I do not see Ellen.

"Charley, I have some bad news for you. Ellen isn't here. She didn't make the voyage with us."

The children haven't noticed me yet. Either that or they don't recognise me. Elizabeth takes me into the hall and says,

"We didn't have enough tickets for the Cope ship. Ellen said that she would take another steamship and meet us here. She didn't want me travelling alone. She had enough money for another ship, the *City of Birmingham*. It was leaving a couple of days after ours."

"You gave me a scare there, Elizabeth. Ellen should be here in a couple of days. I'll take yis home and come back for her."

"I hope she has a safe voyage. Come in and see the children."

Of course, the children look older to me than when I saw them last in Ireland. Bridget is the biggest surprise. She is only eleven years of age but looks mature for her age. There are lasses working at the mill who look younger than her. Elizabeth is in charge of the children, but Bridget has a big hand in disciplining them and it shows.

I welcome Jimmy and Eddie and see that they remember me well. They never stop talking about their trip to England and to America. They tell me that they had been going to the Gleneely School and can read and write a bit. It is through them that I learn later about the hardships they faced on the voyage from Liverpool.

Katie, at eight years, is a bit shy. She pulls away a bit from my embrace. I tell her about the house that is waiting for her in Kellyville, and finally she smiles.

The young ones, Paddy and Charles, just look at me and try to remember me. When I talk to them, they just ask about their mother. They seem to believe that I was to bring her with me when I came to the hotel. I explain that she is coming in a couple of days, and that I'll bring her to their new home.

I spend the night sleeping on the floor with my two older sons. Elizabeth, the wee boys, and the girls are crowded into three beds in the large room. I am tired from my long walk and fall asleep immediately.

The next day, I have a word with Mr. Gallagher. I learn that Elizabeth and the children have been here for four nights. I offer to pay for the room, and he tells me that he would be happy if I paid for only two nights.

"You should go to the port and ask about your wife's ship. It may be arriving any day now. You are welcome to stay here until her ship arrives."

"Who should I see about the ship's arrival?" I ask.

"It is easy. Look for a man wearing a suit at the port office on Market Street. Look for someone who seems to be in charge."

I walk to the waterfront and see the sign for the Port of Philadelphia. I enter the office and walk to the desk of a man who seems to be the busiest.

"Sir, could you tell me when the *City of Birmingham* is expected to arrive? My wife is aboard.

I expect to be insulted by the gentleman at the desk. At first, he appeared to resent having his work interrupted. I am surprised to see a change in his countenance. Those within earshot of me turn and look.

"Your wife is aboard the *Birmingham?*"

"Aye, she is."

"Sir, the *City of Birmingham* was expected to arrive yesterday. So far we have heard nothing of her new arrival day. She must have been held up by a storm."

I decide that I should bring Elizabeth and the children home. I really can't afford to stay at Gallagher's any more days.

There are three ways to return to Kellyville now. There is a new train from the Market Street Bridge that stops at the Kellyville Station. There is also the stage coach that runs from Market Street to Kellyville. And there is the walking. Guess which one we choose? Here is a hint, the train and the coach require a great deal of money.

On the road to Kellyville, I learn more about the hardships Elizabeth and the children faced coming to America. First was the sadness of leaving the families. Nothing is sadder than an American wake when children are involved. After saying their goodbyes, they had a long walk to Belfast where they took a steamship to Liverpool. As expected, they had to fight off the runners and villains in Liverpool who wanted to separate them from the wee bit of money they brought with them. They had to put up with filthy accommodations in Liverpool until their ship was ready to sail. Eddie told me of the rats he had seen in the halls of the guest house where they stayed. Their ship, the *Saranak*, was a steam ship and the duration of their voyage was shorter than mine; nevertheless, they still had to put up with poor food and poor toilet accommodations. I had warned them to bring a commode with them. They did, but they tell me that washing it presented some disgusting moments.

Our new home in the Kelly Village is ready for us when we arrive. It was vacated months before when the old fellow who lived there died of consumption. Previously his children had moved away, and his widow left Kellyville to live with them at another mill town called Rockdale.

The house is a wee cottage with two bedrooms, a parlour, and a separate building for the kitchen. My children love it. Having a company house means that more money will be deducted from my pay. Normally, other members of the family work to help pay for it. In reality, I have no one who can help me with the extra expenses until Ellen gets here. Elizabeth had expected to work at the mill or as a housekeeper, but she can do neither. I need her to watch the children until Ellen arrives. I think about Bridget, nevertheless. She will be twelve years of age soon. The Commonwealth of Pennsylvania passed labour laws to protect children just before I came to Kellyville. A child must be twelve years of age to work. Bridget, although short in stature, looks old enough to work at the mill. I think that I'll fib a bit and tell my employer that she is twelve now. Children of that early age are restricted to only ten hours a day, sixty hours a week. This is two hours a day less than adults.

I inform Mr. Kelly that my wife didn't arrive with the children. He tells me that he will have his people let him know when the *City of Birmingham* arrives at the port.

Days pass and there is no news from Mr. Kelly. There are tears every day when I return from work and tell the children that their mother isn't in America yet. I regret that I didn't negotiate eight ship tickets instead of seven, and I secretly resent that Elizabeth replaced Ellen on their ship. Ellen is on my mind constantly, and I can't sleep at night thinking about her and seeing her sweet face. When will this waiting be over? Where is her ship? I wish that I could be at the Philadelphia docks day and night until her ship arrives.

Two long weeks pass and finally I get a message to visit Mr. Kelly. My hope is that he has heard that the ship arrived, but it is not to be. I am invited into Mr. Kelly's office.

"Charles, please sit down. I have some bad news." The air suddenly goes out of me and the room spins a bit. "The *City of Birmingham* is missing. It is believed to have sunk in the North Atlantic Ocean. The crew and over 400 passengers are believed to have perished."

chapter 18
[1853]

The wait is over now; Ellen is gone. I will never see her lovely smiling face again. I wish that I had died with her. There seems to be no point in living without her.

Mr. Kelly tells me to go home. He will send Father Shiels to our home the next time he is in Kellyville.

What will I tell the children? Here they are in a strange land without their mother. Should we go back to Ireland? We should. There they will have more family to love them.

I arrive home and meet Elizabeth at the door. I tell her quietly, and she rushes off to her bedroom in tears. I can hear her sobs as I watch the children before me playing in the parlour. I was hoping that Elizabeth would help me tell the children. It looks as if I have to do it alone.

Bridget is watching Charles and Paddy sharing their few toys. Jimmy and Eddie are practicing their writing, playing school perhaps before they start at the Springfield Road School in September. Katie is cleaning the dishes outside at the pump. I don't know how to tell them. Ach, I'll start with Jimmy and Eddie.

"Boys, could I have a word with yis?" They stop writing on the scraps of paper when I walk over to them. "It's about your mother and I'm afraid that it isn't good news."

They both look at me alertly with wide eyes. From watching Elizabeth run past them in tears, they seem to know that they will be hearing the worst news that they have ever heard in their young lives.

"There is no easy way of saying this. You know that your mother left England in a different ship than all of yis. Well, that ship has sunk in the ocean, and your mother is now with God and the angels. I am terribly sorry...terribly sorry."

Eddie lets out a cry that frightens both me and all within earshot. Bridget comes in and the young ones follow.

Jimmie tells her, "Ma is dead! Ma is dead!"

The crying starts and lasts throughout the rest of the day.

Kate is the last to hear. She comes into the house and puts away the dishes while this terrible wailing is going on. When she enters the parlour, she is informed by all the children at once in a babble of sobs. I rush to her side and embrace her. She says nothing, but I feel her tears soaking my shoulder.

All day, I try to console my children. Eventually, the children start talking with each other. All of them want to return to Ireland. I do, as well. I planned a bright future for Ellen and my children here in this grand country. It doesn't seem possible now with Ellen gone. I tell them that we will start saving money for a trip back to our homeland.

Elizabeth tearfully asks me to notify her parents about the tragedy. I tell her that I'll have one of the Cullen children write a letter. It will have to be worded carefully. I believe that Mickey's daughter Margaret will do a fine job of it.

Reluctantly, I walk down the street to the Cullen home. When she sees me, Nell Cullen knows that there is something seriously wrong. I report the sad news to her, and her shrieks bring the rest of the family to the door. They welcome me in, and Mickey offers me a whiskey, which I much crave but refuse.

Over and over, we discuss the proper way to tell the Bradleys of their daughter's death. Eventually with the help of her mother, Margaret composes and writes a kind letter. It is the best we can do under the circumstances. I will post it tomorrow at the mill.

The neighbours start visiting later that evening and paying their respects. I don't know what to say to them other than to thank them for their prayers.

My mind is torn with sorrow, but I try to think of my next action. There is no body of Ellen for me to have a proper wake, and there is no one to bury in the churchyard. At best, I will have a memorial Requiem Mass at St. Charles. I must discuss this with Father Shiels.

I leave our home of sadness the next day to go to work. George Palmer walks with me and offers his condolences. I thank him, and we walk through the gate into the mill.

When I arrive at my work station, the fellows there tell me that Mr. Kelly wants to see me. I am grateful for his sympathy, except I don't know what this is about.

Once again, I enter Mr. Kelly's office.

"Charley, I have a newspaper here that reports on the missing ship. The names of all the passengers are listed. I don't want to give you false hope, but your Ellen isn't among them."

"Ach, she was in steerage class. I doubt if their names were recorded."

"No, here it lists first class and then steerage. The names of all 406 passengers are written here."

I would like to believe that Ellen wasn't on that ill-fated ship, but I know that many passenger lists of immigrant ships are inaccurate. I for one was not on the passenger list for the *Barbara*. Ellen could have been listed under a different name or inadvertently omitted entirely. I thank Mr. Kelly for the information and tell him that it has given me some hope. I don't believe it for a minute. If Ellen wasn't on the *Birmingham*, where is she?

I hand the letter notifying the Bradleys of Ellen's death to the office clerk and ask her to post it with the other mill letters going to the Kellyville post office.

Mr. Kelly's information gives me no peace. I don't even tell my family about it. We continue our lives with plans to return to Ireland.

August arrives and we begin trying to earn money for our return to Ireland. Bridget starts working at the mill. Her tasks are easy, carrying cloth and spools of thread from one area to another and sweeping the floors. For this she gets 2 dollars a month which helps a bit with our housing costs. Elizabeth is still minding Paddy and Charley, and she also washes clothes and linens for the richer residents of Kellyville. For myself, I've given up my leisure on Sundays. After Mass, my afternoons are spent picking vegetables at the farm of Tommy Lindsey. Tommy is a weaver at the mill but owns a vegetable farm on a street far to the west of the Kelly Mill. His children are young and can't work the farm yet, although they help with his planting and harvesting. Lindsey has Irish immigrants working for him during much of the year. I am considering working for Tommy with full time wages, except I'd have to leave the Kelly Mill housing if I did so. Right now, the money can't justify the change. Also, there would be no work in the winter.

Tommy believes that just owning the land of his farm will pay off in the future because of the rising value of property in America. He hopes to turn his farm over to his sons someday. Right now they have a few years left in school.

George Palmer has taken a fancy to my sister-in-law. We invite him for supper, and he is all smiles when he arrives. George is a tall, handsome fellow and a perfect match for Elizabeth. Of all the lads I've met in Kellyville, he seems the most kind and generous.

When George hears of our plan to return to Ireland, he tries to talk me out of it. I'm sure that Elizabeth is the main reason for his panic. He would hate to lose her. I assure him that Elizabeth is reconsidering returning to Ireland now that she has a friend like himself here. I tell him that we may have to return without her. He informs me that returning to Ireland will not be easy for anyone. For one thing, it will take years before we earn enough to pay the passage. Most ships returning overseas do not have steerage passenger accommodations. They need the space for cargo. By the time we earn enough for a cabin on a ship, the children won't want to leave. Sure he has a point there.

I leave work at six o'clock on a Tuesday in late August. George Palmer joins me and five of my friends as we walk up the hill to the mill housing. George leaves us at the street where my home is, and he continues on his way to his parents' home. The rest of us wearily walk through the rows of houses to our homes, where we expect that supper will be waiting.

There is something strange going on at my place. A number of women and children are congregated at my front porch.

One shouts, "Here he comes."

What in God's name is happening here? I leave the lads and hurry to my porch.

"Wait till you see who's waitin' for ya in the parlour," someone yells.

I rush through the doorway and then can't believe my eyes. Is it a ghost? My children are sitting on the floor next to a chair where a smiling woman stares up at me. My God, it's Ellen!

Everyone is talking at once. I can't make out what they are telling me. I just rush to her and pick her up and hold her tightly as the chatter surrounds me.

"Thank God you're here and alive," I whisper in her ear. "Don't speak. Just hold me."

We embrace until we feel the children tugging on our clothes. I look down and see Charley and Paddy trying to get Ellen's attention. I notice the smiles of the other children. They seem like the happiest children on earth. This is the most wonderful day in my life.

I try to see what changes have come to Ellen's appearance. She still has the kindest face I have ever known, pleasant if not beautiful. She looks a bit older around her eyes, but her eyes still twinkle when she looks at me. I ask her if I have changed.

She says, "At first sight, I wouldn't know you for yourself. You just look like any other Yankee. Then I saw your ears. Ah sure, it's me darling husband."

I think she is joking with me. She definitely hasn't lost her biting sense of humour. She is dressed too warmly for August in America. She is wearing a plaid woollen dress that she never owned in Ireland. It looks new. Her bag is a new large canvas valise that looks heavy.

The children show her the rest of our house. I turn to our next door neighbour, Mrs. Whalen.

"Alice, how did she get here?"

"I don't know exactly, Charley. I was sweeping my porch and saw a group of people walking with a strangely dressed woman, apparently showing her the way to your house. When they arrived, she introduced herself to me as your wife. 'Mother of God,' I blurted out. 'We thought that you were dead.' She then explained to everyone that she took the wrong ship, and it went to New York."

"Ach, so that was it. Alice, I'll tell you everything when I get to talk with her."

Supper this night is wonderful. Elizabeth prepares a delicious meal of sausage and vegetables, including fried potatoes. Ellen never had such a meal. After dinner, Ellen thanks Elizabeth for the supper and then tells us of her big adventure.

She arrived at the Liverpool docks too late to board the *City of Birmingham*, but she had enough money to board the next ship to depart. It was another steamer, the *Trenton*. She asked if the ship was going to Philadelphia. The agent told her no, it was going to New York, and it is just a short coach ride to Philadelphia from New York. He told her that there are no ships leaving for Philadelphia for almost a month. She decided that she couldn't wait that long, and she boarded the *Trenton*.

Onboard, she worried about how she would get to Philadelphia once the ship docked. She told of her predicament to whomever she met. Finally, an Irish couple, the McFaddens, took pity on her. They told her that she could stay with them until they could find out how she could get to Philadelphia.

The McFaddens took her to their cousin's apartment on the 4th floor of a tenement building near the docks. Ellen said that it was a dreary place. For a week or more, she asked everyone she met about how she could get to Philadelphia. A helpful soul told her that coaches run every day to Philadelphia from Manhattan. When she found out the cost of the coaches, it was more money than Ellen had. The McFaddens said that they would lend the money to her. They also found some American clothes for her to wear and bought her a new bag for her belongings to replace her old shabby one.

"The McFaddens are lovely people. Of course, we must find a way to pay them back. They have written their names and addresses on this paper," Ellen says.

"Sure we will," I reply. "We'll use the money we saved for our return to Ireland."

Ellen seems puzzled by that remark.

In the coach from New York to Philadelphia, Ellen asked her fellow passengers how to get to Kellyville. No one ever heard of the place, so she asked how to get to the Gallagher Hotel on Front Street, and it turned out that the driver knew, and he told her. Ellen carried and dragged her new bag to Gallagher's where she was welcomed by the proprietor. She stayed two nights at no cost at Gallagher's before being directed to the coach for Kellyville. One of the Meenreagh Gallens walked her to the coach station at the Schuylkill River.

She boarded the wrong coach. She was on the Woodlands coach to Darby before she realised it. When it arrived in Darby, she asked how she could get to Kellyville. Finally a gentleman agreed to take her in his carriage. She recalled the bumpy ride up the Lansdowne Road to the turnpike. The gentleman appeared to be smitten by Ellen, even though she kept talking about getting home to her husband and children. Fortunately he was a gentleman, and he took her directly to the Kelly Mill, where he asked if he could help her further. Ellen said no and thanked the man as she left the carriage. As soon as the carriage departed back to Darby, she asked the first person she saw if they knew where the Gallens live. There was no one who could help. She went inside the mill office and asked there. A clerk there, not knowing who she was, gave her directions to the mill housing. Ellen then followed the directions up the hill to the housing. People passing asked where she was going, and she told them she was going to her husband's home. They asked who her husband was and she told them. They seemed shocked by this and walked with her into the village, gathering more women and children as they passed by.

"So, here I am. Did you miss me?"

We are silent for a moment, then young Kate starts to wail. The rest of us, including myself, start weeping. They are tears of joy.

"What is this about returning to Ireland?" asks Ellen.

It is late October. The leaves on the trees along the Darby Creek are changing colours. They are yellow, red, and orange. They are gorgeous. I don't remember Donegal ever being as colourful.

Bridget and my sister-in-law, Elizabeth, are working with me at the mill. Jimmie, Eddie, and Kate now go to school, and they seem to love it, although Kate doesn't talk about it as much as the boys. Ellen is home with the young ones. She thinks that she is pregnant again. I am not surprised.

George Palmer comes to our home for supper often and is almost a member of our family now that he is courting Elizabeth. I can think of no finer man for Elizabeth than George.

My memories of Donegal are starting to fade now. Sometimes, when I'm dreaming, I can see the face of my Da and Ma and the misty green hills across the river. These dreams are becoming less frequent. I send letters to home when I think of it and include some money I know they can well use. I can picture the excitement when our American letters arrive at the Killygordon post office.

I am happy here in America. My children are safe and they have a grand future in this lovely country. I know that I'll never return to Donegal. At Mass and at evening prayers, I pray for the people we left behind there and for all the people of Ireland. I pray that they will succeed in getting the rights to own their own land and maybe even getting their freedom from England someday.

Charles Gallen 1853

Printed in Great Britain
by Amazon